# NEIGHBORING LIVES

# NEIGHBORING LIVES

*Thomas M. Disch*
*&*
*Charles Naylor*

CHARLES SCRIBNER'S SONS

NEW YORK

Library of Congress Cataloging in Publication Data

Disch, Thomas M.
  Neighboring lives.

  1.  Chelsea, Eng.—History—Fiction.  I.  Naylor,
Charles, joint author.  II.  Title.
PZ4.D615Ne    [PS3554.I8]      813'.54      80–19021
ISBN 0-684-16644-5

3 5 7 9 11 13 15 17 19   F/C   20 18 16 14 12 10 8 6 4 2

Printed in the United States of America.

# FOR OUR MUSE
*Laurie Graham*

*Readers who please to go along with us . . . shall wander . . .*
*as in wintry twilight, through some poor stripped hazelgrove,*
*rustling with foolish noises, and perpetually hindering the eyesight;*
*but across which, here and there, some real human figure is seen*
*moving: very strange: whom we could hail if he would answer;—*
*and we look into a pair of eyes deep as our own,* imaging *our own,*
*but all unconscious of us; to whom we for the time are become as*
*spirits and invisibles!*

—*Thomas Carlyle,* Past and Present

# Contents

# NEIGHBORING LIVES

# Prologue

Chelsea beneath a sky of whitest light diffused, a timeless sky, a day
torn free from calendars to glide across the face of waters. The river
serene and his heart equally. He laid the peacefulest of washes across
the paper, so . . . and raised his eyes to the whiteness overall. As sky
and paper hung in the balance of his mind, he placed a long broad
horizontal band of ocher across the first mass: a shore. At the left of
the sheet, where the wash had not completely dried, the ocher bled
delicately at its upper edge, feathering into the void above, as though
the land were to breathe its soul into the air and be transformed to
elemental energy. Light spilled from the sky, pressed against the shore
—now a splotch of sienna within the ocher, confronting, wall-like, that
pressure of light. He worked more intently in quick gradations of
umber, ocher, green, shaping a world from the void, only glancing up
at intervals to witness the world already so shaped. He stopped, added
a slanting stroke of muted blue in the upper left corner, a blue demanded by the particular green below. It was finished. He hung his
hand over the splintery bow and let the current wash his brush clean. A
mile or two farther downstream the Thames's waters would have lost
their cleansing properties. He looked at his painting, looked at the
Chelsea shore, and realized, with chagrin but with real pleasure too,
that he'd made his own house the center of the composition. And more:
the green he placed above it was not the green of greenery, as a viewer
of the watercolor might suppose; it was in fact (squinting he could just
make it out) the more insistent green of Mrs. Booth's dress. She had
gone up to the gallery on the roof. Like the great Apollo, he had turned
a woman into a tree!

He took the gin bottle from the basket underneath his seat, pulled out the cork, and took a long deliberative swig. Greaves eyed him balefully. The boatmen always seemed to expect to share his bottle. On the grounds (one had actually said so) that he did not otherwise provide a pourboire.

"Good light," he announced, corking the bottle and replacing it in the basket. "Not strong, but good. We'll make for St. Mary's."

"Very good, Adm'ral." Greaves pulled up the anchor, then began to row, with quick, sharp strokes.

His eye flitted, swift-like, over the water, under the wooden pilings of the bridge, across the jagged profile of roofs, and lighted, lovingly, on a barge piled with ponderous bales of rain-sodden hay destined for the stables of London. It brought the upper reaches of the river—the daisied meadows, the ripening corn—intensely before him: achingly, as for a lost chance, a forfeited career. Those meadows and fields would never be his. He had lived his life on the waves, made his conquests there, as well.

"Adm'ral," said Greaves, taking the unlighted clay stub of a pipe from his teeth and pointing to the Battersea shore, where an oxcart loaded with tar barrels was being drawn over the muddy sloping shore toward the loading platform of a warehouse. A child was seated on the back of the straining ox. ". . . That little wench, Ann Alexander?"

He squinted, but it was too far off. He felt a stirring of resentment against the boatman for reminding him of his short-sightedness. "Be-like it is," he said curtly. "I cannot put a name to the face of every urchin in the parish."

"It's a dangerous game for a lass to be playing. If I was 'er father, I'd give 'er a 'iding, I would."

"Europa!" he said, thinking suddenly of a picture he had seen. But whose? And where? A suave, untrue concoction. Venice. The bull decked out in garlands, Europa in a fancy dress.

"What's that, Adm'ral?"

"Nothing. I was thinking of what you said, of dangerous games."

Even Titian's wanted truth. The water should predominate and dwarf the figures. A fearful, louring Giorgione sky, not like today's, but on the order of the one he'd seen last winter off Sheerness. Last winter? Whenever; he'd make a note of it.

When they reached the shingle shore, the embanking wall, and, above, the church, he could not go in at once to his usual seat in the bay window that looked out across the river, for there was a funeral service in progress. John Ambrose, the sexton, was deep in conversation with the gravediggers beside the freshly opened grave. The new stone had been propped slantwise against its neighbor. He waited in the corner of the churchyard under the lime, taking rather more gin than was altogether wise so early in the day. The mourners filed out of the left-hand door, the mutes following. The coffin was lowered and a few last words spoken before the earth fell over it. Finally they left, all but Ambrose and the gravediggers, and he was free to take up his usual station at the window. Just in time, for it had begun to rain.

The gravediggers cursed their ill luck.

# CHAPTER ONE

# *Arrival*

## JUNE, 1834

### 1

The creaking hackney into which they were all crammed—people, parcels, and barrels of crockery—was ferociously hot. The tall girl on the seat facing the Carlyles, with the canary on her lap, was the only one of them who evidenced any interest in the streets through which they were passing. She'd arrived in London only the night before, seen none of its fabled wonders but the long expanse of unswept, cobbled street between the inn where the mailcoach had left her and the Mileses' house, to which Mr. Carlyle himself had taken her, a curious kindness in an employer. But the Carlyles *were* kind; meeting them when she was still a child, she had sensed that. Dr. Baddams, her mother's employer, had said that he was a curious man, even insisted that he was a "great" man, though to judge by her master's trousers, which were discreetly mended at the cuff, and by his boots, relics of a rough, country life, it must have been a curious (and not very prosperous) kind of greatness. Still, he was great enough to have brought Bessy here to London all these many miles from Birmingham; to London, the greatness of which was unquestionable; or, if not to London precisely, to Chelsea, which the doctor's wife had assured her was much the same thing.

Mr. Carlyle turned a page of his book. How ever could he read with such a jolting and jouncing? His wife lifted her eyebrows, parted her lips, then pursed them tightly. She seemed always to be carrying on an imaginary and rather lively conversation, of which these facial tics were the silent evidences. Her eye met Bessy's by chance and Bessy

looked down, embarrassed, into the birdcage, where Chico, the Carlyles' canary, performed, like a little circus entertainer, endless feats of
balance, holding to his perch despite all that the rolling of the coach
could do to dislodge him.

"And who is my bravest bird?" said Mrs. Carlyle, as she put off
fanning herself for a moment and bent down over the cage. "All the
way from Craig-o-putta, over as many bumps as wheels have yet made
known, and still holding fast!"

"I fancy it has been a hard journey for both of you, missus," said
Bessy deferentially to her still-youthful mistress, "but it will soon be
done, and you shall be in your new home." Then, to the canary in
particular, "And you shall have a place from which to hang and sing in
peace." Hesitating, "He does sing, doesn't he, missus?"

"Without relenting," declared Mrs. Carlyle. "All the considerable
distance here from Scotland he sang aloud wherever he might be and
put great heart into me. I am mystified by his present silence."

Mr. Carlyle turned a page of his book—backwards—and his forehead crinkled with the slightest of frowns. Mrs. Carlyle sat upright and
began to fan herself again, while Bessy looked out the window of the
coach at London's strangely monotonous magnificence. Terrace after
terrace of identical stately houses passed in review, every facade the
same except when the scale of stateliness was too vast to bear repetition.

The coach had arrived at just such a noble pile.

"Oh my," said Bessy, straining forward across the birdcage for a
better view through the coach's narrow window. Then more emphatically: "Oh my!"

As though responsively, the coach came to a stop. Mr. Carlyle
looked up from his book and peered ahead down the broad—and, it
seemed, unobstructed—highway that swept so grandly round the private park at the center of the square. The treetops, aglow with the
vivider green of early summer, stirred in the wind like a flock of folded
Brobdingnagian sheep.

Bessy, made reckless by awe, whispered to her new mistress, "Is it
the king's palace, Mrs. Carlyle? The Doctor said the king has built a
new palace in London, and this does seem so very grand. . . ."

Mrs. Carlyle smiled with the innocent vanity of a newcomer who
has been asked, by chance, the way to the single street in the neighbor-

hood that she knows by name. "Oh, Buckingham Palace is many times grander even than these buildings, Bessy."

"And what is this then, missus?"

"Carlyle, what did you inform me this square is called?"

Mr. Carlyle looked away from the wind-tossed masses of foliage, in which he had seen, as in the briefest lightning flash of *déjà vu*, some green immensity from his lowland childhood. "Belgrave Square," he replied, with a smile in which there was mixed regret for the fast-fading vision and pleasure in his wife's enthusiasm for the spectacle of the bustling, bedizened city. He scrutinized the stonework under discussion, or was it—there, and there—mere stucco simulating stone? At the rate that this Babylon was growing, such time-saving deceits were only to be expected; had the force, indeed, of venerable tradition.

The breeze which had lately moved through the treetops entered, briefly, at the windows of their crowded compartment.

Mrs. Carlyle snapped her fan closed, and took a deep breath of the cooler air. "That is some relief," she murmured, the words seeming more to have escaped from her continuing inner monologue than actually to have been spoken.

Chico, as though in reply, chose that moment to burst, with quite Covenanting conviction, into an entire Italian aria of the most ornately mellifluous warblings, which they all sat listening to, as to a prophet just come down from a mountaintop to give them God's personal assurance that He is good and all is well in His world.

Then, unaccountably as it had stopped, the old hackney coach heaved into motion, and Chico, having all he could do, once more, to hold to his wildly swaying perch, fell silent.

Mr. Carlyle returned to his book, Mrs. Carlyle to her fan.

Bessy, after sufficient meditation, could not forbear to ask: "Missus?"

"Bessy."

"Do you believe in signs and such as that?"

Mr. Carlyle looked up from his book. He, it may be said at once, surely did believe in signs—and in his own especial canniness in their interpretation. Bessy could not have asked a more acutely interesting question; it seemed, itself, a sign. But of what? Of her being a capable, honest girl, let it be hoped. He could see already that it would be useless to hope her a *quiet* girl, as well. But if she were a chatterer, that would be Jane's concern. Jane might even like a chatterer, if the chatter were not too inane.

"What a rare *craiture* you are, Bessy. Supernatural signs? Apparitions?"

"No, Mr. Carlyle—plain, natural signs. It seemed to me that when Chico burst out so at Belgrave Square, that *that* might be taken for a sign."

"A sign of what, Bessy?" Mr. Carlyle asked in, it seemed to Bessy, a rather snappish way, though what his altered tone betokened was merely his having brought her into focus.

The girl blushed and looked down at the ever-precarious bird as though he might save her from those clear eyes with an answer. "I . . . I don't know, sir," she murmured.

"But say what is in you to say," Mr. Carlyle coaxed with schoolmasterly condescension.

"Well . . . it seemed that as we have nearly arrived at your new home, sir, it seemed that it might have been a sign that we should be happy there."

"Speak up, Bessy," said Carlyle a little impatiently, "we can't hear you when you mumble."

"He did sing so cheerfully," she added hastily and with some effort to be heard, "and for no reason I could see, but that it were meant for a sign."

"There, was that so difficult? With some exercise we may produce a fine auguress." His eyes met those of the ungainly servant girl (she was quite five foot nine). "And a fair soothsayer you would be, Bessy. I picture you now, wrapped in samite robes like a sibyl of the ancient world, listening to the chirlings and mutterings of birds, picking awful meaning from the troublesome flight of the lapwing."

"I daresay, Carlyle," his wife put in, ostensibly to champion Bessy, but really for the sport of bandying words with her husband, "that Bessy is an excellent reader of omens, just as Chico, as I've always known, has a most infallible and mystic sense of what lies beyond the veil of futurity. He knew," turning to Bessy, "long before we did, how urgently we needed to leave behind the endless silences of Craigenputtock. And I am quite sure that he is right as to the larger happiness we may expect to find in our new home."

"Happiness!" said Mr. Carlyle dismissively, which Bessy found altogether unaccountable, for what he seemed to be dismissing was not so much her fancy about the canary as the very idea and possibility of happiness. What made it all so much odder was that he seemed, for all that, one of the happiest men she'd ever encountered; happier, certainly, than poor Dr. Baddams, drinking himself to death while the family stood helplessly watching; happier even than the Reverend Flanders of All Saints' Chapel in Birmingham, who had preached three separate times on the text (Deuteronomy 33:29): "Happy art thou, O Israel. Who is like unto thee, O people saved by the Lord." If even God were concerned to promote human happiness, it did seem rather more than peculiar for Mr. Carlyle to be so offhanded about it.

## 2

Sloane Square, the beginning of Chelsea proper, was, at this late morning hour, a busy, thriving, clamorous tangle of humanity and horseflesh. The weather, gloomily undecided at best, was now becoming squally, and the sky above the brick facades darkened to an undifferentiated iron gray, bespeaking hours of downpour. Already umbrellas were opening, tarpaulins were being thrown over stalls, and the few unprepared were making for doorways.

"Oh, Mrs. Carlyle," Bessy burst out in the excitement of discovery, "do you see that!"

Jane Carlyle, alarmed by the rain and the effects it was certain to have on their moving in, nodded absent-mindedly. Pickford's, the movers, had promised to be at Cheyne Row no later than two, and possibly much earlier. In short, there seemed every likelihood that the furniture would be drenched before it could be moved from the trackboat. . . .

"Oh, missus, *do* look, before they've passed."

Mrs. Carlyle smiled. "Yes?"

"There, do you see—she's carrying the market basket for the lady in the capote bonnet."

"Yes . . ." Mrs. Carlyle said, nodding, "Oh yes. There are a great many good stout leeks in the basket, and I believe I see the feet of a chicken—but there is nothing unusual in that, Bessy."

"But *missus!*" Bessy leaned forward to keep the two women in view. "Don't you see what she is *wearing?*"

"You mean her bustle."

Bessy rolled her eyes expressively.

"Surely, Bessy, women are wearing bustles in Birmingham? The custom has established itself long since in Edinburgh—even in Dumfries, which is but a small port."

"Oh yes, missus, among the fine ladies and the quality. But that was just a servant girl," she whispered.

"In London, Bessy—I've been told on good authority—the maids are as free to make fools of themselves in the name of fashion as their mistresses. Only last night, Eliza, the daughter of the Mileses with whom we've been staying, told me that their own serving girl, not two Sundays ago, was so desperate to cut a figure before the world that, lacking a suitable cushion, or sheepskin (for I'm sure I don't know precisely *how* the madness is achieved, no more than Mrs. Miles's Katie knew), she pinned three feather dusters under her skirts, and they seemed to serve quite well."

Bessy was beside herself with laughter, and even Mr. Carlyle, reading away at his book, couldn't resist a smile, though he had been present when the anecdote had first been told by Eliza Miles, in whose account of it, however, Katie's ingenious vanity had appeared to be a source of scandal rather than of amusement. It was wonderful how Jane's tongue could so reshape the trifles of existence that they became, in her telling, jewels—and sharp ones at that, fit to etch a pane of glass. Truly a wonderful tongue, his Jeannie's—providing it wasn't turned against anyone present.

"Are you intending to follow the fashions yourself, Bessy?" Mrs. Carlyle asked.

Bessy's blush developed to a serious crimson. "Oh, missus," she protested, half in earnest, half still given over to the idea of feather dusters. "La!"

"And yourself, Jeannie?" Mr. Carlyle asked.

Mrs. Carlyle gave her husband an arch look. "La," she said drily.

## 3

A city is such a solid-seeming thing; more solid-seeming, perhaps, in 1834 than since, though the great sprawl outward from center to suburb had already been in progress since the days of Henry VIII, who himself had a share in the ever-continuing process by which the village of Chelsea was to become, in due time, an appendage and, at last, a part of London. Not much remained of Henry VIII's presence except certain courses of brick dividing one stretch of market garden from another and some legends attaching to these walls. Sir Thomas More had left rather a more personal mark on the village, having consigned his first wife to burial in Chelsea Old Church, whose great stone tower marked the western end of Cheyne Walk. Of More's home, Beaufort House (as it would later be known), there was no longer a door or window, although for two entire centuries it had been the central wonder of Chelsea. Indeed, Chelsea was, in these days, in the ashy stage of its phoenixdom, and the Carlyles' coach, as it groaned on riverwards along Paradise Row, passed a rather dreary succession of once stately houses, their facades crumbling, their gardens gone to seed. Soon, clearly, these must share the fate of Beaufort House. Chelsea had become as little fashionable as the perukes and periwigs that were quite certainly to be found (by moths and worms) in the damp attics of those houses on Paradise Row.

This was, of course, precisely the attraction of Chelsea for the Carlyles. At £35, the rent for their house on Cheyne Row was a significant £10 cheaper than its nearest contender in Brompton, farther inland, and for no better reason than that Chelsea was considered unfashionable. The Carlyles, while not entirely indifferent to fashion, valued such amenities as light and living space higher than the right address, and in these regards the house on Cheyne Row was clearly the best of those they'd seen to choose from. In the end, however, it was the rent that was decisive.

An oddly prophetic decision, this choice of neighborhoods, for Chelsea was to become—and much more rapidly than even the most optimistic speculator could have supposed—all the fashion once again. Of course, it would never rival Mayfair or Belgravia—for fashion is finally a matter of money—but among the various suburbs then being formed, either in brick and mortar or in the airier stuff of the financial imagination, none would enjoy quite so happy a destiny as Chelsea.

It would be difficult to say exactly why. Perhaps because all the city's railways—the first of them was being built in this same year of 1834—were to pass it by, and so wouldn't bring the doubtful blessings of commerce and industry. It had even then its undeniable charm, but there were neighborhoods all about London whose charms were at least potentially no less considerable. Charm, a neighborhood's charm, is by and large man-made, though Nature can be encouraged to assist. It is true, of course, that trees and vines have been allowed to exert their theories of beauty over the more overt artifices of stone and brick that have accrued through the centuries, but trees and vines must be planted, nourished, and pruned by those who possess them. Only the river is there without invitation, and though the river is a powerful presence, it cannot account for the place's singular charm. Chelsea is charming because the people living there have felt the need for charm and so created it. Pimlico, lying just to the east, though it shares the Thames and is nearer the central city, is decidedly less charming, seems always to have been so. At least Carlyle, when he would walk eastward to Westminster, systematically avoided the direct route by way of Pimlico, which he found "squalid, confused, dirty, and detestable."

In any case, whatever the reasons for Chelsea's still-nascent fashionability, it is not to be wondered at that Thomas Carlyle, being by profession a prophet, should have caught some scent of it and cast his lot with this good-omened neighborhood, where he would live for nearly the next half century. Perhaps his prophecy was even self-fulfilling to a degree; perhaps by coming here and settling in and becoming, as much as any lime or oak, part of its landscape, he was, in effect, setting the fashion. No one, of course, can set a fashion all alone, but someone has to be *noticeably* first. And the Carlyles would be, distinctly, noticeable.

## 4

Jane Carlyle was not one to delight in water, except in its most domesticated forms, such as in a tumbler on a hot day. The calmest sea could make her ill. The very thought of voyaging, were it only by ferry, or in a skiff on a lake, could provoke her digestion to the most unpleasant alarms. Nevertheless, she was resolved (as she viewed the expanse of water at Chelsea Reach) to change. The steamers that now plied the river east and west, snorting and spewing smoke, were the likeliest, most economical means of reaching the more august or lively precincts of the City. The future, Mr. Carlyle insisted, belonged to Steam and Smoke; though the present, as much as could be seen of it from the window of the coach, belonged entirely to three young men in white jackets and trousers darting in their light boats across the gray and slow-moving river.

Home lay not far away now, and each fact and facet of the observable neighborhood seemed to possess new and desperate significance:

the man sprawled in front of a tobacconist's shop, drunk or asleep, bespoke the more disreputable character of the westward reaches of the village, while, a short way on, a servant girl with a pitcher of milk on her head seemed a very allegory of the older, more rural Chelsea. Well, the good came mixed with the bad. A world that was *all* milk-maids would be decidedly less lively. Indeed, Jane Carlyle had spent the last six years of her life in just such a bucolic and humdrum world, and London (she made no distinction in her mind between London and Chelsea) promised to be a redemption from the longueurs and desolations of life in Craigenputtock. She was sure, furthermore, that her husband was of the same disposition, however much he might exalt the virtues and blessings of their life in Scotland. But mum was the word: Jane had long since learned such simple rules of domestic management as not to provoke needless controversy. She would join with her husband gladly in rewriting the history of those eight weari-some years—now that bridges were safely burned behind them and there was no danger of their *returning* to that Golden Age (golden, chiefly by virtue of its silence!).

But the coach had stopped. With a last shake of the reins, the overburdened drays were made to turn in to Cheyne Row, and the Carlyles, their maid, and the more fragile portion of their furnishings passed in review before their neighbors' curtained windows. A serving girl, in ribboned mob cap and canvas apron, stood agape on the fresh-scrubbed doorstep of No. 4, then took alarm and dashed inside to announce the event to her mistress. A mender and vendor of old pans left off crying his wares. The coach came to a stop again—its final stop—before No. 5.

There it was, and there were they. Carlyle opened the door of the coach, stepped down to the pavement, and looked about him with proprietarial satisfaction—neglecting to offer a helping hand to his wife. While he stretched his legs, the driver hurried round to Mrs. Carlyle, and then to Bessy as well, who handed him the birdcage.

Chico, graciously, answered with song, and at the same instant the house door was opened from within (Jane had forgotten that the car-penters were to have preceded them). What a splendid house it was. She could have stood there for an hour, solemnly admiring, but already the carpenters were occupied with helping the driver take down the small, unsteady pyramid of goods roped to the roof of the coach, so she followed Carlyle and Bessy into the house.

In the first room on the ground floor—their dining room, they had decided on that first visit—Carlyle set down the birdcage, and Chico, left to himself in all that uncanny emptiness, was in the greatest consternation. Jane took up the cage and looked about for somewhere to hang it. The ledge above the fireplace was too narrow, and in any case, in the hurly-burly of moving, once Pickford's men arrived with the bulk of their possessions ...

There was a crash. She rushed to the window, fearing the worst: the good blue china! But no, it had been one of the posters of her red bed, the one in which she first had seen the light of day—and no harm seemed to have come to it.

A carpenter staggered into the room with a barrel of crockery. "This would be china?" He pronounced the word the old-fashioned way— "chainy"—which was also the way one was supposed to say the name of their street. "Where shall I put it, mum?"

She checked the number chalked on the top of the barrel to be sure. "Through here." She advanced beyond the great arch into the next room and pointed to the dark storeroom off the northeast corner. Out the back window she could see Mr. Carlyle already smoking in the garden. A breeze wafted the faintest odor of his cigar through the open window. Chico loved breezes. This would be the room for him then, at least in the summer; but not now, not till he would be safe from the arms of wandering chairs, the shoulders of carpenters.

She carried the birdcage into the back garden, where, as though waiting to be used for this very purpose, a hook projected from the brick wall separating their garden from that of a neighbor.

"Jeannie," said Carlyle with a grumble, "take note: we need a tinderbox. I have just lighted the fire for Bessy with one of these lucifers, but we must not be put to that expense every day."

"I shall see to it, Carlyle."

He nodded, and the thought of a tinderbox evaporated from his consciousness at once, dispersed into oblivion like the smoke from his cigar. Jane could be relied upon to remember housekeeping details, thus freeing his mind and memory for larger and loftier concerns: a parsimonious, practical arrangement that suited them both quite well.

"Where is the famous walnut tree you spoke of?" Jane asked, facing an unlikely contender bearing a few green cherries. Like the poor, pollarded lime trees that stood across from the house on Cheyne Row, this must, by necessity, be cut back if it were one day to bear real fruit.

She hadn't realized on her first visit to the house, only five days ago, how desperately in need of tending the garden was, for it had rained steadily all during that preliminary survey. And all gardens look alike in the rain.

"There is thy nut tree, Jane—with sixpence worth of nuts upon it."

Behold, there it stood, their very own walnut tree. Needless to have asked, needless to have answered—but a kind of sweetness evidenced itself in such decorums, a pleasure in the tidy and temperate accretion of the words with which they had begun to build their nest.

"And is that not mint growing wild by the wall?" she asked.

Carlyle bent down, broke off a sprig, and sniffed. "Spearmint, yes."

"You will be wanting garden tools. We passed an ironmonger just before we turned in to the Row. And we'll need other pots beside the great copper in the back kitchen."

"In good time," said Carlyle, contemplating the even-burning tip of his cigar with satisfaction. "For the moment let us enjoy our nut tree, our flagstones, our good fortune generally, and, if it suit thy appetite, let us also enjoy Mrs. Miles's good cold boiled beef—that is if she remembered this morning her promise of last evening."

Jane smiled. "I'll find the basket. If I spread a cloth over one of the box-lids we can enjoy our meal . . . like gypsies!"

She considered for a moment whether she might spontaneously kiss her husband, but the cigar was back in his mouth and his thoughts seemed already to have flown elsewhere. In any case, at three-and-thirty one was perhaps a little old for such effusions, and so she contented herself with waggling a finger inside Chico's cage as she passed on her way into the house.

Chico responded with an enthusiastic flutter of wings, but all uselessly, for in a moment the finger was gone and there were still no seeds in his dish, no water in his cup.

---

## 5

While the carpenters reassembled the red bed in the back room of the first floor, and while Carlyle himself was busy positioning and then repositioning that most sacred article of furniture, his desk (which had belonged to Jane's father, Dr. Welsh, and so was doubly sacrosanct), in the front room, Jane, in the small, windowless, many-shelved room at the back of the ground floor, stood contemplating an unopened barrel of china; at the same time she was contemplating the first minatory twinges of a headache. In truth, she could not allow herself such dreadful luxury. Not with so much still to be done. She must fix her mind on a task that would leave no room in her consciousness for this inconvenient ache. The china waited—but the barrel was nailed shut and Carlyle had the clawhammer.

She called up the stairs. "Presently," he answered. She retreated to—might they not use it as a breakfast room?—and stared, with grave suspicion, at the wainscotted walls. Her mind inhabited the darkness behind the paneling with legions of tiny, tormenting creatures, all lying in wait for the larger darkness of night when they might consolidate their victories. She had not seen any clear evidences yet of the house's actual infestation, but it seemed all too likely. If they weren't already here, they might be picked up from the trackboat and come riding in triumphant upon the furniture; they might be in her own clothing, even—for her uncle's home in Liverpool (where she'd passed a night in transit) was not above suspicion, nor could she be sure of the Mileses' house in Ampton Street. In short, Bessy must air everything in the garden, shake out the clothes and linens, and then, as for these cracks and crevices in the walls, a way must be found to *seal* them.

Her head was becoming insupportable.

"Mrs. Carlyle?"

"Oh, Bessy! You startled me."

The girl had changed into a washdress of striped cotton and put aside her bonnet for a mob cap. "Did you call me?"

"Did I?" She had to think. "No, I called upstairs to Mr. Carlyle. He has the hammer, which I need in order to get the tops off the crockery barrels. We must set to work and put things in order." She placed a hand back below the small gathering of hair, where the pain seemed to concentrate itself.

"Yes, missus—it will all be done, never worry. I've made a nice fire in the kitchen grate—you know, it is very damp down there. I wonder how long has passed since there's been a fire down there. I do hope it dries out before my bed arrives."

Her mistress nodded abstractedly.

"You *do* have so much room," Bessy observed, making a mental comparison of these relatively spacious rooms with her own tiny cave of a back kitchen, airless and lightless, below—not without the wistful hope that some other corner of that three-story house might be ceded to her.

The hint passed unnoticed. "Would *you* get the clawhammer from him, please, Bessy? We cannot do a thing without it."

The hammer was got, the barrels were opened, and the blue china and other fancy pieces were deployed upon the shelves of the china room, to the accompaniment of a steady patter of praise from Bessy and a single pronouncement from Mr. Carlyle who, coming down to retrieve the hammer, agreed with his wife that the soup bowls might better go on the shelf *below* the dinner plates.

Before returning upstairs, Mr. Carlyle demanded to know the time. Jane took from its fob in her waistband a thick, staunch old watch that had been her mother's and (consequently) the envy and fascination of her girlhood, though now that it was hers, she found its cumbersome size not a little embarrassing and often wished, unloyally, that it were not quite so impervious to the ordinary mischances of its kind. Still some minutes must pass before the promised hour when the furniture would arrive.

"Everything that can be done *has* been done," Carlyle declared, "and your bed only wants its coverings for you to have your inaugural nap upon it."

"I should love nothing better," Jane said with a sigh.

"Then let me find my shawl to cover you," Bessy hastily volunteered, and darted off.

"Do you know," said Jane, when Bessy was gone, "I think there has been a special providence in her having come to us."

"She seems eager to please, puir lassie. Doubtless her mother reared her to a healthy sense of duty."

"Coupled with kindness—she is not of the serving class, I may remind you—no more than was her mother."

"For all that, Jeannie, she appears thankful for the work; thankful too, no doubt, to have such a mistress as yourself."

Jane smiled skeptically and shook her head.

"I believe she talks to herself," he added significantly.

"I think most servants do, my dear. They spend so much time with no one else to talk to. If it weren't for Chico, I suppose I would be talking to *my*self. I hope that does not mean that *I* am mad!"

"And there am I, if you will think of it, sitting at my desk, scribbling away, which is another form of soliloquy, and may be the maddest of them all. What o'clock does thy watch declare now? Pickford's men should be here."

She removed the old watch once again. Bessy could be heard mounting the steps from the kitchen. She paused in the doorway to show Mrs. Carlyle her shawl of fine gray Cotswold wool, a treasure of a shawl. "I'll spread it out on the bed, mum." Her footsteps counted the steps to the first floor above them, crossed the bare floorboards to their bedroom and the red bed directly over them.

"Our first order of business," commented Carlyle drily, "must be to lay carpets." He had remarkable hearing and a capacity no less remarkable to be driven furious by the least rustle and whisper of other people's activities. It was, to say the least, no blessing. Jane wondered how much her own hypersensitivity in such matters might owe to her husband's fine-strung nerves. Did she listen, sometimes, on his behalf? Wasn't it, even, her duty to do so? "And I believe," he continued, "not a moment ago, coming from the garden, I heard—what think you?—chickens."

"Oh dear, I hope not!"

"Chickens," he repeated, nodding morosely.

Like a deliverance there came a clatter of wheels and horses' hooves on the flagstone-paved street, followed presently by the loud rap of the brass knocker on the front door: the men from Pickford's with the furniture.

The headache was forgotten.

## 6

After the carpets were laid (the old red one from Craigenputtock stretched tight across the floor of the front drawing room, and tacked); after the piano, the beds, tables, and chairs had found their ways to their rightful places; after the presses had been filled with linens and the overflow of books, the former having been aired in the garden between intervals of rain; after the beds were made; after a supper had been prepared and eaten, and water heated, and dishes washed, and the pantry shelves scoured (by candlelight) a second time, with greater thoroughness; after, in short, all had been accomplished that might be accomplished, Jane, not to her surprise, felt considerably better. The headache was quite gone, and the tone of her thoughts accorded pleasantly with the tarnished gilt of westerly clouds. Chelsea's sunsets seemed quite as satisfactory as those in Scotland.

She was, for a while, alone. Carlyle had gone to take an initial survey of the neighborhood, to make it, by the act of vision, his own. Bessy had gone in search of milk for Carlyle's evening bowl of porridge. Jane debated whether to leave the house herself—an unseemly idea for any other day—to seek out her husband, who would doubtless be found somewhere along the riverbank; but no, better to let him have this moment of peace. A quite sufficient view of the Thames could be had from her own doorstep. Before she could reach even that vantage point, however, she was deflected from her purpose by finding, slipped under the door, a note, which she knew unerringly was from their friend Leigh Hunt: the bit of pale blue ribbon with which it had been tied declared it, as much as a seal or signature, to be his. Slipping the ribbon into the pocket of her apron with a completely unconscious thrift, she read the single page, folded it, and smiled.

The kindest, the most charming of men, this Leigh Hunt, and also, sad to say, one of the unluckiest and most bedeviled. He was the editor, currently, of a brand-new periodical bearing his own name, *Leigh Hunt's London Journal*, priced at three halfpence and printed on one of the new steam presses. All Hunt's friends—and they were a multitude—had the fairest hopes for this latest undertaking, and (according to Carlyle) the gravest forebodings. From the literary point of view, Hunt was the most brilliant of editors. He'd been the first champion, virtually the discoverer, of Shelley and Keats, a friend of Byron, Lamb, Coleridge, Hazlitt, and a host of others; no one was more generous with his approbation; no one's approbation counted for more among the literati of the day. But the public, along with the critics in the more established journals, were dismissive of Hunt, when not actually excoriating. His first fame had sprung from the same bitter soil as his first grand misfortune, when he'd been imprisoned for two years on a charge of libeling the Prince Regent in his brother's newspaper, since which time his life had been an almost steady succession of disasters—financial, critical, and personal. For the sin of having been born within "the sound of Bow bells," he'd been labeled a cockney, the ringleader, thereby, of an entire "Cockney School." His recent memoir about the years spent in Italy with Lord Byron had been savaged in *The Times* itself by no less a luminary than Thomas Moore, the title of whose satire told it all: "The Living Dog and the Dead Lion." Against such currents it was hard to make headway, as much as one could do to stay afloat. Hunt wrote and wrote: poems, essays, a novel, leaders for newspapers, introductions, an endless flow, sometimes brilliant, sometimes workmanlike, and never successful. The magazines he edited sank under his fatal captaincy like so many doomed ships. Though he had by now outlasted his most virulent enemies, had even begun to receive something like his due among the newer critics, his personal finances remained in a state of permanent crisis, keeping him never more than a step away from bankruptcy and debtor's prison.

Jane had met Hunt twice, briefly, on her first trip to London two years ago, and had felt—as anyone would—the most immediate liking, a liking that passed well beyond being charmed by his graces and pitying his misfortunes. He *amused* her. Usually in society Jane felt an obligation to be amusing herself, and she'd become, by natural gifts and by dint of practice, almost legendary. In the Carlyles' early days together in Edinburgh, before a misguided desire for adventure had led them to Craigenputtock, Jane had been as celebrated for her wit as Carlyle, though of course his style was much grander. For someone who is under the constant onus of amusing others, it is both a delight and a relief to *be* amused. Jane, therefore, could not help but be pleased by Mr. Hunt's note and the expectations it awoke of being near this kindest, most charming, most amusing of men; but it must be admitted that, for all that, she felt a certain apprehension too.

It was the use in his note of the first-person *plural* that made her uneasy, his mention of *Mrs.* Hunt. Jane had not met the woman. Few people had, apparently, of late, for she was reported to be a semi-invalid and kept very much to her home; and Hunt, by virtue of his straitened circumstances, did little entertaining. But those who had seen Mrs. Hunt had little good to say of her, and often considerable ill. That she was a slattern who lived in a state of dismaying disorder, that her numberless children had been allowed to make the Hunt residence into a kind of gypsy encampment—this much seemed undeniable, in that Carlyle had lately witnessed it all at first hand. But there were more damaging reports, which Carlyle could not so certainly confirm, that her invalidism and incompetence in domestic management were the result of an incurable addiction to gin, that no little of her husband's misfortunes could be traced directly to her improvidence, and that the reason she did not go out was that there were few respectable households that would receive her. All in all, a very doubtful sort of neighbor.

But, after all, the rumors might be unfounded. Think of all that had been said in print against Hunt himself, quite vicious things, and how unjustly. As to Mrs. Hunt and her tribe of gypsy children, it was too soon to judge. The wilder sort of children, those who are accustomed to the largest liberty, are often the most delightful to meet with; though to live *near* them may well be something else. If she and Carlyle were to have a child—a wee bairn . . .

But that was out of the question, impossible.

Of course all parents—all potential parents, she corrected—must doubt the possibility of parenthood before they are simply engulfed by the fact of it. This house was large enough, surely. By Carlyle's report, the Hunts had half the space.

She knew beyond all doubt that her husband was not as other men. It had been his curse and his blessing in equal measure; now it was her curse and her blessing, as well. When she considered the alternatives—the various rejected suitors and the lives *they* were leading—she thought that she had, on the whole, made the best bargain she could. She would never have enjoyed a common happiness; it would have made her sour and shrewish, a malcontent like her mother, whose weathervane moods bespoke a deep and undying dissatisfaction with the swift cutting off of her active life at the early death of Dr. Welsh. Jane, whatever else she might complain of, could not complain of that. Having married a genius, she was entitled (as much as any queen) to consider the world and history her stage.

------

7

------

The day's last light was being wrung from the clouds in the west, while in the eastern sky a stranger, stronger luminescence gathered—the garish, inspissated glow of the Infernal Wen; Fog-Babylon; London, Gargantua of Cities. How much tallow, coal gas, bee's wax, and whale oil had to be combusted in how many rooms to account for the unnatural, turbid radiance of those clouds; it was unthinkable—of a magnitude to rival in its awful immensity that other imponderable mystery, which lay beyond this nearer one as beyond a painted curtain, more pure, more terrible, unfathomable: the Starry Heaven. But for these intervening clouds, Carlyle's mind would have delighted to reach out, to wander in, to sail through those immensities, where he felt as much at home (some nights) as a country child at play upon the commons. He'd come within a hair's breadth, once, of holding the chair in astronomy at Edinburgh University; *would* have done so, if Lord Jeffrey had not so unaccountably withheld his support; and a brave astronomer he would have made too, not like these new French clockmakers who understood of the sky above them only what they could *see* there, only the million gleams of as many far-off furnaces, and not the Seal and Signature of the Hand that had lighted those fires, whose Breath still kindled them! Blind, blind—who are more blind than those who call themselves natural philosophers?

Not Science then, and not Philosophy (what was *called* Philosophy): it must be Literature. But even here he found that what *he* considered Literature and what the world looked for in that commodity were, similarly, irreconcilable. The world, as represented by Lord Jeffrey once again, had lately spurned Carlyle's first overt Master-Work—*Sartor Resartus*, as it would come to be titled—as being somehow unsuitable for the pages of the *Edinburgh Review*, where most of his earlier articles had appeared. Jeffrey had found the style too "personal," too "ideosyncratic," not quite the right cut for reforming Whigs. Instead, the work was appearing in a quarterly of the most violent Tory principles, *Fraser's Magazine*, and Carlyle was to receive £83, at which rate he calculated that he would be in debtor's prison within four years, if he continued to produce Master-Works instead of what the world preferred—novels, and sketches of sporting life, and other such humorous froth skimmed from the bubbling pot of Daily Life.

Nevertheless, he was determined to produce another book—one so vast in conception, so epical in scope and execution that the world would simply be subdued, would be forced to its knees; or would not, as the case might be. It was all one to him. He would set down the Truth in its flaming letters, and the world might read them or not, as it chose.

What truth? Which truth? That was the poser: the first Master-Work had tackled Truth headlong, in the manner (Jeffrey had told him) of a rustic wrestler, confident that he will overcome all challengers by mere brute strength. This time he would adopt a more douce strategy; he would have a Subject, and declare it, so that the world would never notice that what it observed in the mirror he held up was its own glorious, mad, woeful face—would not recoil, therefore, from what is, after all, the world's chief fascination.

Was it to be the French Revolution then? Would he aspire to that? An historian? No, more than that! A prophet! than which no human profession is more honorable, or loftier, except (perhaps) the profession of Kingship. For the recent convulsions in France (though they were now forty-five years past, were still, in the mind of every thinking Englishman, as urgently contemporary, as "recent," as yesterday's catch of eels) were only a chapter from a book that was far from being concluded. The great changes then begun were still going on in France and Germany; among the Carbonari of Italy; in Greece, too; in Portugal and Spain. Everywhere one read the same flaming letters. And *not* in England? Not here, where the gulf between the Old and New, between rich and poor, between the Justice of the Thundering Heaven and the Injustice of some few corrupt and reprobate men, was widest and most alarming? Oh no, never suggest it! He would call his book "The *French* Revolution," and let the letters of fire scorch whose hand they would.

It was decided then, and he took his vow upon it. He had resolved both his outward and his inward course at one stroke; had fixed his home and chosen his task, and the fixing and the choosing were a single act, a single choice. He chose Society: the hubbub and hurly-burly of an urban existence, with all the whirligig pleasures and distractions that flowed, naturally and inevitably, from such a choice. Madness, even that: it could not be ignored, nor frowned out of existence. London was one endless Bedlam of lunatics, some raving, some melancholy; all mad. You could hear them, even now, on both sides of the river, bawling and brawling in their alehouses. The *Adam and Eve* on the Chelsea side; the *Red House* on the south shore. The words of a song floated over the water from the rickety wooden balcony at the back of the *Adam and Eve*—a ballad commemorating the hanging, on the Newgate scaffold, of a popular murderer. With more of gin and less of ale; with more of suffering and less of—comfort? nay, it was not comfort that sustained them—call it, rather, hope; with a Danton or a Robespierre to stir them up and urge them on, would not these same alehouse bawlers soon be out upon Regent Street or the Pall Mall, dancing the carmagnole, leading on the tumbrils, drinking their enemies' blood even as it poured down from the guillotine, as from an opened wine barrel? Nothing prevented it; nothing but the natural torpor of humankind, and the natural fear of what peril there might be to their own necks, should the experiment fail.

What a theme it was! How its unfolding would bring all classes and conditions of men within his reach, quite as though he might scrawl his letters of fire upon the very underbellies of these lurid, louring clouds for all of London to look up and read his *Mene, Mene, tekel upharsin!* Which is to say, the Lord has judged thee and numbered thy days; thy kingdom is divided; thy house is on fire, thy children burning!

Returning to the Chelsea shore, he had to pass the toll booth once again, where the guard had the temerity to demand a *second* halfpenny for the privilege of standing upon *his* bridge and gazing at *his* heavens. Carlyle berated him soundly, called him a scoundrel, demonstrated with mathematic rigor the utter illogic of the demand, and paid him the damned halfpenny. For such thoughts as he had pondered, it was a small enough price; and in the future he could have his meditations just as well from the shore *without* the payment—twice over—of a toll!

# CHAPTER TWO

# Of Porridge and Nightingales

### 1

Following a succession of his blue-ribboned notes (one accompanied by a single pressed flower), and having received encouragement in the form of a flutter from Mrs. Carlyle's handkerchief after having slipped the latest communication beneath the heavy oak door, Leigh Hunt called on the Carlyles.

He had calculated nicely: Carlyle was done with his "useful pacing" and had descended to smoke in the garden, for relaxation, one of his twenty-inch churchwarden clays (which he preferred to cigars) and then, coming into the front room, had interrupted Jane where she sat addressing a letter to her mother.

Hunt pulled the doorbell and waited.

The Carlyles, despite an evident paucity of chairs, were oddly disposed to show off their small world. And Hunt, made by parenthood and editorship an indulgent and overcooperative audience, was ingenious in finding new ways for them to do so.

He was a trim, graceful man, with hair beginning to gray—a sweet-natured child of fifty, one would suppose—and contrary to the reputation of his household, *he* dressed scrupulously, though not ostentatiously.

He applauded the house for its commodity, the furniture for its unpretending solidity, the carpet and Jane's cheeks for their color; the very floorboards he would have praised for the excellence of their grain, indeed, were they not already so excellently covered. He contrasted Jane's lingering country color, in a garland of well-chosen epithets from both English and Italian poets, to his own citified, literary pallor, diplomatically avoiding mention of Carlyle's complexion, which was, as ever, sallow. Having eulogized one Carlyle, he proceeded, more seriously but no less gracefully, to do the same for the other. For fully fifteen minutes (Jane kept track by the clock on the wall) Hunt held forth on the merits of Carlyle's essay on Cagliostro, which had come out last summer in *Fraser's Magazine* and which he had picked up only the night before and found himself "unable to resist rereading." He praised its drollery; he praised its dispatch; he even praised (which few critics did) the prose, which he didn't think "at all eccentric" but rather "intensely individual." Most of all, he praised it as a vision of history. "Carlyle, you make the old scoundrel come alive," he concluded, "quite as much as any novelist. Scott himself has no vivider colors in his paintbox, despite that he has all the resources of fancy at his command. *You* have imagination—as, indeed, did Scott, at his infrequent best—what is more, you have applied it not to some trivial melodrama but to History itself, which is a task no historian before you has ever dared aspire to!"

Carlyle, of course, was ravished by this lyrical, unstinting appreciation. He was always susceptible to a well-framed compliment, but Hunt had managed to light upon the single aspect of his new undertaking, the first pages of which he'd written that very morning, about which he was most anxious—this business of enlivening History by judicious application of the Imagination. It was as though Hunt had dictated a manifesto for his personal use and inspiration. If he'd been of the Covenanting persuasion, he'd have laid his hand on Hunt's fading locks then and there and called upon the Maker to shower him with assorted blessings; but being of a more secular and latter-day disposition, he contented himself with insisting that Hunt stay to supper.

Hunt demurred. It was late; he'd best be going home. Carlyle insisted. He rang for Bessy and told her that Mr. Hunt was staying to supper and to bring an extra setting.

A very short while later Bessy returned to announce that the table was laid, and Hunt followed his host and hostess down to the ground-floor dining room. There, in a homely china tureen, was a great steaming gray mound of oatmeal. To one side of the tureen stood a pitcher of milk; to the other a bowl of sugar. It must have taken, Hunt figured, fully a pound of meal to make such a mess of pottage.

They sat down, and Jane served herself a quantity of the stuff, then offered the ladle to her guest, who helped himself, with great delicacy, to a much smaller serving. Carlyle took twice again as much as his wife.

Jane passed the pitcher of milk to Hunt, who passed it to Carlyle without pouring any over his own porridge.

"Does milk not agree with you?" Carlyle asked.

"Only a bit of sugar, if I may." Hunt sprinkled sugar on his oatmeal, and then, as though absent-mindedly, retained the teaspoon from the sugarbowl for his own use, ignoring the larger spoon by his plate. "How delicious," he said, smiling at Jane after his first taste. "What a delightful . . . earthy flavor. And the consistency—extraordinary. What do you call it?"

"Porridge, Mr. Hunt," said Jane with some satisfaction. "Brought all the way from Annandale."

"Ah, I see," he said, smiling reflectively. "I was sure it must be something you had brought here with you. I assure you there is nothing like it in London."

"Aye," said Carlyle, "there *is* none like it here. Ground by the Satur mill—and we've brought fifteen stone with us. But ye must take more on your plate, my good man. What ye've taken would not suffice a bird."

"Indeed, I could not." He laughed, though it was really (thought Carlyle) more of a titter than an honest laugh. "I shouldn't wish to spoil such perfection through superfluity. But I shall certainly suggest to Mrs. Hunt, who, I see at once, lacks your lovely wife's sagacity in the arts of domestic economy, to serve it to our little tribe. An excellent and frugal repast this—I fancy old Cincinnatus would have relished it, were porridge known to the Romans."

Jane smiled.

"You jest," said Carlyle affably, "yet here is simple justice and plain truth: my Jeannie is the best of managers. If she were not, we would not have survived eight long years in the wilderness. You must know as well as I—literature is not the securest of bulwarks against adversity."

"True, true." Hunt scrutinized the tureen of porridge, determined to find some sunnier significance to Carlyle's observation. Finding such silvery linings was, after all, his special gift. He looked up with a smile of triumphant optimism. "But 'sweet are the uses of adversity,' and no less sweet—that is, when one puts sugar on it—the good porridge of Annandale."

To this they all raised imaginary glasses. In the sudden silence they were made aware, by its warbling, of the prophet in the breakfast room.

"Ah," said Hunt (laying aside the teaspoon), "listen—how he sings. Tell me—" He leaned in the direction of Jane. "—has the bird a name?"

"His name is Chico."

"Chico," he repeated. "His singing brings to the darkness of a room at dusk an invisible light. Such a cheerful little presence."

"Chico," said Jane, turning in her chair to address the canary, "dost thou hear how this gentleman flatters thee, Best of All Birds?"

"He brings to mind," Hunt continued, "a nightingale I heard once, one morning walking Londonwards from Surrey." He paused.

Carlyle had returned to his porridge. His wife, however, was charmed by the fancy, despite her better judgment, and smiled to encourage Hunt.

When Chico at last fell silent, Hunt continued: "With each florid variation a half-forgotten experience from our youth is told again, and in each retelling some new element of remembrance is introduced— plaintive, remote, and yet clear as the roulades of a fountain, all unseen, deep in the wood. One's impulse—my own, I confess—was to kneel there by the hedgerow, so that my soul might memorize that unearthly song; which, of course, it never will be able—or what would be the use of nightingales?" He laughed. "You must, Carlyle, some morning before daybreak, come with me to the Surrey hills. The experience is essential to our lives!"

Carlyle cast a doubtful look at his wife. He hadn't expected Hunt's peroration to lead to so tangible a conclusion; one which, moreover, posed a threat to his sleep.

Jane did not choose to help him out of his dilemma. "What say you, Carlyle?" she asked with a mischievous smile. "Will you arise before the sun and accompany Hunt in his quest after Supreme Beauty?"

"Might a nightingale not come to our own bit of garden?" Carlyle temporized.

"Oh no," Hunt assured him, "paved streets and nightingales are incompatible."

"I fear that if we did go off, as you suggest, your woodland fountain might choose not to burble on cue. Jane will tell you how difficult I become when I am disappointed in my hopes."

"Oh, he is a veritable Mountain of Wrath when he is *vaixed*!"

Hunt pondered this with seeming gravity, then persisted: "One must be patient, of course. If our first expedition fail, we must undertake a second."

Carlyle laughed. "Better and better. I shall lose not a single night's sleep but an entire week's! All well for you poets to wait on inspiration —I have sorrier duties, and must keep business hours to perform them."

"I see." Hunt looked as downcast as a child who's been told he's not to be allowed out of doors.

Carlyle felt abashed. "Well, well," he said in a mollifying tone, "we may, for all of that, sacrifice a few hours to such essential beauty, though I'll be much surprised if your nightingale's song surpasses our Chico's. Or Jenny's, for that matter."

Hunt, who had taken up his spoon again, paused with another morsel of porridge suspended before his lips. "Jenny?" he repeated in a questioning tone. The blush on Mrs. Carlyle's face, however, answered at least the most basic of his questions. "But only a moment ago it was 'Jane.' And a moment before that, 'Jeannie.' If I may say so, Mrs. Carlyle, you rival Cleopatra in your infinite variety."

Jane laughed. "There are still more, Mr. Hunt. I am Janekin, Jeanniekin, Wifekin—"

"Not to forget," Carlyle interrupted, "Goody—that is my sport name for her."

"Yes, and Goodykin—for whoever or whatever I am, I am also the diminutive of it."

"I realize, of course," said Hunt, with one of the seraphic smiles with which he prefaced most compliments, "that in Scotland manners are more . . . formal, than among us London cockneys. . . ." He paused to take a spoonful of the porridge and continued. "So I should not venture to address you, madam, with undue familiarity, whatever warmth of friendship I may feel. Yet I shall, with your permission, *think* of you as 'Jenny.' Somehow that suits."

"By all means, sir," replied Jane in the same mock-courtly tone. "In your thoughts, or wherever else it may please you, let me remain—" She inclined her head coquettishly. "—Yours most affectionately— Jenny."

## 2

Was it that the house was more than usually a shambles, or was his dismay, as he crossed the threshold, the effect of the immediate contrast to the Carlyles' tidiness? The hallway was strewn with *shoes*, for Jacey had lately discovered a similitude between footwear and boats, and entertained herself by sailing navies of old shoes about the various oceans of the house. He would like to have read for a while in the sitting room, but Thornton—at twenty-four, Hunt's eldest son—had already unfolded the screen and retired behind it with Kate, his newly-wed bride; consequently the room was dark. As to the rooms upstairs, those were inviolably the children's—just as his niche of a study was inviolably *his* (and was, as a result, the only room in the house in which something like order obtained, if only the order of books on shelves, alphabetical by author). That was where, any night but to-night, he would have betaken himself—but his lamp had exhausted its last drops of midnight oil late last night and he'd not succeeded in refilling it. According to Mrs. Whitfield (who was usually right), there was no oil in the house and few candles—a shortage that might explain Thornton and Kate's retiring so early. Still, there might be a stub discoverable in the sitting room; and if he were very quiet . . .

But before he'd ventured a single step into the darkened room, he was brought short by Marianne's voice: "Henry?" for so she was wont to call her husband, "Henry, is that you?" There was no resisting that peremptory tone. It was too much to hope that she'd have gone to bed without first receiving a postmortem of his visit to the Carlyles. And so, with a sigh of resignation, he proceeded down the hallway to their bedroom.

Marianne, sprawled sideways on the bed in a wrinkled nightgown, drowsed over a book. She seemed, by the light of a single candle, so inert as to be lifeless—as though she were the spring's last, vast mound of unmelted dirty snow, preserved in some shadowy northern declivity. Hunt looked at her with a brief, ineffable flash of hatred, which a sense of moral duty quickly modulated to an impulse of conscious pity:

poor, sick darling. For her part, Marianne, from the moment she'd heard her husband at the front door, had felt an answering and equal aversion, not so keen as his perhaps, since she had labored under no inner necessity to transform her resentment and animosity into affections of a less reprehensible cast. It had been many years since she'd tried to have principles.

"How was the party?" she asked languidly.

"In fact," Hunt said, unbuttoning his waistcoat, "I had a lovely time. Carlyle is a noble talker, and his wife the most charming creature —and not without a mind of her own."

Marianne grimaced, but she did not protest against her husband's implication: that *she* did not possess a mind of her own. "And the house itself?"

"Oh, very modest, though of a well-nigh nautical neatness. Their best furniture seems mostly to have been handed down from the family —hers, I fancy. The carpet is pieced out with bits of, I believe, flannel in one room. All done up with the greatest care."

"It sounds respectable, at least."

"Yes, it manages that much, but just barely. I could swear, Marianne, that I smell prawns." He lifted the spread delicately, like a seamstress at a fitting, and looked under the bed. There was a half-empty mug of porter, but no sign of the prawns.

"The bowl's on the commode," said Marianne, affecting to read again, "but I don't think there are any left."

"*How* did you get prawns? When I left here, three hours ago, you said there was not a farthing in the house. Have you found a way to arrange terms of credit with shrimp girls?"

"I sent John round the corner with the first volume of this." She tapped the open book before her. "Round the corner" was family slang for the pawnshop on Lombard Street near *The Rising Sun.*

Hunt picked up the bowl, which contained now only the brittle, bitten-off tails of the prawns.

"Oh, Marianne," he said in a tone of quite genuine disappointment (for he would have liked some prawns himself), "how can you *do* such things? When Mary Shelley was so kind as to lend you the book . . . "

"One must eat, my dear. It's all very well for you: you can always invite yourself somewhere in the evening and stay on till they have to invite you to supper. What am I to do?"

"Where is the ticket?" Hunt demanded.

"I'm using it for a bookmark."

"Let me have it, please, before you pawn the second volume. And in future would you please pawn what belongs to us before you dispose of goods that our few remaining friends have lent to us."

"If I did, you'd never redeem them. Percy's suit is still round the corner. For three months now. If he wants to go into the City he has to borrow Henry's, which is too small."

"My dear Marianne, it ill behooves *you* to reproach me when it was undoubtedly you who pawned the poor boy's suit." He held up his hand to prevent an anticipated protest. "Please. We've discussed this quite thoroughly before; indeed, the ground is all as familiar as the floor of a prison cell. Let us not rub salt in the wound. And speaking of salt, what *is* there to eat, do you know?"

"Nothing, unless John left some scraps of bread on the plate on the mantel. He won't eat crusts, you know."

Hunt went in search of the crusts and found, instead, a hard-boiled egg that someone had shelled and taken only a single bite of. He finished it off in three mouthfuls.

"I thought you'd had supper."

Hunt smiled and shook his head. "I had what the Carlyles are content to eat for supper, which is a bowl of oatmeal porridge."

"Really, Henry, they can't be as poor as that! Their rates are thirty-five pounds a year. They have a kitchenmaid."

"It isn't poverty that compels them but prudence—something you would know nothing of, Marianne."

"You're a fine one to talk."

Hunt wiped crumbs of yolk off onto the bedspread and proceeded to untie his cravat. "I shall tell you this, Marianne: the Carlyles will be one too many for you. To borrow so much as a cup of sugar from that household you will need the wiles of a diplomat. They are as close . . ." He searched for a metaphor. ". . . as close as Croesus."

Marianne could not keep from smiling. "And that was *all* they had? Oatmeal?"

"They claim to consume a pound a day—and Carlyle (in confidence, of course) complained of his bowels—that they won't move!"

Marianne laughed. "A fine pair of neighbors you've found for us! Tell me, is he in person at all like that essay of his you tried to make me read?"

"At his best, you would suppose he were reading aloud from one of his own manuscripts."

"Worse and worse. I pity the poor wife."

"Oh, Jenny *venerates* her husband. It is wonderful to see."

"Jenny is it? After just one visit."

"As to that, Marianne, you need feel no anxiety. I could flirt with her till Doomsday, and she'd be proof against it. You see, she believes in her husband's Genius, and a wife who does that is more certain to be faithful to him than if she were in love."

Marianne shook her head. "Everything you say only makes me realize that, after all, there are others more unfortunate than myself. Do stop dawdling and come to bed. I'm cold."

# CHAPTER THREE

# A Rival

---

1

Within the drawer of his writing table the pages gathered, each day's work adding to the tangible thickness of the manuscript. In his duller or darker moments he would comfort himself by taking the pages in his hands to feel the actual weight of so many words. Louis XV was made to die, the Dubarry to flit, alarmed, from the scene of that royal death; one by one the final set of scoundrels entered onto the stage of the Ancien Régime; fine ideas collided with the vanities of Versailles, with its perpetual bottomless need for money, preferably in some other form than paper. Inexorably France moved toward its self-created doom.

If any further proof were wanted to attest to his book's satisfactory progress, it may be noted that he was once more suffering all the torments of the damned—such times, at least, as he thought to confide his condition to the pages of his diary. Carlyle never wrote well except he suffered. He suffered from dyspepsia; he suffered from the heat; he suffered from the cry of "Shrim-m-mps! Shrim-m-mps!" outside his window; he suffered from depressions that struck suddenly and with hurricane force; now, however, he suffered chiefly from neglect. For him the move to London had not been attended by its looked-for consequences. Editors of periodicals had not sought him out. Fraser was now quite determined not to bring out the Teufelsdröckh essays *as* a book, and Carlyle had to content himself with binding the magazine installments together to produce, for his own satisfaction, a simulation of a proper bound volume. The only real encouragement came from

Boston in America, that is, from young Emerson, and even he qualified his praise of the book's "celestial truths" with deprecations of its quirky "spendthrift style." Spendthrift—of all pejoratives for *him* to be saddled with! Emerson meant well; he only lacked a sense of humor.

Jane (her husband's sufferings notwithstanding) was enjoying these first weeks in Chelsea. After the solitudes of Craigenputtock, how could she feel other than redeemed by so much Society? Whole afternoons and evenings of speech; a veritable parade of faces; a sense— not to be found on northern moors—of some infinitely vast plot unfolding. She had become, in brief, a Londoner.

The third resident of No. 5, Cheyne Row, felt no such redemption in her altered circumstances. For Bessy Barnet the life of a London domestic (say, rather, Chelsea, for of London itself she'd seen but a glimpse) differed in few respects from the life of a Birmingham domestic, except that it was harder, since the Carlyles had no staff besides herself. But Bessy was not, like so many million of her sisters in the attics and sculleries of England, obliged to be mutely miserable. When she could find the time and the paper (the latter a much more available commodity in the Carlyle household), she was quite capable of chronicling her own unhappiness in a letter home. Such a letter as this, begun on a July afternoon when an unaccustomed ferocity of summer weather had brought the perpetual motion of domestic drudgery to a temporary halt:

*Dearest Mamma,*

Please forgive me for not answering sooner but there is so much to do, for we are still settling in, as Mrs. Carlyle says. You say you miss me—how much more I miss you! I cannot go on pretending to you, as I did in my first letter, that my life here is what we wished it would be when we were so full of hopes last winter. It is not the work only, though there never seems an end to it, and I cannot say the Carlyles have been unkind. They never remind me of what I have come here to forget. At first I thought I should be as happy as ever I was with Mr. B—happier, since there is no shame in the friendship *they* offer. And they are kind in their way—I have tea *with* them on Sundays, we read aloud afterwards, sometimes he reads his own work, and Mrs. C is very confiding sometimes when we are alone. But that is not often, and for most hours of every day I am alone, with *no one* to talk to. That is, of what I *feel*, of what Mr. B's death has meant to me, of how much I *loved* him. When I try to speak of such things to Mrs. C she refuses her sympathy and turns away, and thinks of some new char to stop my tongue. It is only embarrassment, I think —not a judgement. She is not like other married women. In any case, she will not listen and there is no one else, for the neighbours' girls are all very *low* and make sport of me for *my* speech! Some times I stand behind the door when the Carlyles have company just to hear their voices. At night, some times, Mr. C will come and sit in the front kitchen because he can smoke his pipe there and he will sit for hours reading his book and I must do nothing all the while. Oh Mamma, anything would be better than this, even Reverend Flanders scolding me after the funeral when I had comported myself so ill, which I confess was very shameful of me. And then during these first days of mourning too. But I am over all of that, truly I am. If you could only . . .

Her pen hesitated, not daring to ask the favor for which this confession had been the preparation.

As though to reproach these rebellious thoughts, the doorbell sounded and Bessy put the unfinished letter into her private drawer, tucking it within the folds of her bedding. Would she dare take it out and finish it ever? The bell rang again. She hurried upstairs, expecting to be preceded to the door by one of the Carlyles, but although they were at home, neither was in evidence.

It was with a sense of quiet dismay that Bessy recognized the man on the doorstep as Mr. Mill. John Stuart Mill was, excepting Leigh Hunt, the most frequent and (without exception) the dullest of the Carlyles' visitors. Today, however, something almost like animation enlivened the young man's mild features, and there on the pavement behind him was the source of this unwonted liveliness. Though the woman had never before been a visitor to Cheyne Row, Bessy could guess who she must be: her fame, better infamy, had preceded her.

"Good afternoon," Mill said. His pale eyes avoided Bessy's while he tried, and failed, to remember her name. Then, with a wan smile meant to excuse the omission, "I wonder if you could announce myself and Mrs. Taylor."

So *this*, Bessy thought, with that mingling of satisfaction and disappointment that comes of witnessing what one has long imagined, is Mrs. John Taylor. She was altogether another order of being from the drab John Mill—a proper fashion plate, and cool as rain (as though there couldn't be a doubt in her mind that she'd be admitted to the Carlyle residence). Perhaps she didn't know that she'd become, without Carlyle's ever laying eyes on her, his enemy—or, more accurately, his rival?

It was not without a sense of mischief, then, that Bessy asked the couple to wait within the dining room while she ascertained, upstairs, if the Carlyles were home. She could not be taken to task for such an initiative, since John Mill was a regular visitor and Mrs. Taylor was not presumably known (to Bessy) to be an unwelcome presence.

The Carlyles, meanwhile, were conducting a quick, furious, whispered argument as to which of them was to go downstairs and receive their visitors, whose arrival they'd witnessed from a window overlooking the doorstep. Jane, who invariably lost such arguments, went down, while Carlyle, in a flush of anxiety and indignation, retreated to the floor above with a book. There he sat staring at a copper-plate engraving of the head of Mirabeau, the frontispiece of an edition of that man's memoirs. One would not suppose from those plump features that the man had once been a libertine of the most abandoned character; nor would one think it of John Mill, but such, to Carlyle's ever-mounting dismay, was the case. Carlyle had it on the authority of Sarah Austin, who was a neighbor of Mill's at Queen Square, John's tutor in German, his sister's in French, and who attended the same intellectually fashionable Unitarian church in Finsbury as the fatal woman for whose love Mill was ruining himself. The woman's name was Harriet Taylor; she was the wife of a prosperous wholesale druggist in Islington and the mother of three children. Worst of all (from Carlyle's view; to Mill it may have been her chief charm), she was a blue-stocking, a woman, that is to say, with ideas of her own.

None of this would have mattered (or it would have mattered no more than the generality of the world's iniquities and follies) were it not for the love that Carlyle bore Mill; a love that until quite recently had seemed to be reciprocated; a love (it must be said at once) of a character both pure and noble, the love of teacher and student, of master and disciple. To teach was the foundation of Carlyle's character, the basis of his deepest friendships; not simply in the sense of delivering lectures that must be attended to (though he insisted on that too), but in a larger and worthier sense. This was the era of self-made men. Behind every such "self-made" man, however, there has been someone who first fired him with the ambition to achieve, who assured him, if only in a smile or a handclasp, that yes, he was built in the heroic mold and might expect to conquer some significant portion of the world. It was in this sense, as an inspirer and firer, that Carlyle must be accounted a great teacher. Even Jane had been his pupil before she had become his wife.

If Carlyle's greatness was to teach, no less was it John Mill's to learn. His childhood had been one endless cram, beginning with Greek and arithmetic at the age of three and progressing systematically through the whole gamut of human knowledge. His instructor in all subjects had been his father, the philosopher-economist James Mill, as exacting a taskmaster in his own way as any mine owner or cottonmill operator of the time, when children no older than John were chained to the carts or the looms. By the age of eleven he was able to help his father correct the galley proofs of his mammoth history of India; by nineteen he was virtually co-author, with Jeremy Bentham, of *Rationale of Judicial Evidence*, in five volumes. He was enabled to perform such prodigies by virtue of a memory that might have been called photographic at a later date, and a mind that had often been likened, for sheer dauntless force of logic, to a steam engine. For all this, Mill had not been a particularly happy youth; quite the opposite, indeed. The element that had been left out of his education (as it had been left out, so noticeably, of his father's many volumes of philosophy) was feeling. John knew this—had known it since his first onslaught of suicidal depression some seven years ago when he was twenty-one. The first remedy he'd attempted was poetry, downing tomes of Wordsworth like medicinal draughts of stout, but after a time he found that Carlyle's work, with its larger frame of reference, was more to his taste. They'd corresponded and then, three years ago, they'd met. Mill was at once swept off his intellectual feet, and Carlyle too, as noted above, succumbed. Not only was the boy the most promising of all his potential disciples (Carlyle would have nothing less than discipleship), he was also the son and, till lately, the spokesman of one of his own *bêtes noires*. Could he ask for a finer trophy for his own all-conquering philosophy?

And to think that his beloved disciple, his John, should now be consorting openly with this druggist's wife, this adulterous blue-stocking! They were almost—so Sarah Austin declared—regarded as "a couple" in the circles in which they moved; circles in which the Carlyles themselves had made some few tentative explorations. It was even whispered that John Taylor made no objection to his wife's liaison, that his complaisance extended to active encouragement! Could such things be? What were they doing now? Carlyle went to the head of the stairs and strained to hear their voices. Useless, wholly useless.

If only the same might be said of Mill! If only the friendship could be cast off like soiled linen! Alack, the nearest similitude would be amputation of a limb, for of all Carlyle's London acquaintances Mill was surely the usefulest. He had been a dependable source of introductions to various literary lions of the day, and more importantly, to editors of a liberal tendency. There was even, Carlyle believed, the chance of Mill's arranging for *him* to be the editor of the leading radical periodical, *The Westminster Review.* What a plum *that* would be, and what an editor *he* would be: the journal would be altered out of recognition, he dare swear to that already!

This, may be, was a daydream and might come to nothing (Mill had already hinted that Molesworth, who funded the *Review*, was not yet fully persuaded of Carlyle's fitness for the task), but Mill's usefulness was both larger and more practical. In addition to the other accomplishments he'd packed into his prodigious youth, Mill had acquired a knowledge of the actual history of the French Revolution (as against the myths then current among most Englishmen) that made Carlyle's own command of the subject seem inconsiderable. He'd lived in Paris, spoken with many of the Revolution's surviving luminaries—including the great Lafayette himself—had mastered the available literature and amassed for himself a library on the subject superior to any in England (though a fair proportion of these books were on permanent loan to Carlyle). What a boon, what a providence, therefore, to have a mind so stocked and an intelligence so keen and scrupulous available on a continuous basis. Mill came by every Sunday, the day he was free from his office, and together they would pursue their one great theme down its thousand tributary avenues, Carlyle setting forth, like so many gold and crimson skyrockets, his free renderings of how it must have been in the days of Loménie-Brienne or at the convocation of the States-General, and Mill either filling in the broad outline from his own richer store of information or annihilating speculations with a sharp inference or a fatal fact. Carlyle would kick against these pricks, at times quite fiercely, but Mill could never be blustered out of what he believed, though occasionally he might be persuaded. The book lost, by this process, many splendid swoops and filigrees of gold and crimson, but it gained immeasurably in other respects. Insofar as it was in his nature, Carlyle was grateful.

His reverie was broken by the sound of footsteps. Was Jane bringing them up here? Heaven forbid! No—she was taking them out into the garden, where, by standing close to the window at the turning of the stairs, he was able to see the stiff brim of the capote bonnet hiding all of Mrs. Taylor's features but two swaying cones of curls on either side of her neck. Mill and Jane remained outside his purview, though he could hear Mill's desiccated voice praising the garden's cooler air. Then in a voice compact of affectation and false sentiment, he heard Mrs. Taylor pipe: "Jessamine!" She flounced to the shadier, north-facing wall and touched a flowering branch with her gloved hand (pink gloves, forsooth) and turned about, arm still lifted, like an actress on a stage. "Jessamine is my favorite flower, Mrs. Carlyle. The *scent* of it in the evening . . . !"

"Yes, despite this poor Chelsea soil it seems to thrive," he could hear Jane saying, as it were, off-stage. "It has come with us all the way from Dumfriesshire, no small journey for a wounded shrub with only a clump of earth to call its own—but Carlyle is an inspired gardener, and I daresay our jessamine shall survive."

Mrs. Taylor lifted her long skirts and swept across the grass to the flower beds. "You mean that *he* has accomplished all this? How remarkable! Literary men so seldom stir themselves outside their dusty rooms. John, how many times have I told you, *you* must take up such a pastime?"

"John!" If Mill made reply to this question, Carlyle did not hear it. "John," she called him, quite as though they were betrothed! And before Jeannie! It surpassed belief.

If Carlyle was touchier on this matter of first names than many of his contemporaries (Harriet Taylor had had no intention of being indiscreet; she called *all* her friends by their Christian names), this was an aspect of his Scottishness. Among the countryfolk of Annandale the familiar forms of the second person still survived, and the distinction between the formal and the familiar, between you the neighbors and thou the family, had a force and a firmness that must be lost whenever the *tutoiement* is abandoned.

There was no help for it—he must go downstairs and defend his sacred hearth. Jane could not be expected (possibly could not be trusted) to deal with such matters. Next this woman would be asking them to dine *chez* Taylor! Then, too, there was the question of *The Review.* Mill had said he'd have word from Molesworth this week, a yea or a nay with no more equivocation. The fact that he'd come calling thus unannounced (albeit with his inamorata) must surely be a favorable augury.

With a deep-drawn breath and such a prayer as soldiers pray before they follow the trumpet to glory or to death, Thomas Carlyle went down to the garden. There, leaning in the frame of the doorway, wiping sweat from his hatband with a dirty handkerchief, was the beloved disciple, unhampered for the moment by the presence of Mrs. Taylor, who was still cooing and swooping about the garden with Jane.

"John," said Carlyle with a quaver of reproach, "is it thou?"

"Ah, Mr. Carlyle!" Mill handled his hat uncertainly. Being half indoors and half outdoors, he did not know if his hat should be on his head or in his hand. "Mrs. Carlyle said that you . . . were occupied, and we, um, assured her we did not want to take you from your work, as we are *both* so earnestly admiring of the productions of your pen. As you know, sir, Harriet especially admires the Teufelsdröckh essays."

"Harriet?" Carlyle inquired.

"That is, Mrs. Taylor. I've wanted so long for you to meet her, and since we somehow lost our bearings in the vicinity of Wellington Street, I suggested we might drop by on the chance you were home. I hope you don't mind: it was my idea."

"Not at all. But you've chosen a very hot day to be peripatetic. Come inside, come inside where it is cooler."

"But the ladies . . ."

"The ladies always require a little time alone. I shall tell Bessy—" He turned and called into the basement. "—Bessy!—to wet the flagstones so that we shan't be baked alive when we take tea in the garden. You will stay for tea?"

"I should ask, um, Mrs. Taylor. I'm not altogether sure . . ."

"Nonsense, John. Remember what I said a month ago: You must

not be disingenuous. A man of your parts, at twenty-eight, has no business being disingenuous. Now, come upstairs, and—" (in just the same peremptory tone to Bessy, who had come up to the head of the stairs) "—Wet the flagstones *thoroughly*. We shall be taking tea in the garden."

Bessy nodded, and John nodded, and Carlyle, feeling himself obeyed, nodded as well.

---

### 2

"Wherever can he have gone?" asked Mrs. Taylor rhetorically, having concluded her tour of the garden.

"Ah, my husband must have come down and carried him off. They'll be up in the drawing room."

But when Jane showed Mrs. Taylor into that room, there was no sign of either gentleman. Excusing herself—and the bell rope, which hadn't worked since its installation, two days after they moved in— Jane went off in search of Bessy. Mrs. Taylor, left alone, went directly to the book press near the fireplace and studied the titles—those that were legible—on the spines of the books. As she scanned the ranked volumes, her expression underwent a profound and rapid change. Gone was the limpid, well-regulated sweetness, the ivory composure, the ever-incipient smile at the edges of her lips; in their place was something nearly resembling wrath. Impulsively, she took out one of the volumes —it was Condorcet's *Vie de Turgot*—and opened it to scrutinize the marbled endpapers. A folded foolscap sheet fluttered to the floor. She stooped to retrieve it and, still stooping, read the lines of regular, neat handwriting, growing visibly angrier with every word.

"Ma'am?"

Mrs. Taylor looked up, her face quite scarlet from the combined influences of anger and embarrassment. It was the Carlyles' maid.

"Yes?" She got to her feet and, with as much composure as she could muster, replaced the book she'd taken from the shelf.

"Mrs. Carlyle said to ask you, ma'am, if you would like to join her in the garden."

"I shall be down directly."

The maid nodded and left.

"The scoundrel," she whispered. "The damned, thieving scoundrel!" Then, taking a deep breath, she composed her features and descended to the garden, where four chairs had been placed upon the moistened flagstones about a small folding table.

Jane, having created this impromptu tea-garden and feeling, as she always did when she'd achieved some new domestic order, much more at ease, greeted Mrs. Taylor with a smile. "The gentlemen have disappeared altogether, but I trust they will be back momently. Come, sit here by me in the coolness, Mrs. Taylor, and tell me about your writing."

Mrs. Taylor took the chair offered and tried to resume her earlier, friendly frame of mind. She felt no animus, after all, against her hostess, who struck her, in her rustic, unpretending way, as a distinct original, certainly by comparison to other literary wives.

"As to that, Mrs. Carlyle, I am still very much of an apprentice. Shelley has been my greatest inspiration, but also may be my undoing. Great poetry, I think, must come in one spontaneous gust or not at all. I labor to produce a sonnet, and the labor I fear shows. But I hope that some day, with practice, I shall develop more facility. In any case, it is the only thing that seems at all worth doing."

"But your work has been published. Mr. Mill has been kind enough to send us copies of the *Monthly Repository*, in which I remember now seeing the name of Harriet Taylor."

"Oh, John is much too eager to trumpet my talents. It is wonderful, of course, to have so sympathetic a critic, but he really is too partial. And as to appearing in the *Repository*, its editor is a dear, dear friend. Have you met Mr. Fox? No? Then you must. There is not a more liberal or more far-sighted man in all England, excepting, of course, John—and Mr. Carlyle. Fox is a friend to all humanity. But sometimes, perhaps, too indulgent a friend, which alone accounts for my poetry having come, so prematurely, to the world's attention." She paused. "And yourself, Mrs. Carlyle? Tell me—honestly now—do *you* not write? Forgive me if I am impertinent, but you seem the sort of person who would."

Jane smiled, remembering with sudden vividness an exchange she'd just recently had with Marianne Hunt. It was altogether apropos to Mrs. Taylor's question, but its gist might be somewhat deflating to anyone who regarded poetry as "the only thing . . . worth doing."

"You put me in mind of our neighbor, Mrs. Hunt, whose company I cleverly avoided yesterday with the excuse, which was quite true, that I was *painting*. She dropped by to invite me to tea. I'm quite sure, had I accepted the invitation, that I'd have been obliged to provide tea, bread, butter, and probably the crockery too—Mrs. Hunt is notoriously *that* sort of householder. Well, after I'd declined her invitation, she wanted to know what kind of painting I was doing. I was vague. She insisted: 'A portrait?' 'No,' said I, 'something on a much grander scale than that. I'm painting a *wardrobe*.' She was dumbfounded—" (As, it would seem from her politely incredulous smile, was Mrs. Taylor.) "Was that the sort of thing that *I* should be doing, she wanted to know. I simply told her that my husband would allow me no dinner if the wardrobe wasn't completely painted by five o'clock. And I perceived she *believed* me! Whatever, one genius of the literary variety is enough for any household, and I confine my writing to letters."

"Jeannie, you are too modest," said her husband, appearing of a sudden in the doorway. Mill stood in the hall behind him, squinting into the brightness of the sunlit garden.

Mrs. Taylor started and, turning round, regarded Carlyle with a glint of the anger she had managed, talking with Jane, to subdue; the minutest fraction of her earlier outrage, but Carlyle's quick eye took it in and answered with a glint of its own. There was a pause during which Mill, had he the presence of mind, might have introduced the two rivals for his affections to each other, a formality the omission of which both Carlyle and Mrs. Taylor had noted. But Mill had just been through the excrucitation of informing his friend that the editorship of *The Westminster Review* had been settled on himself (as, indeed, he'd always intended it should be), not on Carlyle, and so the moment passed. Carlyle and Mrs. Taylor were to remain, in a formal sense, strangers thereafter.

Before his wife could correct this breach of etiquette, Carlyle seated himself and continued: "Before we married, Jeannie would turn all her tenderer feelings into couplets. I've often wondered what ended the rhyming."

"Hush," said Jane acerbly. She didn't like her husband to contradict her, even if a compliment were intended.

"Just as I thought," said Mrs. Taylor. "You *do* write."

Jane avoided her eyes. "Only, as I say, letters."

"If it be your nature to write, you must follow your nature. That is the cardinal rule, is it not?—to follow one's nature? But I see that we must discuss these matters another time, when we have more leisure, and when—" She turned in her chair to confront Carlyle, who met her challenge with unruffled equanimity. "—we are alone."

After tea Jane took Mill for a turn about the garden, and Mrs. Taylor was left with Carlyle. She had been able, during the polite inanities of teatime, to compose a compliment for the inevitable moment when they would be left on their own—a very rosy compliment, though the rose was not without its thorn.

"I have begun to read your series of papers in *Fraser's Magazine*, Mr. Carlyle—with, I may say, the liveliest pleasure, and even, when I think of it, some edification."

Carlyle inclined his head, accepting the praise as his due—and not much crediting it. If Mrs. Taylor had actually apprehended his message, he believed, she would cease being Mrs. Taylor.

"Perhaps it is premature of me to say it, not having read the entire series yet, but I do believe you should collect them together in a single book. With only the smallest adjustments they would make a perfectly fluid sequence."

"Thank you, Mrs. Taylor. They were *written* as a book, so I do not much wonder that they have that appearance."

"Splendid! And what shall you call it, in its entirety?"

"I have thought of it as simply 'Teufelsdröckh'—that being a somewhat cut-down version of the original and full title, 'Thoughts on Clothes; or The Life and Opinions of Herr D. Teufelsdröckh, D.U.J.' But I've had second thoughts since. What think you of 'Sartor Resartus' for a name?"

"That is the Latin . . . for?"

"Yes, 'The Tailor Re-patched.' "

"Of course." She wondered—but did not ask—what *that* might mean. "What has most struck me in your . . . book, is its 'philosophy of clothes.' We women are so much more under the tyranny of fashion; such unnecessary importance seems to attach to the way we dress our hair and to the use of cosmetic agents, that when I began, gradually, to apprehend your meaning, it came like the sun out from a bank of clouds."

"That is a reasonable enough meaning, ma'am, but it is Mr. Rousseau's, not mine. *I* am not saying we would do better to imitate the savages and shed our clothes, or even that we must simplify them, though no doubt a case could be made for the latter. On the contrary, what I am saying is that clothes are the essence of civilization—clothes and what they stand for—a code of behavior, a set of proprieties, a moral Law."

"I appreciate that. But are you not also saying that we have, in our century, worn out the clothes we've inherited from the past; that, accordingly, we must fit ourselves out with new clothes—and new moral laws?"

This was, indeed, the message of *Sartor*, but it did not at all suit Carlyle to hear it proceeding from the lips of Mrs. Taylor. He was certain that the first moral law *she* meant to reform was the one concerning adultery, and it was most emphatically not *his* meaning to be a spokesman for profligacy and sin. On that point he could be as unyielding and uncharitable as his Calvinist ancestors. He did not like blue-stockings. Emphatically, he did not. So, to her question, he accorded only a dour grunt of acquiescence—and promptly changed the subject.

"And when shall we have the opportunity of meeting *Mr.* Taylor? Soon, I hope."

"Oh yes, I share your hope, and indeed earlier I told Mrs. Carlyle that we mean to have you both to dinner with us at the earliest opportunity. But we should like to have our dear friend William Fox of the *Monthly Repository* present as well. However, unfortunately, at just this moment that presents a difficulty, for Mr. Fox is involved in a small conflict with certain members of our church. This has taken up much of my husband's free time, additionally, since *he* is very active in the affairs of the church. We are Unitarians, you know."

"Yes, I know."

He knew, as well, the nature of Fox's "small conflict" with the members of his church. Fox had reportedly taken his young ward Eliza Flower as mistress, and Mrs. Fox (a less complacent spouse than Mr. Taylor) had lately raised a protest among the members of her husband's congregation. There was a movement afoot to remove him from the pulpit. It was wonderful, thought Carlyle, how all these Unitarians apparently had no other motive behind all their free thinking and liberal philosophizing than to justify their own ungoverned instincts.

Feeling herself and her religion dismissed, Mrs. Taylor asked: "And what religion is yours, Mr. Carlyle? *Sartor Resartus*—which, incidentally, *must* be the title—has the stamp of Enthusiasm on it, yet I should be hard pressed to say that it reflected any known faith."

"I've often been asked that question, Mrs. Taylor, and my answer is always the same. My faith is a matter of confidence between the Almighty and myself."

3

"Well, Jeannie, what thinkst thou of Mrs. *Platonica* Taylor?" Carlyle demanded of his wife the moment that their guests had left them.

It was clear from his tone that *he* had no very high regard for her; but Jane, though prepared to accept the nickname with its various implications, was not yet ready to consign Mrs. Taylor to the outer darkness of overt ostracism. For his own good, Carlyle himself must be brought round to a friendlier state of mind.

"I thought her rather a pleasant woman, as a matter of fact," said Jane blandly. "Admittedly, we talked of nothing very important—the garden and her children . . . and, of course, she *dresses* beautifully. Mr. Taylor must be a very prosperous man."

"A bitter man, too, I should judge."

"As to that, we shall have occasion to judge for ourselves. 'Platonica' wants us to dine at their home in the near future, and means to have Fox on hand to meet us."

At his wife's adoption of his own sarcastic epithet, Carlyle smiled with satisfaction. "Yes, she held up the same bait to me."

"But we should meet him, for he promises to be, at the least, a very characteristic fool, of a type not much met with anymore—'a friend,' Mrs. Taylor avers, 'of all humanity.'" Her eyes narrowed, glinting, as with the sheer pleasure of taking aim. ". . . A description that put me in mind of that droll creature you lately dug up for your History, the one who wished to make the world a Universal Republic and convened a kind of Babel-Congress toward that end. What was his name?"

"Anacharsis Clootz."

"Anacharsis Clootz. If you hadn't shown it me in cold black print, I should never have believed you had not simply made him up out of whole cloth."

"These 'friends of the species,'" Carlyle scoffed, "they are all the same. All their cant about freedom and the everlasting 'happiness of the greatest number' reduces to a sordid desire to shrug off every uncomfortable or inconvenient *duty*."

"Just so," said Jane, in a tone of soothing, concordant sarcasm. "And *why* they are all so anxious to believe that you are such another I shall never comprehend. Mrs. Taylor seems persuaded that *your* views mirror those of Mill and Fox, which I suppose she means for a compliment."

"When the handwriting appears upon the wall, those who can read will read it, though they will do their best to read their own meanings *into* it, as well."

"Shall we *not* accept the invitation, then?" Jane asked demurely, in the assumed role of his "Goodykins." He had, she calculated, reached that height of self-satisfaction at which he was most tractable.

"Not go to the Taylors'? Nay, what have we to fear from them? So long as there has been no *public* scandal, such as has sprung up around this Fox and his Miss Flower, so long will the Taylors be visitable. And candidly, I expect no scandal. John Mill is too canny to go that way. His blood is cooled as it passes through that fine head of his. He will finally see Mrs. Taylor for what she is."

"And what do you believe she is?" Jane asked.

Carlyle thought a moment. "She is the *heroine* in a *novel* by a *lady-novelist*."

"Do you know, you could tell her that to her face and she would take it for a compliment?"

Carlyle smiled. "I shall."

4

They had walked as far as St. Luke's, the new-minted "Gothic" church on Robert Street, before Harriet would deign to break her baleful silence and explain the one ferocious remark she'd made on departing from No. 5, Cheyne Row, that she would willingly and with pleasure see Thomas Carlyle struck down by lightning and reduced to a heap of smoldering ashes. John, though he had not expected her to be won over at once by Carlyle's rough manner, had certainly hoped for better than this. Until now his whole concern had been for the Carlyles' reception of his All-in-All, his Life and Soul, his own angelic Harriet.

"*Why* am I angry? Can you ask me that, John? Can you look into your own heart without being consumed with anger against that man? Can you?"

"My dear Harriet, 'that man,' as you style him, is one of my dearest friends."

"So much the more shameful, then, that he should steal from you!"

"Steal, Harriet? Whatever do you mean? Carlyle is the soul of probity. I rather feared you'd censor the stiffness of his principles than the contrary."

"Oh, John! Are you blind to what he is doing? Probity? *His* probity! Oh, I suppose one would never catch him pocketing a teaspoon. But good heavens, John, he is stealing your life's work from you."

"Oh, that."

"Oh, that!" she echoed, aghast.

"It wasn't for me to tell you, Harriet, what Carlyle—or anyone else—is writing. Writers are often so sensitive on the point. But rest assured, my dear, that he did not undertake such a work without consulting me as to my intentions."

"Of course. If he knew you meant to write the book that you have in you to write, he would never dare tempt comparisons. He knows nothing on the subject. *I've* read his essays on Voltaire and Diderot, on Cagliostro, as well. They are *thin*, John, transparently so."

"Oh, he has tremendous powers of assimilation. You would be astonished how far he has come in so short a time."

"Having commandeered the better part of *your* library. *That* is how I found him out. I recognized your books filling his drawing room. I took one from the press to be sure. In its pages was what I presume to have been an abandoned draft of a passage on the death of Turgot—in the man's scarletest rodomontade."

"I remember the passage."

"Do you lead him along, then, page by page?"

"Not any longer. We both agree that it is too constraining. When he has a substantial part of it complete, I shall read that. For the time being, we simply discuss his ideas. Really, it has given me enormous pleasure to do so. His *vision* of the period is quite vivid. It will be a fine book."

"But will it be *his*? It seems to me that he is picking ideas from your brain as one would pick ripe apples from the tree!"

"Harriet, I long ago explained to you why I find myself *unable* to undertake a history of the Revolution. It would lead me to say things I dare not say in a public forum, concerning especially the decay of established religion. I believe the Revolution came about because the Enlightenment of the educated classes had penetrated to the meanest hovels, and men no longer had any reason for deferring to any authority whose claim to allegiance was that *le bon Dieu* required it. England is not ready to hear such things, and I have no intention of jeopardizing my livelihood, my career, even my ultimate *usefulness*, by calling down Mrs. Grundy's thunders on my head. I do not wish to be a martyr. Carlyle, however, is in no such difficulty."

"Because he temporizes, do you mean?"

"Not at all, Harriet. Because his own soul is profoundly divided between the old way of thinking—faith, let us call it—and *our* way of thinking. That is why he is the ideal person, at *this* moment, to write such a book, and why I am prepared to offer him every assistance I can. If he gets the facts right, then let the mystic winds blow as they will, he will have written an immensely useful and important book."

Harriet laughed, as if conceding him the point. What made her laugh, however, was the absurdity of his trust in that charlatan Carlyle. Faith? There was no faith blinder in all England than Mill's in Carlyle, unless it were her own in Mill. She believed in his genius with a fervor and fullness of faith beside which the faith of Jane Carlyle would seem like skepticism, and it made her, as faith will, a dangerous woman.

## 5

"It is now—" Bessy resumed on a fresh sheet of paper expropriated from her mistress's writing table,

> —a day later. The sun isn't up yet, but I woke an hour ago and lay awake writing this letter over and over in my thoughts, and now, before I must put on my apron and light the fire, I must put an end to what I have to say. I fear you will judge me lazy or undutiful, that you will consider the fault *all mine*, that I'm still giving over to grieving what was never mine and never could have been. But truly, Mamma, the difficulty is with the Carlyles and not with me—if you could be here and *see* our lives, you would have no reproaches. I don't lay blame on Mrs. C. I feel as sorry for her as ever I felt for poor Dr. B. There is a madness in her ways. She takes up each task

here so furiously, and when there is no work that needs to be done, she will invent some new undertaking. *Often* she will set me to washing stacks of dishes that have never been used. And two weeks ago, when the doctor Mr. Julius came to look at Mr. C, whose liver was more than usually upset, and stayed on until he was asked to spend the night in the spare bedroom—well, next day Mrs. C insisted that we must take apart the bed and look for bugs, as though Mr. Julius were not a respectable gentleman but had come from some low doss house! And then after these commotions she'll be come over by one of her sick megrims and must take to bed for hours at a time. And, Mamma, the food! We eat according to Mr. C's needs—broth and boiled meats—*never* roasted—potatoes, sometimes a pudding, and *always* porridge. Many servants fare worse than I, no doubt. I admit that I have been spoiled by living with Dr. B, who was so very liberal—too much so, you often said. But never to have a single sprout or runner beans and to see the stalls now overflowing with them!

Please don't scold me, Mamma—don't say that I complain about nothing. I don't know how to say what is so upsetting—do you remember the dreams I had when I was a child—how I would awaken screaming and all in a fever? I have begun to have such dreams again.

There was a lady here, yesterday—she arrived while I was writing the beginning of this letter—and I saw her scarce at all, but it was her I saw in the dreaming. Yesterday I came on her by surprise, when she was alone in the study, looking at one of Mr. C's books—and the look she gave me, the look in her eyes—and she a stranger I'd never seen before. And again in the dreaming there was that same look, only I *understood why* the hatred flushed up out of her. I must have screamed when I woke, and I was afraid I'd awakened the Carlyles upstairs, and that made me still more afraid. Living in this house is like living inside those dreams.

Please, Mamma, I entreat you—write in your next letter that you need me at home. Write that your health is worrying you and I am needed. I would not ask you to tell a lie but that I cannot bear to hurt Mrs. C's feelings, for she really wants to be good to me. But I cannot go on living here and seeing their unhappiness. If you do not let me come back to Birmingham, I don't know what I shall do—I shall have myself taken to Bedlam. Truly, I will. Please let me come home. I love you.

*Bess*

# CHAPTER FOUR

# Through the Market Gardens

"Now see here, Martin," he said, with all the authority of greater years and larger girth, "if we don't cross this field of cabbages, I don't see how we can hope to reach the house by teatime, and Mrs. Booth can be a fury when she's thrown out of her reckonings. She'll have both our heads on pikes. Or rather—" He looked back over his shoulder at young Leopold. "—our three heads."

Leopold Martin, though he could scarcely be considered a child any longer (he was twenty-two and already betrothed), had remained a lad of ten in the near-sighted eyes of his father's old friend—a role he was content to accept, since the man, by his own admission, preferred the companionship of children to that of most of his peers.

"Yet this is not our field, old chap," the elder Martin countered, with a worried look at his shoes, "and no cabbage I can imagine would grow the leafier for being trod upon by such as we. A cabbage has quite enough work resisting worms and—damn me!—flooding. Look out there, where the ground dips—the field is still sodden. 'Tis well for you, in those thick boots, but what of us?"

"Hear, hear," murmured Leopold, for his own shoes, though not so new, were the best he had.

"If you'd been so concerned for the time and for Mrs. Booth's temper," John Martin urged, in a tone of smooth reason, "we could have mounted the omnibus when it went past. Then we might have avoided these iniquitous market gardens altogether. But to cross them: no, not in these shoes, please!"

"Very well then," he said grudgingly. It was not a matter worth contending over. He even was able to sympathize with Martin's con-

cern for his shoes, since they must have cost over a quid, being, like
the rest of his rig-out, of a rather dandiacal stamp. His own clothes, by
contrast, were so modest as to seem almost a disguise, albeit a disguise
he preferred to the clothes that Martin and his kind considered more
"fitting" to his station: a heavy pea coat, a much-abused top hat, and,
instead of the usual walking stick emblematic of gentlemanly status,
a spyglass that swung by his side on a cheap watch chain. At a
glance, one would have taken him for a retired seafaring man of the
lower order—the captain, say, of a Thames barge—and so the Chelsea
residents did take him, according the elderly eccentric the honorific
rank of "Admiral."

The three men set off along a lane between the rows of ordered
cabbages that glowed, under the changing light, with the most intense
and various greens. Nothing could touch cabbages for the splendor of
their greens—except the sea. Pity, then, not to be marching headlong
through them; but Martin had no conception of the poetry of *ordinary*
things. He could paint great sprawling vistas of Babylon or the Deluge,
paintings that were really rather good in their way and that sold, when
they sold at all, for prices of corresponding magnitude, but he was
blind, apparently, to the coruscations of a muddy field, the celestial
gleams that the sun may strike from the merest mire.

He stopped short.

Martin stopped behind him, breaking the silence: "I say—" (trying
to restore the earlier tone of bonhomie) "—you can smell the river
already! What a stink it makes in summer, eh? A regular open sewer."

He looked up from the mirrored sky, transformed within the spaces
of a puddle, azure, brown-gray, its single cloud etched with amazing
clarity, to take the direction of the river. "Sewer? Yes, on a summer
afternoon it does get boiled rather, sewage and tar." He wrinkled his
beaklike nose and sniffed at the air. Could Martin really smell the river
already? *He* couldn't catch a whiff of it, though he was not about to
say so to Martin. When one is sixty-four one doesn't fancy making
such admissions to someone who is fifty.

"You know, John," he said, walking again, "I don't believe it a bad
smell. Not bad at all. And the sky on such days, have you noticed?—
not so much today, but—how the light seems to collect into a thick
yellow. A clotted yellow, not a healthy color. Yesterday it was so, but
this morning's rain has cleared the atmosphere, and we shall have a
fine sunset this evening."

"It is strange," said Leopold, "but *I* can't smell a thing."

Both older men glanced sidelong at Leopold, and then at each other.

"If it were not that you smelled it as well, sir—" Leopold nodded deferentially in his direction. "—I should suppose that Father were riding his hobbyhorse again, for he is perfectly capable of smelling the pollution of the Thames from a distance of five miles or more."

"And so I can, Leopold, and it is a disgrace to the government and every citizen of London that such a thing should be allowed." John Martin continued in a vein of prophecy and denunciation, but for all his eloquence, neither of his companions paid him much heed. All that he said was true—the Thames should not be turned into an open cesspool; London had grown too large for such simplicities—but he had said it too often in both their companies for the message to seem in the least urgent. Leopold was even somewhat anxious that his father should have lighted on the subject at all, for it had not been many years since his father had hovered on the brink of bankruptcy as a result of diverting all his working energy from painting into his schemes for creating a modern system of sewage disposal for the entire metropolis.

"Oh, Father," Leopold ventured, when Martin had begun, in an oddly impassioned way, to set forth his scheme for combining a railway line with his ideal sewer system along a hypothetically embanked Thames, "we quite *agree* with you. Preach your gospel to the Philistines, please, not to us."

Though Martin reacted with silence, his diatribe had set a train of thought in motion in the "Admiral's" head: "I'll allow there are days when the water is foul, but there are other days when it is clear as it might be upstream—in Hammersmith. Chelsea survives more a country village than you would think. And this is not so when the current is swift, but when it is slow. Curious."

"You have lived in Hammersmith?" said Leopold, still trying to move away from considerations of sanitation.

"Ah yes. But many years past—I daresay, before you were even born." He smiled broadly, revealing the dark ruins of his teeth. "And I was a lad *your* age, pursued by many the lass—had my way with them, you can be sure." It occurred to him, immediately, that he had been older then, a man in his mid-thirties, and that it was odd how very young, from the viewpoint of one his age now, thirty-six could seem.

"And yet you never married," marveled Leopold, with the very torches of Hymen's altar glowing in his blue eyes.

"Say rather, my boy, that I did not become ensnared. For how can a man want, when he is young and has the world before him, to become tangled in the deceits of womanhood—eh?"

The elder Martin produced a dry admonitory cough, which went unheeded. It would do young Leopold no harm to be told a fact or two of life. Everyone else these days seemed bent on talking nonsense, particularly on the subject of women.

"They're all mad, you know. Women. After a certain age, every one of them succumbs. I regret it, but the fact remains."

Leopold tried to receive this pronouncement with a serious expression and managed not to smile *too* broadly. There could scarcely have been a madder family in England than the Martins, but the taint seemed to infect the blood of the men only. And *such* men! The most harmless of the lot was his uncle William, who contented himself with such innocent follies as dressing up as a knight-errant in breastplate and brass-mounted, tortoise-shell helmet, a genuine Don Quixote residing (thank Heaven) in Newcastle, whence issued an incessant stream of his broadsides and pamphlets. Uncle Jonathan had begun in the same pamphleteering vein, but progressed from that to direct action: when the clergy of York Minster were deaf to his warnings anent their balls, card-playing, and other abominations, he had, with calm resolve one night, burned the age-old Minster down, becoming thereby the greatest arsonist of the century and the principal celebrity of Bedlam for many years thereafter. Recently, Jonathan's son, who'd been apprenticed to learn painting with his uncle John in London, had persuaded himself that his breath was poisoning his adoptive family and turning them all black! To bring these proceedings to a swift halt he had committed a most spectacular suicide. Still other Martins would have been accounted mad in any less prodigiously endowed family, and the chief of these (alas) was Leopold's father himself, if not on account of his vast canvases devoted to the more scenic catastrophes of human history (after all, he did earn a handsome living from his designs, and isn't earning money the very opposite of being mad?), then on account of his various schemes, the new sewer system preeminently, for reforming the world into the semblance of his own dreams of Babylon and Nineveh. Even this might not have been adjudged entire folly if the world had shown greater interest in having itself transformed; but as it did not, there was always a danger in John Martin's sacrificing himself and his fortune and his family prospects (including Leopold's) for the sake of one of his hobbyhorses. A brilliant parent can be a terrible trial.

As Leopold dwelled upon these familiar worries, his father must have been having very similar thoughts, for when he did speak again (they had proceeded from the cabbages to ranks and rows of brilliant flowers destined for the markets of Covent Garden), it was to controvert his friend's theory.

"No," insisted Martin, "it is the *men*."

The man with the spyglass shook his head emphatically, incontrovertibly: " 'Tis women."

"Is it women who populate Bedlam and Gateshead? What is madness? A fever of the mind. Men are, by their natures, more susceptible to such fevers, for they are more in the habit of overtaxing their mental faculties. Women have their moods of melancholy, I will grant, but on the whole they are more sane."

"I insist 'tis women, John, who are constituted, in all ways, the weaker sex. Whether they live as spinsters or wed and have children, it comes in the fullness of time. I have seen it (though it was no relation of my own, of course). I have seen a woman break to bits like a foundered boat in heavy seas. And it was childbearing that brought her to it. Then the drabs one sees, sometimes, the older ones, sitting alone in public houses discoursing with themselves. . . ." He shook his head mournfully.

"Ah," Martin replied in earnest, "one may see more men muttering to themselves in the stews than women. Enough porter will loosen the tongue of either sex, and if they are not so fortunate as we in being provided with genial company—" His friend awarded this remark a quick, wry, grateful smile. "—then they will talk to themselves." He heaved a sigh. "I could do with some porter myself."

Yet the other was not to be denied the last word on the subject: "But men, you see, are better able to resist the *temptation* to be mad, even when they have cause. Men . . ." Something, some element in the landscape had changed: the ancient oak that announced, cresting as it did against the sky, a long sloping off of the land; the hedgerow; two low cottages and the regular columns of smoke that climbed up into the highest air from their chimneys; the flowers everywhere. Even with his poor vision, he could tell that something in the composition had shifted. "I thought I saw . . ."

"Yes," said young Leopold quickly, "a fellow and his wench were there behind the hedgerow. We startled them with our talking."

"And they are gone?"

"Yes."

The old seafarer moved on in silence, inwardly distressed, feeling that the pair might have been known to him. Yes. It had been young Ann Alexander. He was sure of it. How suddenly she had grown, all in a summer—now, a woman.

"Ah," he said, breaking the reverie, "I meant to tell you of a notion I thought you would fancy, John: Europa—but not such a one as Guido might paint, in a ball dress and mounted on some bull you can't see for the flowers he's draped in, the pair almost lost in the landscape, more on the order of your *Destruction of Pharaoh's Host*. Do you see?"

"Mm." Martin didn't see. Further, he resented being offered "ideas," as though he were incapable of producing his own.

"It is a noble theme, but one which is never handled nobly. Europa, what is she but our own Europe—the mother of our civilization, of our very race—and the bull that carries her across the waves (towering, thunderous waves you would paint, I should think), what is he but the principle of manliness, ready to dare all, to meet any challenge? Do you see it now?"

"I see that it contradicts what you have been saying about the relative sanity of men and women."

"Ah, this would be no mad bull, but a sober, purposeful brute, while she . . . she might be in extremities—*might* be, nay, would most clamorously be—"

"A very original conception."

He nodded, remembering as though it were yesterday the ox hauling tar barrels up a sloping Thames shore, the child upon its broad back.

As he passed the hedgerow he thought of the same girl, a woman now, lying with her lover there among the yellow flowers, blind to their color, blind to the dappled summer sky.

# CHAPTER FIVE

# A Contest of Endurance I

## MARCH, 1835–JULY, 1837

### 1

A Friday night of mizzling rain, of a rain so enduring and unchanging as almost to seem an unalterable law of nature; therefore to stay within doors and as close to the fire as one could approach without risking the upholstery of one's chair or the hem of one's skirt. So sat the Carlyles: he, in a dressing gown of blanketlike substantiality (its plaid of his mother's own spinning and weaving), reading the twelfth volume of the *Histoire Parlementaire*, a work as perdurable as this March rain and—for long stretches—as numbing in its effect; she, wrapped in a shawl, had abandoned for a while the duty of reading the latest book by Harriet Martineau, a friend of their London friends, though not yet their own, since only Carlyle had met her and she was presently in America, witnessing slavery at first hand. Miss Martineau was a woman of tremendous character, but having been stone-deaf since adolescence, her fictions—this one, in four volumes, was entitled *Illustrations of Taxation*—had a tone of strident monotony, as of a trumpet voluntary endlessly sustained, the consequence (Jane maintained) of poor Harriet's supposing that all the rest of the world spoke and thought as she did, with the same earnestness and lack of humor. Novelists ought not to be deaf. A relief to turn from these debilitating *Illustrations* and simply sit by the fire, conscious of its warmth and of nothing else. She ought, perhaps, to have taken up her sewing, but truly, Jane did not like to sew and would have preferred even the longueurs of Miss Martineau's *Illustrations* to those of basting a seam.

While the Carlyles thus serenely wore out the hours till bedtime, secure within their habits as within some high redoubt, the destroyers of that serenity had drawn up in a carriage just around the corner, outside the tobacconist's on Cheyne Walk, and were debating (in whispers, so that the coachman might not overhear them) how, if it could be done at all, they might escape a complete, annihilating, and (so Harriet Taylor insisted) entirely deserved disgrace.

"Deserved?" John repeated, in stricken tone.

"For my part, yes, but for you, surely, not at all. That is why I *will* not let you take the blame on your shoulders."

"Harriet, we have been through this all before. I thought you had agreed to the course we must take."

"The fault is mine, John; then, let the shame be mine as well."

"You were beside yourself. There is neither fault nor blame in that."

"If I had the opportunity to do it again at this very moment, I would act no otherwise than I did. *I hate him!*"

"Hush!"

"I would! As for his book, it deserves no better. And I shall tell him so with the greatest pleasure."

Mill gripped Harriet's chin and turned her head so that she could not hide her eyes behind her bonnet's wide brim. "You will say *nothing*, nothing whatever, and I shall tell you once again, for the last time, *why* you will not. If he knew that you had acted with malice prepense, he would have no compunction in taking you to court."

"And you would testify against me?" Harriet demanded.

"I should have no choice."

"So be it. I deserve no better."

"And your husband, does *he* deserve no better? And myself, do I?"

She began, once more, to cry. Her feelings swung wildly between extremes of anger and anguished remorse.

"You know," Mill persisted, "that whatever you aver, the deed, and its shame, will be laid to my account. It will mean my utter ruin. I shall have to leave India House. There can be no question, either, of my continuing as editor of the *Review*. Everyone we know will cut us: Carlyle would see to that. Quite rightly, too."

"John, I am sorry. Truly I am."

"Yet you say you would do it again."

"No. That was . . ." She brushed away tears with her mittened hand. ". . . bravado. A moment after I'd done it, I knew I'd been a fool. Tell me what I must do and I shall do it."

"Only support the story I told you."

"Oh, please!" She caught hold his hand. "Don't make me go in there and face them. Not tonight!"

"Harriet—it was you insisted on accompanying me here."

"Because I could not bear to sit home at such a moment. But equally I cannot bear to enter his house in the state I am now. I could not trust myself. If they should notice me, do say I am upset and prefer to wait outside in the coach. Once you explain why you have come, they will have no thought for me."

"You must give me your solemn word, Harriet, that you will not suddenly change your mind and try to ease your soul by ruining your life."

"If it were my life only, I would not care; but I will not act to harm *our* life, John. You have my word to that."

"The flesh about Mill's eyes crinkled into a grimace, but only for an instant—almost a tic of satisfaction—and he tapped at the roof of the cab with the handle of his cane. The coach rolled forward ponderously through chill, drizzling blackness, turned into Cheyne Row, where the darkness seemed to reach its completion. The iron-plated wheels ground out a low, thunderous tattoo in counter-rhythm to the shambling hoofbeats of the dray. Before each door along the Row the coach slowed hopefully. At No. 5, Mill gave another tap with his cane. They came to a stop. Mill got out, explained to the driver in an undertone that the lady would wait within the coach, and then, before the Carlyles' door, paused to gather his wits and his resolve.

The door opened without his knocking. They had heard the coach, and seen Harriet within; insisted that they both should come indoors.

"Harriet would rather not, I think. This is not . . . a social call. I've come—but I scarcely know how to tell you, the news I bring is so terrible. Can we go upstairs?"

The Carlyles exchanged a look of swift, mutual understanding. They had already, at the window of the drawing room, conjectured as to the meaning of this oddly timed visit, and their working hypothesis was that Mill had finally resolved to run away with Mrs. Taylor, a theory that Mill's stricken look and bumbling speech seemed further to confirm. The Carlyles could only concur that such would, indeed, be "terrible news."

"Do that, both of you," said Jane. "And let me, meanwhile, have a word with Mrs. Taylor."

Carlyle led Mill, protesting, up the stairs; and Jane, drawing her shawl about her shoulders, went outside. At her first footstep onto the damp stone doorstep the night's cold pierced the thin soles of her carpet slippers. She fairly danced across the paving stones to the coach and was inside before Mrs. Taylor could protest.

"My dear Harriet," she said, with an expressive squeeze of her mittened hand, "what has happened? What brings you here at such an hour, on such an evening?" Though Jane had heretofore resisted calling Mrs. Taylor by her Christian name, despite being repeatedly urged to, this friendlier form of address did not seem to generate any perceptible warmth. Indeed, her "dear Harriet" had unmistakably *cringed* at Jane's touch, and in answering her questions would only mutely shake her head. To escape Jane's inquiring gaze, she averted her head so that the bonnet's brim masked her features. Even so, Jane was fairly certain her first supposition must be in error. This was not the behavior of a woman on the eve of running off with her lover. There was all the guilt but none of the excitement.

From being solicitous, Jane became alarmed. "Harriet, please, whatever is the matter, you *must* tell me. Surely you did not come all this way only to shake your head? Come in by the fire. To the kitchen, if you would rather we be alone."

"You must excuse me, Mrs. Carlyle. You had really best leave me by myself."

"Very well, let us talk here—now that you have found your voice."

"It is not for me to speak," said Harriet in the raggedest of whispers. "John will tell . . . what must be told."

Though she could not have said why, Jane was convinced that this bad news, whatever it was, concerned Harriet Taylor more closely than she cared to admit. She felt herself becoming piqued with the woman's obstinate equivocations; felt, at the same time, a kind of diffuse, wondering pity for the hidden eyes, the breaking voice, the heart enveloped in its coils of an untellable emotion. Perhaps it would be kindest, after all, to leave her to herself.

She made one last attempt: "At least come in where you'll be warm, Harriet."

She shook her head.

"Then you'll forgive me if I do. I am not dressed for this weather."

As Jane made to leave the coach, Harriet's head turned; their eyes met. In the deep shadows of the coach, Harriet's face took on the stony likeness of a tragic mask. The lips of the mask parted. Jane stood on the wet pavement waiting for whatever oracle should issue from the darkness.

"You will never speak to him again."

"Oh, I daresay we shall though," Jane replied—perhaps too brusquely, but really, how *is* one to answer enigmas? She had no patience with mysteries. Her husband was right. Harriet Taylor was an actress. She had cast herself in the role of romantic heroine, and now was endeavoring to involve the rest of the world in the same foolish melodrama. Jane would have no part of it.

She closed the door of the carriage. "Good night, Mrs. Taylor. If you should change your mind, you know where to find us."

Jane's hopes of solving the evening's riddle when she joined her husband and Mill in the drawing room were promptly dashed, for the scene she discovered there simply made the mystery a degree more mysterious. Mill was in tears. Not sweet-flowing, heart-easing tears of the kind a novel may elicit from a susceptible reader, but racking, convulsive, heart-broken, bitter tears of the sort it is always a bewilderment to have to deal with; tears such as Jane had never cried herself, nor ever expected to; tears the sincerity of which, however, it was impossible to doubt. Had Mill's father died perhaps? But why would *that* have brought him to Cheyne Row—and with Mrs. Taylor in tow—at so late an hour on so vile a night? No, whatever his sorrow, it must concern themselves: that much she could read in her husband's face, who, for all the awkwardness of his commiserations, had been stricken no less than Mill, though nonconvulsively.

"John, my dear good man, come, there is no *cause* for this," Carlyle urged, placing his hand on Mill's narrow shoulder, which seemed, for all such steadying, only to shake the more. "The world is not at an end, nor yet my book."

His book! Jane caught her husband's eye. Disbelief confronted raw dismay. His book? He had lent Mill, a month ago, the manuscript of the first completed volume of his history.

Carlyle answered the unasked question. "It seems, my dear, that there has been an accident. The Mills' maid has mistaken my manuscript for wastepaper and used it to light a fire."

Jane stared at her husband, then at Mill, who had been thrown into more strenuous paroxysms by Carlyle's words. Clearly, her husband meant she should accept this preposterous story at face value. He, evidently, had already chosen to do so.

"And how much, then, has been lost?" she asked.

"All of it."

"All—" Mill choked out, "—but this!" He withdrew from his surcoat pocket a scrap of paper, which Carlyle accepted gingerly and without examination.

Jane, under the sway of that ungovernable curiosity which attaches to objects of a deathly significance, took the small slip of paper from her husband's hand. It was something over two inches in width; in length, a little less. The edges evidenced tearing rather than burning. There was no doubt, however, that it had come from the borrowed manuscript, for there—her eye sought out individual words, incomplete phrases—in her husband's crabbed script, ". . . Champs Elysées . . ." and ". . . turn another general; the Quais . . ." above, at the edge of the tear.

"How . . ." Jane brought out numbly, "did she . . . ?"

Mill seemed to freeze in mid-convulsion. In the manner of a tic, his eyes squeezed—ever so briefly—shut, and fresh tears ran down his cheeks.

"The maid," Carlyle explained hollowly, "mistook it for kindling."

"I had stayed up quite late," said Mill, with sudden self-composure, "reading it a second time—my admiration was so great—that's just the pain, you see, the particular pain. . . ."

Carlyle winced.

Mill seemed to falter, but went on until his voice became too choked to permit further elaboration: "And when I went to sleep I left it, by inadvertence, among some papers I had no more use for, notes of my own, drafts of already published reviews. . . . Or rather, I think, I thoughtlessly placed *those* papers atop *your* manuscript. And the maid took them . . . all together."

"And burned them," said Jane, not so much to drive the point home more emphatically to Mill; only that she might begin, herself, to comprehend it.

Mill nodded, and from nodding began to tremble again, more violently than before. One might doubt his story; not his remorse.

For half an hour the Carlyles were obliged to concentrate their sympathetic attention on Mill, who seemed truly to be beside himself. Yet even as they ministered to him, with hot tea and warm reassurances, they could feel a weight of dismay, almost of horror, settling over and pervading their own spirits.

Five months of Carlyle's best work, lost beyond retrieval! The manuscript he'd lent Mill was his unique draft; there were not even notes from which it might be built up again. Five months; all those foolscap pages; thousands of words, and those the most impassioned and incisive he'd written in his life. If there were cause for weeping and carrying on, then surely it was for her husband to do, Jane thought bitterly, even as she soothed and assuaged the self-confessed agent of this catastrophe.

The oddest moment in this evening of consummate oddity occurred when Jane, remembering Mrs. Taylor still waiting outside in the coach, offered to go down again and urge her to come within. To this suggestion Mill reacted with undisguised alarm, forgetting his sorrow and evidencing what Jane could only suppose to be fear. He did not wish, Mill declared, to have Harriet witness him in his shattered condition; she had been so upset when he'd first arrived with the news of the disaster that he'd not dared leave her by herself; or rather she, in her agitation, refused to part from *him*. The more he sought to explain, the less sense there was to any of his explanations. All one could understand was that he was as anxious as Mrs. Taylor had been earlier that she should not join them.

The awkwardness of the situation was relieved when, at ten o'clock, the coach, with Mrs. Taylor in it, drove away. Thereafter it became distinctly easier to deal with Mill. He gave over shaking and soon even his tears were only intermittent. Carlyle spoke bravely, even blusteringly, of how he would repair the damage. Jane, though not without inner misgivings, seconded her husband, insisted, in the most matter-of-fact tone she could command, that of course the book would simply have to be rewritten; that Carlyle's having already written it once was the proof that he could do it again. Mill listened with evident eagerness to all such reassurances, but would then relapse into further self-recriminations, some in a vituperating vein, some more melancholy. As the hours wore on these outbursts gradually waned in force, until it finally seemed possible to let him set off, at midnight, back to his father's house in Kensington.

"Well," she said, as she followed her husband back into the drawing room, "do you credit his tale?"

"That is to say, Goody, am I a fool? Nay. Though I may, for all that, pity him for the poor wretch that he is." He collapsed onto the sofa and kneaded his face with long, strong fingers.

Jane sat beside him.

He smiled, a weary, stricken, grateful smile. "And what did *she* tell thee?" he asked.

"Very little. Only that you would never speak to Mill again."

"Ah, that is her hope, is it? And her aim too, no doubt. Well, we will not let her triumph as easily as that. We will go on speaking to him so long as ever we choose to; and to her, too—the strumpet!"

"You believe she did it then? Quite deliberately?"

"Do not you?"

Jane bowed her head, concurring.

"Why else would she have come with Mill, answer me that? Why would *he*, when he discovered his 'accident,' hasten at once half the length of London to apprise *her* of it before coming here?"

"He never did contrive any explanation for that," Jane observed.

"The reason is clear enough, is it not? The deed was not done in Kensington, but at Kent Terrace; in the grate, I would suppose, of Mrs. Taylor's boudoir; where he learned of the matter at the hour he came calling at the end of his day's work."

"I drew the same conclusion, I admit. But still I can't understand why *she* would act so. It was not a month ago we dined at Kent Terrace. Mrs. Taylor was cordial then, to say the least."

Carlyle's smile grew more bitter, threatened to become an outright snarl. "No doubt, Jeannie, there were guests of the Borgias who had to ask themselves the same question."

"But even the Borgias had motives."

"Oh, Mrs. Taylor has motives. We are enemies, she and I, from first laying eyes on each other—and probably before that. It was John's soul we were contesting for. And I must allow—she's won the contest. She has secured him, I should think, forever. And may they both rot in Hell."

Jane bit her lip. It had been easier to comfort Mill in his distress than to sit like this, sharing her husband's helpless rage.

"And the book?" she asked after a long silence.

"I shall write it again—with what miseries, teeth-gnashings, and tearings-out of hair, no one knows better than thee, Jeannie. But I shall do it. Somehow I shall find the strength."

To which, with forebodings as dark and a conviction as unshaken, Jane, laying her head upon his shoulder, agreed.

He dreamed that night—he who never dreamed, or never, at any rate, remembered dreaming—and of this dream all that he took with him out of the caverns of sleep were the faces, swollen and dumbly sorrowful, of his father and his sister Margaret, faces not to be seen again but in dreams, for both were dead. He lay awake under the warm, damp bedclothes, staring at the homely objects about the bedroom, each, in its dim, pre-dawn reality, a kind of refutation of the occluded horrors of the dream world—until, with a start, reality supplied him with a prospect no less terrible. His book was burnt, his work all undone.

Yet he was not, when he considered of it, unique in that. His father, who had farmed the stony, unyielding soil of Annandale, could have told him of cornfields beaten down by hail or withered by drought. Against such acts what recourse has a man but to sow new crops and pray that he may be allowed, this time, to harvest them? Acts of God, so called; but are the acts of men and women any less the acts of God than flood or famine? Carlyle's God was not, in any case, quite the same God as the one his father had worshipped. His was Nature, Necessity, the All-That-Is; this God of Carlyle's was, no less than his father's, unfailingly just, so that all the world's events, from the fall of a sparrow to the fall of a Louis XVI, must reflect that divine justice. It was, at best, a bracing creed, with little of comfort in it, but if it would brace him now, at the moment of affliction, then it would serve its purpose. He felt so small, a bairn again, whose copybook has just been torn up by some stern, invisible schoolmaster—who tells him, with a flourish of his rod, that he must sit down and write something *better*. For that, if God were truly just, must be His meaning.

Accordingly, Carlyle sat down at his desk that day at the usual hour and set to work—not returning at once to the rebuilding of what had been destroyed, but continuing with the chapter he had been writing yesterday, "The Feast of Pikes." All the material was still, for a wonder, ordered in his mind; his fingers gripped the steel-tipped pen quite as before; and when he fixed his eyes upon the blank page before him, the words issued at their usual unsteady pace, sometimes in a spate, oftener with painful slowness. He described what he'd left off describing on the previous afternoon—the building in the Champs-de-Mars of a great open-air amphitheater, where Paris means to celebrate the first anniversary of its Revolution with all possible pomps and splendors—a moment of unaccustomed lightness among so many dark events, though not without its irony; a moment when the laughter of Olympus had almost a kindly ring to it. Carlyle was determined to convey the exact timbre of that laughter, and that, for three hours of slow, squint-eyed concentration, he did. The result was a triumphant three-quarters of a page of prose in absolute defiance of his own abjection and down-heartedness.

When he put it into the drawer of the desk, he thought, "*There*, John Mill—that is for thee and thy strumpet!" Instantly, he cringed at his own vindictiveness, which he'd supposed he had transcended by the virtue of that morning's work. His impulses refused, as impulses gener-ally do, to be governed by his principles. Well, he would tame them! He would become, like the God he worshipped, sublimely impartial, Olympian; he would *laugh* at himself, at Mill, at Mrs. Taylor. He would spit in their faces!

It was not an easy task, governing impulses such as these, but that afternoon he was offered his first opportunity for self-mastery. A letter was slipped beneath the door—it must have been delivered by one of Mill's servants—in which Mill argued, with ponderous diplomacy, that although no amount of money could compensate Carlyle—or the world—for the loss of a work of genius, yet even genius must pay grocery bills. He asked—he demanded!—to be allowed to give Carlyle £200, and a bank check in that amount was enclosed with the letter.

Carlyle's impulse was to refuse this offer of conscience money out of hand, but after discussing the matter with Jane (who pointed out how perilously low their savings had sunk), he wrote back to Mill, thanking him for his too generous check. Half the sum, he insisted, was *all* he could allow himself to accept, as representing the wages of five months' labor. Carlyle didn't know how much Mill earned for his work at India House (in fact, his salary was shortly to rise to £800 per annum), but he was certain that it far exceeded the "wages" he was to accept. In short, Mill was not being let off the hook. If anything, the hook was only to be the more securely lodged. By way of giving it a further twist, he added (truthfully enough): "I have ordered a *Biographie Univer-selle* this morning; and a better sort of paper. Thus, far from giving up the game, you see, I am risking another £10 on it. Courage, my Friend!"

Mill, reluctantly, replaced the £200 check with one for half that amount. He insisted, however, on supplying the *Biographie Universelle* himself, together with further cargoes of books. But not the "better sort of paper."

As soon as the "Feast of Pikes" chapter was finished, Carlyle turned to the immense task of reconstruction. Louis XV was made to die a second time and the Dubarry, once more, to flit from his deathbed; again the final set of scoundrels entered on the stage—the set of which had begun to seem, to its designer, distinctly tattered. It was a nightmarish task. He racked his brains to *remember* what he'd originally written; to re-create a particular turn of phrase; to paint with just the same few telling strokes one of the myriad fleeting faces. It was never possible. It had to be done afresh, and the result, invariably, failed to satisfy him. For all his agonies (agonies no less keen for his having been able to predict them) the work would not march, the words would not come. At last he gave up trying and passed a week reading the lightest fiction he could lay his hands upon. He walked all over London, attended parties, avoided by every conceivable means the basilisk gaze of the blank paper on his desk. He emitted rumblings of giving up writing altogether, while his stomach treacherously emitted rumblings even more dire. Not only was he to give up writing—he would emigrate to America! He could never go into the City and behold the many-masted forests of the sailing ships crowding the river's lower reaches without imagining himself and Jane making their lonely way across the world-ocean, consigning the corrupt, unredeemable Old World they left to its merited perdition. But really, it was not London he wanted to put behind him, but his book. In brief, he was beset, as never before, by the "blue devils."

Poor Jane the while suffered sympathetic pangs in strict proportion. If *he* could not write through most of April and then through May, if *he* despaired of ever taking up his pen again, what could she do, as his helpmeet, but bow her head and whisper counsels of patience? What upset her most (though she stoically forbore to say so) was his talk of setting off, with an ax on his shoulder, into the western forests of America. Life in Craigenputtock had been a Purgatory of loneliness; life in America promised to be a very Hell. Dread kept her awake for hours, as she imagined their new existence at the edge of some vast swamp, a vision she'd borrowed (via Mrs. Hunt) from Prévost's black fable, *Manon Lescaut*, with only red indians and nigger slaves for neighbors. Eventually, the strain proved too much. Digestion failed, and shortly afterwards her nerves gave way, and she was obliged to keep to her bedroom. Her mother was sent for, and arrived just in time to restore a semblance of order to a household bereft not only of its mistress but, suddenly, of its maid, the second since Bessy Barnet had been summoned by her mother back to Birmingham. Bessy's successor had been a genial slattern whom Carlyle had dismissed the morning he'd discovered her deep into reading his translation of *Wilhelm Meister* instead of engaged at her proper task. The next had been irreproachable, the best servant Jane had ever had. Alas, after only two months of service, she was summoned home, like Bessy, to attend a sick mother!

By this time, however—August of 1835—Carlyle felt flame stirring where there had been only cinders these many months. The work was under way. If his agonies continued undiminished, at least they were productive agonies. With Mrs. Welsh on hand to look after (and pay heed to) Jane, he was able to give himself over wholly to writing. He knew he'd completely subdued his "blue devils" on the day he set down, in one single stupendous burst of inspiration, the grand Homeric catalogue of the members of the three estates that concluded Chapter Four. What a day! What a chapter! What an amassing and compacting of facts and foreshadowings! And what a collapse the following day!

In September the book was done. Or rather, the first volume of the three. In effect, he was back where he'd been in March, and accordingly his sense of triumphing over a host of enemies quickly degenerated into the familiar abjection and dismay of knowing all that still remained to be done. To continue without respite was unthinkable. Leaving his wife in her mother's care, he took the coach for Scotland, where in his own mother's sinewy arms he fell completely and gratefully to pieces.

# The End of an Era and of a Reign

---

### 1

Just as the histories of neighboring peoples are divided into eras according to their differing destinies, so that an Englishman will speak of the Victorian Era, a Frenchman of the Second Empire or Third Republic, and an Italian of the Risorgimento, so in any marriage, however loving and accordant, a husband and wife may divide their life histories into eras and epochs that are radically unlike. The eras of Carlyle's life were simply his books, and as these were generally long books, so too were the eras. Jane, like a nation in turmoil, had briefer eras—thirty-nine of them during the years she was to live at Cheyne Row, one for each of the servants who came to work for her. Jane would have preferred, naturally, to have but a single servant, one consecrated to the Carlyles' service for a lifetime, like her mother's irreplaceable Betty Braid, but that was not to be. She could never establish the proper distance, was either too tender or too tyrannical, would not leave them in peace—and always paid for her too great involvement in migraines, colic, and less specific (though no less horrendous) vastations.

She was undergoing one of the worst of these one afternoon during the summer of 1835. (Our readers should note that we have turned back the calendar some three weeks from the date of Carlyle's departure for Scotland, since this prior date marks, by another historical principle than Housemaids, the commencement of a new epoch in the life of Jane Welsh Carlyle; by the principle, namely, of House*guests*.) Her mother was to be arriving at the St. Katharine Docks in the City, whither Carlyle had already gone on the steamer to meet her. This would be Mrs. Welsh's first visit to her daughter's Chelsea home and, indeed, to London. The suspense of waiting together with the earth-quakes of housekeeping required in the Carlyle household before re-ceiving any visitor had reduced Jane to a state of nerves that would translate itself, at the least provocation, into either lightning pangs of migraine or showers of tears. At the moment it had prostrated her in the bedroom prepared for her mother. This room possessed the red bed of her girlhood, the bed in which she had been born and whose curative properties she judged superior to the broader bed upstairs. She was prostrated—but unable to rest. Weak as she felt, she arose from the bed, smoothed the covers, crept down the stairs, and burst in upon the dining room, as though to startle it into revealing the impression it might make upon her mother.

The room was not so grand as that in the house at Haddington (in which she'd grown up), or the dining room at Templand, where her mother lived now. The furniture, in the adjoining breakfast room, was as miscellaneous as one might encounter at a Methodist bazaar. But clean and in good repair. The very crevices of the woodwork gleamed. Window glass rivaled the air for sheer transparency. Moreover (though it was nothing to tell her mother), Jane had done it all herself.

Feeling a sudden determination to confront Fiona, she crossed to the fireplace and gave the bell pull a purposeful tug. The clock on the wall ticked away an entire minute before Fiona was to be heard mounting laboriously from the basement. Upon reaching the head of the stairs, the large housemaid leaned on the banister, blacking brush in hand, and sighed like a mass of bedding.

"Yes, mum?"

"Fiona, are you still blacking the grate?"

"And it's tired I am, too. The heat down there is enough to make me turn to water. It's the dailiness of it, now, don't you see? There's never been such a summer." With her bare forearm she pushed away damp strands of red-blond hair from her eyes. If only she would tuck it into her mob cap, thought Jane. But of course she couldn't with the tin of Warren's blacking in one hand, the brush in the other.

"Here, let me," she said impatiently, and disposed Fiona's hair properly. The woman accepted the courtesy with the usual ill grace.

"I must have some coffee," Jane announced, remembering second-arily that she should have a reason for her summons. "I don't know anything likelier to stave off a headache, do you? But I see you're in no condition to make it, so I'll go down and do it myself."

"I'm sure you will, mum," was the laconic reply. Fiona's coffee was invariably criticized as being either too strong or too weak—even, upon occasion, as *both*, for she was not above reheating what was left of the morning's brew and serving it, without admission to her mistress, as though it had been freshly made.

Sullenly Fiona thumped down the staircase, followed by Jane. Seeing the way her maid's belongings were littered about the two basement rooms, she wondered how it were possible for anyone to own so little and yet make such a display of it. What would be the result if her mother were to see the kitchen? One of the heroines whom Mrs. Welsh had long ago commended to Jane as a model of good behavior was a certain Mrs. Fisk of Dundee, who had not set foot into her own kitchen for seven years. Now that was a lady! Mrs. Welsh had never demonstrated such rarefied refinement herself, had probably not gone seven *days* without venturing below stairs, but while she was a guest in someone else's home she would surely not do so—or so Jane fervently wished. Her fervor of wishing at this moment represented the nearest approach to prayer that she was capable of, and immediately the wish was made, it recoiled into a practical consideration: if the household were to seem properly organized, Fiona must be made to learn to brew a pot of coffee! So once more the process was set forth: the measuring, the timing, the precise color of the coffee when in a cup and when in the shallow hollow of a spoon; and all the while Fiona on her knees before the fire speculating dully to herself as to how Mrs. Carlyle could bear to drink the bitter concoction she made. There was not a stall in London that didn't make better coffee. She could be quite sure that her mistress's coffee was the source of her megrims, just as the oatmeal *he* consumed in such quantity must be the ruin of *his* bowels. But to suggest that would be to invite a half hour's harangue on either of two subjects—the Carlyles' digestion or her own impertinence. So she waited till Jane had said all that could be said on the subject of brewing coffee and then replied with her standard, "Yes, mum, I'll bear that to mind."

Jane, knowing she had *not* conveyed the secret of good coffee (but not knowing what more could be said), returned up the stairs.

"Shame on you," she said, hearing Chico and his young bride Philine disporting themselves in their wire cage in the breakfast room.

"Shame on you both. If the *cat* that ate your baby were capering so gaily, I shouldn't wonder—but his parents!" To give credit where it was due, the honor of parenthood belonged as much to herself as to either Chico or Philine, the Carlyle canaries, who had both disdained the work of brooding. The wicked cat had been banished up the street to the Hunt house, where there were no canaries and a great many mice.

Breathless, they were all now seated in the parlor. The various ceremonies of arrival had been accomplished—the loud salutations and embraces in the street that had apprised the neighbors that a member of Jane's family was at hand, the procession of trunks and boxes up the stair, the exclamations as, in sequence, each of the rooms of the house was revealed (excepting, of course, Fiona's basement demesne), the admiration of each window's view, the recognition of the various Craigenputtock furnishings disposed about the house, and a quick and entirely symbolic "nap," during which Mrs. Welsh contrived to hide the gifts she'd brought with her (unless her daughter were altered out of recognition, there were sure to be many occasions in the weeks ahead when such concrete testimonies of her motherly love would be of the utmost practical necessity). " . . . And then," Mrs. Welsh continued, "we passed the gutted ruins of the Parliament buildings and Thomas told me how he had actually been there on the night of the fire and seen it with his own eyes."

Jane nodded enthusiastically, but bore in mind the many rehearsals his good tale had enjoyed—and which she had endured.

After Carlyle had excused himself and gone upstairs to work, Mrs. Welsh took up again the subject of her son by marriage. "I had forgotten his eloquence. Somehow, now he is older, it seems a more becoming attribute. But *he* has changed, the Thomas Carlyle that is Changeless—I am sure you have done what I told you once you would never be able to, taught him manners."

Jane smiled. Partly her mother was making up to her. "Oh, it wasn't I, Mother, it was London. What use had he for manners, after all, in Craigenputtock?"

"To be sure. And now, dear—" She rose from her place on the sofa to shake out the flounce of her skirts and settled back some few inches closer to her daughter. "—tell me of all your London friends. Thomas says you have become quite *tête-à-tête* with the Sterlings—the editor of *The Times?*"

"Yes, but it is their son, really, who is our particular friend, *John* Sterling. Carlyle believes he has the making of a disciple."

"And does he want disciples? I should have thought that in his present situation he would rather want *connections*. No concern of mine."

To divert her mother's attention, Jane catalogued their London acquaintances new and old. Among the many names that would be known to her mother only from their correspondence, there was one that might be more familiar: "Do you remember Susan Hunter? She has come to London for the summer."

"Susan Hunter, Susan Hunter," the older woman repeated, "I'm sure I *ought* to remember."

"Professor Hunter's daughter," Jane prompted. "She is staying in Edmonton, not an hour's drive from here, and I have been meaning to invite her to tea while you are here."

"Oh, yes, Professor Hunter of St. Andrew's University. And what has life made of her?"

"She is yet unmarried—but has the prerequisite disposition for a prospective bride: she can be a terrible flirt."

"Then you must take care to invite some suitable gentleman on whom she may practice her arts."

"I doubt she will let me—not, at least, until I have fulfilled my promise of a year's standing and introduced her to Leigh Hunt. Quite regardless of his wife and countless children, I fear that she has fallen *in love* with him and only considers *our* company of any value because we know *him*."

Certain literary lions were unknown to Mrs. Welsh, whose appetite for literature had been amply satisfied until recently by the yearly offerings of Sir Walter Scott. Oddly, she was impressed to learn of their recent acquaintance with a pair of titled Italians. "La Contessa Clementina degli Antoni," said Jane with such a purity of vowels as to make it seem an exceedingly short Italian aria; "we've agreed, *la contessa ed io*, to teach each other Italian and English. We've already begun, and I study for at least an hour every morning. She says I have '*un divino talento*'—'a *divine* talent,' as you may surmise. And really, I do have a facility. You'll meet her, the Count as well, Conte de Pepoli—they've become regular visitors. He is one of the first poets of Italy, a handsome, well-mannered man. Unfortunately, we shan't be having many callers until Carlyle has rewritten this part of the book."

Mrs. Welsh leaned forward to place her hand on Jane's. "I didn't come to London for the Season, dear, I came to take care of you until you are quite well again."

Even as Jane smiled, the headache which had been present all the while as a dull possibility suddenly declared the full extent of its authority. She gasped with pain.

Mrs. Welsh patted her hand.

"You must excuse me, Mother. The excitement, and—" She arose and winced.

"Of course, dear. You had best lie down. I shall see you in the morning."

The three of them soon settled into a routine of serene simplicity. Jane languished upstairs. Carlyle did his work through the morning and early afternoon; on good days he would continue well into the evening. When he was done, he would devote himself to amusing Mrs. Welsh, who quickly learned how to direct his conversation away from the graver issues of history and toward those subjects that interested her.

During the first days of this new regimen it had seemed possible that Fiona might have turned over a new leaf. She had had the presence of mind to make the downstairs tidy for Mrs. Welsh's first tour of inspection. Her coffee improved dramatically, and if her bread more often served to feed the sparrows in the garden than the residents of the house, she had learned to boil meats to the Carlyles' satisfaction, her porridge was above reproach, and her potatoes commendable. Her fate, however, had been settled at the moment, some time ago, when she had chosen to defend herself from her mistress's meddlings by adopting an attitude of sullenness. Sullenness was as rooted in Fiona's nature as were her short nose and freckled complexion. She could not have changed now if she'd wanted to—and she didn't want to. She wanted to be left alone. But Jane would not leave her alone, and Mrs. Welsh, who was accustomed to making companions of her servants, was even more relentlessly intimate. She spent hours at a time in the kitchen, supervising the scouring of pots, the wringing of sheets, and upstairs, the making of beds—and all the while prying, spying. It became impossible to draw a breath—or a draught of ale—under the old woman's ever-watchful eye.

Down came the soup plate with furious report, breaking into three neat pieces in front of Carlyle.

"Mutinous Irish savage!" he roared at her.

Fiona stood her ground, glowering at Mrs. Welsh, who, without looking up, murmured an apology and left the room. Jane, though white with expectation of the explosion still to come, could not stir from her chair but watched, entranced, as her husband sputtered with rage.

"Have you abandoned your senses, woman?" he demanded, his voice becoming shrill. "Do we pay you wages in order that we may have nerves *and* china shattered by a creature so ill favored that it can only be a charity ever to allow her to show her face outside a scullery?"

Fiona lifted her chin defiantly.

"Lazy, mismanaging, more animal than human-like, worthless being! Dupe of unholy Popery and Do-Nothingness-Know-Nothingness! Creature from Hell! Polar bear!"

Fiona, partly in fear and partly out of pique at having her own gesture surpassed by the histrionics of an employer, gave her utmost snort of defiance and turned to leave the room.

"WOMAN! I have not finished with thee! Thou shalt remain in this room until thou hast been dismissed by me."

She paused at the very threshold, indecisive.

"It is clear you have actually made your choice. Possibly such decisions *may* be reached without the faculty of reflective intelligence. Go then! We relinquish your grudging nonservices with collectively glad heart. Go. Gather your paltry pathetic possessions. Pack your duds. Depart!" He looked down at his wife, who raised her eyebrows. Taking a deep breath, he nodded with inward satisfaction, reached across the table to the soup plate Mrs. Welsh had abandoned, and began calmly to ladle soup from the tureen.

On the next day Carlyle slept late and then coming down to breakfast announced that he had finished again the burned first half of his book. To reward himself, he would be setting out for Scotland immediately.

"Immediately?" repeated Jane with surprise.

"This afternoon at six. That is, unless you would like me to stay on until you have found a suitable replacement for—"

"In fact," she hastened to say, "a replacement has already been found. I was up betimes asking at the baker's, and learned of a girl who might help us through the time you are away. I haven't seen her—she's to come by at four—but I fear she may be quite young, for the baker's woman tells me she's not been out yet. So, I must implore you, while you are in Scotsbrig, to find us a good, unspoiled, hardworking, and *docile* woman."

"Who may say," mused Mrs. Welsh, "but that the girl who arrives this afternoon will not be just the paragon one requires? Youth need not be a drawback. My Betty was young when she came to me. I believe a good servant is *born* efficient and trustworthy."

"And polar bears," Carlyle added balefully, "are born covered with white fur."

"If she is so young, she will not have developed a bad temper," said Mrs. Welsh reassuringly. "Who knows but that you may have this— what is her name?—for years and years, a treasure to pass on to—" She broke off, embarrassed.

"I don't even know her name, Mother. She shall be entirely a revelation."

At four o'clock precisely the revelation arrived. Mrs. Welsh was in the garden with her needle and thimble mending a shirt; the Carlyles were still engaged in packing his luggage in their bedroom; all three converged upon the front door within moments of the first tentative jingling of the bell.

And there she stood, on the front step she would have to be taught to scrub—not older than seven, not taller (Jane would measure her the next day, just to satisfy her curiosity) than three feet and nine inches. A child. A very poor child, with a pinched, even emaciated face, and a dress that was the merest motley of old rags, though someone had taken the trouble to starch these rags to the stiffness of a wing collar and iron them flat as a board. "Missus Carlyle?" asked the revelation quietly, addressing herself to Mrs. Welsh.

"I am Mrs. Carlyle," said Jane, as pleased with the little creature as she might have been with a hand-embroidered foot-cushion—yet abashed, at the same time, at the thought of *employing* such an infant. How would she ever be able, small as she was, to wring sheets? Or even make a bed? How would she carry a pail of ashes up the stairs? "What is your name, dear?" she asked after rather too long a pause.

The girl, succumbing to shyness under the influence of their triple stare, murmured something so inaudible that neither Jane, who heard everything on this earth, nor Carlyle, who was cursed with preternatural auditory powers, could decipher a syllable of it.

"How was that?" Carlyle asked.

The child gripped her worn cloth bag with a convulsive feebleness. A bird of a girl.

"Your *name*, child?" Jane insisted, and then bit her tongue—for it would never do to go about addressing one's servant as "child."

"Sereetha . . ."

"Sereetha?" Jane repeated, with an air at once of disbelief and of acceptance. However queer, it was a name to call her by. "Come in, Sereetha, and I'll show you to your quarters. Does your family live nearby?"

"Yes, mum." The girl brushed against the wall getting by Carlyle, who hadn't moved from the doorway; her starched rags positively grated. "They lives at Waterloo Place, over the fishmonger's."

After Jane and her little minion had disappeared down the stairs, Carlyle turned to Mrs. Welsh and said, "That is a very fantastical, not to say Arabian Nights–like, name for such a wee peesweep of a lass, don't you think? Sereetha? Have you ever heard such?"

"Never," said Mrs. Welsh positively. "Her mother must have found it in some novel."

"I should not have thought her mother would be a reader of novels. Sereetha . . ."

He returned upstairs to finish his packing, which he accomplished quickly now he had not Jane at hand to complicate the process. At last, with the final leather strap drawn tight and buckled, he could not resist going down to the kitchen himself.

The child had been set to work already—her sleeves rolled up to reveal thin, matchstick arms, her lank mouse-color hair pushed up into the too large mob cap she'd inherited from Fiona—washing the tea things at the sink. Jane had had to provide a stool for her to stand on.

"Does the lass read and write?" he whispered to Jane, to her no little surprise. This was not like Carlyle—neither the reluctance to be heard nor, especially, the taking an interest in the lives and characters of the servants, at least until such time as their dismissal was imminent. One would as soon expect him to be curious as to the construction of the bodice or the receipt for a pudding he'd enjoyed.

"I'm sure I don't know," Jane replied with an amused smile. "We have been otherwise occupied, as you can see."

"Well, I must plumb the depths of this mystery before I go, else I shall be troubled by it all the while I am gone." He went over to the sink and stood beside the girl, who put down the soapy cup and turned to him with a look of wonder and willingness.

"Sereetha," said Carlyle, "for that *is* what you call yourself, is it not? Mrs. Carlyle and I have been whispering and speculating between ourselves how possibly your name might be written down. In the letters of the alphabet, you understand?"

Sereetha's eyes widened alarmedly.

"Let us suppose," he continued, "that your mistress were to write to her uncle in Liverpool about how nicely and neatly the new girl had been washing the tea things. Now, you do have an unusual name. That has already been established to our common satisfaction."

"If you please, sir—"

"Now, I was half hoping, Sereetha," Carlyle persisted over the timid attempt to answer, "that we might coax you to say your name very slowly. And clearly. You see, we are from Scotland, and often have difficulties with the cockney speech. So, if we might hear you say your name once again?"

Clearing her throat, she articulated as best she could, "Sarah'eatha."

He pondered this a moment, then fairly shouted, "Sarah Heather!" He turned to his wife. "Sarah Heather!"

"What is that!" Mrs. Welsh exclaimed from the bottommost step of the stairs.

"Sarah Heather," he repeated once again with satisfaction.


2


Somewhere in the neighborhood, observed Jane to herself, there must be a cow. Ordinarily milk could be obtained only steps away from their door at the Brimlicombes' dairy; however today, according to the notice posted in the Cheyne Walk window, all three Brimlicombes were ill and the dairy would be closed until further notice.

It was in the search for this actual cow that she came upon the beggarwoman with the "cobweb" shawl to whom, only three days ago, she'd given a penny on New Street. Hoping now for some return on her investment, Jane asked her if she knew where there might be a cow. The old woman furrowed her sun-darkened brow, as though listening for a tell-tale mooing from behind some nearby garden wall, then revealed what nearly all the rest of the neighborhood already knew—that the king and queen were to be visiting Chelsea Hospital within the hour.

There was no time to spare. Milk forgotten, and having hurried home to alert her mother, Jane was impatient to be on their way. Even a hundred yards away from the entrance to Chelsea Hospital, Mrs. Welsh (herself now infected with excitement) was in a flutter of apprehension lest they had arrived too late. Jane assured her that that could not be the case, and offered in evidence the crowd that had gathered about the iron gates, some thirty or forty strong. When they were closer, Jane recognized a few figures in the gathering as local shopkeepers, while the rest (not counting a dozen or so children) were servants, to judge by their dress; servants or outright rabble, of which Chelsea had more than its share.

"So few . . ." Mrs. Welsh observed in a whisper.

"So cold," Jane suggested.

"But, dear, it is not every day one may see—oh, I'm certain we're late. These few have stayed on to see them again when they leave."

"Then there would be a coach within the gates, would there not?"

And in fact there were only four of the pensioners in view behind the stout ironwork, looking much warmer than anyone in the crowd in their long blue coats and cocked hats, a costume reserved exclusively for such visits as today's. For their particular holiday, Oak Apple Day, late in the spring, they might be seen wearing the traditional red, but today was insistently autumn and the grounds of the Hospital looked deserted with only the four bluecoats. Usually, one would have seen many more residents about the grounds. Indeed, they were so common a sight everywhere in the village, summers, that it quite altered one's conception of the glories of the military life: scarlet frock coats and visored caps served only to emphasize the pathos of their reduced circumstances.

While they waited, Mrs. Welsh exclaimed dutifully over the immensity and nobility of the building complex within the enclosing pilings. Her eyes, all the while, never left the road along which the royal coach must make its approach.

At last it appeared: first the guardsmen on horseback; then the royal carriage resplendent with gilt; then a single more modest carriage in the rear. Not at all the degree of pomp Mrs. Welsh had looked for in a royal cortège; nor did the sight arouse the assembled crowd to the pitch of enthusiasm she would have thought their duty, as subjects, required. Instead of lifting a cheer at the sight of the royal couple (who were now clearly visible at the windows of their carriage), they, rather, fell to talking among themselves.

When the carriage had stopped before the gates, the onlookers began to crowd together for a closer view, and Mrs. Welsh heard the youth beside her (his face as dirty as any sweep's) ask his equally shabby elder whether he thought "old Billy would spout at them today." Moments passed before Mrs. Welsh realized that "old Billy" was not one of the pensioners, now busy shooing children back from the opened gates, but King William himself. "Naow," replied the older man, "hit's not worth 'is while. What's 'e 'ave to say to the likes of us?"

Once within the grounds of the Hospital and the gates securely barred behind them, the royal couple descended from the carriage. For all her determination not to be impressed, Jane felt an absolute aching of curiosity, as though the darkest mysteries of time and history might be read in the faces of the royal couple, had one but the gift of reading them aright.

The king seemed unable to decide whether to address the crowd outside the gates or to proceed directly into the Hospital. He whispered into the queen's ear. She shook her head.

He turned toward the crowd, rubbing his hands together briskly. "I am very glad to see you all here today to greet us," he said in a loud voice, "though we should all be a damned sight warmer, I'll wager, sitting before a fire down at the *Swan*."

The crowd applauded, and some of the men huzzahed.

"What is the *Swan*?" Mrs. Welsh asked earnestly.

"A public house that looks on the river." Jane indicated its relatively close position with a gesture. "People watch the river races from its balcony—and they say that *he* was in the habit of attending, himself, years and years ago, when he was still the Duke of Clarence."

The applause had died away. The king waited, offering his arm. The queen stepped forward—anxiously, it seemed—and quite unexpectedly curtsied to the crowd.

The crowd made no response.

Jane looked at her mother. A tear was forming at the corner of Mrs. Welsh's eye, then lost itself among the wrinkled deltas of her cheek. Could it be the wind? Jane wondered, for the wind was bitterly cold. Or was it pity for the poor woman, with her rough, red, frost-bitten face and her look of uncertainty?

### 3

In the afternoon's declining light Marianne Hunt took account of her front parlor as soberly as she might. She had begun the day with the firmest of intentions not to have so much as a glass of beer before the first guest rang, but confronted by the several cheerless tasks party-giving entailed, it had been impossible to resist the cheer implicit in a bottle of brandy. God bless Thorny, her eldest son, for thinking of his old mother! It had begun with a single judicious sip shortly before noon; then a second sampling, by way of honoring its excellence; and who knew how many more? But why *have* guests if one cannot at the same time amuse oneself?

All was in order. Sally had proven her tractableness in a myriad unaccustomed ways. The window glass, where it could be seen at the parting of the rather dirty curtains, showed unmistakable evidence of having been washed. The grate had been cleared of ashes and a new fire begun.

Had it gone out? Marianne nudged the log with her slippered foot and greeted the flame that leapt up with a gratified smile. And the floor? All clear now (with Jacey's help). No more shoes, nutshells, breadcrusts, magazine galleys, the various *trouvées* the children had excavated from the mud by the steamer pier last August when the Thames was so low. Not that the clearing away solved *all* problems of housekeeping—in fact, it only exposed more glaringly the deplorable state of the carpet. She must tell Henry: if he meant to begin entertain-ing again in earnest, they must have, at the very least, a new carpet. And curtains. The broken stair and missing banisters could wait, as the hallway was too dark, even in daytime, for public scrutiny. And with winter almost upon them, carpeting would hold the warmth better than these scraps.

The view through the window of the various back gardens of Cheyne Row at once contradicted her mood of optimism. Brick walls boxed in each little green space, the string of them resembling the celluli of a catacomb—was such monotony necessary? For all Italy's discomforts (especially in the winter, which the Italians pretend does not exist), even the meanest alleys of the cities were never so actively, so *oppressively*, ugly. Ah . . . that was what she wanted—not a new carpet—Italy! The Italy she had loved! As soon as there was the least money set aside. She would sculpt again. She would walk again through the woods of Vallombrosa and watch the leaves whirl about her feet. Her health would return. They would eat beautiful peperoni, roasted out of doors on a wood fire. The scent of them in the clear Umbrian air at evening. . . . "Henry? Henry, are you there?" she called. Silence. "HENRY!"

"Yes . . . my love?" came the reply at last. He was in the kitchen—that she could tell by familiarity with the house and it sounds—helping Sally, or rather, to judge by the 'cello-like quality in his voice, *amusing* himself with the girl. No housemaid, however young, old, or ill favored, escaped his amorous attentions. He was as indiscriminate as a butterfly. If they had hired the Carlyles' *child* serving girl, she had no doubt but that he'd have been after *her*. Before Marianne could say what she'd had in mind, he added (in less dulcet tones), "We haven't enough cups. Are there any about the parlor?"

"I can say without looking that there aren't. But there might be one on the mantel in our room. And another possibly in the garden where Jacey was digging?"

She could hear him begin to mount the stairs.

"Use tumblers," she continued in as loud a voice, "if need be. Henry, what I meant to ask you, why don't we return to Italy? We wouldn't need to take *all* the children. Just Jacey and Vincent. Surely someone there would give us lodgings?"

Hunt entered the parlor with a theatrical laugh. "Dear love, what wild fancies you have today! There is no one in this *world* so foolish as to extend his hospitality to us. Put it out of your mind. As to the 'garden' teacup, it has, as I recall, no handle, and is accordingly suitable only to support the crust of a meat pie. It wouldn't do, I fear, for the likes of this evening's guests. No. What *I* was wondering—what of the two cups borrowed from Mrs. Ronca? Sally has just dried their saucers."

"Broken," said Marianne tersely.

The bell jangled and Hunt went down to admit the first guest. Marianne stood by the staircase until she'd identified the caller's reedy whine as that of Mrs. Olivia Burton. Mrs. Burton had been a neighbor of the Hunts' (and indeed a very useful neighbor) in their days at St. John's Wood, since which time they'd seen nothing of her until this evening. A nuisance to have to see her at all, for she belonged to that most tiresome breed of artist—the writers who never write, or rather, who keep endlessly rewriting the first twenty or so pages of what they call their "novel," and who expect you, what is more, to read each new draft.

With a step almost as light as her husband's, Marianne Hunt crossed the parlor to where she had secreted the bottle of brandy in a drawer of the defunct secretaire and quickly poured out an antidote to the thought of Mrs. Burton. By the time Hunt was showing the woman into the parlor, Marianne felt much more companionable. "Olivia!" she exclaimed.

"Marianne," said Mrs. Burton.

They touched cheeks.

Mrs. Burton's eyes began to explore the walls of the Hunts' parlor. She hoped to see (and quietly *seize*) the two Martin engravings, illustrations of *Paradise Lost*, which the Hunts had borrowed a week before leaving St. John's Wood. Alas, the walls stood innocent of all art except for four black-on-gray silhouettes of Marianne's own cutting. She would have to screw her courage to the point of asking—later in the evening—for her prints' return. She wished with all the force of her wilting spirits that she had never come. But no, that was not so, for there remained a second sound reason for being at hand: Hunt had said that Mrs. Thomas Carlyle would also be a guest, and Mrs. Burton had a boundless appetite for writers. Knowing them and talking with them made her feel so much closer to being one herself. Admittedly, Mrs. Carlyle was only a writer's *wife*, but Hunt had assured her that Mrs. Carlyle was to the last degree kind-hearted and susceptible, especially toward praise of her husband's work. Having won over *Mrs.*

Carlyle, she would have, in effect, a foot in the door of the lion's den,
and then . . .

The bell jangled once again.

There were, with Thornton and his wife, ten; and ten more uncomfortable and ill-suited people there could not have been assembled in
any room in Chelsea that night. The parlor was not only too small for
them, it was too low as well. Mrs. Burton stood nearly as tall as Jane's
exceedingly tall friend, Susan Hunter; the brims of their two bonnets
practically scraped the flaking paint from the ceiling. Such a gawk she
was! But that was all the more reason, Marianne knew, to be watchful:
her husband was as indiscriminate in his triflings with the fair sex as
Mozart's Don—and as cynical. He could gauge the susceptibilities of
serving maids and blue-stockings as accurately as a farrier would estimate the temper of a horse. Ones like this—tall, whey-faced, and
smitten (by Jane's report) with the "romance" of Literature—were
foredoomed. A good thing she did not reside in London; while she
visited at the Carlyles', Henry would have time only to sniff at the
bloom, but not to pluck it.

Jane, though not so forthright in her self-communing, was also keeping an eye on Susan. It amused her to think what a *little* warmth and
banter could serve to set the female heart to fluttering. Miss Hunter
and Mr. Hunt had enjoyed no more than a quarter hour of each other's
private company during the course of the little gathering at No. 5,
Cheyne Row, when first they'd met, and now they both behaved like
experienced intriguants, winking and smiling and glancing away the
while they pretended to converse with other guests—she with Hunt's
son Thornton; he, in mellifluous (if imperfect) Italian, with Count
Pepoli. It would not do, however, to be so transparently curious, and
so by way of avoiding her mother (who was in a querulous temper,
having quarreled with Susan only moments before leaving the house
over some political matter), Jane joined her hostess and that other
woman whose name she'd forgotten the moment she'd heard it. There
were as many matters she'd have liked to discuss with Marianne Hunt
as there had been items borrowed from her household and never returned, but this was not the moment to inquire after them. Ah, but
there had been one transaction that had been a gift outright and not a
"loan."

"How," she asked, "is that murderous cat?"

"*Oh-he-thrives!*" declared Marianne, shaking her head in admiration. "He goes slinking about every corner of the house. We have mice *everywhere*. Or I should say, we *did*. Truly, a treasure of a cat. You may come begging him back, Mrs. Carlyle, but you shan't have him."

"Cats make me sneeze," said Mrs. Burton in a melancholy tone.

"Really?" said Marianne with evident good cheer. "And why is that, do you suppose?"

Mrs. Burton turned earnestly to Jane: "I must say while I have the chance, Mrs. Carlyle, how much I admire your husband's work."

Jane smiled numbly.

Though she had been warned many times over by her daughter, Mrs. Welsh couldn't believe the ruinous condition of the Hunts' household. She had known careless housewives in her time (her neighbor Mrs. Gilmour was a notorious slattern), but none so absolutely abandoned to shame as Marianne Hunt. She had seen crofters' cottages neater and better looked after than the Hunts' parlor. Everything seemed to be falling apart—or coming, unnaturally, together. Two bound books peeped out from a cachepot. The planking, where it showed at the carpet's ragged edge, had never known the passage of a broom. And the smell! Months, years, generations of foul odors had been compounded into an inexpressible attar so malignant that one was actually thankful for the gusts of smoke that the drafty fireplace puffed into the room at intervals.

Hunt, having Italianized for the requisite several minutes, turned to Mrs. Welsh to ask how she was enjoying her stay in London.

"Very well, thank you," was the curt reply.

"Our Sally informs me that you were at Chelsea Hospital on the day of the royal visit?"

"Yes." This was the second time today that the subject of her seeing the king and queen had served as a conversational gambit, and she heartily hoped that Hunt would leave her feeling less "whirled about" than had Susan Hunter not an hour ago, for the royal visit and Susan's talk of "the coming revolution" had been precisely the topic of their quarrel.

"I understand," he continued with hardly concealed delight, "that on that same evening the queen was hissed at the theater."

"Oh, no. Really? I had not heard that—the poor woman!"

"I daresay, if I had been at the theater, I might have joined in myself."

"You?" Mrs. Welsh gasped incredulously, for Hunt seemed to her the mildest-mannered man alive. "You are surely having sport with me, sir? I cannot believe, whatever your views, that it could be within your powers to show such unkindness—if you had seen the poor little woman . . . I'm sure you'd have done no such thing!"

"Ah, but I spent the better part of two years in jail in my youth for having libeled the Prince Regent in my brother's newspaper—and while I'll allow that Queen Adelaide may be Georgie's superior with respect to physiognomy, her politics are at least as reprehensible as his. Yes, I believe I *would* have hissed."

It must be revealed here that Mrs. Welsh's chief interest in seeing the queen had not been political, one way or the other. Rather, it was to be armed against a certain neighbor at Templand in Scotland who never stopped telling the tale of how *she* had been present on the occasion of Princess Caroline's trying to obtain admission to Westminster Abbey during her husband George IV's coronation.

"Ah, Jenny!" Hunt said, dipping his head toward Mrs. Carlyle, who had at last escaped Mrs. Burton on the pretext that she must see to her mother, who suddenly looked faint. "We have just been speaking of your jaunts about the city now that Carlyle has left you two to your own devices. What sights *have* you taken to viewing beyond—which we were just now discussing—the ruins of Her Majesty?"

Jane gave him a chiding glance before speaking. "On Tuesday," she began, "*I* satisfied a long-held ambition and took Mother to see the Elgin Marbles. You *have* seen them, Mr. Hunt? I was deeply affected by them. Something about the rubble of it all, trying to contain it in so small a space, when what it demands is air, light! Great broken pieces of sculpture, hardly recognizable forms mingled among even larger blocks—the base of a column! As I stood there imagining—or trying to imagine—what these fragments might be like in their pristine wholeness, I could only be amazed. Indeed, I don't believe that the entire Parthenon, brought here in sections by a thousand ships, could have given me such feelings of awe and wonder as that room full of those shards of its surviving beauty."

"Yes," exclaimed Hunt, "they abound with the most beauteous, frozen rhythms. Their very silence is eloquent. Did you observe how, as one followed the 'drama' of the panels, the procession moved . . . ?" He directed his attention this time to Mrs. Welsh.

"Truly we were part of a great procession," that lady said laconically. "The British Museum was thronged."

Hunt took Mrs. Welsh's sarcasm as a challenge to his own powers of rhapsody and developed a paean to the Elgin Marbles that left no possible doubt as to *his* capacity for sublime appreciations. Jane, listening simply to the music of his speech, was quite enchanted; but Mrs. Welsh, who had experienced the Marbles as little more than badly damaged goods, became more and more impatient. It occurred to her that there was *no* substance to *anything* the man said. Flute-playing, all of it! She felt no regret when he eventually excused himself to go to Susan Hunter, who had until now been speaking with Marianne.

"Well," said Jane brittlely, "you may be sure we shall hear no more of Hunt *this* evening. See how he takes her directly to the window seat, to be praised in privacy. Have I ever told you what Carlyle calls her?" she whispered.

Mrs. Welsh shook her head and bent closer.

"A very youthful old maid."

"Jane, I do declare: you're jealous of the poor girl."

"I! Jealous? Nonsense. Though whether Mrs. Hunt might legitimately harbor such feelings, I should not venture to say."

Some while later efforts were made (by Mrs. Hunt) to rearrange her guests, but Hunt and Miss Hunter proved inseparable, as did Thornton and his young wife, though the latter pair did admit Mrs. Welsh to their own smoky enclave before the fire.

Mrs. Burton, meanwhile, exercised her charms upon Count Pepoli (who spoke little English) by resurrecting her memories of Italian verb forms and other basic elements of that language—all learned twenty years earlier on a wedding tour. From what Jane could overhear, it was not a conversation she cared to join: Florence, it was agreed, was *"molto bello!"* and so on through Rome, Naples, Venice, Perugia, and others. One would think every town in Italy were either *"bello"* or *"bellissimo."* So, perforce, Jane rejoined Mrs. Hunt upon her bergère.

She had heard in the morning post from Carlyle, who had already found a promising servant in Scotsbrig. "Her name is Marion Hay, and she is twenty-four, possesses good health, declares herself ambitious to earn London wages, will wash, sweep, scour, cook, and do all that I require of her for five pounds the half year!"

"Indeed?" Mrs. Hunt saluted this paragon of industry with a raised eyebrow *and* raised teacup (which was curious, since no one else had been offered tea).

"Nor does she expect, as others have, an allowance for beer."

Mrs. Hunt set down her teacup on the floor beside the bergère and nodded with solemn approval.

"Of course, there is the cost of bringing her to London—two pounds —the half of which sum she must return if she leave us before the sixth month."

"At the wages you are offering, I see no reason why she should ever leave. I hope our Sally doesn't learn how much you are paying—she gets much less from us. Even so, it is more than the lazy slipslop is worth. Soon, I shall have to hire a second girl to perform the duties Sally disdains. Only this evening she said she would not answer the door to guests. 'Too much to be done in the kitchen.' The cheek!"

"Cheek?" repeated Jane.

"One of *her* words. 'Unexampled insolence'—a gloss I learned when she accused *me* of having cheek because I'd told her she could absolutely not receive gentlemen callers in my kitchen! This new girl is unmarried?"

"Not precisely. She's not wed, but I am prompted by hints in Carlyle's letter to believe there has been a misfortune."

Mrs. Hunt heaved a sigh. "Isn't it always the way?"

"Oh, it matters not to me, so long as the bairn isn't brought to live with us. And a girl is usually more cautious after one such accident. On the whole it need not be a bad lesson."

"Truly, but it will not do, you understand, for we—their mistresses —to say so. For my part, I should like nothing better than to live, as Thorny says we shall all live one day soon, in great phalansteries where everybody is both maid and mistress, turn and turn about. In the meanwhile, however, I must have a girl to help me so that I may be free for my own work."

A look of confusion passed over Jane's face.

"My work, that is, as an artist."

"Of course." Jane turned to the bust of Shelley on the mantelpiece to bear witness.

But Marianne sensed her skepticism. It *had* been many years, after all, since she had put her hand to any task larger than the scissoring of a silhouette. She must show Jane Carlyle that her gift was not utterly spent: she would make a copy of the bust of Shelley and give it her as a present—a present that would haunt her immaculate parlor ever after! She would! But in the meanwhile she must say no more of her sculpture, for she knew too well, from a husband's example, how tiresome it can be to hear any artist puffing his own creations—whatever their merits.

Mrs. Burton's "tour of Italy" with Count Pepoli had reached the city of Genoa, and overhearing her, Marianne interjected, "*I've* lived in Genoa."

The Count looked over with relief.

"When we were Lord Byron's guests," she continued. "As Mrs. Burton aptly observes, it is a very beautiful and a very interesting city. Also, very, very damp. I vow that for *wetness* it must rival London. Weeks of uninterrupted rain—torrents! The wind comes off the Ligurian Sea with the force of a hurricane. Once—Percy was still an infant—I remember a window was blown out of the children's room in the middle of the night, and the bedcovers were tangled in the limbs of a cypress a hundred feet away. Tiles and chimneypots disappeared from the roofs quite regularly. The bedding and food were always damp. Ditto our clothes. We had colds constantly!"

"How terrible!" Jane broke in. "You must have been glad to return to England."

"Yes, but at the same time, as Mrs. Burton says, *l'Italia è molto bella e molto interessante.* I have never been happier than I was there. So long, that is, as I kept my health. When one is bedridden, one may as well be anywhere. I developed pleurisy and it went deep into my lungs, remained through the summer that followed. I became a skeleton, even feared for my life. Work, of course, was out of the question. The sight of the worms I crushed with my hands, working the clay, was enough to make me violently ill."

Jane blanched.

"Health . . ." Marianne sighed. "Once you lose control, it is difficult to turn the course of things. Health does not return with its first heedless, blessed strength. Not, at any rate, to me. I implore you, Mrs. Carlyle, look to your body's health! *You* want color in your cheeks. You stay within doors too much. It is the lot of all us London women, yet we must resist it. Once youth and health are gone, life has no joys. One is left with—" She reached down for her teacup and drank the last trickle of the brandy. "—very little. The expectation of the dinner hour, the amusement of the few novels that *are* amusing, and—" She gestured to where Hunt sat *tête-à-tête* with Miss Hunter in the window seat. "—the spectacle of a husband's inconstancies. You will excuse me," pressing Jane's hand, "but I must see why the tea has not come up yet."

Directly Marianne had left the room a great crash of breaking china resounded from the basement. Though there was no knowing what had actually happened, Jane had the most vivid mental image of Marianne Hunt walking to the kitchen dresser, taking the tray with the tea things on it, and dropping it, with utter deliberation, onto the floor.

Instead of tea there was music. Amazingly, in a household where so little was intact, the Hunts' piano was in better tune than the Carlyles' and Hunt's talent was such that his playing seemed as naturally enchanting as the music. The broken chord which introduced the familiar strains of "Faithfu' Johnny" on the piano, and the lingering high A, which he floated through the parlor's smoky air in his ineffable silvery voice, were beguiling. Each phrase seemed artlessly perfect in its formation. Simple, too often used words drew wealths of new meaning, and each time he returned to the phrase "When will you come again . . ." it was as though one were suddenly seeing and hearing another Leigh Hunt, who had lived twenty or more years before.

Jane forgot while she listened the grudges and resentments she bore toward Hunt and his family. Nor did she grudge Susan Hunter her particular raptures. Even Mrs. Welsh, who had just had the most appalling conversation of her life (concerning the nature of matrimonial relationships in an ideal commonwealth) with Thornton and his bride —even she succumbed to the irresistible charm of Hunt's voice; and when asked if *she* would care to sing or play, she shook her head and said what they all were feeling—that her only wish was that Hunt would sing just one more song. The air he chose was one they all knew:

> *Oft, in the stilly night,*
>    *Ere Slumber's chain has bound me,*
> *Fond Memory brings the light*
>    *Of other days around me;*
>      *The smiles, the tears,*

*Of boyhood's years,*
*The words of love then spoken;*
*The eyes that shone,*
*Now dimmed and gone,*
*The cheerful hearts now broken!*
*Thus, in the stilly night,*
*Ere Slumber's chain has bound me,*
*Sad Memory brings the light*
*Of other days around me.*

After that encore, however, the party broke up—largely at the insistence of Mrs. Burton, who declared she must depart. She could not bear to continue making idle talk (especially in Italian), having earlier discovered that her Martin engravings were irretrievably gone, the set of them forever broken. Mrs. Hunt had *sworn* she had no memory of borrowing them; that, indeed, she never would, as a general principle, borrow an engraving or anything so small and easy to misplace in the turmoil of her housekeeping. Not content with these perjuries, Marianne had then made her husband attest to their truth as well. In the end, Mrs. Burton almost wondered whether *she* might be mistaken. A second disappointment, and one much the keener, had come when Mrs. Carlyle, after hearing her husband's work lauded to the skies, had made it unequivocally plain that Mrs. Burton would *not* be a welcome visitor at Cheyne Row when the great man returned from Scotland. Far from helping her into the sanctum sanctorum, Mrs. Carlyle had stood at the threshold with a flaming sword to bar the way! The more she pondered the matter, the more bitterly unfair it seemed, but there was no remedy except to say good night.

Directly Mrs. Burton had gone, Count Pepoli arose to take his leave. Jane then exchanged signals with her mother and they announced their intention by rising and approaching Hunt, who had already resumed his earlier conversation with Susan, without quitting the piano bench. Miss Hunter reluctantly declared that she must join the general exodus.

Jane and Mrs. Welsh preceded Hunt and Susan down the dark staircase in order to give them a last word together. (Thornton and his wife had already left to accompany Mrs. Burton to a hackney stand on the King's Road, and Mrs. Hunt was too inebriated to negotiate the stairs, so Jane and her mother were left quite to themselves.)

"*Such* a goose," whispered Mrs. Welsh as Susan, in the hallway above, audibly procrastinated, fussing with the knot in her bonnet strings until Hunt, in his silveriest tones, offered to assist.

"Hush!" said Jane. "She will hear you."

Footsteps slowly descended the steps—paused midway. "God bless you, Miss Hunter," he whispered—not a single time but thrice in succession, each time more quietly. Then Jane distinctly heard (cursing the keenness of her hearing) the meeting and reluctant parting of their lips in a kiss, the rustle of Susan's skirts as they embraced.

Jane sat at the breakfast table and soon her pen nib was scratching away at the paper in her usual nervous rhythm, long line of the slanting script following long line. So much to be said: an account of Sereetha's progress, and of John Mill's visit of duty when he'd scrupled to stay gossiping with Jane for as long a time as he would have spent philosophizing with her husband. She filled page after page, saving the account of the party at the Hunts' till the last, then bringing it forth like a flaming pudding. ". . . Now you remember," she wrote, "what sort of looking woman is Susan Hunter; and figure their transaction! If he had kissed me . . ."

Just as this chapter began with a turning backward to events occurring before those which brought the previous chapter to a close, we must now violate the principle of strict chronology by leaping years ahead to a new era, when King William was dead and his niece Victoria was monarch of England—this by way of taking our leave of Leigh Hunt, who is about to quit the neighborhood of Chelsea and to remove his numerous household to the cheaper environs of Hammersmith. Life has not been kind to Hunt. Yet another magazine has lately collapsed under his editorship. The verse drama which was to have inaugurated his career as a playwright has ended it instead. And if these disappointments have not sufficed to brim his cup, he had lately, for the first time in his life, been seriously ill. For weeks his life had lain in the balance. Jane had known this through the intercourse of her latest maid with the Hunts' maid, but she had resisted her impulse to visit him upon his sickbed. Even if there had been more communication between their two households in the intervening years, she would have hesitated; to have surprised Hunt at a moment when he was not armored to meet the world in his embroidered waistcoat and kid gloves seemed somehow an injury worse than simple neglect.

These were her feelings—or rather the background to her feelings—at the moment when Hunt, in waistcoat and kid gloves, entered the parlor where Jane had been sitting going over the domestic account. At the sight of him—the illness had wasted his face, which showed for the first time the ravages of its sixty years—she rose from her chair and held out her arms to welcome him.

That was all. Except that an hour later, after he had returned to his own residence round the corner, there came, through the letter slot of No. 5, Cheyne Row, another of his distinctive notes, tied with a bit of blue ribbon. Within the envelope was a poem eight lines in length:

> *Jenny kiss'd me when we met,*
> > *Jumping from the chair she sat in;*
> *Time, you thief, who love to get*
> > *Sweets into your list, put that in!*
> *Say I'm weary, say I'm sad,*
> > *Say that health and wealth have miss'd me,*
> *Say I'm growing old, but add,*
> > *Jenny kiss'd me.*

# CHAPTER SEVEN

# A Contest of Endurance II

In December Carlyle returned from Scotland and resumed work upon *The French Revolution.*

Mill, in the long meanwhile, moved from success to success, a progress that tended to challenge Carlyle's faith in the unfailing justice of the All-That-Is. True, some of Mill's more rigidly respectable friends had seen fit to cut him for the openness of his liaison with Mrs. Taylor. True, his father's article attacking the Church, which appeared that July in the second issue of *The London Review,* provoked a scandal among the pious (then a more numerous and powerful party than now), and the magazine's circulation suffered a consequent decline. But John's own contributions showed him in top form; sure-handed, clear-headed, even-tempered essays that were not at all the sort of thing one might expect from a man pursued by avenging Furies. In the best of them he placed a laurel wreath upon the young brow of Alfred Tennyson, becoming, in effect, the "discoverer" of the future Laureate. Molesworth, his publisher (despite that the magazine's attack on the Church had cost him the hand of his fiancée), was so satisfied with Mill's editorship that he bought out his only radical competitor, the old *Westminster,* and joined the two journals into a single *London and Westminster Review.*

Carlyle, who had accustomed himself to the disappointment of not being asked to edit the *Review,* had now to swallow the bitterer pill of not being courted for a contribution. This, even though years ago before the days of his editorship Mill had read, and praised, Carlyle's long essay concerning the "affair of the necklace" at the Court of Versailles; he had even offered to bring it out as a book at his own expense! The essay, as Mill knew, remained unpublished. Finally, Carlyle himself suggested that Mill should bring out "The Diamond Necklace" in the new conjoint review. Mill shillied and shallied and at last said—No. Brilliant it might be; perhaps too brilliant for the generality of readers. Mill was terribly sorry, of course, but . . . No. This rejection was somewhat sweetened by his asking Carlyle to review Mirabeau's memoirs, which Carlyle agreed to do for two reasons: first, because in the course of his research, Mirabeau had come to seem to him the Cromwell of the French Revolution, its single largest heroic figure; second, because he was desperate for money. It had been four years—or even longer!—since he'd earned a farthing by his writing. Mill was offering £50; no one else was offering anything. So, with a sense as of pulling his forelock in deference to the lord of the manor, he wrote his "Mirabeau" and, afterward, to relieve his spleen, in a letter to Emerson, a brief anathema: "As for Mill's *London Review*, I do not recommend it to you. Hide-bound Radicalism; a to me wellnigh insupportable thing! Open it not: a breath as of Sahara and the Infinite Sterile comes from every page of it." A wonderful convenience, this young Emerson an ocean distant in America: one could say anything to him without fear of repercussions.

The Furies, meanwhile, had finally found Mill out. Early in 1836 his health began to give way, and by the first anniversary of the burning of the book—the 6th of March would never henceforth pass without Carlyle's raising a glass to it in sardonic salutation—Mill was said to be dangerously ill. It went beyond the mere collapse of energies he'd suffered at twenty-one, but it was similarly (Carlyle was certain) a crisis of the spirit much more than of the flesh. In June, Mill's father died, and shortly after Carlyle helped his friend make the journey to Dorking, in Surrey, where he was to convalesce. During his stay with the grieving family (a wonderfully moderated grief they evidenced, the lot of them; one might even say a "utilitarian grief"), Carlyle could not help noting the symptoms of Mill's so-visible decline: the sallow flesh, the precipitate baldness, the nervous spasms of his eyelids, the droning flatness of his speech, as though the very last wrinkle of feeling had been ironed out of his bloodless heart. He had the spiritual presence of an old shoe, and Carlyle returned to Chelsea with the conviction (half wish, half premonition) that he would not see much more of his friend and betrayer.

Mill refused to die forthwith; the Furies had not such a firm grip on him as that. Instead, he set off for the Continent with Mrs. Taylor, bringing her three children and two of his siblings as chaperones; which to Carlyle's eye was tantamount to running off to a cholera hospital to avoid the plague. His health did *not* improve in Paris, nor in Geneva, nor in Lausanne, and upon his return to England in November he promptly came down with influenza. But still stayed alive; and still, in despite of the Furies, Fortune went on smiling, in the massive form of a promotion to a position of third in command at India House with a salary, now, of £1,200. The All-That-Is could scarcely have been more accommodating, short of slaying John Taylor outright in order to allow Mill and Harriet the condign satisfactions of a legitimated love—and who shall say that that would have suited the lovers better than the more fraught relationship they presently enjoyed?

Not that Carlyle was so blindly bent upon some classic retribution of eye for eye that he ever lost a saving sense of what a trifling affair it was, after all—under its eternal aspect. One could not spend two and a half years chronicling the most awesome event of modern history without seeing how small one's own woes bulked against those of all Mankind. Even so, something of his personal outrage might be seen to shine forth from his pages. Surely in his treatment of the Girondins, those champions of the Revolution who were to become, so spectacularly, its final victims, Carlyle took a not altogether secret satisfaction in establishing their likeness to the reforming, legalistic "radicals" who were the mainstays of Mill's review, Mill himself not the least among them. There were moments as he penned his final pages when he could virtually see Mill stepping onto the tumbril and being carted off to the guillotine—eyelids twitching, the voice droning on, all reasonably, concerning the un-Constitutionality of his execution. There were moments, as well, when the original conflagration—of his manuscript in Mrs. Taylor's grate—would spread, as it were, through the unburnt pages; when it became a Universal Holocaust; never more notably than on the night—a Thursday in January, near the hour of ten o'clock—that he finished the book. The Revolution—that which had been and that which had yet to be—shuddered into sudden apocalyptic fire, consuming every injustice, every corruption. "IMPOSTURE," he wrote, on this last page of all,

> is in flames, Imposture is burnt up: one red sea of Fire, wild-billowing, enwraps the World; with its fire-tongue licks at the

very Stars. Thrones are hurled into it, and Dubois Mitres and Prebendal Stalls that drop fatness, and—ha! what see I?—all the *Gigs* of Creation: all, all! Woe is me! Never since Pharaoh's Chariots in the Red Sea of water, was there wreck of Wheel-vehicles like this in the Sea of Fire. Desolate as ashes, as gases, shall they wander in the wind.

And then—wondrously—it was done. The flaming letters faded from the wall; the Prophecy had been spoken, in three completed volumes! He went out walking in the brisk night air feeling like a man released from prison. Two and a half years! He never need write another book again! He never *would*! Every star was visible above the river. The edges of puddles were crisp with the first forming crystals of ice. A horse trotted by on Church Street, making the cobbles ring. He felt a sudden urgency to be on horseback himself, though it was splendor enough, for the moment, to stride through the wide darkness of the streets, breathing the air, feeling his freedom: knowing he was *done*! As he passed one of the last houses of the village, he ran his walking stick, rataplan, along the iron rails. Only moments later he found himself taking refuge from the cold inside a bright, noisy public house, not his usual custom, but surely this was a fitting moment for a libation of thanksgiving? He took a glass of the house's best brandy, and while he savored it, watched the unfolding of a small drama that seemed to become, with each enfiring draught, the epitome of his own life these last two years. There, hand locked in hand, foot braced against foot, two youths, in shirtsleeves, contested to see which of them would subdue the other. Their strengths were well matched; the contest had already gone on, he learned, half an hour; might go on the night. Now the lad in green trousers seemed in the ascendant, but the clasped hands would tremble with a new burst of buried energy, the balance would sway, and for a while his rival, a shorter but stouter youth, seemed to have a clear advantage. The other drinkers had already grown bored with the spectacle and turned away to smoke their pipes and talk among themselves. Carlyle watched transfixed. The two arm wrestlers seemed a living allegory of his struggle these two years with Mill. There had been no violence in it. They had met, and spoken, and dined together, and their eyes had met a thousand times; and every moment of those thousand times Carlyle's inmost thought had been of his friend's black guilt, which his friend (except by the twitching of his eyes) steadfastly denied. For a while it had seemed that Mill would triumph, that Carlyle would collapse beneath the task of rewriting the destroyed manuscript; then, the balance had swayed, and it seemed (the work progressing) that it was Mill who would collapse. And even now, tonight, the final issue of the combat could not be surely known. Even now. Carlyle finished his brandy, placed the glass upon the bar, and went out again into the night air, leaving the two wrestlers locked, perpetually, in his mind.

# CHAPTER EIGHT

# A Bundle of Letters

1841–1843

*Oh My Dear Geraldine,*

I have been hindered from writing to you neither by the impromptu visits of American lion-hunters, nor *yet* by headache, but rather by a keen intuition of our Solemn Vow's probable outcome. Lo, I, who have resisted the 'problematical luxury' of a diary these many years in which to record my multivarious and errant ills—I, who have kept heart and mind *valiantly* sealed!—must now succumb (for having sworn an Oath!) to divulge and confide in letters All my most secret thoughts—and to a *woman* friend! It is really, as Helen would say, 'most insinuating!'

A thought that made itself known to me soon after your declaration and proposal (but proved unwilling to be framed in speech at so tremendous a moment) demands now to 'step forward'—Dear Eternal Friend! What will become of my *letters* if you should suddenly be found *dead* beneath an omnibus, and not presciently have thought to destroy them before departing from your house. Will my 'diverse and various' confessions then become (like a murderer's court testimony) part of the public record?

And—to continue in the same vein—how long may I be given to believe your 'passionate devotion' to me will last, when a similarly Eternal Devotion to my husband (for bringing about your 'intellectual awakening') remained only long enough for the name of George Sand to be uttered in his presence? Wait till you have experienced *my* 'vicissitudes of nature.'

And how, precisely, do you suggest I play-act the part of your older, wiser sister—for I shall need some coaching, never having known a younger. Better you should play my 'unknown daughter' and submit to a thrashing out of all Romantic Notions from your enthusiastic red head. I am not, by all evidence, the woman you see! Much less the woman you would have me *be*. Consider my well-established singularity in this world: it is a *waeful* process to reform the spoiled only child. More advantageously assault the course of a swift-flowing river!

But enough. The time not passed in anxious concern about my promise to you has been weathered after a fashion despite the ringing of bells (the entire night long—at Chelsea Old Church) and multivarious beginnings and stoppings and *grumblings* from Carlyle related to the Cromwell book, which, it seems, cannot be written until he has travelled thither to 'Cromwell Country' and *walked* all the Actual Paving Stones touched centuries past by the foot of the Lord Protector himself.

Whenever Carlyle is made too familiar with the state of *my* head and heart, I too am promptly advised to walk! Walking having become the sanctioned panacea in this house for all ills to which the loquacious human (or half-human) person is heir—*idleness* especially (to which he attributes the greater part of my discontent). Yesterday, immediately following breakfast (at which *no* kind words were passed, among not a few of *the other kind*), I sallied forth, choosing arbitrarily for destination the London Library, as providing a Real Purpose of returning yet another triple-decker, for the most part unread (all twaddle), when just as I was about to enter St. James's Square, whom should I hear *running* up behind me, calling my own name as might not be confused with any other voice, 'Mrs. Carlyle, Mrs. Carlyle!' Mazzini— looking (hair flying every way) like the world's *cheerfulest* child, black garments notwithstanding (worn in deference to Italy's current ills), and dissuading me (with little effort, you may imagine) from signing out another book, but instead—the perfect succedaneum, to his mind —to *walk* with him! As though I had not already had sufficient walking for the day. And where? Well you might ask—To the City! No novel suggestion on his part—rather one he, with renewed *studium*, has been known to put forward three times in a single week! I gave only the least resistance—having nothing more pressing at home than such letters as this to indite!—and off we went, he negotiating *my* way over every crack and puddle as though I were blind, and returning me home by four-penny steamer in time for tea. . . .

I must, as a certain Quakeress once said 'in all innocence,' beg a clarification of terms—what *is* an Hermaphrodite? Have you ever known one? Fully half my adult life (and my *entire* childhood) have passed in fear and perplexity of such beings—yet without ever understanding their true nature.

It is clearly not their True Nature to live a normal life (normal to be construed as you will), yet must such a one suffer God's Wrath in solitude, with no lover or friend to share the 'flying carpets of the imagination'? Can she not, as I have heard (I know not where), occasionally find some other being, similarly unique (!), with whom to live out her days on earth? And what of George Sand? One supposes she is not one, though she dress like a man and smoke cigars.

There was a being (by name Mysie Hamilton) in Haddington when I was a girl. 'Meal Mysie' we called her (as continuing her mother's flour trade). Whenever we would come near the barrow where she stood, day in, day out with her sacks of meal, and I would hear her loud *man's* voice, I would run in terror.

Not even now, after all these months, can I think of places from my childhood—Haddington, eating preserves from Templand this morning!—without the heart's breaking a little more. How little I understood my mother—how many questions now I would ask her. Once—I remember not when nor why—she gave a great tea party and, possibly as a gesture of kindness (not without interest in making the party *memorable*), she included poor Mysie. Yet what talk was served up by way of 'wits' in such a guddle I cannot imagine, we children were so occupied that day with our clattering from room to room. And now I cannot ask.

What would Carlyle make of such a *craiture*? . . .

*ᴏᴠᴏᴠᴏ*

Ach! I have just passed two hours in the company of Mazzini discussing—what think you? (feet warm on the fender, tea and biscuits warming our insides)—*my* impending invasion of Italy by balloon! And what a surprise I should be to the occupying Austrians, whom M. envisions pointing their cannons to sea in expectation of the *usual* form of attack!

Now not a word of this to another soul (for so, in hushed tones, it was presented to me). A certain Mussi, it is revealed, has developed the means by which to manoeuvre balloons as easily and perfectly as any steamboat or railway carriage, in confirmation whereof I was shown a mass of certificates, each bearing the *segnatura* of one or another Grand Duke or *Estimabile Professore* before whom the *model* had been displayed. Little did I realize at the outset of this exposition that I had inspired such folly, but lo, that was to be revealed to me in good time—my rôle personating a 'fallen angel' casting benevolent dark-eyed glances over all the subjugated populace as I *calmly* lighted down had been suggested by my *dis*ability to travel by sea! I was further reminded—Heaven help me!—of the *suitability* of such an invasion, as I should be descending from the very realms of *God* (Dea ex machina) bringing hope to a suffering people! The man is mad!— yet in the credulous, lovable, *truthful* way of children—and I had my *hands* full keeping my *tongue* silent.

The only obstacle preventing the realization of Mazzini's Grand Scheme, you may believe, is the trifling sum of two thousand pounds! which represents not the cost of fabricating such an airship, nor even the expense of furnishing *me* with a suitable gown in which to perform my solemn duties, but rather the price for which the above mentioned Signor Mussi will deign to part with his secret! . . .

It is one matter to write actual letters to verifiable beings, and quite another to realize a novel of letters—even for such a 'brilliant letter-writer' as I. And, as to 'filling the day with useful activity,' My Dear Geraldine, I can ruminate on no activity *less* useful to mortal man or woman than the activity you propose! Consider—You and I, and Betsy Paulet putting off our *natural* household duties to collaborate *à trois* in the making of this mad several-armed tale, as yet plotless and leaning heavily in the direction of remaining so. The idea makes me want to scream! You confuse writing books with pulling taffy—a plot cannot survive the tugging of three wills from as many directions of the compass.

"I am not, be assured, *dis*interested in the project as it may proceed forward from *your* pens. Indeed, I await the first chapters by post with a keener anticipation than even Mr. Dickens's creations can inspire. Do I understand your plan correctly—you will write the first letter yourself—then Betsy will indite the second? And will you discuss the contents of each successive section before committing words to paper?

You appreciate, I could not, at such a distance, undertake a fair share of the duties.

I may, some uncharacteristic day, set down a novel of my own devising and be wholly responsible for the contents therein, 'foul or fair,' but this idea of yours and Betsy's I must resist for the present—at the double-risk of my brain's decomposing for want of active exertion and—Good Gracious!—of falling into madness when I learn you are 'now in your seventh printing!'

As for the general drift of things, I continue on Brother John's course of blue pills and enforced walking despite the pain in my side and no little lack of faith in his ministrations. The pain and exhaustion is never half so bad as the task to follow of cleaning mud from my cloth boots—such weather!

I have not yet viewed the portrait, finished or unfinished, yet Carlyle has made it known that I must, at my convenience (in plain English, immediately), stop by at Gambardella's studio (another of 'my' Italian refugees) to give verdict on the image thus far committed to canvas, as there is evidently some problem a-foot, Carlyle complaining that he has 'never before' been obliged to *sit still* so long, and the work 'still not finished!' 'But,' ventured I in all promptitude, 'you have never before sat to be painted!' In any event, I am confident that this Gambardella is the best of portrait painters, and accordingly have arranged with my family in Liverpool that he should go there as soon as possible —that is, directly after the portrait of Carlyle is done and varnished— to paint my uncle. Shall I send him to you in Manchester thereafter? Tell me as soon as is convenient because I foretell matters here will soon reach a crisis pitch in the portrait department. . . .

The bundle of manuscript from you and Mrs. Paulet arrived safely this morning, however (I add with tremendous haste), I shall not be in a position to peruse this fascinating work nor 'reconsider the matter' of my own participation in the project until after I have read and commented upon an even larger bundle of papers 'arriving' almost simultaneously from Carlyle! These are not, as you might imagine, the first pages of the planned book on Cromwell, but rather concern that old Abbot of St. Edmonds Bury, who has recently, through the now-penetrable mists of time, pressed himself upon the public consciousness. You understand, of course, my logic in 'preferring' to assault wifely duties before those in which I have only a *friend's* interest. . . .

My dear, I have still not dared to open your parcel as, with each day's passing, a new sheaf of papers is thrust upon me by Carlyle. He is working on this trifle (as it began) with a madman's fury!

But on to your urgencies and—I must say—misapprehensions. Your long, *dense* epistle of 5th December has me in fits, not knowing whether to shriek with alarm or cry-out in righteous indignation! What cause do you have to suppose I sent Gambardella to you as a prospective husband! That I purposed you should fall *in love* with him! He is a mere, hard-working painter and—yes—decidedly 'overproof.' I had not the slightest intention . . . but one would think that because Betsy Paulet found herself a merchant from Genoa for husband, you, and all other marriageable young women must necessarily be disposed of similarly by the Fates! The idea—Geraldine! It *interests* me (in a manner of speaking) to learn that you managed 'in a day's time' to 'love him very sisterly' but no—I am not *pleased*! There *is* such a thing as too much passion, and, it is evident, you must learn to cultivate other facets of your being than this. The less *passion* in the world the more *virtue* and *good-digestion*! How do you know but that you should be bored for the rest of your life with such a man? Just because a male being presents himself on your doorstep is not reason enough. Ach!

No, of course, I won't mention a word of this to my niece Jeannie— and don't you either! . . .

~~~

Finally! Oh Geraldine, it was with such relief that I read the novel—I cannot tell you! Relief and astonishment. There are moments of brilliance exceeding even the powers of Dickens in their radiance. Sense and insight shine throughout, revealing a degree of Genius that even Carlyle would admire (if he were not so buried in the past as to prevent him from stepping forward—into the present—to read what is 'beneath his nose'). I had no idea that you were hiding so dazzling a light beneath your bushel. In point of fact, I must now, in all Finality, excuse myself from any further commitment to the project for want of Native Aptitude—and daring!

Indeed, there is an element of rushing headlong into uncharted territories of the imagination that proves both admirable and dangerous— an *indecent* undertaking when one considers the readers whose religious sensibilities will be offended—better, *dashed* to bits by the Original (my word!) ideas of Morality which you attribute to your heroine!

Understand, my dear, I speak quite directly to you (whose handwriting I know so well, and who I pray will not be wounded by my sharp tongue) and not to Betsy. (Her contribution accords better with my abiding and abidingly unfulfilled desire for calmness and peace in all things, and can, therefore, be neither so severely faulted nor so excessively praised for cleverness as those sections which I know to be your own.) On both your parts I suspect a superabundance of Actual Truth, encompassing everything from Moral Principles of a dubious variety (Geraldine, your heroine does express her desires, at times, with the most dangerous transparency!) to unadorned Seaforth Gossip, which will not pass *un*detected by others. A fig-leaf of conformity judiciously painted in throughout would not be ill-advised.

I am returning the manuscript (with apologies for keeping it here unread so many days) not directly—incomprehensible creature that I am—but tied and marked to your *personal* attention within a general parcel bound for my cousins (and Alick's wife) in Liverpool, to arrive before Christmas—as I know you will be seeing each other within the week. . . .

Have I mentioned to you, or have you heard talk of a certain Society pair, friends of Carlyle unknown to me (except from common report) —he, the son of Lord Ashburton, William Bingham Baring, will himself one day (if the Fates cooperate) take on the title?

For the present, he and his capacious, apparently clever wife Harriet (known in *my* circle as *la belle laide*!) give large extravagant parties and entertainments at Bath House to which they summon Carlyle regularly. (I, as you know, am wrecked by such gatherings and have established a policy of not attending—not that I am ever invited!) Carlyle recovers no better from these evenings of 'snob ambition'—yet, having given himself ample practice, he grows accustomed to 'the next day's biliousness.' These Elevated Affairs are nothing new here, to be sure, though of late they occur with unthinkable frequency. They are not 'in my line'—that is a truth not to be denied. Yet, however little first-hand experience I have had with such 'lionings,' I have begun to feel a powerful antipathy for this Harriet Baring.

What breed of monster must she be, I ask myself—with her passion for novelty, gathering about her all the male wits London has to offer —and corrupting them? I live in terror of the day when, finally, I do meet her. The hold she keeps on Carlyle (her favourite, it seems) is of such strength that he will swiftly drop all other obligations and promises at a moment's notice should he learn of her desire to see him. Oh Dear Geraldine! What think *you*? Please do not delay in considering this. I am so confused some times that I only want to dash out my brains! If the woman were more than a phantom, if I only were once blessed with a distant view of her, or might overhear the sound of her Actual Voice! A want of Real Evidence has me ready for Bedlam! And all the while Carlyle is 'vaixed' with my involvement in the affairs of the 'Young Italy' people, complains of my seeing Mazzini too much (Mazzini's mother, in Italy, knowing me to be a married woman, expresses the same worry!), and yet I am expected, for the sake of *our* rising in Society, to swallow whole my reasonable apprehensions concerning his comings and goings.

Rising in Society! If my mother could see us now, if she were still alive! Her daughter, once the country's Most Desirable Commodity—the irony is excessive! He, who would not bend an inch to accommodate her 'notions of gentility'—he, who sneered at 'tuft-hunting,' now speeds off to Mayfair every evening with his boots gleaming!

Geraldine, oh my dear, I have cried entire evenings by the fire, indisposed to speak to any son or daughter of Adam. My life here is become a barrenness of solitude—growing worse daily. I lived six years without society in the wilds of Scotland for his sake, managed a house on pennies and sheer hope. I forgive him years of not caring, not feeling. *My* feelings have been ignored so much (I, the spoiled only child!) that I worry lest I forget the meaning of tenderness and the idea drop away from my consciousness forever!

Not that it matters. However bleak, silent, and empty of feeling, life proceeds. There are the small joys stolen from who knows where—and yet some times I wish I could hear the voice of *my own child* calling me. If there were only the gentleness in this man that a woman needs and understands, the feeling sense that I might not wish to hear each of this siren's words of wit repeated and held up for my admiration as though they were aphorisms newly brought down to earth from the dining tables of Olympus. You must, when we are together again, teach me to curse like a man. . . .

*Ever your own,*
*Jane Carlyle*

# CHAPTER NINE

# Maids and Wages

## JANUARY, 1849

"Anither wee drap," the more portly figure insisted, refilling her companion's glass before she could say aye or nay. " 'Tis but ha' four."

"Oo, Missus Booth," purred the Carlyles' maid, Helen Mitchell, congenially, "I dinna dare." Only a moment earlier the winter sun had penetrated the dusty window of her hostess's sitting room. Now the clumsy furnishings of the darkened space bore muffled shapes like cairns beneath snow: the solemn mantel clock on the chimneypiece, a single rude table and pipe stand beneath the window.

Mrs. Booth, better known in the waterfront houses for her coarseness than modesty, topped her own glass to the brim before setting the bottle down upon a ravaged back issue of *The Illustrated London News*. Having done this and taken a thoughtful drink, she leaned heavily in the direction of the dying embers and beckoned with one hand for Helen to do the same.

Helen, a wee wiry woman in her fifties, stared hard at the clock face without finally discerning the information she wished. "Ha' four, and the bedding no' sae muckle aired. . . ." The bedding had, in fact, been aired, the lumps dispersed after a fashion, and both beds remade that morning. But the kitchen—and Mr. Carlyle's supper!

"No mairr is mine," returned Mrs. Booth, in a tone rather of satisfaction than of self-reproach, "but then I'm no' sae partikler as your Mrs. Carlyle. Dairrt is *my* element, as water is the Adm'ral's."

"Aye," said Helen with a sigh," 'tis my alement too—"

"*El*ement, not ailment," the other retorted with a raucous laugh.

Helen, in many ways as wise as her master and as witty as her mistress, had meant simply, in this instance, neither the physical condition nor a pun. "I dinna say 'ailment.' I *said* 'tis my 'a-lement,' too . . . as gin has aye been and aye will be my failing." She lifted her tumbler with the melancholy dignity of a sibyl who reads, in entrails or a crystal, the ruin of empires. Then, with a quick smile, which showed a row of blackened stumps, she emptied it.

And there was no gainsaying the confession, for Helen, however discreetly she timed her drinking bouts, was a drunkard. She was also less than careful about her personal cleanliness. The neckerchief crisscrossing her bodice was as soiled and even-mottled a rag as many that had been used for a week's washing up, and one suspected by the fugitive odor when she moved to one side or the other, an odor not to be mistaken for the thick and all-pervading wintry smell of soft coal burning, that the condition of her nether garments was still more deplorable. Yet, as Helen herself said, to look as though she had cleaned the many rooms of No. 5 with her own person was only fitting at her age. To her credit, she was the first maid of promise the Carlyles had found in many years, and her lack of interest in cleanliness and finery —whatever its consequences—stayed more in keeping with their notorious thrift than any alternative thus far.

Mrs. Booth (whether or not her diplomacy might extend itself to matters of personal cleanliness) could find room for equivocation concerning drink: "Nae, nae, there maun be moderation in all things. There's mair t' the topic o' drink than a' the demons and deevils 'at Father Mathew an' sic as he thunderrs aboot. One man may drink for the tang it gi'es his toong, anither t' keep warm on sic bitterish days as we have noo, an' anither drinks in the place of vittles, as the Adm'ral maun do syne a' his teeth's been extrackit."

"Oo, the puir man," Helen commiserated.

"But nae to stupefy hissel', Helen."

"Nae," Helen agreed dourly.

Her companion's conversation having taken this uncomfortable and uncharacteristic bent toward edification, Helen bethought herself of other subjects of discourse. Something jolly, by preference. "Did I tell ye, Mrs. Booth, o' the time Mrs. C. brung me round to where Father Mathew was preachin' in the Commercial Road?"

Ordinarily Mrs. Booth would have listened to this retold tale with pleasure, for Helen only rose to the full heights of her narrative powers when the theme was her mistress, that queer young woman whom

Helen venerated for her kindness, cared for and pitied when adversity
took the form of headache (as it did with some frequency), but whom
she disparaged at such moments as this for her manifold eccentricities
—but today Mrs. Booth had her own tale to tell, one with a bloom of
freshness upon it and no little pathos, and so she dismissed Helen's
counter with a peremptory, "Aye, ye've told me."

"She had been once to see him hersel'," Helen went on undeterred,
"an' got sae fired oop by a' his braw talk and pother (for she's aye a
susceptic soul sic as runs after every will-o'-wisp new notion) 'at she
nairly took the plaidge hersel'. Oo, the tear in her ee when she told me
how he gi'en her just a wee sil'er trinket—I weesh I could show it
ye—sic as Papists wear aboot their necks."

"Ye've told me, Helen—saivrral times!"

"Have I, then? Well, there's nae harm in telling a tale o'er. A good
tale's like a good dram. The taste is aye grateful." She fixed her eye
meaningfully on the gin bottle where it stood catching the ever-rarer
light from the fire.

Elizabeth Booth, despite a fondness for company, chose not to see
this. Helen would drink herself insensible quite every day if there
were gin and time enough—particularly now in her disappointment.
Two years ago, Helen's brother, having become prosperous selling
coach fringes to the railways, had summoned her from the Carlyles' in
London to serve as his housekeeper. And so, Helen left her position of
nine years, thinking to become genteel as mistress of her brother's own
great house in Dublin; but he, a tight-fisted Scotsman, had had no such
apotheosis in mind for her. He was simply after a slavey who would
not require any wage but bed and board. Helen returned to London
and the Carlyles' service a changed woman. And though Mrs. Booth
had been glad to have her neighbor back again, she could not help but
be conscious of the changes Helen's disappointment had wrought in
her. Before, even in her most slatternly moments, there had been a
touch of something majestic in her manner, an air of natural authority
that Mrs. Booth ascribed to her Highland ancestry. Carlyle himself
attributed to her "an intellectual insight almost genial." But now it
could not be denied that Helen's mind and character were altered, and
all for the worse. Drink, which had been her weakness, had become
her undoing. She would drink herself to death now, there would be no
doubt of it, and any tempting of her must be wrong; yet if Helen were
not here gossiping by Mrs. Booth's fire, she could be found in the

*Cross Keys* or the *Rising Sun* and several degrees more sodden. What would be would be.

Mrs. Booth poured some more gin into Helen's glass.

"Chayrs," said Helen.

"Chayrs," said Mrs. Booth. She paused, allowing Helen a moment to savor the gin—this time she made an effort not to bolt it down—and said, "Hae ye hearrd wha's become o' the Alexander gurrl? Puir Annie?"

"Puir Annie!" hooted Helen. "She has juist wha' she desarves, the slut!"

"Then ye hae hearrd," said Mrs. Booth in a tone of disappointment.

"Only 'at she's run aff these two days syne."

"Three. Nicht one worrd to her puir father."

"Wha' word's t' tell?" Helen asked rhetorically. "It's aye the same story when a lass runs aff, an' she winna tell *that* word to her father."

"Hae ye nae pity, then?"

"Pity? 'T's rail insipid! Whar's the pity for *me* then, 'at's lived nigh forty years a kitchenmaid?"

"Thee?" Elizabeth Booth demanded sardonically.

"Aye—me! Wha' matter I fell once as a wee slip of a lass—I've nae doon it agin, nae though I be drunk aneath the table."

"Well, 'tis yourr ain likin', Helen, 'at keeps ye sae uncommon pure. 'Tis nae partikler vairrtue."

Helen considered of this, and of her glass. "Truly spoken, Missus Booth: I dinna ken why any lass would commit sic folly mair than one time."

Mrs. Booth permitted herself a smile of conscious wisdom. Then, since it was a devilish sort of wisdom that didn't bear pondering, she observed, "The raison is nae far to seek, I dairr say."

"Aye?" Helen inquired politely.

"Where else but Cremorne? Wha' shall a wee lassie think o' a' the tarts gaen an' coomin' to the Gairrdens, an' coomin' an' gaen, ilka nicht, in frocks as fine as the finest leddy?"

"I dinna ken. Wha' shall she think?"

Elizabeth Booth's bosom swelled with a sudden access of respectability. "Shall she think, as we're told in the Scripture, 'The wages of sin is death'? Nae, nae. She thinks, 'The wages of sin is fine frocks and the sicht o' fireworks in the nicht sky'!"

"A braw sicht!" Helen protested indignantly, for she had often shared her mistress's pleasure in watching the Cremorne illuminations from the topmost windows of Cheyne Row. "I dairsay lasses have lost their vairtue in Chelsea lang afore there was fireworks in Cremorne Gairdens. An' as for tarts, Missus Booth, tell me where a lass may grow oop an' nae see tarts—nae in Chelsea, nae Rotterdam!"

"Naetheless, Helen," said Mrs. Booth portentously. "Naetheless . . ."

Helen was about to point out the inadequacy of such a refutation as this bare "Naetheless," but the benign and all-prevailing presence on the table of the bottle with quite five fingers of gin in it brought her up short. No need to roil Mrs. Booth with too much controversy. For all her warmth of heart, Elizabeth Booth could be "most lit'ral-minded." Helen might even go so far as to say the woman was slow-witted—which suited her, no doubt, to living with Admiral Booth. Though the old man was thus known, Helen had long ago wormed out the admission that he was neither a naval officer of whatever degree nor, for that matter, was his name even Booth! His only relation to Elizabeth Booth was that once, when she had lived at Margate, he'd been her *lodger*. Now he could be called, at best, her guest, for (so she maintained) it had been four years since he had paid a farthing for food or lodging. The man was a worse miser than Helen's brother: Helen had said as much to Mrs. Booth, and Mrs. Booth agreed. And yet—despite all insistence, Helen found this hard to credit—the Admiral was supposed to be a man of considerable wealth: evidently wealth in some mysterious, unspecified form that was neither money nor property, nor yet railway bonds. A strange companion for such as Mrs. Booth, who set such store upon what she was pleased to call appearances!

"Oo, aye, naetheless," said Helen equitably, "though 'tis a sad thing for a lass to live close by sic stews and behold sic sinfulness on her ain doorstep, wha's to be doon? The wairld gaes on juist t' same, for a' we shake our heads o'er sic as Annie."

Elizabeth Booth considered this fragment of fatalism and found that it accorded well with a strict predestinarian view. "Aye," she agreed, though still with a trace of melancholy.

"Weel," said Helen, "I'd best be gaen hame. 'Tis a'most dairk."

Before Mrs. Booth could reply to this with another grudging finger of gin, Greaves the boatman, without bothering to announce himself by so much as a knock on the door, burst into the room and said, "Missus Boof, you best come to the riverbank down back o' the *Adam an' Eve*. The Adm'ral's there, and 'e's got 'imself in a spot of trouble."

Mrs. Booth, having opened her mouth to reproach Greaves for his manners, could only gape, speechless. Then, clamping her jaw resolutely, she grabbed her shawl from the back of a chair, her bonnet from a peg on the wall by the door.

"Wha' has he doon?" she demanded, as she pushed her loose hair roughly into the bonnet.

"What 'appened was, the Adm'ral an' me 'ad just come back from over across the river, an' 'e said somefing about the 'aze in the air an' 'aving to go up on the bridge to 'ave another eyeful, which 'e does according. Well, when 'e's up there, the peelers, who've been draggin' the river since the sun come up—"

"Is he in trouble with the police, then?" Mrs. Booth asked sharply.

"No, no, nofin' like that. It's wif old Alexander, what's lost 'is Annie—"

"To the point, mon!"

"That *is* the pint, Missus Boof," Greaves replied aggrievedly. "If you'd let me get on . . ."

"Oh, losh!" Mrs. Booth fretted. She motioned Greaves out the door and had almost followed him outside when, remembering her companion, she turned round and issued a peremptory command to Helen to take up her own shawl and bonnet and come with her.

Helen, who had intended to linger, forgotten and cosseted with the double warmth of bottle and fire, rose and did as she was bidden.

As the two women strode along beside Greaves down muddy Davis Place, he continued his explanation. While the Admiral had been watching the wintry sunset from Battersea Bridge, the police had recovered the body for which they had been dragging the river all through the day. He had followed the other curiosity-seekers down the Beaufort Stairs and across the riverbank to where the corpse lay, belly up, neck twisted violently about, so that half of her face was black with mud from when she had been dragged ashore. A child's face, Greaves said, but already in the family way. Not content with looking on, like the other neighborhood residents who'd gathered about the body, the Admiral insisted on kneeling beside it.

"Blimey, I thought," Greaves said, as they passed before the signboard proclaiming his own name in scaling black letters two feet high, " 'e's goin' to kiss 'er. 'E was bendin' closer an' closer, an' squintin' the way 'e 'as when somefin' takes 'is fancy. Well, I should of known what 'e was up to, 'cause the next minute 'e's takin' out 'is pencil an' that black book of 'is an' 'e's scratchin' away. Not in 'is usual way, fast an' furious, but all neat an' finikin' so you could ackcherly tell when 'e was done what it was 'e'd drawn. Surprised me, that did."

"I still don't understand," Mrs. Booth said impatiently, "what this has to do with Will Alexander."

"Ah, well—Will 'ad 'eard this mornin' about the peelers lookin' for the girl what was seen to jump off the bridge last night, and natcherly wif 'is Annie gone out of the 'ouse, 'e couldn't be sure as it wasn't 'is own lass they was draggin' for, could 'e? So when 'e 'ears they've found 'er finally, 'e comes runnin', an' when 'e gets there, there's the Adm'ral tellin' 'im not to touch the lass cause '*e*'s not finished drawin' 'er—can you believe it!"

"But it *wasna* Annie, was it?" Helen demanded.

"If it 'ad o' been, old Will would of killed the Adm'ral then and there. No, it *weren't* 'er, but wif Will's finkin' it be, and wif 'is not fancyin' the Adm'ral special much to begin, old Will was in a fair way to breakin' an oar over 'is 'ead. An' the Adm'ral just goes on scribblin' away an' won't pay Will a bit o' mind. I tell you, Missus Boof, there wasn' a man of us would 'ave tried to stop Will, the state 'e'd got 'isself into."

"What did the man *do?*" Mrs. Booth insisted.

"Up to the pint I went off to fetch you, Missus Boof, nuffin' but rant at 'im, sayin' as 'ow it was 'im and 'is like what ruined Annie."

"As auld as he is?" scoffed Mrs. Booth, though not with her wonted authority.

They had reached the head of the stone stairs beside the bridge. Will Alexander was to be seen squatting on the bottommost step, smoking a long pipe of blackened clay. Mrs. Booth descended the steps carefully —they were slimed and treacherous—and stood before the robust, red-faced boatbuilder but did not address him until, after long meditating on the bowl of his pipe, he looked up and met her accusing eyes. "Shame on ye, Will Alexander—to torment an auld man! If ye've done him any harm—"

Alexander spat into the mud. "It was only 'is age that stopped me. 'E's bleedin' loony, 'e is. They should lock 'im up in bleedin' Bedlam. Drawin' pictures of a girl layin' *dead*, an' not even the dirt washed off 'er face. Hit ain't decent!"

"Those drawings," retorted Mrs. Booth, piqued in her pride, "are worth, ilka ain o' them, more than any boat ye've ever built or ever will!"

Greaves made a quiet but nonetheless audible snuffle of incredulity.

Mrs. Booth turned on him, grateful to have a safer focus for her anger and anxiety. "And what's *that* supposed to mean?"

"Oh, 'e's 'armless enough—I don't say 'e's not—but I've seen 'im makin' them pictures of 'is, Missus Boof, an' you can't tell me they's wurf a farthing. 'E slops on some red, an' 'e slops on some blue, an' 'ey-presto, 'e's frough! I don't know much about painting, Missus Boof, but I know the Adm'ral's no painter. Why, my 'Enery, what's on'y four years old, can make a better likeness of a face than 'im, for all 'is airs." He turned solemnly to Helen Mitchell and added, "Hit's the God's troof!"

"The truth?" Mrs. Booth echoed, conscious of having an advantage over Greaves with regard to the fricative "th." "Shall I tell you the truth? That man you're scoffin' at is a dignitary. He is Joseph Mallord William Turner!"

"That may be as it may be," replied Greaves. "I don't care if 'e's the bleedin' Prince o' Waoos—'e still can't paint a picture so's anyone can tell what 'e's painted."

"He was Praisident of the R'yle Academy, an' would be still if he wished it."

"An' I'm Ole Boney," Greaves retorted, sticking his right hand into his jacket in the manner of Napoleon and crossing his eyes.

"Oh, shut yer traps, the both o' yer," said Will Alexander morosely. "You're worse than a pair o' curs."

Such an injunction would ordinarily have had no more effect on Mrs. Booth than to provoke her to fresh scolding, but being brought up short, she had time to reflect on her own indiscretion. To gratify her vanity she'd betrayed the man who'd sworn—solemnly sworn—it was only her ministerings kept him alive. She had betrayed him, and it was only by a quirk of fortune that she hadn't been believed. Unless . . .

She stole a look at Helen, standing on a higher step. Impossible to tell, from the glazed look in her eye, whether Helen had grasped the significance of what she'd just let slip. She had a gleg wit, Helen Mitchell, but at the moment the edge of it was dulled with gin.

"Whaur is he, then?" she demanded harshly of Alexander.

"Still gawkin' at the girl's body, when I left 'im." Alexander gestured with the stem of his pipe to a part of the shore concealed by the massive wooden pilings of the bridge.

Mrs. Booth regarded the path she would be obliged to take with dismay. One could tell, from the depths to which the various small craft were sunk in it, that the shingle silt was of an unusually oozy consistency due to the rains of the last many days. The boots she was wearing had only that morning been cleaned and polished. The hem of her dress already required wiping from where it had brushed the steps, but if she were to attempt to cross this quagmire . . .

"Helen, my ain dear goody, would *ye* fetch the Adm'ral for me?"

"Oo, aye," said Helen, with only a hint of sarcasm, for she had been making the same calculations as to the relative harm the mud might do her boots and Mrs. Booth's.

" 'Tis a kindness I winna forget."

Helen set a foot into the mud, sank into it to within two eyelets of the top of her boot. She caught up the stiff canvaslike cotton of her skirts, tucked a corner in the crook of her elbow, and set off across the shore, threading her way among the beached boats and barges. When she had almost passed from sight beneath the bridge, Mrs. Booth called after her: "Tell him I'm in a black temper an' he maun come at once."

She could see him now, in all his oddity, sitting, stooped low, on the gunwale of a small lighter. The body, if it were still there, was hidden by the boat. The merest mite of a boy had crawled into the boat to observe him at work. As the pencil in his hand slid over the paper, or scratched, or wriggled, he spoke to himself in a toothless mumble. Even standing close by, she couldn't unriddle any sense from what he said—but there were no riddles, so far as she could see, in what he drew. A girl's face, deeply shadowed on one side, seeming to smile, asleep. The corpse was gone (the police had taken it away), but he still would look up from time to time at the patch of mud that bore its imprint.

A face as meager as her own, thin lips, a pointy chin, the eyes recessed: the more she looked at it the more it seemed that it might be herself, for she had often dreamed, poised on the lucid edge between an everyday despair and swinish drunkenness, of just such an end. Someday, perhaps, she'd have the strength. It seemed, looking at the jumbled lines that formed the face on the paper, almost within her reach.

She remembered her mission. "Adm'ral Booth, ye'd best gae to the stairs. Your missus is waiting."

He made a gesture of impatience with his left hand and went on drawing.

"Adm'ral Booth—" she began again, but was interrupted by another voice, far off but strident with urgency.

"You down there, 'Enery! Git 'ome, d'you 'ear?" It was Greaves, above them, on the bridge.

The boat lurched as the boy jumped from it—the lead pencil broke, leaving a black scar on the woman's temple.

"Adm'ral Booth—"

He drew a deep breath, closed the sketchbook with a sigh. "Yes, yes. I heard you."

# CHAPTER TEN

# Breakfast for Eight

## 24 JUNE 1846

Gräfin Hahn-Hahn's blind left eye stared, sightless and unmoving, at the crisp center-parting of her hostess's hair. The pupil had contracted to the merest pinpoint, giving the cornflower blue of the iris an uncanny limpidity. Jane's gaze kept returning to it, even when the other, livelier eye was not turned away. Twice already she had been caught out in this indecorous fascination: the seeing eye had seen, and glanced away; the full, rouged lips had smiled, amusedly.

The talk, though in German, had not yet advanced from the secure terrain of platitudes and commonplaces to loftier regions of articulacy, and accordingly both she and Browning were able to straggle along in the rear of the conversation. Her own contributions were in the main limited to agreeing that, yes, London was very big; that, no, she could not agree with Byron Bystram that it was also notably clean (Edinburgh was *much* cleaner); and that, yes, the weather was *very* hot. The German for "intolerably" escaped her. They were all fairly melting away, like candles in a draft. Mrs. Jameson, being the stoutest, was melting away at the most prodigious rate, and the pink summer-light foulard of her bodice had darkened, here and there, to a dusky rose. The ladies' fans were in perpetual motion, but the heat, the intolerable heat, made a mockery of such polite solutions, and there was no help, at last, but handkerchiefs. Even these, soon enough, were wringing wet. Yes, it was very hot; it was (she remembered it) *unerträglich heiss*!

With ritual inevitability the conversation moved from topography and weather to exchanges of compliments as the various authors praised each other's books. As this could not efficiently be done en

masse, the party broke up into pairings, a process initiated coura-
geously by Amely Bölte, who drew aside the redoubtable Mrs. Jameson to exclaim over her latest offering to the public, *The Relative
Position of Mothers and Governesses*. Both Mrs. Jameson, in her early
years, and Amely (who was again seeking such employment) had
drunk from the particular cup of bitterness that Mrs. Jameson's book
rather obliquely hinted at, and soon the two women, in suitably hushed
tones, were swapping tales of former charges and employers, each
more horrific than the last.

The Gräfin Hahn-Hahn, meanwhile, was setting forth, like evidence
in court, the grounds for her admiration of Carlyle's not-quite-biogra-
phy of Oliver Cromwell, which had appeared scarcely two weeks ago
in a second edition of three volumes. The Gräfin, justifiably proud of
having made her way through such a quantity of prose—and English
prose at that—was determined to be credited for the effort she had
made and so was very circumstantial in her praises. Carlyle, whether
from mere authorish delight of applause or from a reluctance to discuss *her* book (which he had *not* read), seemed content to be praised
at whatever length the Gräfin was prepared to go. He listened to the
slow unfolding of her appreciations with an expression of tolerance
and benignity, which was ruffled only once or twice by the need to fix
his attention elsewhere than on the Gräfin's blind, blue, pupilless left
eye.

Browning had not caught the name of the young man who had come
with Amely Bölte, due to the Gräfin Hahn-Hahn's having accidentally
spilled a glass of sherry over her dress at the moment the introduction
was to have been effected, but the young man had evidently caught his,
for at the first opportunity of speaking privately, the fellow had come
up bold as bold, and begun to lavish the most unqualified praise on him.

"There has not been a collection of poems in the last ten years," the
young man declared with an earnestness that seemed altogether fever-
ish (for he suffered almost as copiously as Mrs. Jameson from the
heat), "not even Tennyson's, none that speaks so clearly and *lucidly* to
the mind of man."

"That is very kind of you," Browning murmured.

He wished the young man (who was not, in fact, much younger than
himself) would speak of other matters; or, if he would go on in this
vein, that he might be more specific. It was heartening to be singled out
for one's lucidity, especially when even the faithful few who professed

to admire one's poems would nevertheless keep worrying the old bones of one's supposed obscurity. Is there a poet in all creation who will concede his poems to be obscure? For what is poetry if not the wresting of matters out of their native obscurity and into the light of full, conscious expression? So this "lucidly" came very sweetly to the ear.

It would have come more sweetly still if its source had not been quite so unprepossessing. Browning felt a dandy's cultivated distaste for those whose efforts to appear smart are misapplied. One does not wear an evening dress coat when one has been invited to breakfast, *nor* does one wear a mammoth Osbaldiston cravat with evening dress, nor does one *ever* wear trouser straps of India rubber. Browning had seen Mrs. Carlyle's critical eye take in that last solecism, had virtually heard the little bell-like tinkle of her delighted disapprobation as the detail registered. Still, there was that "lucidly," for which he was prepared to overlook whole wardrobes and jumble sales of error.

The young man went on from singling out his companion's merits to hinting at his own. He was himself a poet, though not a poet *precisely*; a lower servant, shall we say, in the Muses' temple: he had translated the *Nibelungenlied*. Browning confessed that his only knowledge of the *Nibelungenlied* came from their host's illuminating essay, and expressed a polite interest in reading the young man's translation when it appeared in print. Alas, the book had yet to find a publisher, there was no telling when it would find its way to print, but if he were interested in reading a fair copy in Miss Bölte's own clear hand . . . ? Browning felt he had been trapped. He would have to read a book he had no interest in reading, in a translation he would probably not like; but if he did like it, and said so, then he'd be obliged to pass the book on to a publisher, and if the publisher in turn liked it, he would demand some sort of certificate of endorsement from Browning, who —didn't all the world know it?—had paid, and still continued to pay, for all his own publications—full five volumes and all eight numbers of *Bells and Pomegranates*—from his own pocket; or rather, his father's pocket. Ironic to think he might be instrumental to aspirants when he could not help himself. And all for one "lucidly," which (he saw it now) had probably been no more than bait on the hook. Really, why had the Carlyles asked this fellow to their party, with his *Nibelungenlied* and his India rubber trouser straps?

He said he'd be delighted to read the young man's translation— provided he could find the time before he set off to Italy.

Ah, Italy! The young man envied him. Land of the vine and (he paused significantly) of palm leaves!

Palm leaves!

And what, wondered Jane from the opposing corner of the room, could they be discussing with such strenuous animation—Bölte's friend and Browning? Two years earlier Amely had threatened to become a permanent fixture at Cheyne Row (as much by her ability to be useful as by her inability to take a hint). Finally, however, she had been found a position instructing the daughters of Sir James Graham. This brusque, short, bulky woman had the peculiar double nature of most governesses—sometimes so quiet and retiring as to disappear completely into the wallpaper, while at other times a perfect Jeanne d'Arc championing in her dearest-held beliefs, whether the iniquity of low waists and tight lacing or the sublimity of Thomas Carlyle's work (an opinion never challenged at Cheyne Row), or yet—and here Jane's eye returned warily to Browning and the young man—the difficult (and, she suspected, dull) Mr. King, *ehrsüchtig* translator of the *Nibelungenlied*. *He* had been Bölte's doing, yesterday in the garden. Nor had Jane, then, felt ungrateful, for without Richard Monckton Milnes (whose telegraphic dispatch announcing that he would be unable to attend allowed only twenty-four hours' notice) they might have had an empty chair next to the Gräfin's. An "indisposition" that had overtaken him while visiting Nettlebed Abbey. She refused to believe that Milnes's indisposition amounted to anything more than a reluctance to leave the relative coolness of the Chilterns for the furnace London had become during the last month.

Browning, for his part, still considering what particular connection he might have to palm leaves, doubted whether he would penetrate so far to the south "as to encounter palms in any abundance." Sorrento was a possibility, but Pisa was likelier, at least for the immediate future.

The young man nodded knowingly. Pisa, he noted, was of course nearer to Germany.

Browning, about to point out that he had no compelling interest in Germany, remembered that that might be thought to reflect on the *Nibelungenlied*; and so let the remark pass.

At this juncture Browning was offered the promise of deliverance by the welcome intrusion of Jane Carlyle. Having first steered Oberst

Bystram toward her husband (at that moment delivering an instructive monologue on the proven inefficacy of the Reform Bill to the Gräfin), Jane now took the reins of the flagging conversation between Browning and the young man with the trouser straps and led it round gracefully to the realm of objective anecdote. She asked Mr. Browning and Mr. King (that was his name then, King), did they mean to continue in London despite the heat? They did. And she? Browning asked. The country did not suit her so well as it did her husband. She had lately been to Addiscombe, the Barings' country home near Croydon, and nearly gone out of her wits for want of sleep—henbane had been quite useless. The noise! Roosters and workmen chiseling granite at five a.m.! Alverstoke had been even worse. The Carlyles had passed a month of the winter there on the Hampshire coast, *again* as guests of the Barings (indeed, Jane noted to herself, the very sherry in their glasses came from the Barings), and Carlyle had been so taken with the infinite perspectives of the sea and its perpetual rumblings and tumblings that he had threatened to build a cottage by the shore and quit London forever. He had only been deterred from his terrible purpose by having encountered, every day, at every turn, a strange old man without a nose who went about shooting at nothing visible. Day after day this walking apparition had become so interfused with the peaceful scene that Carlyle, mercifully, lost his taste for the seaside. An example, Mrs. Carlyle declared, darting a teasing smile at Browning, of how Providence may derive good even from what seems unmitigated evil, for if that unfortunate man had not suffered the loss of his nose, who could say but that they might not be living at Alverstoke already?

"Indeed," said Browning a trifle humorlessly (Mrs. Carlyle was not one of his favorite persons). "God works in mysterious ways. And are you quite secure from being rusticated in some other direction? London should count it a great loss if you were to leave."

"For the time being. Carlyle speaks now of setting off for Prussia—specifically, Berlin—but in the interests of scholarship; not, I pray to the heavens, to seek some new domicile."

"Berlin?" Browning inquired.

"Having quite done with Cromwell, he is considering Frederick the Great. At least on Tuesdays and Thursdays that is his idea. Other times he speaks of confronting the evils of the age more directly, in which case he means to go to Ireland, where the age is now assuredly at its evilest. I wish you might fire his imagination with Bembo or a Medici or some other of your fine Italian *cavalieri*, for in that case I might be tempted to accompany him upon his researches. But he is not to be tempted south of the Alps, I fear. The Italians are not of sufficiently heroic stock, and he must have heroes if he is to write. It will be Prussia in the end, inevitably."

"A pity," said Browning.

"Come, come," Mr. King chided. "Will you, sir, speak against Prussia after your own experiences there?"

"*My* experiences in Prussia? I took a coach through it once, on my way to Russia, but that was thirteen years ago, and I recall little more than a weary, wintry flatness, gray skies, and a great discomfort from being bounced about in a coach. That is all the testimonial I can give on behalf of Prussia."

Mr. King looked puzzled to the point of alarm. "But your article in the latest number of the *Edinburgh Review* ... ?"

"Oh, that was not by Mr. Browning," Mrs. Carlyle gasped. "That was by Monckton Milnes."

"And you are not ... ?" Mr. King's mouth gaped.

Now he understood why the fellow had given such an unnatural emphasis to "palm leaves." *Palm Leaves* was the title of Milnes's latest collection of poetry.

So much, then, for that "lucidly"; so much for *all* his compliments.

He smiled and made a little bow of self-acknowledgment. "Robert Browning, by your leave."

From flattering her host, the Gräfin Hahn-Hahn had come by imperceptible degrees to teasing him. There were men of a certain self-assured and self-important stamp who attracted and annoyed her in equal measure and whom she could not resist baiting, though she knew from sad experience that such men were not likely to take her quizzing in good part. Of all people the British seemed to nourish this type in the greatest abundance, and Carlyle, of them all, had brought it to the completest, oddest flowering. A handsome man, still in his prime at an age (late forties, she judged) when most men are but the phantoms of their youthful selves; conscious of his advantages without seeming vain; with a manner, a mien, a carriage that would have been the envy of a king. One of Nature's aristocrats, just as Mrs. Jameson had said. What she had not said was that his opinions could be so absurd, his arguments so tendentious, so wanting in that imaginative sympathy that made what he *wrote* (what she'd read of it) fairly glow with the warmth of its humanity. What a conundrum—and how impossible to resist leading him on!

It had begun when Bystram joined them. Carlyle made polite inquiries about the journey to London. Bystram had mentioned their stop at Ghent for the sake of its sublime Gothic altarpiece. Carlyle, having spent a morning in the town some three or four years ago, proceeded to lecture them on the unimportance of the art of painting, then on the iniquity of the Catholic Church (despite the Gräfin's pointing out, as delicately as she might, that she was herself a Catholic). Finally, by way of an anecdote to do with the churchbells of Ghent and his insomnia, Carlyle had got onto the subject of pianos, which he declared to be emblematic of "the hollow triviality of the present age." Herr Oberst sniffed, exchanged a look of arch incredulity with the Gräfin, and looked down at the tips of his boots, disdaining to contest such a patent absurdity.

"Surely," the Gräfin urged in slow but perfect English, "you are not serious, Mr. Carlyle. The age we live in may be trivial, but the piano itself is the noblest and most expressive of musical instruments."

"I am most darkly, yea, woefully serious, Gräfin," said Carlyle. "If the Devil were to wield his hammer at this very hour and smite into smithereens all and every pianoforte of our European World, I would count it a blessing, true and shining. You would soon come to agree if you lived in this house, let me assure you. We have neighbors: two hapless, fanciful young women whose characters have been ruined by the piano. They pass all their young, bright days not in learning to darn stockings, knit wristikins, starch wing collars, sew up a dressing gown, bake bread, or in any other profitable art, but rather—to the distraction and bellicosity of All—in taking fitful, desultory notions to practice upon the keyboard of a pianoforte. The jangle of their playing, as it comes through the walls of this house, has become an emblem for me of the unwholesome and distracted misery of this era. So I say again that the world would be happier if there were not one spinet left soundable in it."

"But that is monstrous!" cried the Gräfin, delighted. "What of Chopin? What of *Beethoven*?"

"Aye, and what of them?"

"Is not their music the very voice of our age?"

"If that be so, then the Age speaks in the voice of a bedlamite. No, I won't allow as much as that. I have been present when someone performed a Beethoven sonata, so called. It was the merest jumble of noises, like a quantity of bricks tumbling down a building."

The Gräfin turned her head sideways, the better to fix her good eye on Carlyle, and spoke in a compassionating tone: "Then, by your own admission, you are deaf to the meaning of music. For no one—not even Goethe—is more full of meaning—lofty meaning, sublime meaning—than Beethoven."

"Is it not strange, in that case, Gräfin, that no one has succeeded in translating these sublimities into cloudless clear and meaningful English—or German, for that matter? Not so much as one sentence."

"It is not necessary. The music speaks so much better; it says much *more*."

Carlyle made a snort expressive of dubiety.

"Very well," she responded, "I shall translate a passage of Beethoven into English. Let me think." She thought quickly and continued, almost without pause: "His Fifth Symphony conveys most forcefully the very same moral that can be drawn from your own admirable *Oliver Cromwell*. It says, quite clearly, that we are entering a new age, and that the leaders of this age are the middle classes, the same classes who were, in earlier times, burghers and peasants. It says, moreover, that it is the duty of this new ruling class to acquire the refinement, the inner cultivation, the spirituality—such a lovely word that is; we have only *geistige Natur*—that formerly distinguished the aristocracy. Finally, he is saying that we must *all* become heroes, aristocrats, and saints. Beyond that, he even shows us, by the example of his divine music, how this may be done."

Carlyle bowed his head in mock submission. A lock of lank hair fell across his wide brow. His brilliant blue eyes sought out the single animated one of his guest. "These are indeed noble meanings, Frau Gräfin. I am glad that you should have read them in my *Cromwell*, and I will accept your authority for their being present in the Beethoven symphony. I will say no more against Herr Beethoven, nor pianos—so long, that is, as the Misses Lambert are not inspired to serenade this morning's breakfast. I fear, though, that the forenoon be a dangerous time of day; the perverse muses of cacophony and disorder may descend on us at any moment. Then—you may judge!"

On the way to the kitchen Jane felt the oddest lightness, a sensation almost of floating, as though her skirts had been inflated with hydrogen like a Vauxhall balloon instead of the common agency of petticoats. Such heat! Poor Helen, slaving below. This was their first proper dinner party. Breakfast—she corrected herself. In the manner, rather the *fashion*, of Samuel Rogers and Milnes, but with hardier fare. Rogers's breakfasts were known to feature strawberries, a sure cause of colic!

The previous day's aching head had graciously left off its throbbing; doubtless, the tonic of company might be thanked for that. However she might dread the prospect of visitors, the actual fact of them seemed to settle her nerves like one's well-remembered first draught of laudanum (before custom has dulled its efficacy). Perhaps, after all, she had been meant for such a life as Harriet Baring's—a whirl of faces, the air ever ringing with the sound of voices. Carlyle, of course, would not abide such a life, in principle (though he liked it well enough, it would appear, *chez* Baring). What a thirst she felt sometimes . . . but for what, she could not begin to articulate. Perhaps to be like Mill and his Platonica—not that they still saw Mill and Mrs. Taylor socially—sailing, doubtless at this moment, down the Rhine. She could feel the very breeze. But no. Two minutes away from her party and already she was fabricating an imaginary life—the actual party, her own, half-heard in another room, extended to infinity. No wonder she had never been able to write five consecutive pages of a proper book. Her mind would not be *fixed*. Two glasses of sherry were not sufficient excuse. *Why* had she come down to the kitchen? She couldn't remember.

Helen (poor creature) glistened with sweat as she transferred the broth from kettle to tureen.

"Imagine," said Jane, "anyone having *such* a ridiculous name—Countess Cock-Cock!"

Together they carried the brimming tureen to the back kitchen and centered it upon the lift.

"And I understand," she continued, "that her companion, the Baron von Bystram, is the original of Andlau in her novel." This bit of gossip was of particular interest to Helen, who had just begun to read *The Countess Faustina* and looked forward to serving the pudding (having bathed especially for the occasion). "Oo, aye," she answered, deep in thought. Jane had borrowed the double-decker from Mudie's Circulating Library and, as often was the case with books by friends or acquaintances, had passed it on to Helen, a curiously avid reader, before returning it.

Helen tugged at the pullropes, hand over hand, and the soup began its ascent to the room above.

Mrs. Jameson, still ensconced with Amely Bölte, considered whether charity required her going to the rescue of the young man who was so mysteriously suffering by the piano. But deciding, after all, to be selfish, she made her way, instead, to Browning, who was endeavoring to take an interest in the engraved face of Oliver Cromwell glowering behind glass.

"And whom do you think," she asked in a tone suitable for teasing small children, "I accompanied to a viewing of Rogers's collection on Monday afternoon? Whom do you suppose?"

Browning knew very well that it was his fiancée, Elizabeth Barrett, who had been to Rogers's gallery with Anna Jameson, for there was no detail of his Ba's life that he wasn't informed of on the day that it occurred, thanks to the conjoint miracles of her indefatigable pen and the London post. The engagement, however, was a secret, and therefore, as well, their correspondence. The reason for such secrecy was ostensibly to avoid the jealous wrath of Ba's father, who was (without exaggeration) the supreme monster of the species *paterfamilias*. Beyond this practical need to avoid Mr. Barrett's suspicions, there was the further sweetness inherent in all secrets, the closeness that comes of sharing them, the drama of leading a double life. Mrs. Jameson, had she known that Browning was daily covering several sheets of foolscap in an effort to persuade darling Ba to fly with him to Italy, for health's sake as well as love's, would only have approved, but it was more exciting to imagine *all* the world against their two sole selves. So he replied: "I can't imagine."

"Our darling Sappho."

"Indeed! It *is* rare for her to adventure so far from the cloisters of Wimpole Street. I had thought she was too much the invalid."

"Oh, she took stirring. I had been weeks persuading her to it. The trip was ever and again postponed. But I was ruthless, while preserving as best I might an appearance of gentleness."

Browning nodded approvingly: this was exactly his own formula for dealing with Elizabeth. "And what impression did Rogers's collection have on her?"

"Not a very forceful one, I judge. She has been so little in the world and seen so little of the better sort of painting, that any brightness, any likeness, any image that strikes some sympathetic chord will excite her admiration. Of painting, itself, she has no ideas. She walked right past a Titian without observing it, took no notice of a Velásquez. . . ." Mrs. Jameson shook her head in solemn deprecation, and the sausage curls that framed her round face translated the motion into a vigorous, affirmative bobbing up and down.

"And quite rightly too," Browning asserted (for Ba could do no wrong). "It is a mark of the highest receptivity that it should be quickly surfeited. Galleries on the scale of Rogers's are an insult to any sensitive mind. Paintings should be seen, as painters paint them, one by one—not ranged like so many hurdles in some mental steeple-chase."

Mrs. Jameson as a professional connoisseur and writer of guide-books to the galleries of Europe could not but take offense at a notion so contradictory to her livelihood, and so, as Browning had hoped, their talk was diverted from Elizabeth Barrett's excursion to the neu-tral grounds of objective controversy, as safe and as exciting as a fencing match.

Edward King stared numbly at the closed keyboard of the piano. The talk whirled about him unheard. Intermittently, flashes of resent-ment would brighten the uniform gray of his misery: against Browning, for having (as Edward supposed) led him on; against Mrs. Carlyle, for having (and with such a glint of *Freudenschade*) un-deceived him, making him look the fool; against Carlyle, for having refused (quite two months ago) Amely's request that he should provide his transla-tion with a few words of judicious praise. How small an effort that would have cost the great man—and how vast a difference it would make in finding the book a publisher. But he'd refused, though Amely (in King's eyes, the most reticent creature in the world) had literally gone down on her knees—or, at least, had threatened to. But his greatest resentment was directed, naturally, against the one person to whom he might express it: Amely herself—who now, having been shaken off by the redoubtable Mrs. Jameson, had finally elected to notice Edward, standing companionless, a pariah beside the piano.

She joined him.

"Well, I hope you're satisfied," he said.

She shrank before his accusatory tone, becoming in an instant the sort of craven governess-like creature she had just been denouncing with Mrs. Jameson. "What is it, Edward?"

"What is it, Edward?" he mimicked nasally. "Only that I spent half an hour talking to Robert Browning on the assumption that he was Monckton Milnes, because *you* told me he would be here."

"I said he *was* to have been here, but then he sent a telegraphic dispatch saying that he could not come. You were to replace him."

"That is not what you told me."

"I am sorry if you misunderstood."

"I look a perfect fool."

Amely hung her head.

"Mrs. Carlyle fairly sneered at me."

"She has a sharp tongue," Amely allowed.

"I am leaving this moment!"

"Oh, please, Edward, don't do that!"

"Oh, please, Edward," he echoed, "don't do that . . . And why not, I should like to know. There's no one here who gives tuppence about what *I* may have to say."

"That is not true," she assured him with a desperate earnestness. "You must be patient. Talk to Carlyle. Lead the conversation around somehow to the *Nibelungenlied*. It will be well in the end."

He paused. "Very well, I shall stay. But only to spare *you* embarrassment."

Amely pressed his hand in gratitude.

The bell summoned them to dine.

He was off again (the soupbowls had descended to the kitchen; the boiled fowl, roast mutton, and sundry removes had mounted aloft) on the still-agitating subject of the Reform Bill. Though quite fourteen years had gone by since its passage, Carlyle was ranting as though he were on the hustings instead of at the head of his own breakfast table. "Reform!" he crowed derisively. "Parliament was not reformed, and never will be. The Reform Bill burnt no more than the dry edges of straw on that dunghill. A huge, damp, putrid mass remains rotting where it is. There is no reform!" Jane gave an admonitory cough. The Gräfin, seated on Carlyle's right hand, was slicing the piece of chicken that had fallen to her portion with a fixedness that the overcooked meat scarcely merited on its own account. Somehow the torrent must be diverted, but Jane shrank from the task.

"And thus it will remain," he went on, "for anything an extended suffrage may do to cure it. Extend suffrage and you extend the rot. What use are votes without Wisdom? And how shall a man find Wisdom in a dunghill?"

There followed in rapid succession a half dozen such rhetorical questions, each more unanswerable than the last. The total effect of them was a sum greater than its parts, and the company, though at a loss to reply, was dazzled into such respectful fear as sheep may experience by the barking of a shepherd dog.

All the company, that is, but the Gräfin Hahn-Hahn, who, having dissected her chicken nearly into its atomic components, turned her one good eye upon her host and observed coolly: "It seems you would prefer to live in a world in which fools were not so prevalent—and so should I. But what are we to do until that happy day? We must be ruled by someone. How shall we select our rulers if not by voting?"

"They," Carlyle snapped back, "must select us." But he did not continue. The torrent had been stanched, at least for the moment.

The Gräfin pursued her advantage. "You believe, then, in some kind of aristocracy? I do, as well, though not for the purposes of governing. I have lived in a country governed by an hereditary aristocracy and have learned its disadvantages. But they *do* have their use, aristocrats. They are free, and so they offer us models for our own freedom. The Countess Faustina, in my novel, has the freedom to dress as she pleases, and she can do so without jeopardizing her position in Society. A woman of the middle classes is, alas, more circumscribed in her possibilities."

"I wish I could believe that were so," Mrs. Jameson said, leaning forward to address the Gräfin across the steadily busy fork of Mr. King. "But the aristocrats I have known have seemed to me as circumscribed in their actions as any chambermaid, albeit by a different code of necessary behavior."

"I speak not of reality, of course, but of theory. Of the Ideal Aristocrat. Of my own Countess, Faustina, and no one else's. But the world is not without its actual examples, some of which, indeed, surpass my heroine. There is Madame la baronne Dudevant, for example. Could there be a freer spirit than hers? A more shining inspiration?"

"George Sand!" Jane exclaimed, aghast and delighted in equal measure. Long ago she had learned not to speak of the popular French author before her husband, for though he would tolerate her reading Sand's novels, he would not allow them to be praised in his presence— not by Jane, not by her bosom friend Geraldine Jewsbury (who worshipped the least paragraph Sand wrote), not by the tragedian Macready, nor yet by Mazzini, whose other liberal opinions Carlyle was prepared to pass over in silence. All of these had one time or other tried to champion George Sand in the drawing room of Cheyne Row, and all without exception had been made to regret their advocacy. It was the controversy of controversies else most calculated to awaken Carlyle's direst thunderbolts.

"George Sand!" Carlyle repeated with the transparent pleasure of a Puritan who has just named Satan by one of his most closely guarded pseudonyms; nor could he resist another repetition. "George Sand . . . an inspiration? Then we must call Clytemnestra an example to her sex, and Phaedra a model wife! George Sand an Ideal Aristocrat? A woman who goes to the opera in trousers, smokes cigars?"

"As to cigars, my dear," Jane interposed mildly, "I have heard on good authority that Harriet Martineau—of whom you largely approve —has been known to indulge in the same vice; not to mention . . ." She waved the name not mentioned away with a sweep of her hand: it might have been her own. Carlyle's own mother smoked a pipe.

He was undaunted. "If Hell still has a meaning in our language, it is such as she we must thank. A creature compact of naught but Appetite. Force of hunger for pleasure of every kind, and want of all other force—like that other chosen vessel of Hell, John Keats, whose life, I understand, is to be celebrated by our absent friend Monckton Milnes, as though the best way to treat such malodorous sewage were not to let it return to its component dust unseen and unremembered."

"What possible harm can you discover in John Keats?" Browning marveled. "Surely he is the most inoffensive of poets, as well as the most musical."

"As to the supposed value and language of music, I will refer you to our visitor, the Gräfin—but as to Keats's offense . . . it stinks to the vast, hardly-reachable-to-such-as-man Heavens! Keats wrote those infamous 'Lines on the Mermaid Tavern':

*Souls of poets dead and gone . . ."*

" 'What Elysium have ye known,' " Browning continued, " 'Happy field or mossy cavern, choicer than the Mermaid Tavern? Have ye tippled drink more fine than mine host's Canary wine? . . .' And so on—*infamous?*" Browning insisted.

"And degrading to the Soul of Man; for what does it say, when you have removed the jingling *music*, but that the supreme good that poets see fit to commend to their readers is drunkenness and oblivion. Keats is a miserable creature hungering after unattainable sweets, and complaining of his hunger—and George Sand is such another, though the sweets she craves are of a character that no decent writer heretofore has ever had the effrontery to hold up to the public view."

"And yet," the Gräfin Hahn-Hahn calmly replied, "we must allow that Sand is the first genius of her sex and the Prometheus of womankind."

"The Lucifer, say rather!" Carlyle volleyed back, managing to hiss and to shout in the same breath.

"I have heard critics in Germany declare that Lucifer and Prometheus may be two aspects of the same being. In an era of change, such as ours, Good may easily be mistaken for Evil. Think of Christ, and how He was crucified for His prophecies."

"Ha! Just as I've said. You will make this Sand the Virgin of your new religion, named of Universal Love, with Sacraments mainly of Divorce, and this Sand in her trousers will be flanked on either side of the altar by Balzac and Eugène Sue for Evangelists, and for a Gospel to read from the pulpit we shall have *Lélia*, perhaps in an Authorized English Version—for I understand one of Mazzini's young ladyfriends intends to translate the entire festering oeuvre—so that no woman, however humble her station or simple her mind, may be prevented from succumbing to the contagion!"

At just this moment the young lady in No. 6, Cheyne Row, began to play upon the pianoforte.

"There! there, as I foretold! She is at it again! Listen and you will hear the death knell of peace. Pianos! There is a pianist enlisted among the many lovers of Madame Sand, is there not? And small wonder—listen to it, the very voice of this lascivious age. Presently she will begin to sing some siren song of the modern Babylon, some simpering hymn at the altar of the new religion of Universal Love. Hark! She stops . . . she begins!"

One could just hear, through the wall of the dining room, the lyrics of their neighbor's siren song:

> *There is a happy land,*
> *Far, far away,*
> *Where saints in glory stand,*
> *Bright, bright as day.*

Bystram, at the farthest end of the table from Carlyle, was first to laugh—the driest, politest twig-snap of a chuckle. Edward King added his own deep-throated titter, like a pizzicato passage played upon a 'cello, to which Mrs. Jameson and the Gräfin Hahn-Hahn soon added their alto and soprano accompaniments. As the hymn took up its second stanza, even Jane and Browning joined in. Only Amely Bölte, with her limitless capacity for suffering a sympathetic pain, refrained from laughing and sat staring at the bones of the chicken wing on her plate.

Carlyle glowered defiance as long as he could and then, unable to resist, laughed the loudest, most convulsive, and longest laugh of all.

# CHAPTER ELEVEN

# A Huge Nose and an Undeveloped Fourth Finger

## JULY, 1848

By the cut of his coat he might have been the Count d'Orsay. Only last Tuesday the mistress, in one of her talkative moods, had been speaking of "the Count" as of some momentarily expected parade. A dandy, certainly, with those yellow nankin trousers, and his air of just gliding along the pavement in his pearl-buttoned boots. But if he *were* the Count, then the woman beside him (more substantial in every respect) would not be stopping at every doorway to check the house number.

Whoever they were, Anne, the Carlyles' current housemaid, was certain that they were meaning to come to No. 5, and so, with reluctance and gladness mingled, she interrupted the butcher's boy, gently kicking him in the ankle, and nodded in the direction of the approaching guests. Taddy, accepting this as his due, went right on telling of the great Chartist meeting on the Fulham Road.

"Taddy," she said, taking the leg of mutton in its paper wrapping from him, "it's *visitors* for our house: be off with you!"

Reluctantly Taddy relinquished the joint, pantomimed a kiss, and set off in the direction of Cheyne Walk.

Anne was about to go into the house (so as not to receive the guests with a leg of mutton in her arms), but the woman with the very floral bonnet was too quick. Lofting her parasol in a peremptory gesture, she obliged Anne to stand at the half-open door while they approached.

On nearer examination the gentleman couldn't possibly be the Count d'Orsay, for this was another breed of dandy altogether. The pallor! And in July! He looked like a proper corpse—with those sunken cheeks and blue lips, his legs, in their trousers, as thin as those of a skeleton! But the oddest feature, and one which her mistress would surely have mentioned in her so thorough inventory of the Count's features, was the gentleman's nose. It was huge, and with a great hump in the middle. Just horrid.

"Ah-ha!" said the woman, in a rasping, rough-tuned voice, for the benefit of her companion: *"Ceci est numéro cinq!"* She turned, addressing him in a voice of an altogether sweeter timbre: *"Frédéric, tu as la lettre...."*

And the gentleman, with a slow, subaqueous movement, such as one might evince under mesmeric influence, reached into his breast pocket, removed a letter, and handed it to the woman, who handed it in turn to Anne. "This is a letter of introduction," she said in the clearest English (but in her earlier grating tone), "to Mr. Thomas Carlyle. We shall wait *here*—" She planted the tip of her parasol firmly on the doorstep, like an explorer taking possession of a new land. "—while he reads it. Say that I hope he will be able to receive us, if only briefly."

"The master's not at home, mum," Anne replied, not a little pleased at being in the position to thwart the woman's immense purposefulness. "He would still be off in the country."

"I see." Frowning, she turned to her pallid companion and translated Anne's message, using those softer tones she reserved for his ears. Anne, though she could not understand French, gathered from the words that the gentleman was somehow unwilling to *accept* this disappointment. Not that he seemed angry, as the woman did; his protest was more in the nature of a tired and fretful child who has been told to move from his place before the fire. It occurred to Anne to wonder whether the woman might actually be his mother. But no, she was not that much older.

In a burst of compassion (for the man was evidently not feeling at all well), Anne asked would they like to come in to the sitting room to rest a while.

"Oh, if we might, please," the woman answered without hesitation. "Our coachman, you see, misdirected us, and we have been wandering in this cruel heat for too long." She turned to her companion and explained in French that they were to be allowed inside. The gentleman's cyanotic lips flexed in a thin, wan smile of gratitude.

Anne opened the door. Then, sensing that the gentleman would not wish to attempt the hall stairs, she showed them into the dining room.

Jane the meanwhile, having feigned a headache, was luxuriating in the farthest recess of the garden. The "headache," though it had already served to turn away two unidentified callers earlier that day, was entirely fictitious, a morning excuse to assuage a sudden "strong desire to bake oatmeal loaves" and, now, to escape Anne's surveillance while she indulged in forbidden pleasures.

Occasionally, still, the smoke from these dark, little cigars (or "cig- aritos") would make her dizzy, even nauseated; but today, with the roses triumphant in the clear light, and the sweet, slightly fermented scent of new hay wafting over the garden wall from the row of stables behind, today the vapors she drew into her lungs seemed to translate instantly into a sensation of heightened well-being and ease, making the blue sky more dramatically blue, the green grass lusher and more moist beneath her stockinged feet (for she was that far gone in volup- tuary delight as to have removed both shoes).

Suddenly Jane's reveries were stopped—the sound of the garden door opening turned langueur to guilty alarm! Anne stood on the flag- stone paving at the other end of the garden, Anne, who had never seen her mistress smoke! She hid the cigarette behind her full skirts. Should she drop it? Would the grass be damp enough? She must risk it, for Anne was approaching.

"Mum, if you please," Anne said in a stage whisper, when she was within earshot, "there is a lady and gentleman—the gentleman is look- ing ever so seedy—not his clothes, you know, but as though he was to faint. So I lets them go into the dining room to rest some. They have a letter for Mr. Carlyle and—"

"Oh, Anne—" Jane interrupted, more in self-defense than in anger, for as she struggled with the shoe buttons she could see smoke still wreathing up out of the grass from the discarded cigarette. "—you *know* . . . my head!"

"Yes, mum," she replied in a quieting tone. "And that's why I came back here to inform you—as I *didn't* tell them you was home. The letter was to Mr. Carlyle. I told them *he* wasn't home, but didn't think to say you was."

"Anne, heavens, you're *impossible!*" Jane answered, already on her way into the house and in a thoroughly good humor. Now that her shoes were on and she was certain Anne hadn't noticed the cigarette, she was ready for the adventure of a visit. But who might they be? Americans, probably, come to do homage to the Great Philosopher— with inane questions and autograph books.

But the surprise was of a quality and dimension altogether beyond her imagination. "Monsieur Chopin!" she cried aloud, causing the great composer to tremble before the blast of her astonishment. As the visitors stood, Jane raised a hand to her face as though to extenuate her outcry—and, smelling the tobacco on her fingers, reddened. "Monsieur Chopin," she repeated, in a moderated tone.

"And Miss Jane Stirling," said his companion, holding forth her gloved hand (which perforce she must accept—with a prayer that the woman's olfactory sense was not too acute). "We had hoped to see *Mr.* Carlyle, but your maid informs us that he has left London. We were suffering from the heat, and she kindly offered us respite here." She waved her hand to where a floral bonnet rested upon the tapestry-covered dining room table. Jane had only enough time to take in this piece of tasteful extravagance (Parisian, beyond a doubt) before Anne had spirited it off into the hallway with M. Chopin's hat and gloves.

"Yes," said Jane, replying to the small, emaciated, still-young man, rather than to Miss Stirling (for she had not been insensible to the emphasis placed on "hoped to see *Mr.* Carlyle"). "*Mr.* Carlyle is gone to Wiltshire with a friend from America." From the blank look on Chopin's face it was clear that he had not understood, and before Miss Stirling could volunteer a translation, Jane provided her own. "And please," she added in a species of French which made up for its want of polish with a warmth of kindness she reserved exclusively for invalids and small animals, "*do* be seated."

Miss Jane Stirling took a seat upon the horse-hair chaise, while Chopin chose one of the chairs belonging to the dining table.

Jane, under cover of the nervous patter she could produce even in French, began taking stock of Chopin's companion. Divested of her *grand bavolet*, Mlle Stirling's chief claim to beauty was one which only a coiffeur would recognize: the masses of curls framing her plain (not to say insipid) features were magnificent. But her eyes lacked the brilliance which alone pardons the imperfections of a mouth too emphatic and a chin too strong for *feminine* beauty. Not that a woman may not be permitted other modes of beauty. Madame Sand, for instance, was no rosebud-lipped sylphid, and yet how many men, both famous and fashionable, had been in thrall to her! And none more notoriously than Frédéric Chopin, for among the great woman's latest literary efforts, *Lucrezia Floriani* had contained a portrait (as all the world knew) of the composer—and not a very flattering one, for (as all the world also knew) their romance was over. How many questions she would have liked to ask about George Sand! But, of course—and alas!—those were precisely the questions that must be avoided.

So Jane spoke, instead, of the inconvenience of the previous week's rain and of the revolutions in Europe, and made compliments to M. Chopin upon his playing.

At mention of his art Chopin seemed to waken from his coma of polite inattention and, with an earnestness all out of proportion to his whispery voice, he began to thank Jane for "the poem she had written" to him. "Miss Stirling rendered your verses into French for me. I was much flattered. You are too kind."

"Oh dear," Jane replied, flustered. "It wasn't *I* who wrote those verses, though they express my admiration for your music much more admirably than my *letter* could have. No, I must confess, that sonnet was the work of my dear friend Captain Sterling, who accompanied us to the concert at Eaton Place."

"Stirling," Chopin echoed with bland confusion.

"Sterling with an 'e,' " Miss Jane Stirling explained.

"Ah. Then please convey my gratitude to Captain Sterling. I was much flattered."

Feeling that her visitor was not yet sated with compliments, Jane bethought herself for others. "Our friends at the same concert, Lord and Lady Ashburton—" Chopin's blue-gray eyes widened receptively at the sound of a title. "—were equally in raptures. There was one 'study' in particular which Lady Ashburton likened to the sound of water welling from a spring and coursing over the pebbled bed of a stream."

*"Oui, comme de l'eau,"* he repeated, with a small grimace as of one swallowing a spoonful of medicine. " 'Leik water'—*c'est ce que disent toutes les femmes."*

"That is what all the English ladies say, invariably," agreed Miss Stirling. "Some German critic or other has written that the A-flat study reminds *him* of a shepherd playing pipes during a thunderstorm. For my part, I regard it simply as a work requiring a formidable evenness of touch—and control. Beautiful, of course, but *so* exacting. To be expressive, yet to limit one's expressive powers virtually to the fifth finger of the right hand!"

"I should say, yes," Jane agreed.

"I see that *you* play, Mrs. Carlyle." She nodded to the well-polished pianoforte gleaming in the corner of the room.

"Heavens! I play Scots ballads at the request of Mr. Carlyle and sundry fools. You, surely, are a *musician*, Miss Stirling."

Miss Jane Stirling inclined her head forward so that her ample sausage curls would conceal the blush that (twenty years earlier) might have suffused her cheeks. Everything about the woman annoyed Jane. It was unfair, illogical even, but there it was. Everything! the sound of her voice, like a pan being scraped, and those hands of hers swooping about in their lace gloves. Even, or especially, the way she'd usurped not only her own name "Jane" but that of her friends, the Sterlings. Maugre the difference of one letter! The Sterlings were, all of them, embodiments of kindness. Consider only Captain Anthony— how he'd put his carriage at her disposal, sometimes virtually on a daily basis, and the gifts he would give, could not be prevented giving, though his magnanimity only served further to agitate his "mad" wife. The poor Captain! Carlyle called him martinetish, but that was because he'd not been allowed knowledge of the Captain's tenderer nature. Wasn't it odd that the same surname (with a vowel of difference) could encompass individuals so unlike as the dear Captain and this dreadful *poseuse*?

"I am a pupil of Monsieur Chopin," replied the woman, all unaware of these terrible judgments. "I studied with him in Paris, and earlier with his distinguished pupil, Mr. Lindsay Sloper."

"How I envy you!"

"I have Miss Stirling to thank for bringing me to England," said Chopin morosely.

"And do you like it here?" She gave the bell a tug.

He seemed not to have heard, for he made no reply. Perhaps the fault lay in her French.

"Do you like London?" she insisted.

He . . . gasped.

Was her question so distressing? Had it been asked of him so often, and was he so sensitive to the necessity of summoning up some polite untruth, that he was stricken quite dumb?

Then Jane noticed that his companion had been similarly stricken, had, indeed, stopped breathing altogether. And she understood: he was dying. The process had long been under way and would continue yet a while. He would not die here in her dining room—but he would soon be dead. His right hand, which had been (with his left) trembling slightly all the while—despite the warm breeze from the open garden door—dipped into the pocket of his jacket and withdrew a handkerchief fastidiously clean. Though when he held it over his mouth and coughed, it might as well have been drenched with blood: its power over Jane's imagination could not have been more terrible. The spasm, though not violent, had a life, a shapeliness, and a death of its own. At its conclusion, to their general relief, he addressed himself to Jane's question quite as though this morbid parenthesis had never intervened:

"London I find . . . expensive. Wessel of Regent Street publishes all of my works. Everything. And yet—" He broke off, seeing Anne, who'd come in answer to her mistress's ring. The maid bent down to receive a whispered order, then withdrew.

He resumed, not altogether sequentially. "They *all* know my name, even the least musical. Lady Gainsborough, the Marquis of Douglas. I have played for the queen herself. Yet these English ladies object to my fee! And the *young* women are the worst: they commit themselves to lessons and do not appear. Nor (needless to say)—" His voice had diminished to the most tenuous of whispers. "—do they pay. What am I to do?" He paused to touch his handkerchief to the corners of his mouth. "I do not feel that twenty guineas is an inordinate fee for playing in a private home. Yet, can you believe when I tell you that Lady Rothschild inquired what I ask, and when I named that figure, she thought fit to advise me that it was too large! *I* must be more moderate in *my* demands! Tell me, Mrs. Carlyle, do you consider twenty guineas an *immoderate* demand?"

Miss Stirling achieved a genuine blush. Jane, though disposed to be sympathetic to any plea of hardship, could not keep from reflecting that her own serving maid earned but half that sum in a year—and with it helped to support an aged mother. Clearly, hardship is a relative matter. He must spend a fortune at his tailor. Where did the rest of it go? she wondered—and he with his odd, un-English lack of compunction in discussing the affairs of the pocketbook answered her unasked question:

"No one has moderated the demands they make on me, I assure you. On the contrary, tradesmen are rapacious. In May I engaged rooms for, as I thought, twenty-six guineas a month, but at the end of the month my landlord demanded twice that figure! There was nothing in writing; I was obliged to comply."

"All short-term rentals have become shockingly dear, I am afraid," Jane said in a tone of sympathetic indignation. "Our American friend,

Mr. Emerson, simply could not find a room within his means *anywhere* in London, and that is partly the reason he and my husband have gone off to survey the mysteries of Stonehenge. The turmoils on the Continent are to blame. Since the French king fled here last winter the flood has not abated. Half the royalty of Europe and all the ministers have come to London."

"And as many musicians as well," added Miss Stirling acidly. "Thalberg is giving *twelve* recitals at the Italian Theatre. Hallé is here, and Berlioz—I know not how many more."

"Let us hope that the strife will soon be over, and order restored. The reports of the fighting in Paris would suggest that the crisis of the disease is past, there at least, though it is dreadful to consider the price that has been paid. So many thousands of lives!"

"Cavaignac is a great man," declared Chopin of the general who had suppressed the insurgent Paris workmen in the recent "June Days."

"Assuredly," Jane agreed. "I was a close friend of his deceased brother Godefroi Cavaignac. A sister could scarcely have followed General Cavaignac's recent career with more suspense or greater admiration. And yet it *is* a terrible task, is it not—the slaughter of one's own countrymen?"

"Cavaignac has done what was necessary."

"Of course. Carlyle would agree with you entirely." Jane bit her tongue rather than risk needless controversy by adding another "and yet" or "but still." But still, she couldn't contemplate Cavaignac's great victory over the workmen behind their barricades without wondering on which side of those barricades her dear Mazzini would have found himself, had his convictions drawn him to Paris instead of to Italy, where now he was fighting with Garibaldi outside Milan.

"If the workmen had not been put down swiftly," said Miss Stirling, "they would have instituted another Terror. They demanded nothing less than the surrender of all wealth and property into their own hands."

Chopin concurred in this judgment with a worried frown. His hands were again, visibly, trembling; and for an uncomfortably long time all three persons in the room seemed to be conscious of nothing else. Then Miss Stirling addressed Jane, in English: "I wonder, Mrs. Carlyle," she said in a more amiable tone than previously, "if we might impose upon you for a cup of tea. I fear that my friend's speaking of money is a certain sign of his fatigue. Our walk in finding our way hither was beyond his strength, and I do blame myself. My appetite for Society sometimes exceeds his—and yet, you know, he can be quite fretful if he does not move among people."

"The girl is already preparing a tea for us. It should be ready now. If you will excuse me a moment, I'll see what is keeping her."

When Jane appeared below stairs, Anne was filling the hot-water pot. The other tea things were arranged in readiness on the best teak tray. Beside it, hot and fragrant, buttered slices of the oatmeal loaf formed a wreath of archetypal wholesomeness on a blue china plate.

"Who is it, mum? The gentleman."

"That is Frédéric Chopin, from Poland by way of Paris, and a man, moreover, in need of hot tea and fresh bread. Let us—"

She broke off, transfixed, as though the first notes of the music had pierced directly to the very core of her. In the room above them the piano spoke with a force of eloquence it had never before possessed. The language of the music was as clear—to Anne as to Jane—as the lamentation of a great prophet: whole histories, entire worlds of sorrowing seemed to have been distilled into this pensive progression of single notes. Then a pause, and when the darkling half-speech, half-melody resumed, it was with a melancholy more poignant. And yet more nearly distant, once removed from the original statement; half remembered, spun out like the song of a thrush. He'd played the piece at both London concerts—it was one of the studies, though not the one "leik water."

How different it sounded here in her own home, upon her own piano. Who would have thought such powers lay within its tightened wires and felt hammers waiting to be released?

Quietly, solemnly, the small procession of Jane followed by Anne mounted the stairs, Jane with the plate of bread and the water jug, Anne with the tray. When they came into the breakfast room, Chopin was still playing like one transformed. The physical exertion, rather than exhausting his waning strength, seemed to serve as surrogate for the mechanical process of breathing.

She knew, standing motionless there, that it must end, and, of course, it did—he turned to acknowledge her return, letting one long, arching, cadenzalike phrase disintegrate within the weightlessness of his touch.

"*C'est désaccordé, vous entendez, madame?*" In demonstration whereof he played the second F# above middle C thrice in rapid succession. The piano badly wanted tuning. How could she not have noticed as he played?

"The tuner was here only last summer," Jane said. Then, feeling the inadequacy of this, she was more candid: "And it is rarely played."

Miss Stirling, helping herself to a slice of the warm bread, arched an eyebrow that conveyed a judgment pitiless as Cavaignac's against the insurgent workmen.

"But now that Monsieur Chopin has played upon it, I shall surely make amends at the nearest opportunity. Truly, Monsieur Chopin, you are a magician."

"*Comment? Je suis musicien, non?*" Then, grasping the word but not yet her meaning, "*Magicien?*"

"In that your playing calls forth spirits."

And still he regarded her with the blankest of blank expressions. Could George Sand's lover and the greatest of contemporary composers be so witless?

"Ah, I see: *demonic* spirits. You mean to suggest that I am like Liszt, the Hungarian. Yes, some of his music is demonic." With a self-satisfied smile, like a child who has acquitted himself well before his tutor, Chopin finished his tea in one long, pensive draught. "He is strong, as well—he has the technique of a Mephistopheles. While *my* poor hands . . ." He held up his left hand, limp as a scrap of silk, and with his other hand lifted and let loose its fingers as though they were the lifeless digits of some supremely well-oiled marionette. Then, he singled out the fourth finger: "You see . . ."

With his right index finger, he raised it high and curved above the others. "This is Liszt." Then let it drop. "And this is Chopin." He placed his left hand on the back of his right and raised the same fourth finger, unaided—less than an inch. "But—" He folded his hands sedately in his lap and smiled. "—my music does not make such pyrotechnical demands as does the music of Liszt."

As though he'd settled a problem the solution of which alone had prevented his departure till now, he rose to his feet. "*Merci, madame.* You will please convey to Captain Sterling my sincere thanks for his verses."

"And," added Miss Jane Stirling, "our warmest regards to *Mr.* Carlyle. I do hope we shall have the opportunity to meet on some other occasion."

Jane echoed this hope with mechanical courtesy, and summoned

Anne (who had remained in the hallway, in the hope that the visitor might continue playing). Soon she again appeared with the lady's bonnet, the gentleman's hat and gloves.

"Will you know where the coach stops?" Jane asked.

Miss Stirling confessed she would not. Chopin, as though set free from all such low considerations by his genius (or faltering health), seemed not to have heard, and deigned no reply.

"Then I shall walk with you to the corner."

And so, "bonnetless as one who would corrupt the Entire Civilized World," Jane accompanied her visitors to the foot of Cheyne Row, set them into a hansom, and bade them farewell.

Returning, moments later, up the shadow-stippled pavement of the Row, she encountered the elder Lambert girl—in a state of breathless agitation.

"Do pardon me for my curiosity, Mrs. Carlyle. I know it is quite out of place, but I couldn't help but hear—the walls between us are so thin, as you have pointed out so often yourself. Such playing, such . . . and then, seeing you go out—"

"Frédéric Chopin, Constance," she said in answer to the unasked question.

"I see, Mrs. Carlyle—and in your own home."

"And in my own home."

# CHAPTER TWELVE

# The Flight into Egypt

---

1849–1855

Rossetti, with his large penetrating eyes, sat, back to the window, so that the light, aqueous from the tinted bullet-glass panes, made a natural halo about his unkempt dark hair. One lock in particular—Hunt's regard flickered up from his sketch to appraise it again—came curling down across the opposing curve of his right ear: one of those felicitous accidents that nature casts up upon the shores of the passing moment. There: in two quick curves his pencil had snared it. His lips tightened with the satisfaction of this fractional achievement, and Rossetti in response (for his pencil was just then defining the bowed line at the juncture of those lips) grimaced annoyance. The drawing already was botched beyond redemption: the nose he'd given Hunt was blunter than any pugilist's, the tangled mass of the beard a bedlamite's, the eyes (caught at the moment they studied his own features, with the light full upon them) protuberant and ever so slightly out of true.

" 'The Truth Seeker,' " Stephens suggested, like some damned tormenting sprite. Stephens, grown tired of his study of the saltcellar, contented himself now with compiling a list of suggested titles for their projected magazine.

Rossetti rejected the idea with a vigorous shake of his head, modifying the relationship of curl to ear, but Hunt's pencil, by now, had passed on to the more problematical contours of Rossetti's eyebrows—problematical only in their ideal, unreal regularity. His drawing was taking on too bland a handsomeness. Rossetti no doubt fancied himself in the role of an errant prince—disguised, may be, in the seedy brown overcoat of a bohemian—but Hunt had no wish to be his court painter.

" 'Aspirations Toward Truth,' " Stephens persisted.

Again Rossetti shook his head, though this time less emphatically.

Hunt, taking pity on his protégé, said, "No, but put it on the list. There's *something* there."

"We want to emphasize Nature," said Rossetti, with an oracular furrowing of his brow.

And there was the detail that had been escaping him: Rossetti's forehead swelled noticeably as it moved down to the ridge of the eye sockets. Hunt darkened the shadow above the base of the nose, the shadows below the brows, and, dipping a finger in his pile of shavings, drew the faintest of demarcations along the line where the forehead bent forward. Would that do?

" 'Truth to Nature,' " Stephens offered.

"Or possibly 'Aspects of Nature'?" Hunt suggested.

"Ah," said Rossetti, "I like that. Write that one down." (Which Stephens did.) "It has a ring: 'Aspects of Nature.' Possibly, possibly . . ."

(In fact, it was only an *aspect* of the nature of Rossetti's features that Hunt had captured. His *character* refused obstinately to shine forth. There was too much of Hunt's own phlegm and melancholy in it, nothing of Rossetti's airiness or *brio*, or—to be quite candid—his conceit.)

"What think you of—" Gabriel paused, laid down his pencil for dramatic effect, and held up his finger in the manner of Leonard's *St. John.* "—'The Anti-Smudge'!"

"Ha!" said Stephens, at once recognizing that this was a joke *and* that it wasn't very funny.

Hunt looked offended. "You can't be serious, Gabriel. Oh, and turn your head back to the left?"

"Let's have done. The light's worse here than in the Academy cast room on a February afternoon. I've made you look a proper Caliban. How'd you make out?"

Hunt turned his sketchbook round in reply.

Rossetti cocked his head and squinted out of one eye, taking its measure.

Stephens said, "Oh, yes. You've got his nose exactly."

"I *am* serious, though," said Rossetti, forbearing either to praise or to criticize, for the picture was both very like and very unflattering. Surely his forehead did not bulge so? But Hunt could not bear to be criticized, so the politic course was to stand mum. " 'Anti-Smudge' says what we stand for—or what we stand against: old 'Sir Sloshua' and the Slipslop School of Ancient and Honorable Incompetence. We might try a decalogue of sorts on the cover, with the names of all the artists who shall not be tolerated under the P.-R.B. dispensation: 'Nature be the Lord thy Guide; thou shalt have no Claudes before thee.'"

"And no Michael Angelo!" added Stephens, oblivious to Rossetti's pun.

Gabriel grimaced agreement and, undaunted, pursued the whimsy. "Instead of a decalogue, what say a guillotine, with the names of our enemies on baskets below it? Correggio, Rubens, Delacroix—we'll cut them *all* down!"

"Gabriel, do be serious," said Hunt, though not without the indulgent glimmer of a smile.

"But they *are* our enemies. Shall you take back the words I heard you speak but a month ago in the Louvre before that rubbishy mulch of a landscape by Rubens—"

"Oh, they're our enemies; but surely the magazine should be named for what we believe in, not what we oppose?"

"*What* words?" insisted Stephens, scenting embarrassment.

"Bill said, 'A bloody ape could paint better than this.'"

The ever-moderate, not to say prudish, Hunt blinked at his treacherous friend.

"And you should have seen the looks he got. He thought we were the only English in the room, but he was wrong."

"Well, Rubens is a fraud," Hunt murmured. "But, of course, that can't excuse such language."

Rossetti parted his lips, poised on the brink of some new sarcasm, but catching the pleading look in Hunt's eyes he was merciful.

"What say—" He paused until Stephens looked up from examining the tabletop. "—to simply, 'The P.-R.B. Journal'?"

Stephens thought it a fine idea, with one reservation: that people would be curious to know what the secret initials P.-R.B. stood for, and the initiated members of their Brotherhood were solemnly bound, on pain of perpetual shame and dishonor, never to reveal the initials' meaning.

"Let them be curious," Rossetti countered, lifting his chin defiantly. "*We* shan't tell them. What did you say, Hunt, when old Egg put it to you—or was it Gibbons?"

Egg was Augustus Egg, the painter; Gibbons the patron to whom

Egg had introduced Hunt and who had bought his *Rienzi* after it had been hung at last summer's Royal Academy show. Hunt, according to the rules of the Brotherhood, had placed the initials P.-R.B. below his name in the corner of that painting, just as a member of the Academy might have added the initials R.A. Unlike a Royal Academician, however, Hunt was sworn never to reveal the meaning of these letters to the uninitiated. Those who shared this secret formed a very small circle indeed. Beyond the three of them there at Don Saltero's Coffee House were only their fellow students John Millais, Thomas Woolner, and James Collinson; plus Gabriel's brother William, who worked at the Inland Revenue Office and showed as little aptitude for Fine Art as any collier or dustman. Young Stephens, for that matter, was still a most unproven quantity, having painted nothing and drawn only such casts, bottles, and tumbles of drapery as he could not, in the course of nature, absolutely avoid drawing. As a cripple he deserved some consideration, however. Further, he was Hunt's dearest friend, and if Gabriel could be allowed to bring in his brother, the taxman, then Hunt could surely be permitted to introduce Stephens, who might, after all, turn out to be a painter—for he had yet to demonstrate an incapacity as absolute as that of William Rossetti. Such, and so oddly sorted, were the members of the Pre-Raphaelite Brotherhood (to reveal, at last, the significance of the mystic initials).

Hunt, who took this matter of the secrecy of their little society as solemnly as any Freemason, looked about uneasily, but as they were the only custom in the room with the river view (and not even the serving man was within hearing range), he could not simply dismiss Rossetti's question with a precautionary finger to his lips. "I'm not sure that Egg ever did put it to me, nor Gibbons either."

He focused, uneasily, at the river gleaming whitely through the dripping denuded branches of the lime trees that bordered Cheyne Walk. Though what he'd said was not a lie, strictly, it was an evasion. He had, in fact, been asked the meaning of P.-R.B.—and, shamefully, he'd offered an explanation.

Rossetti, with his usual keen instinct for the vulnerable spot in another's armor, pressed the attack. "But *someone* did, or you wouldn't suddenly look away like that. Confess, Bill—who was it, and what did you tell him?"

"Well, it doesn't signify, really, as it was only my father, and I impressed on him the need of secrecy in the matter. Being in trade, he's not likely even to have an opportunity to mention the matter to those of our circle, and in any case what I told him wasn't the *real* meaning of the letters, which he'd not have understood—just some nonsense I invented on the spur of the moment."

"Out with it!" demanded Rossetti.

"I said it stood for 'Progress, Riches, Beauty.'" A blush spread across Hunt's broad and pimpled cheeks.

"Riches!" crowed Rossetti with delight. "Riches? I shouldn't have expected that from you, Bill, of all people!"

"I couldn't, for the life of me, Gabriel, think of anything else suitable beginning with 'R.' I suppose it's because my father tried to keep me in trade for so long fearing I should become a pauper if I made a career of art. So perhaps I said 'Riches' by way of demonstrating that I'm not wholly unworldly. I regretted it, you may be sure, the moment I'd said it. I ought not to have betrayed our oath, even thus far."

"Well, you're forgiven. Isn't he, Fred?"

Stephens nodded.

"In future we must be prepared with some formula that will serve for the curious. And something less candidly Philistine—" (Hunt's mind shriveled into one bright flame of shame.) "—than 'Progress, *Riches*, Beauty.'"

At that moment, muse-like, a single Chelsea pensioner (seen through the distorting glass) crossed Rossetti's field of vision and, after a suitable pause, the bell above the coffee house door jangled. "I have it! When we move into the vacant mansion next door—for a mansion it verily *is*—we shall affix our mysterious monogram to the gate, above the bell, where it will signify to the profane no more than 'Please ring bell'!"

Stephens laughed; Hunt smiled in a worried way.

"But who would believe we'd name our magazine 'The Please Ring Bell Journal'—or would read a journal with such a name?"

"True, true—we shall certainly have to find another name than that."

"I like the idea of Progresss," Stephens volunteered. "It shows we're not simply harking back to an older kind of art, which is the trouble, you know, with 'Pre-Raphaelite.' What think you of 'The Progressist'?"

Rossetti, merely by not taking exception (as he had to all of Stephens's suggestions heretofore), seemed to approve.

"Wouldn't that be more suitable, really, for a political journal?"

Hunt cautioned. "People would think we were Chartists or some other sort of radicals."

A silence ensued.

"We could name it after our place of residence, like *The London and Westminster Review*. 'The Chelsea Review'—that has a pretty ring. I like it!"

"But, Gabriel, it isn't certain that we shall be taking the place. Seventy pounds is rather dear, even if we divide it four ways."

Stephens hastened to share Hunt's alarm. "Indeed. Moreover, Collinson and I won't be able to come in with you until April at the earliest."

"And though Deverell might *fancy* to, he can't quit his present quarters without giving notice. Nor for that matter, Gabriel, can I."

"Ah," Rossetti answered airily, "you're speaking practically. I'm speaking ideally. If we're to be a proper Brotherhood, we must have a common home—our own monastery. The garden, though it's been allowed to get rank, somewhat, would grace a proper cloister, and as for the light, there's floods of it. In that respect alone it surpasses our old crib on Cleveland Street—you'll admit that."

Hunt did admit it. He did not, however, express his deeper reservation about this latest freak of his friend's fancy—namely, that after the experience of sharing his last studio with Rossetti, an experiment as short-lived as it had been disastrous, Hunt would as soon have undertaken to set up house with the anti-Christ. Not that he didn't still admire him mightily for his brilliance and treasure him for the sheer good will and exuberant spirits he spread about him. Rossetti was unarguably the major cohesive force behind the Brotherhood, a source of untiring, perpetual energy, a kind of human steam engine. The difficulty with steam engines, however, from a domestic point of view, is that they demand one's entire attention, and even so they will explode from time to time. No, for all its broad gardens and floods of light, this dwelling together in a house on Cheyne Walk was not to be thought of, though for the time being Hunt did not intend to say so. The plan would fall apart of itself in all likelihood.

So it did; and so, very nearly, did the Brotherhood. Gabriel found a studio in an older, more central quarter of London, near Oxford Street; Hunt, more fortunate, took lodgings at 5, Prospect Place, farther along the riverside upstream than the house they'd originally considered—yet still in Chelsea. His room faced on the river and the noonday sun, which he required for his latest assault on the heights of Parnassus, an historical painting of Christian missionaries escaping from Druids. The painting was already begun when the first number of *The Germ* (as their magazine finally came to be called) appeared, heralding the new demi-century of 1850, and when the fourth and final number came out in April, Hunt was still slaving away on the minutiae of his microcosmic world: rendering the feathered ends of arrows, the furs girding the central Druid's loins, the texture of the peeling beech bark supporting the thatched roof of the hut, the sparrows restless in that thatch, the very dirt upon the ground—all with a patient devotion to detail that verged on obsession. He worked from the morning's earliest light to the final glow of sunset, taking little intermission even when his friends came to call, which they did often during March's long stretches of overcast weather, claiming (Rossetti especially) to be unable to work.

Hunt was always able to work. He was quite as susceptible to depressions as his friend—there were weeks at a time when his painting seemed as stiff and lifeless as a waxworks—but he worked on regardless, trusting to his few, foggy verities—Truth to Nature, Strength in Faith—to see him through to the happier days when the painting glowed at him like God's own fiery handwriting.

At last it was done, just in time to be hung at the annual show of the Royal Academy—and to be reviled and pilloried. Rossetti had told a sculptor friend the meaning of the P.-R.B. initials and that friend, in turn, had passed on the information to Angus Reach, a gossip columnist on *The London Illustrated News*. The knowledge seemed to drive the critics of the R.A. show into furies of denunciation. Millais's painting of a pubescent Christ in his father's carpentry shop was decried by *The Athenaeum* as "a pictorial blasphemy," and no less a personage than Charles Dickens devoted the leading editorial of his immensely popular magazine *Household Words* to an excoriation of the same painting. Dickens described Millais's Mary as "a woman so horrible in her ugliness that (supposing it were possible for any human creature to exist for a moment with that dislocated throat) she would stand out from the rest of the company as a monster in the vilest cabaret in France or the lowest gin shop in England." By comparison to the abuse Millais received, Hunt was let off relatively easily.

There was, however, another aspect to this controversy not immediately evident to the wounded communal ego of the Pre-Raphaelite brethren, and that was that their notoriety was attended by an undeniable commercial success. Millais's *Christ in the House of His Parents* sold for a smashing £350, and with Millais's assistance, Hunt's Druid painting was placed with an Oxford collector for 160 guineas, a palpably better price than the £100 he'd received for his *Rienzi* a little time before. Admittedly, this represented Hunt's wages for a year, and when deduction was made for cost of materials and models, it was not enough to redeem him from a vegetarian diet of potatoes, carrots, and swedes. But what of that? Shelley had been a vegetarian. So long as he survived, Hunt was not one to be subdued by mere physical hardship.

The threat to the Brotherhood came from a different quarter, however, than that of their bad reviews; it came from that ancientest and most immemorial enemy of all exclusively male societies—womankind.

Her name was Lizzie Siddal. She was the discovery of a friend (but not a member, for they *were* exclusive) of the P.-R.B., the American-born Walter Deverell, who'd found her in a milliner's shop near Leicester Square. Lizzie was beautiful to a degree that seemed almost eccentric, with thick, inveigling hair of that devastating Celtic red Rossetti had been known to follow (in other contexts) about the city for hours at a time; an unearthly neck; eyes like a message direct from Paradise; limbs that would fold of their own volition into poses that seemed predestined from all eternity; and, withal, a social manner so retiring that the enigmas suggested by her long, languorous gaze were not easily to be solved. In a word, a born model. Soon she was sitting for all of them: as Deverell's Viola; as a Druid maiden, for Hunt, and then as his Sylvia; and, fully clothed in a brimming bathtub, as Millais's Ophelia. For Rossetti she was Rossovestita and then, in watercolor after watercolor (for he had not yet acquired properly the knack of oils), as the Beatrice to his adoring Dante.

When they met Lizzie, Deverell and Hunt were twenty-three, Rossetti twenty-two, and Millais but twenty-one. She was seventeen. For six months they loved their Viola/Sylvia/Ophelia/Rossovestita in a truly communal spirit. Then Hunt, inspired by a whim, upset this delicate balance by persuading Lizzie to adopt a new role—all in the spirit of fun and only for an afternoon—that of his wife. Rossetti, thrown into a rapture of confusion, insisted that Hunt write a letter of apology to the gentleman he'd taken in by this innocent hoax, which Hunt, smarting with bewildered embarrassment, accordingly did. The upshot was that Lizzie's activities as muse and model were to be devoted in future exclusively to Rossetti. Thereafter, an autumnal coolness pervaded the friendship of Hunt and Rossetti, though there was no actual falling out, only a gradual, never-acknowledged falling away, and for Hunt (though not for the feckless, smitten Rossetti) a falling *back* on the anodyne of work.

His first task was a labor of love—or of love's labor lost. There had been a letter in *The Times,* by the young critic John Ruskin, written in defense of the P.-R.B., whose works at that year's Royal Academy show had once again been savaged by the press. While proclaiming Hunt's "marvellous truth in detail and splendour in colour," Ruskin had taken significant exception to the figure for which Lizzie had posed: ". . . all this thoughtful conception, and absolutely inimitable execution, fail in making immediate appeal to the feelings, owing to the unfortunate type chosen for the face of Sylvia." In an exaltation of regret, Hunt blotted out the "unfortunate type" of Lizzie Siddal and replaced it with the face of another model; the painting went on to win £50 as the most approved entry in that autumn's Liverpool Exhibition. A modest price for a broken heart, but there was something savory even in the smart of his chagrin, like a wine that bites the tongue and leaves it thirstier.

Seen close, Christina Rossetti's skin was not notably delicate, but her eyes possessed, even more than her brother's, the uncanny property of shifting from azure-gray to hazel according to the warmth and angle of the light they reflected.

Gingerly, for it was hot, he moved the tin lantern closer to her skirts, reversing the ordinary pattern of shadows on her face. She glanced down nervously at the smoking lantern, then with an azure glint of irony back at the painter, who returned to his easel with a premonition of his own mastery. At first, when Gabriel had suggested that his sister should pose for the face of Hunt's Christ, Hunt had supposed him jesting; then he'd suspected him of matchmaking. Now he understood his friend's deeper meaning. There was a reproachfulness mingled in her melancholy that exactly suited his subject: Christ, in kingly robes, knocks at a weed-grown garden door, summoning sinners to repentance.

"Where am I to look?" Christina asked.

"Directly at me."

"So?"

He considered the cast shadows on the right of her nose. "Lower your chin just . . . yes, just so."

"When I told my sister Maria that I was to pose for your Christ," she said, with a ventriloquist's knack of articulating words without seeming to move her lips, "she felt I should have scruples. But I have been the Virgin Mary and any number of angels already, for my brother, and so I thought the risk to my natural humility was one I might dare incur."

"Christina," said her mother in a tone of habitual, mild reproof, "if you are concerned to have scruples, it would be more apropos to scruple about chattering whilst Mr. Hunt is trying to draw you."

"Really, ma'am, you must both feel free to speak. It is the eyes and the skin tones I am particularly concerned with. The mouth I have taken, so to speak, from her younger brother—*and* his brow, though in that there is also something of Gabriel. See there, on the table beside you, that is the head I have been working from. In any case, even when Miss Rossetti speaks, her lips can scarce be seen to move."

"As I said, I have served my brother as a model so often that if I had not learned this way of speaking—"

"Your lips distinctly moved then, Christina," Mrs. Rossetti broke in. "Really!"

"Plosives are the most difficult. One must think ahead to avoid them. But Mother is correct: mum's the word."

"Could you lift your eyes just a bit?" Hunt asked her.

Her eyes level with his own (for she stood on a pedestal), Christina acccepted his scrutiny as coolly as if it had been a squirrel in Regent's Park who stared at her. Such sang-froid was not invariably her response to being painted by one of the Pre-Raphaelite brethren. Indeed, no. What a difference there had been when she had sat for James Collinson! What histories of eyes meeting and glances deflected, of smiles starting and fading away, of questions asked and unasked! Though finally he had asked even the one question gentlemen hesitate longest over, and she had answered yes. Now, at twenty-two, she had nothing to show for those ardors but her own and her sister's completed portraits and the doubtful consolation that these represented the best work James Collinson had ever done. The ardors had been too intense, and the young painter had fled from them, alarmed, into the arms of the Roman Church, whither Christina, the staunchest of Anglicans, could not pursue him. How she had suffered, and then, which was more amazing, how insubstantial that suffering had come to seem —a vanity, the merest peppercorn. Now, in retrospect, her regret was rather for having been a cause of the first falling apart of the P.-R.B. (in whose company Collinson could not continue as a Papist) than for the loss of love. Love so easily lost could never have been true.

Hunt dabbed the smallest of his brushes in the darker flesh tones mixed on his palette and flicked it onto the canvas.

Mrs. Rossetti had begun to knit, since the darkness of the room (the curtains were drawn, the morning wintry gray) did not allow of reading.

It occurred to Christina (as it had lately occurred, as well, to Thackeray) that no English novelist had ever taken the lives of *painters* as his theme. In French there was, of course, Murger's *Scènes de la vie de bohème,* a book that Christina, at nineteen, had defied her mother's interdict and her own ordinarily steadfast conscience in order to read, chapter by guilty chapter, disguising it behind the pages of a grammar. Doubtless no *English* novelist would dare (not Thackeray certainly in the yet-unwritten pages of *The Newcomes*) to hint at— much less describe—the facts of artists' lives. Such a fact, for instance, as Lizzie Siddal, the shop girl whose relation to Gabriel could surely be more accurately described as "mistress" than as "betrothed." Miss Siddal no longer lived with her family, and Gabriel was determined to achieve a similar independence. No, one could not with propriety turn such a life as Gabriel now led into a novel.

And Hunt? Though it was perfectly unfair, somehow she could not suppose him—on the basis only of his fleshy lips—as more upright than her brother. Lizzie Siddal had captured Hunt's fancy as well, Christina knew, and if the little milliner had chosen Gabriel it was not to be wondered. His spirit was livelier, his figure trimmer, his features smoother, and who could say but that he might some day even learn to paint as dexterously as his friend? Miss Siddal belonged to Gabriel as certainly as Venice, alas, belonged to Austria, but doubtless Hunt knew another young lady—if not a milliner, a barmaid; if not a barmaid . . .

"Christina!" said her mother, without seeming to look up from her knitting. "How ever do you expect Mr. Hunt to be able to paint you, if you smile so absurdly?"

"Was I smiling?" said Christina.

She recomposed her features and tried to remember if among all the paintings and engravings she had studied she had ever seen an image of Christ smiling.

Christina's suspicions were altogether justified. Hunt did have a mistress, whose name was Annie Miller. She was fifteen years old when Hunt had first encountered her and already a prostitute.

Hunt had, quite independently of his regard for Annie, divided feelings toward prostitutes. That they existed at all was regrettable; that they existed in the metropolis in such numbers was deplorable. But he did not think, because *he* was virtuous, that there would be no more cakes and ale. Nor, for that matter, was he always virtuous, though his falls from grace—up till the time of Annie Miller—were remarkably few, considering the opportunities offered a bachelor in London; a bachelor who is, moreover, an artist at liberty to ask models to enter his studio, and his landlady never the wiser. So many models seemed to assume that their wage of a shilling an hour entitled these employers to any degree of license, while the world at large took the cynical view that one became an artist precisely to enjoy a licentious life. Hunt's own father had implied as much. What the world at large so signally failed to understand was how jolly and kindly and essentially *innocent* this bohemian community of artists and models really was (apart from those respects in which it might be, after all, vicious). The transaction between an artist and a model was not the swift, brutal, demeaning exchange between two strangers above some coffee house that posts a notice of "Beds"; it approached the condition, rather, of courtesans and their lovers, with the difference that there was not much money to be spared for ornamental purposes. However, such money as there was was shared about with a liberality that would not have disgraced a commune of early Christians. Even when there was no money, there were high spirits and freedom of converse that made the usual fare of polite drawing rooms seem tepid indeed. What there was not, however, was the prospect of marriage as the culmination to these days of wine and roses. True, Hunt's colleague Brown was educating his Emma to the standard of civility he required in a wife, and upon her attaining such standard, he was to marry her. There was talk now of Rossetti doing the same for Miss Siddal. But there was the rub—Lizzie was *Miss* Siddal. One could no more think of Annie as "Miss Miller" than one could think of the Cross Keys Court, in Chelsea, where she had

grown up, as other than a sink and a stew. Annie was not marriageable
—not by the ordinary middle-class standards of his father nor even by
those of the P.-R.B., for she had an ineradicable coarseness of manner
that could never be papered over by a change of clothing and vowels.
Now that he'd introduced her to bohemian life, she did not go about in
the wooden clogs and verminous rags she'd worn when he'd first seen
her, cleaning the floors of a public house, but the clothes she chose
for herself, once choice became possible, were the plainest declaration
of her availability and even, if one knew one's way about, of her
price.

Why *did* he love her? He could never understand. She was a stunner,
certainly, but so were a hundred women one might encounter every
day. She had a cheerful disposition, but that led her into nattering, and
Hunt had no taste for listening to the endless jingle of her small
change. As to her laugh, he found it withering—so loud, so likely to be
provoked by the lowest ribaldries. As a social animal Hunt had little
use for so uncivilized a creature as Annie Miller. His love proceeded
almost entirely from mere carnal instinct, from looking and longing
and remembering a touch, a tremble, a taste. He was insatiable.

Though not invariably. There were weeks at a time when he never
thought of Annie, when he believed himself quite cured of his affliction. Then it would recur, like malaria—and always a degree worse at
each recurrence, and the fever persisting for a longer time before it
once again abated.

Because it was love he did not resist it as he would had it been any
other disease. He succumbed willingly, welcomingly, letting the presence and possibility of his beloved flood all the streets of Chelsea. He
would visit and revisit the monuments of their moments together like
a tourist on a pilgrimage to the Holy Land. Here, on Justice Walk, was
the very doorway, its arsenical paint slivering from the warped wood,
into whose shadow he'd seen Annie pass on the first night he'd followed her home. Here was the *Cross Keys* pub, its floors littered with
sawdust, where he'd watched her, hours at a time, flirting with the
carters and costermongers of the neighborhood. Here was the Chelsea
Hospital behind whose high iron pilings her father could be seen almost any bright day, in his scarlet uniform, drowsing in the sun or
playing at bowls with the other pensioners. Here, most tormentingly,
were the graveled paths and tinseled pavilions of Cremorne Gardens,
where, for a shilling's admission, she might now be seen, in the eve-

ning, among the multitudes of her fallen sisters and the greater multitudes of their clients; and here was the very spot, beneath a trellis of trained roses, where she'd first allowed his kiss. Every street held its own heart-wrenching reminiscence. The very river and the sky above it seemed to commemorate the flowing tresses of her unbound hair, the lustrous silken sleeve of a dress glistening in the lamplight of his studio.

The danger in all this (apart from the obvious danger of the pox, which Hunt chose to ignore, on the same principle that he ignored the dangers of equestrianism—that all the more vivid pleasures of life entail a proportional risk) was that he might, in a moment of supreme intoxication, succumb to the temptation of *marrying* Annie. It was an idea that he found supremely arousing, a symbol—like the severed head of Holofernes at the feet of a triumphant Judith—of a final, absolute surrender to the demon of his sexuality.

The idea appealed equally to Annie, though she had the good sense not to count matrimonial chickens on the basis of the daydreams a bottle of claret might engender in Hunt's fancy. He was, after all, an artist by profession, to whom imagination is a professional tool. Still, they were lovely fancies, which might be enjoyed as harmlessly as the dresses in the fine shops of the Haymarket and Piccadilly—not that she'd have been foolish enough to waste her money in such places when virtually the same gowns might be made up here in Chelsea for half the price, but a cat can look at a queen, and who could say but that, with further improvements in her situation and her wardrobe, she might *not* be able soon to enter the same shops as the quality and buy her bonnets—at Madame Bonfoix's? Who could say but that her Billy might not be brought round to making an honest woman of her?

They discussed it—how she would no longer pick her nose and wipe the snot off on the underside of her skirts' ruffle but use a cambric handkerchief instead; how she would wear drawers beneath her petticoats and change them every day (though they did not discuss how she was to dry such a quantity of wet clothing during weeks of damp weather); how she would learn to read (in fact, he went so far as to find her a kind of governess for this purpose, and she had actually progressed to the point that she could make fair sense of a pamphlet entitled "The Diabolical Practices of Dr. _____ on His Patients when in a State of Mesmerism," a truly spine-tingling story and all quite true!); how she would learn to dance in the slower, statelier, sillier manner of her betters; how she would learn history, geography, needlework, arithmetic, and the pianoforte. Truly, a transformation to put Cendrillon to shame, and it was to be accomplished (here was the clause of the contract that provoked her greatest skepticism) while Hunt was away in Egypt and Syria.

After he'd shown her, on a globe in a curiosity shop, where Egypt and Syria were and explained the distances involved, Annie assessed the odds of marriage at roughly 20 to 1 against.

If, that is, he actually carried out his plans. Rossetti, to whom Annie also sat, was of the opinion that Hunt's projected pilgrimage was a pipedream. Hunt would be a fool to leave London now at the very dawn of success and acceptance. A Belfast shipping agent had just bought the reworked Sylvia painting, sight unseen, for a walloping £425, on the basis, Rossetti speculated, of Ruskin's public panegyric. Still better prices were in the air. The P.-R.B. might soon be challenging the likes of such lords of the showroom as Landseer or even Maclise; £1,000 per picture was easily within reach. More, when one sold one's copyright to an engraver.

Annie did not ignore Rossetti's tacit advice. Better a bird in the hand than a flock of them in Egypt or Syria. Hunt must be kept in London even at the cost of sacrificing the enticing fancies of matrimony. To be the mistress of a painter so well set up as a man of Hunt's promise was no little stepping stone. Accordingly, while she continued her reading lessons with the patient Miss Bradshaw, and her ballroom lessons at the Cleveland Street Academy for Young Ladies, she did not encourage Hunt in his more connubial fantasies for fear of precipitating him at once into Orient lands.

In the autumn of 1853 an opportunity arose, or was arranged by God, for delaying his ever-threatened departure by the surest of means.

They were in his studio, Hunt at work upon the figure of his Christ (which stood—a wooden lay-figure draped in the damask glory of his grandmother's best tablecloth—beneath a specially constructed canopy in the corner of the cluttered room), she lazing in a nightgown on the horse-hair divan, when through the window that faced on Prospect Place came the strains of her favorite song, "Oft in the Stilly Night." She sat up, attentive. Hunt laid down his palette and brushes to stare at her.

"It's lovely, in'it?" she remarked, when the organ grinder had gone away.

But Hunt was already at work on the sketch which the song and her response to it had just inspired. By noon of the next day the sketch had already been transferred to canvas, and he had asked her to pose for the central figure, a kind of modern Magdalene seen at the blessed moment when the scales fall from her eyes and she beholds, as though through the parlor walls to the bright spring day outside, a vision of her lost innocence, now found again. She would be arising from the lap of her lover, who is seated before the keyboard—a *new* pianoforte, each article in the room has the gleam of new money about it—and he is unaware of the momentous change that has come over his mistress. A most uncomfortable pose, no matter what arrangement of cushions they attempted, but Hunt could not be persuaded to alter it. He was unable to make up his mind, however, what Annie ought to wear. It must be something *négligé*. She naturally would have preferred a gown that would do service out of doors. Hunt had his way, but agreed that as all of Annie's own nightgowns were either too plain or too tatter-demalion, she would be allowed to have one made up specially to pose in, hemmed with broad scallops of moderately fine lace, with, as a concession both to Annie and to the sensibilities of the respectable, a Paisley shawl in chaste disarray where modesty most required it. Scarcely as elegant as the embroidered silk gown Lizzie Siddal had modeled in for Sylvia, but a cut above the old tablecloths that Druid maidens had had to be contented with.

The nightgown was ordered from one Dolly Withers, a companion of Annie's wild youth (for Annie was now all of eighteen) and already the proprietress of her own little dressmaking establishment above an umbrella shop in the King's Road. Thither, on the evening of the 12th of September, Annie took her lover to secure his approval of the completed work. Arriving in advance of the set hour, they were shown by Dolly's assistant into a small back room populated by a little harem of limbless, headless mannequins, some naked, others clothed in gowns in various stages of construction, the prettiest and most complete being a bridal gown of sheer, white organdy. Its hem, as Annie was quick to observe, was made from the same scalloped lace as her own night-gown.

Dolly looked in at the door, and after a moment of innocent banter, took Annie away to a chamber beyond to change into her costume. Hunt, left alone, began to sketch the wedding gown, working with quick, careless strokes of a blunt pencil. He drew as another man might have drummed with his fingers on a tabletop, or tamped a pipe, from simple nervousness. By the time Annie had returned, be-night-gowned, his sketch was complete down to the imaginary details of veil, bouquet, and—shadowy, top-hatted bridegroom.

"Well?" demanded Annie.

"Not yet! Not yet!" Dolly opened the Paisley shawl (which she'd bought for £3, nearly new, from a client who'd grown disaffected of it) and spread it over Annie's shoulders. Annie revolved in a slow pirouette, making the nightgown flare out and settle in spiraling folds about her full hips.

"Well?" she demanded again.

"Just the ticket," said Hunt.

"You don't fancy," said Dolly solicitously, "it's a trifle too full? If I was to take an inch in here—" She demonstrated. "—and another here . . ."

Hunt smiled approval.

The shawl was deployed to varying effect. The loose sleeves of striped silk were modeled hanging loose, then bunched about the wrists. The bow about the neck was tied so, and then so. The two women cooperated to stretch out the fitting into a little drama of full five minutes' duration, at the conclusion of which Annie again left the room to change back into her dress.

Dolly, alone with Hunt, went to the table upon which he'd laid his sketch of the bridal gown. "Oh, my," she purred, holding it up to the light of the flaring gas jet. "Oh my, yes—doesn't that do for it, just! Annie said you was a painter, but I didn't suppose—Oh, my. The lace looks just like *lace*! And the flowers must be out of your 'ead, as there ain't flowers about the room, but so real . . . you could almost smell them. My."

"Would you like it?" Hunt offered.

"Oh no, I couldn't," Dolly protested even as she accepted it. "It's *so* lovely. If I was to put it in a frame and hang it in the other room where it might be noticed, it *would* cause a stir. But really, no, I couldn't."

Hunt dismissed this half-hearted refusal with a wave of his hand. "And when is the happy day to be?" he asked.

Dolly cocked her head to one side. " 'Ow's that, sir?"

He gestured toward the mannequin. "The happy day of the wedding."

"Oh, that! That's only my own idea, sir. When I have no other work at 'and, I busy myself with that. It shows my skill, and it's cheery to 'ave around. If you should ever want to borrow it—"

Hunt looked alarmed.

"I mean, to make a picture of."

Hunt looked at his hasty sketch of the imagined wedding. A sequel to *The Awakened Conscience*? There was the same type of lace around the hem of the gown as had been used to trim the nightgown.

"No, that is very kind of you. But I doubt I'd be able to, even if . . . I shall be setting off momentarily for the Holy Land."

" 'Ow's that, sir?"

"The Holy Land: the lands of the Bible—Syria, Egypt."

" 'Ow exciting for you, sir. Well, if you'll excuse me . . ."

Dolly swept from the room, leaving Hunt to the faceless interrogation of the wedding dress.

The greatest man of the neighborhood and possibly of the era was coming to the studio at noon to see the two completed paintings. Lacking palms to strew upon the floorboards, Hunt had commandeered his landlady's slavey to see that the place was properly scrubbed in honor of the occasion. The paintings leaned, facing in, against the stacked packing cases, modest as eastern brides. Hunt had passed the last nervous hour and a half stenciling his name and destination—CAIRO, EGYPT—on whichever sides of whichever crates were not yet blazoned with this tremendous information. In a month's time or less he would be living in the midst of pyramids, bulrushes, crocodiles, in a land of cloudless skies and unimaginable light. He: William Holman Hunt, painter of this very *The Light of the World* and of such further masterpieces as were certain to flow from his immortal hand and eye. Such a feeling! To know oneself so young, numbered among the highest echelons of Parnassus, the brother of Leonardo, of Raphael, Bellini, and Tintoret! And more—to know that others knew it no less certainly. The great Carlyle (who was now five minutes late!) had said of his last year's R.A. offering (for this would not be his first visit to Hunt's studio) that *The Hireling Shepherd* was "the greatest Picture that he had seen painted by any modern man." He had it in a letter from the man's own wife (though he would have preferred a more direct testimonial, as it was the only instance in Hunt's life when a critic had found a superlative sufficient to match his own high sense of his accomplishment). And *The Hireling Shepherd* was to *The Light of the World* as the first buds of May to the full-blown roses of June. The glow of the lantern mixing with the moonlight and spilling across the white column of Christ's robe: sublime! The jewels of the breastplate, the leaves of the weeds that choke the doorway: exquisite! The magisterial *simplicity* of that single vertical thrust: the audacity! He did not need to turn the painting round from where it leaned against the packing crates to feel the influence of those eyes, at once so mournful and so inspiring of hope: the painting was as ever-present in his eyes as the shape and color of the crockery from which he'd eaten his meals as a child. Not as the gross image commonly visible to sight, but as his *knowledge* of that image, the ways in which he'd formed it and transformed it. There was the rub—despite his ironclad certainty that he'd painted a masterpiece of wholly objective excellence he might, after all, be mistaking his own painterly concentration during all the weeks of its creation for the force of an innate radiance. Painters are forever falling into such error. How was Hunt to know, then, that this glow of accomplishment wasn't in the nature of self-deception? The only test, damn it all, was what *other* people might say—the critics of *The Athenaeum* and *The Times*, or the critics of those critics, such as (bless him) Ruskin, or, most potently, the people who *bought* paintings. However, except a painting were engraved, one could only know the satisfaction of selling it a single time, and *The Light of the World* was already sold—to the faithful Mr. Combe, for a modest £400. Lady Canning had been willing to pay more, but Hunt disdained acting as his own auctioneer.

Though he could not resist, when asked by the likes of Carlyle, to act as his own gallery. If only the man would arrive. Noon had been announced by the bells of Chelsea Old Church seven minutes since.

He stood at the window. The light was as strong as January ever allows, but southward, above the tiles of roofs, black nimbus clouds threatened to darken the sky momentarily.

At last he could be seen down on the street, unmistakable even bundled into a winter greatcoat, with his head hunched forward on a bent spine, like an owl perched upon a wind-warped tree. His wife walked at his side in a manner at once independent (she did not take his arm even when they came to the curb) and yet somehow wholly connubial. They disappeared behind a neighboring house, and within a moment the bell sounded below. As arranged, Hunt's landlady saw them up to the studio.

Formalities were limited to a brusque handshake on Carlyle's part, a nod and tight-lipped smile from his wife, who kept her hands well buried in a muff.

"Unveil, unveil," Carlyle demanded, pointing his stick peremptorily at the smaller and nearer of the two canvases.

Hunt turned it round.

Carlyle took a step forward, furrowing his prominent brow; his wife stepped backward, lifting her eyebrows quizzically, then (as though a question had been answered) smiling thinly, and then (thinking better of it) erasing the smile. Hunt wondered if she had recognized Annie Miller, and if so how much of her story (and his own) she was acquainted with. He began to blush.

"I call it," Hunt hastened to announce, *The Awakened Conscience.*"

Carlyle nodded sagely and looked to his wife for guidance. Unseen by Hunt, Jane Carlyle pantomimed with her thin lips the word "moon."

Carlyle cleared his throat, stepped closer to the painting, and pointed to the reflected gleam of the springtime foliage in the tabletop. "The moonlight is well given," he declared with an authority all the more forceful for the fact that the painting was meant to represent the light of noonday. "And the other?" he demanded.

Hunt revealed his masterpiece, from which the moonlight did seem veritably to stream forth.

Carlyle grimaced. His hand gripped the handle of his stick as though he meant to strike at the picture before him. "And do ye call this phosphorescence and putrescence a representation of Jesus Christ!" he proclaimed in a tone of heart-withering scorn. "It is the merest papistical pandering. Why, in the name of all that's noble, have ye tricked Him out in sic brummagem fripperies and furbelows? A crown, ha! Meteoric glitter on his breast—and of a heathenish imitation gem variety, at that. This is not the Christ who trod the earth in mortal flesh, but the image priests have made of Him so as to lure men's wayward and imbecile souls into the abomination meshes of idolatry! Would ye have the Whole Species of Mankind believe what ye know yourself to be false? This—" He shook his stick at *The Awakened Conscience.* "—though it give alarm to certain persons by its boldness, nevertheless presents, for All Men, a Reality—albeit the reality of a shallow, idle fool and his wretched victim. But this—this Christ! It is naught but inane, *Grimmsmärchen* make-believe and untruth, the which to fabricate and bring-to-view is a heinous occupation for a painter who would respect his own soul."

Hunt could bear no more. Carlyle did not understand the *poetic* truth of his painting, its *spiritual* reality. But when he opened his mouth to reveal these buried meanings, Mrs. Carlyle removed a hand from her muff to raise an admonitory finger, signing Hunt to be silent. All Hunt's resistance wilted before her gesture—and Carlyle went on, in a calmer manner, as though he were tutoring an obtuse child.

"I have in my study, at home, a screen, upon the which I have put portraits, the best I can anyhow get (often I must content myself with very poor ones, but that is by the by). These portraits are a kind of private Pantheon of all the men who have ordered, improved, or otherwise civilized this junglelike world, but the greatest of such men, alas, has left no record of His countenance for me to place upon my screen."

Mrs. Carlyle, all the while, could hardly disguise an ironic smile. *His* screen, indeed. She had found the naked screen malingering on a dust-heap, conceived and executed its rebirth, filled up with faces and scenes (among the former, his particular *bête noire*, Madame Sand). As a dutiful wife, however, she must not amend his misappropriation of credit due. The screen was presented to him—was it the autumn of 1849?—and now it must be "his" to deal with as he pleased.

"Think how many sculptors," Carlyle continued in the same vein, "lived contemporary to Him and squandered their hard-gained skill bodying forth trumpery Jupiters and Apollos, their venal emperors, their mincing Venuses and bovine Junos. What a later age might have given—would give!—of praise and fame for one faithful portrait of the Son of Man. Lacking that, what is the worth of a million conjectures such as this?

"Oh, yours is not the only such offender—I well know that. I have seen in our National Gallery the picture of *Christ Disputing with the Doctors* by Leonardo da Vinci. That is no Christ, that puir, weak, girl-faced nonentity, decked out in a finer silken sort of gown than even this latter-day courtesan, with a small jewelry shop in stones crusting its hem, as though He had been the darling of some despot's court and not a boy who worked in a carpenter's shop. To which I say—as I say to you, sir—thank you, Mr. da Vinci. That may be *your* idea of Jesus Christ, but I've another of my own which I very much prefer."

Hunt was stricken dumb. Carlyle's criticisms were all the crueler for their running so closely parallel to the announced program of the P.-R.B. It seemed but yesterday that the public had been denouncing Millais's painting of Christ in His father's carpentry shop for its painful excesses of realism. Carlyle's words seemed the ghosts of Hunt's abandoned principles, returning to haunt him.

Hunt's silence in no wise deterred Carlyle from developing a rounded homily on the life, character, and probable physiognomy of the Son of Man, who would have looked, it developed, remarkably like the speaker, with large and piercing blue eyes (Carlyle was emphatic as to the color of His eyes), with shaggy hair and beard of premature gray, and a nose of pronounced but not Semitic character. Hunt could not resist an inward smile at the philosopher's expense. He remembered Rossetti one day hooting over a passage he'd happened upon in *Past and Present* wherein Carlyle had saluted Rossetti's countryman Columbus as a Norse sea-king. Carlyle's Pantheon of World Heroes appeared to be so exclusively Teutonic in its composition that when a great man insisted upon controverting these theories by being born of the wrong stock, Carlyle made an Aryan of him by simple fiat.

Carlyle rounded off his peroration by commending Hunt to study the work of one "airtist" whose conception of Christ was not wholly absurd, Albrecht Dürer. Then he and his wife took their leave.

For the rest of that afternoon, and for many days and weeks thereafter—as he studied the ranked masterpieces of the Louvre, as he sailed down the Saône, even at the foot of the Pyramids—he would renew the internal debate with Carlyle, in the same obsessive spirit in which Macbeth must have mulled over the witches' prophecies. Hunt would not admit that there was anything lacking or false in his Christ, yet he could not exorcise the Carlylean voice within and its relentless harping on the same few literal-minded demands. Indeed, its criticisms gradually became more general. It questioned others of Hunt's paintings in the same authoritative tones. It wondered, for instance, whether *The Awakened Conscience* represented an enduring transformation or a passing fancy on the part of the conscience thus awakened. It could not (as Carlyle could not) clearly distinguish between the ideal and the literal, between the scene fantasied and the life lived. Hunt's ability to call to mind clearly the absent image of his own paintings became a liability. He would study the face of his modern Magdalene, of his dear Annie, alert to any trace of weakness and irresolution that would allow her to sink back after this moment of illumination to her earlier, sinful life. He knew from letters that she was sitting to Stephens, to Millais, to Rossetti. How easily and naturally might Annie, with her light ways and careless laughter, be led to stray from the virtuous path upon which Hunt had set her—especially in such company as Rossetti's. For Gabriel, though he was a boon companion and a fine fellow, had susceptibilities. The flesh, as Shakespeare has noted, is straw.

Nor was it any comfort to read the press cutting, which his father thoughtfully sent him, of that summer's Royal Academy show. *The Light of the World* was pronounced a failure; *The Awakened Conscience* was condemned as sordid and repulsive. One critic found Annie's face "inconceivably painful," just as an earlier critic—Ruskin himself—had deplored the "unfortunate type" of Lizzie Siddal. The remembered face haunted Hunt like a revenant of peculiar obstinacy. Upon his return to England after an absence of two years, the new owner of *The Awakened Conscience* (for Combe had sold it to Sir Thomas Fairbairn) confided to Hunt that, despite his great admiration for the work, he too found something inexpressibly distressing in Annie Miller's face. Would Hunt consider altering it? Hunt agreed to take it to his studio, where, even before he unpacked his clothing, he proceeded to scrape his beloved's face into nonexistence. She had betrayed him—he had heard of her shameful behavior from a hundred sources, and there was no doubt that she was unworthy of him. Marriage was out of the question.

Sir Thomas was delighted with the amended painting and complimented Hunt on having found a new model of such striking soulfulness.

Hunt did not mention that the new face had been painted entirely from his imagination.

# CHAPTER THIRTEEN

# *Betrayals*

## NOVEMBER, 1854

The garden had been set for tea.

Geraldine Jewsbury, plump in her accepted middle age, sat patiently upon the uncomfortable Chinese porcelain drum, waiting for Jane, who arrived with a dismissive wave of the hand, intended (Geraldine realized) for the maid.

"She *cannot*," Jane said airily, "so much as put a biscuit on a plate without a page of instructions."

"But I thought you were *happy* with Ann!" said Geraldine, rising. "You know, you were right—it is *not* too cold."

"No, indeed it is not. Imagine—November! But—" (squeezing her friend's hand and forcing her back down on the hard drum) "—you shall not escape my indignation by praising the weather. Geraldine! Oh, Geraldine!"

"What have I done?" said Geraldine, genuinely alarmed.

"Can you pretend not to know? What have you done but left me alone through four long *weeks* of rainy October—and after moving to London just to be *near me*!—four weeks of silences only relieved by the thunder of pronouncements from—" She lifted her eyebrows to indicate the windows of Carlyle's new-built study. "—on High!"

Geraldine laughed, relieved to know that Jane was merely speaking in her usual hyperboles.

"And you dare laugh? Geraldine! You fly off at the first invitation— to the arms of Lady de Capel Broke. I know that I have no title to offer, no country house, no carriage to put at your disposal; nothing but what you see here, a few square feet of turf for garden—"

"The heather you transplanted looks admirable."

"Never mind that (and, indeed, it's dying). The *fact* is that you deserted me for Lady de Capel Broke!"

Geraldine insisted on having one of Jane's hands and then on squeezing it earnestly, as though to drive away all misgivings and tumults, real and theatrical. "I insisted, did I not? I begged you, as it were, on my knees, hands pressed like a good angel, *and*, more important, I petitioned Lady de Capel Broke to indite the nicest invitation to Oakley Hall (which, in point of fact, I confess to having written *all* myself for her to copy, since she does not know how to *think* with a pen in her fingers)—then, after I had done all that—"

"You *didn't*! But *I couldn't* have come—and that's true too."

"Rubbish. You *could* have. Imagine, if you can, the impression it made on me to read that you must stay in Chelsea 'because Carlyle's trowsers want mending!'"

"*Daily* mending," Jane insisted wryly, pouring the tea.

"Well, I had a lovely time—missed all the rain—and lo, the day I return, out obligingly comes the sun as though it were August! Jane, you *could* have come, and then *I* shouldn't have had to write you all *her* ghost stories. You know they aren't half as effective written down . . . truly. It is one thing to read *my* second-hand accounts of departed spirits picking their ways through dusty halls at every hour, and quite another to hear Lady de Capel Broke deliver the same tales in her sepulchral voice just when you are feeling most dished and ready to believe Anything. There were nights when I went to bed in terror!"

"And you desired *me* there to be frightened out of *my* wits, misery demanding company!" Then, in a manner subdued and parenthetical: "Here's your tea. I'll never put out of my head the story—do you remember?—of the two sisters sleeping in the haunted room? It was years ago you told me—and the one is awakened by a spirit, and has to be revived with smelling salts? And while all and sundry are occupied with bringing *her* about, the other awakens and happens to look toward the press and sees the head of a woman—head and torso, clothed in gray—grinning and nodding. Ach!" For punctuation she took a sip of tea. "Had you sufficient heat?"

Geraldine (who had entirely forgotten the two haunted sisters, and now had only the vaguest recollection of drafts) restrained a frown. "No, it was not comfortably warm—though *I*, as you know, can make do with little in the heat line. I know I should have to have given *your* feet a good rubbing every night!"

Jane laughed. "Are we warm enough *out here*? Would you rather go indoors?"

"On what must be the last day of good weather this year? Nonsense!"

"Geraldine, I may be absolutely candid with you, may I not? We are sisters."

"Absolutely."

"Then I shall ask—have you brought any of your 'cigaritos' with you? The little mild ones with the yellow paper about them."

"*That* is why you've had us take our tea out of doors. It's not the weather at all!"

Jane pantomimed her shameful admission.

"They're in my bag, together with the lucifers. *And* my dark spectacles, without which I cannot go on. Excuse me while I fetch them—they're on the piano."

They were, in fact, on the breakfast table where she had left them. At the very moment she found them, a carriage drew up to the door of 5, Cheyne Row, a carriage that for sheer profusion of ornament surpassed even that of Lady Morgan. This wedding cake of armorial trappings could only belong (Geraldine knew at once) to one person in the world and she the woman now languidly addressing the footman who had dismounted from his post at the rear of the mammoth, gilt-encrusted voiture—Harriet, Lady Ashburton, the nemesis of Jane Carlyle.

Before the footman could dismount, Geraldine, afire with curiosity, had preceded him to the front door and flung it open.

"Ah-ha," said the footman, who was young and confident of his own charm relative to hers. "Lady Ashburton, by your leave, miss—" He winked, by way of punctuation. "—desires the company of Mr. Carlyle, and hopes he'll come with her in her carriage—" His hand indicated the voiture, as though its presence might have escaped her attention. "—to Addiscombe."

"This moment?" Geraldine could not resist marveling.

The footman shrugged, and smiled, and nodded.

"I see. Well, if you will ask Lady Ashburton to come in and rest in the garden, where Mrs. Carlyle is taking her afternoon tea, I shall be pleased to convey her desires to *Mr.* Carlyle."

"Beg pardon, miss." Again, to her annoyance, he winked. "But I don't think my lady quite fancies stepping out of her carriage."

"She is not well?"

"You might say that. Also, she's wanting to be home as soon as possible. Her words."

"Very well. I shall tell Mr. Carlyle. Excuse me." With a perplexed smile intended to seem sarcastic, she closed the door in his face, wondering whom to approach first. Ann, the serving girl, emerged from the stairway with a plate of biscuits and rescued her from the dilemma.

"Ann, would you tell Mrs. Carlyle that there is a visitor for *Mr.* Carlyle waiting, and that I've gone upstairs to inform him."

"Oh, mum, I wouldn't if I was you. Mr. Carlyle doesn't fancy—"

"Yes, I know that, Ann. But *I* shall answer for him." She took one of the biscuits from the plate and popped it into her mouth. "Thank you."

The biscuit was a kind of shortbread made from oatmeal, with little currants in it, all still quite warm and moist; a pity to think (as she mounted the three flights of stairs to the soundproof study) that they would be cold and brittle by the time she could sit down to eat another.

At the sight of his door, which stood ajar, she had consciously to overcome the sense that she was intruding on the Master's dominion. Carlyle was not to be interrupted when he wrestled with his newest book, *Frederick the Great*—this was the arch-decretum of the household. Geraldine knew she would be as welcome as Lara, the neighbors' long-lost parrot, were she miraculously to reappear and roost upon the bust of Schiller.

She cleared her throat, preparatory to speaking his name, and at once the door opened wide to show the Master himself, an open book in one hand. But something was wrong. She gasped.

"Geraldine!" he shouted affably, reaching out his free hand in welcome. "Whatever has—Ah, you've not seen me before with a dirty gorse common sprouting from my chin, is that it?"

"It is a change, rather. Though . . . I believe it may suit you, when . . . yes, it does, already. And then, so *many* men have taken to growing beards."

"That extenuates mine, eh? Well, I had no choice. Lord Ashburton stole in one morning and pilfered my razor. No choice at all. He achieved clearance with Jeannie below, and the next I knew . . . no razor."

"It suits you. But you must, you know, let Jane trim it."

"There's naught to trim, as yet. But don't stand in the outer darkness: enter the sanctum sanctorum. You'll not be struck down. I'm glad to see thee, Geraldine. Jeannie's closest and dearest friend cannot be a stranger to me."

"Yes, yes, Carlyle, and I am *inexpressibly* glad to be here again myself. Truly—but I must immediately inform you that Lady Ashburton sits out in her carriage at this very moment waiting to know whether *you* will go off to Addiscombe."

"To Addiscombe? Now?" His brow furrowed. "I *had* been writing this damned book. What of Jeannie?"

"What of Jane? When I last saw Jane she was in the garden waiting for me to return with a supply of my infamous cigaritos. Since when Ann has surely told her that you have a visitor. I rather gathered that Lady Ashburton did not wish to cross her path—but whether Jane will indulge Lady Ashburton in her disinclination . . . that I somehow doubt."

Jane was just closing the front door when they came to the foot of the stairs. She looked up with a gleam of defiance in her eye, and on her tongue the venom of sarcasm: "Christmas! Lady Harriet requests *our* presence at the Grange for Christmas. *She* is not free, however, at this moment to step inside *my* sitting room, which is doubtless too small to contain so regal a presence—nor does she request *my* company this evening—and how many evenings more she does not say— only yours, my dear. And promptly, too. How dare you stand dawdling when your Lady has declared her pleasure!"

"Jeannie!"

"Jane," Geraldine implored, "you mustn't! This talk cannot possibly lead to good."

"*I* mustn't? I? What *must* I do, then? Must I be silent, simply that?" She crossed her arms tightly over her bodice. "Sometimes, Geraldine, I think this whole mad world of ours, with its butcher-cart wheels and steeple bells and twopenny post raps, is *too* silent, that we never say what *we* feel in our hearts. But for once I *will* say what is in mine—she is a monster! Nothing more nor less. Doubtless that is why she dare

not show herself away from her own dim rooms and attendant luxuries, where she can spread herself out like Lalla Rookh while she
settles down to be wooed by Feramorz's newest, cleverest tale! Which
I, less than a scullery maid, *a wife*, am not fit to deliver. No, *my* tales
do not sufficiently glitter."

"Jeannie, say what you will, the woman is good, and your suspicions
unfounded. She never says aught but good of thee, Jeannie. I swear
it."

"You're a fool."

"Jane," Geraldine whispered warningly.

"I shall pack your carpet bag. I've nothing more to say."

"Carlyle, you must say something, *do* something," said Geraldine,
after the sound of her friend's footsteps had passed into the mingled
creakings of the higher floors. "I don't care what you presently feel in
heart and soul. I moreover don't care how innocent your dealings with
the Ashburtons may be. They treat *her* badly and *she* is the helpmate
of your life. She gave up the world of comforts and luxuries she was
born to in order to be with *you*—not to spend entire long evenings here
sealed up in a *small* house, in a *small* village, while you are off making
wits with such as her, and—Carlyle, *listen* to me—"

"I am listening. But keep your voice down. You are not upon the
stage of the Haymarket."

"You reserve all your energy, your vitality and glory, for another.
You owe it *her*. How shall she not resent that?"

Unaccustomed to criticism, he stared at her with the full force of his
prophetic fury—a very Moses coming upon the Golden Calf.

But Geraldine was not to be cowed. "Carlyle," she continued, "it
was you who raised me up from the depths of do-nothing-ism, your
*Sartor* which taught this flighty creature to live more cautiously, to
weigh each word I heard or uttered; you who taught me to put off
pleasure and not to be so foolish as to expect happiness. Yes—there is
none; you were right. There is nothing before us all but sickness,
loneliness, and death. And yet you . . ." But how could she go on?
Carlyle's not-yet-confirmed decision to go off for an evening of good
talk was not, at heart, unkind—much less criminal. She knew the Real
Issue, the source of all rage and tears, and that issue was, gratefully,
not hers to discuss.

"I don't know," she declared with a sigh. "I have not been an ideal pupil. I don't weigh each word before I speak it. I am too passionate, as you and Jane ever remind me."

The man stood painfully still, his arms hanging limp. "Geraldine," he said after a short silence, "you are my *best* pupil. But there are elements in this Polar Ocean of a World that you cannot know as I do—not without treading each dark step known to me. *Frederick* remains with me like a tumor. I, who speak and write of man's need for solitude, for silence, at times myself must needs scamper off for Society. And when I do return with a fresher view of present and past . . ." He trailed off.

She did not venture to contradict him, and after a moment of melancholy self-communing, he resumed: "The moral of your book (not a work without merit) *The Half Sisters*, which significantly you *half*-dedicated to my Jeannie, tells the same tale: that every living person must find something to *do*. There is no happiness, but there *is* occupation, and that is what my Jeannie lacks. But you must excuse me—my lady waits."

"Yes."

Entering the garden, she closed the door behind her. The tea in her cup had grown cold, but that in the pot was still warm, so she emptied the cold tea over the dying heather plant and poured a second cup. She divided the biscuits on the plate into two equal portions and ate the one she'd allotted to herself. Then, as irresistibly as Carlyle succumbed to the invitation of Lady Ashburton, she ate each of the biscuits she'd set apart for Jane, thinking each time that *this* would be the last culpable bite.

Clouds covered the sun, and the day's unseasonable warmth seemed to turn at once to a known November chill. She would have gone indoors but their quarrel had just then reached its climax, and she dared not intrude.

At last Carlyle departed and Jane returned to the garden.

Geraldine rose to offer her arms and bosom to Jane, who did not seem disposed, however, to avail herself of the comforts of a good collapse. Geraldine felt foolish and then hurt. Jane, for her part, did not notice.

"He looks like an escaped maniac. With that *drizzle* of a beard. The fool." She spoke with a seeming composure at which Geraldine, having listened to her screams only moments before, could not but marvel. "Are you warm enough? The sun's gone."

"Yes."

"I'm not. We *can* go in, but first, if I may, one of your cigaritos. Please."

Geraldine took out two of the thin yellow cylinders, lighted each from the same lucifer, shielding the flame with her cupped hand, and handed one to Jane, who was sitting stiff as an Egyptian statue on an iron garden chair.

"The *beard*—" (after a lungful of the narcotic smoke) "—is *her* doing, Lady Harriet's—like everything else I despise. It was she put the idea in her husband's head and then prompted him to come here and enlist my cooperation. She may be responsible for the entire Beard Movement, for aught I know—or care. Leigh Hunt now sports a great weedy *white* beard, and complains that the children of Hammersmith laugh at him in the street—as well they might. Carlyle, to avoid similar abuse, hides within doors and only dares go out in the streets by night."

She was silent a long time, concentrating her outrage on the cigarette. In her nervousness, she smoked it too quickly and began to cough violently. When she'd quieted, all her composure was gone.

"Geraldine—oh, Geraldine, what am I to *do*? Where shall I go?"

Geraldine, though she'd have much preferred tears or convulsions to such unanswerable questions, tried to steer an honorable course between kindness and honesty. "Whatever do you mean—where shall you *go*? Have you quite lost your mind? Carlyle is under an enormous strain finishing that horrid book. Do you suppose for a minute that he's enamored of Lady Ashburton? *I* don't. I've never in all these years seen any evidence of his feeling affection for *any* woman. Any but *you*," she thought to add.

"But, you see, he doesn't. He doesn't at all. I'm not speaking of today as representing the unique moment when he—" Tears drowned out her speech.

Geraldine drew out a handkerchief from her bag and handed it her.

"*Dear* Geraldine—when I brought down his bag, packed (as only I know how—he can't do the simplest task for himself), I don't know what came over me—I screamed every wretched idea that came into my head, so intent was I that Lady Harriet—sitting without—should hear (the door stood ajar)—and it was then that he, in terror (I suppose) *lest* she hear, took me by the shoulders and gave me the worst shaking of my life! I—I could feel nothing, think of nothing but the Enormity of his Anger toward me. And—" Here she paused. "Do you know? That was the first time he had touched me—in any wise— for as long as I can remember—so that I wanted to shriek for Joy! I felt such a rush of confused emotions, I thought I should die on the spot!"

"Are you hurt—Jane?"

"I can feel his hands, see the rage blinding his eyes." She took a puff of the cigarette, then stamped it out in the grass. "I will confess something to you that I have never told another mortal soul."

"I demand that you tell me all, Jane—everything! Has he *beaten* you?"

"Heavens, no—and do keep your voice down or we shall have the police here to investigate what must sound to be a murder in progress! —no, do you recall some time ago I revealed to you that Carlyle and I had not coupled (as married people do) for all the years we have lived here in Chelsea?"

"Yes."

"I'm afraid I lied to you." She took a sip of Geraldine's cold tea. "My fate, like that of poor Mrs. Ruskin, has been *never* to experience the perhaps pleasant, perhaps *un*pleasant display of animal and Real affection (so it seems in absentia) that we women are taught by our mothers to expect from a husband. Never. Not at Comely Bank. Not at Craigenputtock. Not here. The first week of our marriage he was made so upset by the thought of it that he was *ill*. A few weeks later my mother came from Templand, casting him into even greater physical distress—they never liked each other. Since then—all these *long* years —I have learned to make the best of things. And that, as they say, is that."

Given leave at last to vent a sympathetic sorrow, Geraldine let out a wail so loud and so expressive that within moments three windows were heard to open—and Jane had to rush her distraught friend into the house. "Geraldine!" she hushed, closing the door soundlessly. "*Do* compose yourself. For shame!"

"Oh My Dear, Oh My Poor Dear!" cried the younger woman, "You must leave him immediately. I will not hear otherwise. You must come and live with me. We shall be happy. Oh! How you must have *wept* when you heard the details of the Ruskin scandal. How you must have despaired to think that *all* your life has passed you by!"

Jane cleared her throat. "'*When I think of what I is—And what I used to was,—I gin to think I've sold myself—For very little cash.*' That," she explained, "is a poem I was made to learn as a girl. It is very apropos, is it not?"

"You *must* come with me."

"Geraldine, you are raving. Stop."

"But—"

"No," said Jane quite calmly. "No, I won't be going anywhere, but—in time—to my grave. I *am* fifty-three. There is no Mr. Millais waiting in the wings to rescue me. I once thought there might be, but no longer. Edward Irving is dead. George Rennie is married. All my old suitors have fallen into one hole or the other. Mrs. Ruskin was lucky to have acted sensibly while she still had her youth and hopes about her. I must sleep in the bed I've made for myself for the customary duration of the marriage vow. And in any case," she added, with her usual bright laugh, "I love him!"

# CHAPTER FOURTEEN

# Tin and Tinlessness

## SUMMER, 1856

It was raining when they finally woke at half past one, and so they decided to be lazy and forgo the expedition down the river to the Chapel of St. Peter ad Vincula on Tower Green. Ned stayed beneath the covers, while Morris, who'd slept in his clothes on the sorriest of sofas, lighted a fire and boiled some water for their tea. He upended the teapot over the slop bucket, scraping out the detritus of old leaves with his bare hand. Ned must not have made himself a cup of tea, or a fire, since his last visit the Sunday before.

The explanation, Morris was fairly sure, was sheer, dire tinlessness, but there was no getting Ned to accept a loan. He was a proud beggar and preferred to starve to death in a garret, which he was now literally in danger of doing, than to ask his father for money actually owing him. The elder Jones did not approve of his son's throwing over a career in the Church in order to become a painter. Being himself a framemaker and gilder, Mr. Jones was of the settled and mainly correct conviction that few paintings were worth more than the frames that held them. What was the use of Ned's having been sent to Oxford, at an expense of £600, if he didn't mean to take orders and earn a sensible return on the investment? To leave Oxford after more than two years of study without bothering even to take a degree! And why? To become a painter! Most boys were apprenticed to the trade of painting at thirteen: Ned was twenty-three. Madness. Mr. Jones had no intention of subsidizing anyone's madness.

Topsy (as William Morris was known among friends), doubtless, was not a jot less mad. He and Ned had shared each other's crises, read each other's favorite books, and dreamed each other's dreams ever since they'd met at Exeter College. When Topsy, inspired by the great Carlyle's *Past and Present*, had planned to reinstitute monasticism on a grand scale (which he'd have been able to do as soon as he'd turned twenty-one and come into his inheritance), Ned had signed on as the first of the holy brotherhood-to-be. When Topsy had lost his faith the following year, Ned lost his too. When, at a bookshop, Ned fell in love with Malory's *Morte d'Arthur*, Topsy bought it and bound it in vellum: their new Bible. When, last summer, Topsy had gone off to Normandy to worship cathedrals, he'd made Ned come along, and then, on the last night of that holiday, as they paced through the deserted quays of Le Havre, they had sworn the solemnest of vows that they would dedicate their lives to beauty. They would be artists—Ned a painter, Topsy an architect. So if Ned were mad, then Topsy was as well, for they were equals in everything—except, unhappily for Ned, money.

If Ned could not be made to share and share alike in Topsy's £900 a year (the result of the late Mr. Morris's entirely fortuitous holdings in a Devon copper mine), he could at least be bullied into accepting stocks of groceries on the pretext that the contents of Topsy's market basket would be their Sunday breakfast—though even in an age of heroic appetites no two young men could have downed such a quantity of smoked fish, eggs, bacon, sausage, biscuits, and cheese as Morris supplied on his weekly forays into London.

"Ned?" he asked, spitting two fat sausages and holding them over the fire aside of the kettle. "No, never mind, it's a foolish question."

"What is?"

"Oh, I keep wondering, does Rossetti *like* us?"

"Of course he does."

"In a way I suppose he must, but that's not what I mean."

"Then say what you do mean."

"He couldn't be more attentive, certainly. And the help he's been giving you is altogether ripping. But we are, after all, the very rawest neophytes, and he . . . well, you *know* who he is. So then—*why* does he like us?"

"In your case it is very easy to say why: he thinks you're a genius."

Morris waved the roasting fork self-deprecatingly and nearly knocked the kettle off its hook. Water sputtered on the hot coals and rose in a cloud of steam.

"He does," the other reaffirmed. "Only Wednesday he made me bring 'The Chapel of Lyonesse' to the studio with me—"

"Ned, that copy wasn't meant to be hawked about like . . . like some broadsheet ballad."

"It's going to be in the magazine next month, isn't it? I'm sure it was in the galleys you showed us last night."

"The magazine! As you love me, Ned, don't talk about the magazine. God's wounds, lad, not the magazine!" With his free hand he struck the side of his head in a gesture of what would have seemed comic despair if it had not been so emphatic and forceful a blow. "What did he *say*?"

Ned smiled one of his elfin smiles. "First he read it aloud to Brown, who'd come with a message from Miss Siddal (but that's another story I must tell you later), and really, Top, you should never let anyone but him read your poetry aloud. No, not even you. And when he was done, and Brown had mumbled some weak cant phrase—"

"Brown didn't like it?"

"He may have, but he's the kind of painter, like me, who isn't notably articulate."

"I'll let that pass—but *what did he say*?"

"He said he thought it was superior, strictly as a poetic conception, to 'The Lady of Shallot.' And you know that is the poem he's chosen to make his design for in Moxon's edition of the *Poems*."

"He also says, if I remember, that since Keats, the whole field of poetry is played out and that is why we must all turn painter."

"If it is not enough to be rated better than Tennyson, then there's no satisfying you, Topsy."

"It *is* rather jammy, ain't it?"

"It is. And as for our being so much younger, and knowing less of the world, I believe he likes that. So many of his older friends seem to have disappointed him. The whole P.-R.B. is rather much a lost cause now, to hear him tell of it."

"That's ridiculous. The Pre-Raphaelite Brotherhood is just coming into its own."

"Well, you should hear the way he and Brown go on about Millais. That is, when they're not at each other's throats. Every one of them seems to think everyone *else* is pinching his best ideas. And then there's the Holman Hunt affair, which I can't talk about."

"What affair . . . ?"

"I'm sorry—I promised I wouldn't say anything."

Morris grimaced. "Then don't throw out hints. How do you like your sausage?"

"Immediately!"

They ate the half-cooked sausages with bread that had been fresh when Morris stopped at the baker's yesterday but was now quite sodden with the everlasting damp of Ned's crib—not that Morris hadn't sworn he was lucky to have the place; Morris did his best not to be critical, since he was, after all, Ned's guest. But he was determined that Ned, for his own good, would have to be taken in hand. They must find rooms together again.

"Have I told you," he asked, as he poured the tea, "that it looks certain that Street will be moving his office to London?"

Ned, with a mouth too full to speak, shook his head.

"If he weren't, I don't believe I could stick it there much longer. I live for these weekends in Chelsea."

Ned looked alarmed. "But, Topsy—"

"It isn't just the drudgery. Indeed, I'm rather happy with the drudgery. It's the profession itself. Architecture isn't what I imagined when I was at Amiens, or Chartres, or Rouen. It's a business, not an art. Build cheap and sell dear—that's the motto at Street's, and he's not the worst of them by any means."

"But, Top—"

"I know what you'll say. I must bide my time. And so I must. But it withers my heart, Ned, it truly does, to be copying his plans for brummagem Palladian villas, which are nothing more, behind their false facades, than the same soulless courses of brick that are covering every city in the country like another Plague of Egypt."

"There's nothing wrong with brick," said Ned mildly, tearing off another piece from the two-pound loaf. "Rossetti, you know, is painting the most wonderful oil of a brick wall. He's been painting it for years and will probably—so he says—never live to finish it. But it's quite wonderful. Each brick just so, as though it had paid to have its portrait painted and meant to get its money's worth."

"Only a brick wall—nothing else?"

"No, in fact, there's to be a figure of a woman. But the bricks are the best part so far. It's a modern subject, you see: a fallen woman who's been *found*—that's the title—too late."

Morris grimaced. "Bricks would be a suitable background for that, I daresay. For my part, Ned, I have no wish to be *modern*. People speak of 'our modern world,' and what they mean is a world from which nobility, stature, romance, imagination, everything wonderful has been subtracted."

Morris, warming to this familiar theme, began to compare the ignoble, unromantic London of 1856 with a lovelier London of his own imagining, to which he assigned the nice round date of 1300. As he developed this contrast between tawdry present and apocryphal past, their breakfast was transformed, by imperceptible degrees, to luncheon. Though the weather had taken an unexpected turn for the better, they remained indoors, sated and lost in the bosky tangles and meanderings of their well-beloved Malory. Morris read aloud in an uninflected sing-song style that he fancied was bardic. Its effect on both bard and listener was mesmerizing, in the most literal sense. The story, such as it was—Launcelot was cudgeling, pummeling, unhorsing, and generally trouncing a succession of characterless knights—mattered not at all. Only the words signified, rare old words like rusted shreds of metal dug up near the site of an ancient battle, courtly turns of phrase, elegant and innocent in equal measure, swatches of the oldest silk. To read them, to listen to them, was almost to leave the smoke and squalor and smallness of suburban Chelsea and to enter the enchanted forest of some ineffable, threadbare tapestry.

As they read, unseen by them but quite visible through the lodging's single window (if they'd either bothered to look), a helium balloon sailed across the Chelsea sky, crimson against the massed grays of high cumulus clouds. Suspended beneath the balloon by a complex network of harness straps and rope, a living bull bellowed in protest against being dealt with so unnaturally, while the lady mounted in the saddle on his back (it was the renowned Madame Poitevin in the costume of Europa) tried to demonstrate a contrary and pluckier spirit to her fellow traveler by singing a comic song that had been much in request a few years before, "Pig's Pettitoes." At the altitude to which the balloon had carried them, the bull's bellows sounded like the mildest, most muted baaing of a lamb, while Madame Poitevin's song was inaudible for the most part even to herself, for the bull was not to be humored into a quieter frame of mind. They floated some minutes

becalmed above Sloane Square, and then the wind picked up and bore
them off in the general direction of the Tottenham marshes.

Moments later there came a rapping on the door of the room, and
before Ned could even wonder aloud who it might be, Rossetti entered
with a flourish of a single gladiolus. Had his beard been trimmer, and
his collar fresher, had his cravat not displayed a telltale glint of emer-
ald green, had his trousers not been so baggy at the knee, had, above
all, he worn a top hat instead of the floppy brimmed soft felt hat he did
wear, he would have looked a proper dandy. Instead, he looked rec-
ognizably what he was, a painter and a bohemian.

"Gabriel!" Morris cried aloud, as rapturously as if it had been the
archangel himself he were greeting.

"Did you see her?" Rossetti demanded earnestly.

"See whom?" asked Ned.

Rossetti crossed to the open window and leaned out. "Ah, too late,
too late, and such a stunner too. I knew I should find you like this,
hermited away from the world, reading—what is it?—Malory, of
course. Well, you might do worse, though what you have just missed,
my lads . . ." He'd found his way to the remains of the smoked
haddock and sat fileting it delicately with his fingertips. "What you
missed was nothing less than a damsel mounting to heaven on a bull."

"Oh yes," said Ned dismissively. "I've seen her. They do it every
Saturday and Sunday afternoon at Cremorne. I must say I can never
think of anything else but how wretched the poor bull must feel to be
handled so—but I say, how delightful to see you here, Gabriel."

Rossetti, taking up the haddock on its chipped plate, plumped down
beside Ned on the bed. "How delightful to be here. I tried to think
where I'd be safest from discovery, and where, as well, I'd pass the
time most pleasantly. The answer came to me in a flash: Ned's crib. So
I paid my four pence, boarded the steamer, and—*eccomi qua*—here I
am!—as you see, not quite in my Sabbath best (I haven't a clean collar
left in my drawer), but well enough turned out, I hope, that we may all
go out to Cremorne in a bit. When the stunners begin to troop their
colors, eh? What say you?"

"A capital suggestion—I've been past, but never inside. Have you,
Topsy?"

Morris shook his head. He felt awkward suddenly, and shy. Yet it was the same every time he saw Rossetti: for the first few minutes he could scarcely open his mouth.

"And whom are you escaping?" Ned asked, sliding sideways in his bed to make room for the bulkier Rossetti.

"Whom am I not escaping? Lizzie, chiefly. Brown stopped by yesterday with an American chap and said she is in a most fretful temper, and though I love my dear Guggums dearly, it is sadly true that when she is bad she is horrid. And lately she is bad. Then there is Norton himself (the American chap), whom, like a fool, I told to call back. He said he would love to, and would bring Ruskin besides, whom of all living creatures I should least care to confront, for he will want to see what I've done on the watercolor I promised him; and I've done nothing at all—for before I can do anything else, I *must* do the woodcuts for Moxon. And I can't. Can not, am incapable, would sooner jump in the river. Short of which I thought I would wrap myself in flannel and sleep through the entire week until you'd come back to London. For it is the God's truth, boys, that there is no one in this whole smoking hell of a city whose company more refreshes me and makes me feel as though I were still animate."

His audience shook their heads in mock disapproval, which served not at all to mask their adulation. Here was Rossetti, the greatest painter of his day, as they both quite fervently believed, escaping from the likes of John Ruskin that he might spend the day with *them*. It could scarcely be doubted, after this, that he did like them, that they could call themselves, legitimately and without exaggeration, his friends!

"Ah, Gabriel," said Ned, "Brown is right to scold you, you know. The way you behave to your patrons is a perfect disgrace."

"Patrons!" said Rossetti, rising to the challenge Ned had posed. "Don't talk to me of patrons. Those who are not dolts outright are *cognoscenti*, which is seven devils worse. To suffer an afternoon of such talk as Ruskin spouts, all the lessons in geology and anatomy, the divagations on Tintoret and Veronese, the endless knowingness of the man, is more than I can bear. An hour of it will set me back a week. God save us all from *patrons*!"

With which, he despatched the last of the haddock.

"Dear Topsy," he continued, in a conciliatory tone, "do not look so stricken! Of course I make exception for you. Money is one of your accidental qualities, like, if you'll forgive my saying so, your beard (which *will* get thicker, mine was just the same at your age, you must have faith); it is not your essence. One could take your money from you—" He smiled self-deprecatingly as one who had, indeed, already done so. "—and the essential William Morris would remain. It isn't so with Ruskin. That man cannot be considered distinct from his pocketbook. Tin has corroded his innermost self, tin and the power of tin, which he uses to coerce everyone he knows, in every relation of his life. The man is a walking parable. I say, can I have some of that Cheddar over there?"

"Feel free to eat what you like," Ned invited. "But surely, Gabriel—" He twisted corkscrew-fashion inside his bedclothes so as to keep Rossetti in view as he cut a wedge from the cheese. (The cheese, Morris could not help reflecting, that was intended to see Ned through the week.) "—surely, it won't serve in the long run? Finally, anyone will resist the influence merely of money."

"Do you think so? I'm always astonished how little we do resist, we who lack tin. Does he want me to paint a different head on my Beatrice? Very well, I obligingly scratch out the Beatrice that was and paint a new Beatrice that looks just the same. A perfect waste of time, but that is what he's buying from me, as much as from any lacemaker. Must Lizzie remove to another climate for her health—and to keep *me* industrious and free of temptation? Ruskin thinks I don't see through his stratagems, but I do. So be it: Lizzie decamps obediently for the South of France, where she has no wish to be, and pines and languishes, and why? Because of *his* tin and *her* tinlessness, no other reason."

"But Gabriel, that doesn't sort with what you said of his coercing everyone. Because if he really wanted to do that, he wouldn't send someone so far out of his reach."

"So we said, so we said. Until the lists began to arrive through the post—of the books she must read while she's away—and a tiresome lot they were—and where *exactly* she must stop all along the road to Nice and set up her sketchbook. He would even tell her, sometimes, which feature of which statue in which tympanum she must undertake to copy. And the tone he takes! His presumption surpasses everything except his condescension. To hear him lecture about color, good Lord! He who can't mix black and white to obtain gray. But he knew Turner, you see, and no one can deny Turner's mastery of color. Ergo, he, through his mastery of *Turner*, is to be deferred to in all matters touching on color. I wonder whether he badgered Turner as he does me. Probably he would not have dared. He was only down from Oxford when they first met. Even Ruskin would not have had that much gall."

"But his book . . ." Morris began hesitantly, "you wouldn't say that it isn't a good book, would you?"

"*Modern Painting*? It's a book of criticism, and criticism of painting at that. What is easier than to talk about paintings? If they are good paintings, and one has a grain of intelligence, it will probably seem good talk. Of course, if it makes someone *buy* the painting, so much the better. What Ruskin doesn't understand—what no *critic* understands—is that though he can talk rings about this or that picture, though he can even buy it, his talk will not encompass nor his tin obtain the dream from which a painting arises, and it is only the dream that matters. While dreams abide, there will always be paintings; it's a matter merely of doing the handwork. That is why I say, Ned, that you must persevere with all the apprenticeship nonsense of anatomy and color mixing. But listen to me giving forth elder wisdom, like another Ruskin—or Polonius! Did I, in *my* prentice days, persevere in *any* unwelcome task? I did not. I fled from the casts at Sass's school as from so many basilisks, and even when of my own free choice I got dear old Brown to take me into his study, and he set me fagging at some still lives of pickle jars and rotting apples, it was no better. I would hide myself in an alleyway and scribble doggerel ballads, or just dream. And do you know, Ned—I was right! Forget all elder wisdom. Work as you can—but dream as you may."

Taking heed of the dejected look on Morris's face, Rossetti thought for a moment of correcting his omission: he *had* been directing his attention exclusively to Ned. "Put on your jackets, both of you. Let's be off to Cremorne: the stunners will all be arriving, and you're not even dressed."

It was, even so, another hour before they got out the door, for as Morris was stooping over to pull on his right shoe, Rossetti cried out: "Stop—just there!"

Morris immediately stood straight.

Rossetti groaned—a splendid, rumbling, poetical groan. "No, no, the way you *were*, bending over to your shoe. Yes! Now tilt your face left, toward me. But not so much. Splendid. Topsy, you shall be my Launcelot."

Morris had demurred (it was a most uncomfortable position to hold for any length of time), but Rossetti had carried the day, and so for an hour, while Ned continued to read aloud from Malory's tale of Sir Launcelot du Lake (and Morris endeavored to keep a look of knightly dignity about him despite the pain in the small of his back), Rossetti blocked out, on a sheet of Ned's best paper, his design for "The Lady of Shallot," and then, on the back of the paper (Morris was allowed to cheat, propping his chest on the back of Ned's single wooden chair), a more detailed study of his head.

"What do you think?" Rossetti asked, when the portrait sketch was finished.

"Ripping," Ned declared decisively. "The very picture of a 'parfit gentil knight.'"

Morris took the sheet of paper in his hands. It was true. Rossetti had performed some unaccountable magic and made of his plain and even (he feared) rather coarse features an image of chivalry fit for the finest book of hours. His spirit spiraled up in a lark-flight of exaltation. At the same moment, by the law of compensation, he felt a new, intenser shyness. "I think," he said, with a grin of radiant gratitude, "that you shall have to carry me to Cremorne Gardens."

A twelve-man band of rather military cast was playing a polka at the other end of the pavilion, but here where they sat in the shadows, beyond the range of the last Chinese lantern, the music could scarcely be made out above the clatter of the dancers galloping over the boards of the platform, a clatter that followed the rhythms of the polka in only the most general way. Morris was insisting, over the uproar, on the pathos and absurdity of a misspent youth at Oxford. Two pints of ale had gone far to untie his tongue.

"And then, as to the lectures, why, they are nothing but imposture and sham. Imagine: seven or eight grown men gathered in comfortable chairs before a cozy fire taking turns translating Horace or Lucretius extempore, which is to say, reciting some snippet they've got by heart from one of Bohn's cribs. Oxford, I think, would vanish into the air if it were not for Mr. Bohn. And the lecturer sits there, nodding solemnly, as if this recitation were an oracle fresh from the lips of Lucretius himself. Then, when the recitation is over, he looks very sage and sips his port—ever so judiciously—" Morris furrowed his brow and pursed his lips at the brim of his third tankard of ale.

Rossetti chuckled appreciatively.

"—and he asks, in chest tones that the great Macready might envy, '*Dum* governs two moods, does it not, Mr. Morris?' I agree that it does. 'It governs the subjunctive sometimes, does it not, Mr. Morris?' Again, I agree. 'And is *qui* ever used with the subjunctive? It is, is it not?' And after my third assent, the man nods gravely and tells me that I have done very well, very well indeed. And this was my education! This was my preparation for a career! And you can look at me, Gabriel, and say that you *envy* me the time I squandered at Oxford? You, who already had an oil hung at the Royal Academy when you were no older than I am now?"

Rossetti nodded. "And at that, you know, I was a late bloomer. But it isn't your education I envy. I daresay everyone's official education is a sham. It is one's friends whom one learns from, and vice versa. You work together, and read the same books, and argue about them, and eventually, if there is tinder, one of these sparks will set it aflame, and if there is fuel, a career begins to take shape. That is all education amounts to, ever. No, what I envy in your having been to Oxford is living among such buildings. They are the manufactories of dreams as surely as Sheffield's foundries are of steel."

"Gabriel?" said Ned. "I don't want to interrupt—"

"Ned, *don't* stand on ceremony."

"Well, then, I *do* want to interrupt. Isn't that Miss Cornforth over there?"

"Fanny! Where?"

"In the green dress, dancing with the fellow—"

"—with the tremendous whiskers! By Christ, Ned, you're right—it *is* Fanny. Fancy our finding her here." Rossetti stood and semaphored across the dance floor with his floppy felt hat. "Fanny!" he shouted. "Fanny, over here!"

Polkaing briskly, Fanny Cornforth signaled, by broad smile and a wave of her fan, that she'd heard and seen.

"There," said Rossetti, turning round to address his two companions, "is the definition of a stunner. Look at that hair. It would put even Rapunzel's to shame for thickness, and for color . . ." He shook his head in mute awe. "For color, all Venice can't equal Fanny Corn-forth's hair. Fetters and manacles, my lads—that's the effect of such hair on me. Fetters and manacles."

"She's very handsome," Morris said agreeably.

"And her lips . . ." Rossetti closed his eyes and traced the shape of the absent lips in the air before him. "Just the hue a woman's lips should be ideally—not really red at all, but with the bluish-pink bloom you see in a rose petal. But judge for yourself. Here she comes—Ned, move your chair. There's room for the four of us."

"Mr. Rissetty," Fanny said, bending a little at the knees in a gesture of civility before accepting the proffered chair, " 'ow surprising to see *you* 'ere. And 'oo are these two gentlemen, if I may be so bold?"

"The young man who is growing a beard is Mr. Morris."

Morris, who'd already risen to his feet, gave a short bow.

"And this gentleman you have already met, I believe: Mr. Jones."

"Is it Ned, then? Why, so it is. If you all 'adn't taken a table in the blackest corner of the place, I'd of known 'im straightaway. Why ever *are* you 'ere in the dark—and why ain't you dancing? That *is* why people come 'ere, you know—to dance. You've been talking, I sup-pose."

Rossetti smiled vaguely.

"And what 'ave you been saying, then? Oh all right, don't tell me—"

"No, let me think: I was just saying that the characteristic product of Sheffield is steel, and of Oxford dreams, and I was about to add that what London seems to specialize in is . . . stunners."

Fanny gave a squeal of laughter and wrapped Rossetti's forehead round with both hands and the fan. "Oh, 'ow dreadfu'! Ain't 'e just dreadfu', Ned? You're all the same, you, though I'll make exception for Ned. 'E's a gentleman through and through; while you, Mr. Ris-setty, are *something else*, which I will not say. Not in the presence of these gent'men." With which she gave Morris the most meaning of winks.

"You mean, I'm a cockney."

Fanny's reaction was still more galvanic and shrill. Morris realized, with something like awe, that she was drunk. He knew because he became just the same when he was very far gone in his cups, but he'd never before known a woman (one could not, obviously, consider her a lady) in the same condition, except for the sort of woman associated with the gutter; never, certainly, a woman to whom one might be introduced.

"You was the one to say it, Gabriel," she blurted out when she'd recovered from her hilarity. "I wouldn't of, so 'elp me God."

"Not even in a charade?"

"A charade?" she asked, wrinkling her nose in puzzlement.

"Well, how would you act out the word 'cockney,' Fanny, if you were playing charades?"

Fanny looked offended. "I'm sure I 'ave no idea, Mr. Rissetty."

The band struck up a waltz. Rossetti offered Fanny his hand, and they rose from the table.

"Is she . . . ?" Morris asked, faltering, when the couple was out of earshot.

"One of his models," Ned explained.

"He's certainly very free with her. Look how they're dancing."

"It's his way."

"If he'd been drinking as we have I could better understand it. But he's sat there with the same half-pint of ale all the time we've been here."

"He never drinks. He says the only effect alcohol has on him is sedative."

"She *is* a stunner. I'll grant that."

"Now you've met her, I suppose there's no harm in my telling you that she's the model he's using for *Found*."

"His painting of the fallen woman?"

Ned nodded.

"Do you suppose . . . ?" Morris didn't know how to phrase the question.

". . . that they planned to meet here?" He nodded again. "Yes, I'd lay odds they did."

*This* possibility hadn't even occurred to Morris. He couldn't say which he thought more shocking: Ned's cynicism or Rossetti's behavior.

"He used to come here a great deal. Not on Fanny's account—he's only met her lately—but to go dancing with Annie Miller."

"And who is Annie Miller?" Morris asked with growing distress.

"Do you remember—when we were talking this morning and I mentioned—"

"This afternoon—"

"Yes, and I mentioned the business with Holman Hunt, and said I couldn't talk about it?"

"Yes."

"*That* was Annie Miller. She was *his* model for *The Awakened Conscience*, and she became, in a not quite official way, his fiancée. When Hunt went off to the Holy Land two years ago, Gabriel was to keep an eye on her. Annie promised she would not sit to any other artists while he was away, except Gabriel; but he, instead of keeping her out of the way of temptation, actually encouraged her to work for any number of artists. And beyond that, they would come *here* all the time. Hunt got word of it, and when he came back this spring, there was a great row at Gabriel's studio. The upshot was that Hunt has thrown her over."

"And has Gabriel thrown her over too?" Morris asked.

"Annie was never more than a lark for him. Like Fanny now. He does still mean to marry Miss Siddal."

"And does Miss Siddal know of these matters?"

"She found out from Brown's wife, Emma. And that is why she came back from France. You should have witnessed the scene she made. Screaming and rolling, literally rolling on the floor, and Gabriel beside himself."

"I don't understand why he doesn't marry her at once. How long have they known each other? Years and years. They've even lived together, so I've heard."

"The reason he offers is tin, or rather tinlessness. But the real reason, I think, is that he doesn't want to."

"But surely he ought to."

"Yes, he knows that, and he hasn't said, outright, that he won't. Only, he puts off the date always. And meanwhile they are at each other's throats like two bedlamites whenever they meet. I can understand his wanting to come off to a place like this for the sake of simply enjoying himself. Though I can't, of course, approve."

"No. Of course not."

It seemed certain enough, from all Ned had told him, that the answer to his unasked question was decidedly in the affirmative. Rossetti's stunner was no different from all the other women there on the dance floor, and Rossetti himself no different, either, from the other men. There were hundreds of them at Cremorne. Dancing in the dim-lighted pavilions. Strolling on the graveled paths. Kissing in the shadowed shrubberies. Thousands, perhaps, if all London were to be combed, from the sailors' brothels at Rotherhithe to the costlier but no less notorious attractions at St. John's Wood. Not that numbers made for any extenuation. It was wrong, that could not be denied. Morris would never feel the same unblemished adulation for his idol again. But must he, in all conscience, surrender Rossetti's acquaintance on that account? At the very moment the man had made such clear proffers of friendship?

"There's something else," said Ned.

"What is that?" If Morris had been more capable of ordinary, civil hypocrisy, he'd have asked, instead, not to be told—for he could see, by the way Ned's eyes avoided his, that the subject had not changed.

"Early this summer, after we'd been together to the Royal Academy; and then, as I recall, walked up the length of Regent Street, just as the lamps were being lighted—I'd just parted to go to my bus, and happened to turn back and saw him talking to . . . her. And then she came after me, and there was simply no shaking her off. He'd told her that I was very shy, which is true enough, and that I had wanted her to talk to me, which was not. I said, 'No, my dear, thank you, I'm just going home.' You know me, Topsy—I'm never haughty with those poor things."

"No, of course not."

"It was of no use. She wouldn't go. And there we marched arm in arm down Regent Street, she complaining all the while that she'd received five bob and was an honest girl who did not accept money on false pretenses, and I in terror of being seen thus by some acquaintance."

Morris found himself smiling, and to conceal his smile took a drink from his tankard, but even as he was swallowing the ale, the laughter came, unbidden, irresistible, a spume of spray across the table.

Ned smiled wryly. "Yes, I see it has its ridiculous side. Gabriel does like jokes, and his jokes can be very rough; for a long while I saw the incident in that light, but now I wonder."

"You think he means for you . . . for us . . . ?"

"He brought us *here*, didn't he?"

"Yes, but—" Morris shook his head emphatically. "No, Ned, no. The man may have, as they say, feet of clay, but he would not set out on purpose to corrupt us."

"Perhaps he does not see it so."

"Nevertheless, he must know that *we* would see it so. You do, do you not?"

"Of course, Topsy."

"And I do, so let us speak no more about it. You do him wrong, Ned, believe me."

Another waltz and a polka later (the polka with Topsy, who didn't know how to refuse, and who, for that matter, rather liked to polka), Fanny disappeared and Rossetti approached the two boys at the table to which they'd moved, nearer to the dance floor.

"Fanny is feeling peculiar," he announced with concern.

"Is she?" said Morris, not knowing what else to say.

"And what she would like is a place to lie down. For a few moments. She's sure to be better directly." When Ned did not volunteer, he continued: "Do you think, Ned, I could take her to your crib? Only till she's on her feet again."

Ned felt in his pocket for the latchkey, handed it to Gabriel. "That's for the outer door. The room itself doesn't have a lock."

Rossetti pocketed the key, squeezed Ned's shoulder appreciatively, and said: "Right then." He began to leave, then bethought himself, and turned back. "I'll wait for you in Sloane Square, outside the *à la mode* beefshop we went to the other night."

"Never mind," said Ned, "there's a nail just over the lintel, in the shadow. Leave the key on that."

"Right then. Topsy, I'll see you next week?"

Morris nodded, feeling unaccountably and eternally damned.

Rossetti cocked his head to the side, smiled in a sad sort of way, and left.

They stayed on at the pavilion till eleven thirty, drinking steadily, saying very little, which was unusual for them, since they usually shared their thoughts with scrupulous equity. Once Morris said "Damn" and Ned said "Why is that?" and Morris said "They're going to eat all your food" and Ned just laughed. Afterwards, and very seriously, he observed that Morris ought not so consistently to try to be his brother's keeper, which Morris realized was perfectly true. So true, and a recognition so painful, that he struck a reminding blow to his own forehead, the force of which he rather miscalculated. Ned became concerned. Morris said he was quite all right, but that they had better be leaving, which was true. Meg and Polly, who had introduced themselves much earlier (they sat at the next table), said *"Au revoir,"* and Ned said "Good evening." Morris couldn't say anything. Just as they were leaving the pavilion the fireworks began to go off. "Eleven thirty," said Ned. From all around them, from every shadowed gravel path, from the shrubbery, they could hear the women. Some would shriek, or gasp; some would ooh; and each inchoate exclamation seemed to Morris's drunken, wondering mind perfectly true and perfectly terrible and beautiful beyond belief.

# CHAPTER FIFTEEN

# *The Novelist's Wife*

## MAY, 1858

While Henry smoked his pipe in *The Magpie and Stump*, Mary waited at the corner of the King's Road and Hobury Street, to the sure consternation of the greengrocer under whose awning she had taken her stand. At this quietest hour of a May afternoon the land of clouds above was more active and alive than the shops below. From time to time she would peer near-sightedly down Hobury Street to No. 7, her husband's lodgings, but no one went in or out. It rained just long enough to put a gleam on the cobbles and then, answering her prayer, stopped.

A perfect curio of a man turned off the King's Road and passed by so close, and so much seeming to be unaware of her, he almost trod upon her skirts. With his hair preposterously red and no less preposterously long, with his parrot-beak nose and blinking eyes, with such dandiacal clothes on such a miniature frame, he seemed odd enough to have stepped from the pages of one of her father's books—or one of Mr. Dickens's even more, since her father would have hesitated to evoke quite this degree of the grotesque. Something about him made her certain (was it simply because he carried a book?) that he meant to call upon her husband. But no, he passed in front of No. 7 without looking up. Then, however, several houses farther along the terrace, he realized his mistake, turned round, approached No. 7, and stood before it the longest while, considering, quite lost in thought.

She did not need so long to make up her mind, but was across the street and almost at the door when Mrs. Frawley appeared in answer to his ring.

"Yes," said that woman peremptorily.

The singular man handed her his card and announced, in a piping voice that corresponded too ludicrously well with his whole mien, "Algernon Swinburne. Please to announce me, madam, to Mr. Meredith, if he be in."

There are those—and he was one—who apprehend the world in generalities. That is not to say either that they misapprehend it or that they are blind to its particulars, but that their intelligence fastens rather on atmosphere than on the several scents composing it.

The atmosphere today was that of spring. Swinburne could almost feel the altered tilt of the earth under his feet—though, in truth, the difficulty was rather to be attributed to the ill-laid pavement under foot and the glass of wine he'd taken with his lunch. Shopfronts fairly whirled before him; clouds hurtled by in the contrary direction. *Such* a gusting wind: already it had taken his hat, but no matter, one could enjoy the wind more without it. And here, already, was Hobury Street.

Turning the corner in haste to escape the wind, he entered one of the more unprepossessing back streets of Chelsea, not to say down-at-the-heels; patently a street of lodging houses—here was even a sign fastened to the rail, advertising a room to let. And yet this street was the abode of genius! Not poetic genius, though: novelistic, rather. Poetic genius would swiftly have perished among such mean surroundings: novelistic genius could survive—would even strive. Only think of Chatterton, the marvelous boy, a suicide at eighteen because he could not bear to await his laurels in a garret. Odd that Henry Wallis should light on Meredith, of all people, to sit (rather, lie) for him when he was painting *The Death of Chatterton*. All they had in common, really, was their indigence and red hair. *He* would have served much better as a model for Chatterton, both with regard to age (three years ago, when the painting had been done, he would have been exactly the right age) and to constitution (Meredith was robust as a trooper, while he, alas and damn all, was "delicate"). Even his hair was that degree more red than Meredith's—which sorts with the fullest efflorescence of poetic genius. A great mistake then, on the part of the Parcae, to have arranged the matter as they had. The moral (for there is a moral to be derived from every daydream): One must gain an introduction to Everyone Who Matters as early as possible, in order that such mix-ups will not continue to occur.

This, and no other, was his reason for calling on Meredith today.

Looking up at the orange 19 daubed on the lintel of the house he was approaching, he realized he'd overshot his destination; and in those brief moments during which he retraced his steps along the terrace, his imagination struck up a conversation—an exemplary dialogue, such as might be delivered by the gods—with the person he was about to meet, a shower of mutual compliments and polite attentions—rendered today in the choicest Tuscan Italian. (Though Meredith was probably unacquainted with that language, in a month he, Swinburne, must stand for the Taylorian scholarship in Italian and French, and so all his fantasied encounters were being conducted in one or the other of these languages, according to whim.) The imagined Meredith, who was beardless as he'd been in Wallis's painting (though the Meredith he had encountered a week ago wore a full beard in the latest postwar style), spoke of his admiration for Mazzini, the savior of Italy, a modern Prometheus, a demi-god. *Evviva* Mazzini! Apropos the failed assassin, Orsini, Meredith, slipping into French, denounced Napoleon III in the most scathing terms. Lapsing back into his native tongue, Swinburne observed how apt the Italian language was for praise, the French for pejoratives. Meredith agreed. He laughed. He grew cordial, throwing an arm round Swinburne's shoulders. He asked —what profession did Mr. Swinburne follow? A cavalryman, by the look of him. Alas, no, Swinburne had hoped to take up the profession of arms, but Providence, and his parents, had been otherwise disposed. He was (or would be, in the fullness of time) a poet, no more. No more! protested Meredith. He was a poet himself and considered it the highest of callings, a vocation more sacred than the Church. Had Mr. Swinburne read Carlyle's *On Heroes and Hero-Worship*? Swinburne— now standing at the very door—lied (to keep the imaginary conversation going) and said he had not. Meredith was therefore free to expound Carlyle's thesis that poets stood in the upper pantheon of Heroism, outranked only by prophets, kings, and gods. With all due respect for Carlyle's genius, Swinburne wondered if this were so. After a pause Meredith voiced the desire to be allowed the privilege of reading some of Mr. Swinburne's poetry, or better, of being allowed to hear it read aloud.

At just this happy juncture the red-haired man with the parrot-beak nose and blinking eyes became aware of another pair of eyes. These, solemn and staring, were on a level a little higher than his own—then disappeared, slithering back into the preconscious dark. There in the window, framed by the tassels of a parted curtain, stood a boy of that angelic shining breed that always caused him a wrench of nostalgic regret for his own vanished childhood. He smiled at the boy, and the boy returned his smile.

He mounted the steps and rang the bell. A woman appeared, immense in bombazine. "Yes?" she demanded. He handed her the card, and after she had sniffed opprobriously at it, announced himself: "Algernon Swinburne. Please to announce me, madam, to Mr. Meredith, if he be in."

"Mr. Meredith is not at home."

"Could you tell me—"

Sudden alarm wrinkled the woman's features and she began to close the door—but was forestalled by a voice tuned to the pitch of perfect good breeding and—more than that—of certain intelligence: "Ah, Mrs. Frawley, good afternoon. At last I have the luck to find someone home."

He turned round to see the source of Mrs. Frawley's alarm: a woman afloat upon a hemisphere of brightly colored silk. He didn't take in detail as a woman's eye might and so could not have said how it was possible from the evidences of parasol, straw hat, and a certain quantity of yardgoods and ribbons to know that the woman, though respectable, was not quite of his own class, not cousined to aristocracy.

She addressed Swinburne directly: "You were inquiring after my husband?"

Before he could reply by more than a bow, she had darted up the steps of the landing to insert the tip of her parasol inside the door, which Mrs. Frawley had been inching closed. "A minute, madam, if you please. I should like to see my son."

Mrs. Frawley swelled with ill intention like a puff adder. "Unfortunately, Mrs. Meredith, the young gentleman is not at home." She glared down at the parasol. "Now, if you would be so kind as to remove . . ."

No sooner had the lie been told than the young gentleman himself exposed it, pushing aside Mrs. Frawley's crinoline cage so that the bombazine skirts seemed at first to be tilting forward, then sideways, of their own volition. Mrs. Frawley pushed back, but not forcefully enough: the boy—the same he had seen in the window—was through and, a moment later, in his mother's arms. Swinburne regarded the affectionate tableau with a sentimental tremor; Mrs. Frawley, with a tremor of a less benign character.

"I have firm instructions, ma'am, that the young gentleman is not to leave the house."

"Not on his own, of course. He shall be with me. And—" Here she offered her arm coquettishly. "—with Mr. Swinburne, if he cares to accompany us."

The gambit succeeded. Mrs. Frawley's horror of a scene surpassed her resentment. Though why anyone should feel other than benevolence toward such a pleasant, plausible woman Swinburne could not conceive.

As they walked away, crossing the King's Road, continuing down in the direction of the river, boy and mother prattled and purred in a kind of verbal embrace the ostensible subject of which was the events in the life of a family of sparrows inhabiting the eaves of No. 7, Hobury Street. There were also, to be sure, some unkind words spoken concerning Mrs. Frawley's puddings, which led to equivocations on the mother's side as to when Arthur was to return to the source of the puddings he preferred.

At the riverside, near enough to *The Magpie and Stump* to be able to make out the white lettering on the blue-painted brick, Mary Meredith turned to the peculiar fuzzy-bearded boy she'd commandeered, intending to dismiss him—now that he'd served the purpose of helping to pry her son away from Mrs. Frawley.

"Oh say!" the bearded child squeaked, forestalling her. "Do you see who is there up ahead, outside the public house? It is Mr. Wallis!"

"Is it indeed?" said Mary, squinting (and unable to prevent a blush). She addressed Swinburne nervously: "Are you a friend of—" (and caught herself before she'd said "Henry") "—of Mr. Wallis?"

"We met at Wallington. The Trevelyans' home?" he thought to add, in case she might not know.

"Oh, yes?"

"He was there with Ruskin, and I—Oh, damn! Excuse me, *please*. He's gone inside. I should be ready to swear he saw us. Possibly he did not recognize me, however. I had no beard two years ago."

She turned away to smile. There seemed just a trace of irony in his coxcombery, as though he too acknowledged the absurdity of the remark.

"I daresay he recognized *me*," she ventured. "He's quite an old friend, you know."

"Of course, he must be—your husband with his Chatterton."

"I was his model as well—for another painting."

"How altogether odd. He must not have seen us after all. I shall go inside and—"

She caught hold of the sleeve of his coat. "Pray, don't, Mr. Swinburne."

"But—"

"Do come along. Arthur." She laid her hand on the boy's shoulder, propelling him forward. "Run ahead of us, do." Arthur obediently trotted on before them.

"You've had a falling out," Swinburne declared, in a tone of guessing the answer to a riddle. While, at the same time, he could only marvel quietly to himself at the mysteriousness that gathered, like dusk, about the pretty Mrs. Meredith. What *could* she be up to?

"Not at all." She opened her parasol, twirled it, set it against her shoulder.

A drunken sailor reached up from where he was lying in a gesture of mendicancy; then, like a seaweed after the passing of some turbulence, subsided back to sleep.

"In fact," she continued, "we were to have met here—clandestinely."

Though he could hear the teasing in her voice, he still refused to take her meaning. "In that case, I shall go inside and inform him you are here."

She caught hold his sleeve again, detaining him. "Henry *means* to avoid us, Mr. Swinburne."

"I gather that. But *why*—that is, if I may be so bold as to ask?"

"Because he is not so brazen as I am."

"I should not say that you are brazen," Swinburne insisted gallantly.

"Then you constitute, with Henry and my father, a very small minority."

"Do you call him Henry?" Swinburne asked, more and more impressed by her freedom of manner, which conformed to his idea of how a gypsy or an American might behave. He would have liked to be a gypsy or an American himself.

"Yes, now we're lovers, I allow myself that intimacy." She laughed a spasmodic, coughing laugh at her own *mot*.

Swinburne fairly swooned with admiration. He looked back over his shoulder at the unprepossessing wooden facade of *The Magpie and Stump*, as though it might be able to offer confirmation of Mrs. Meredith's amazing assertion. "You . . ." He waited for her to be done coughing. "You speak of it so casually! I find that—if you will pardon my saying so—rather uncommon. I don't mean to be critical, not at all—but . . ." He concluded his incoherency with a blush.

"Oh, it will soon be common knowledge. If you knew my husband at all, you would have learned: Henry and I are going off to Capri."

"Capri!" The word summoned up a hazy amalgam of a hundred half-remembered paintings. How nicely she would be set off by all that: the strawberry-colored ribbons that trimmed her parasol just matched the strawberries he might offer her, if he were there himself. On Capri . . . "When will you set out?"

"As soon as I am well enough. This autumn, at the latest."

"Are you not well?"

"A little unsteady—no more. Today is the first I have stirred out of doors since I was delivered of my son."

"Your . . . ? But . . . ?"

"Oh, not *Arthur*." Hearing his name, the child, who was never out of earshot, turned. Then—not to seem to have been listening—raced ahead to the little square before the village church. "His little brother," she continued, "or rather, I should say his half brother, Harold. *Henry's* son." The last added as a crowning shamelessness and supreme audacity.

"Really!" shrieked Swinburne, in a tone of wonder rather than reproof. Then, thinking how poorly his outbursts and exclamations sorted with her own cool manner, he repeated it an octave lower and tuned to her splendid nonchalance. "Really?"

She replied with a glance and a half-spin of her parasol, then set off toward her son, who had found an imposing furry caterpillar in the churchyard and was anxious whether he would be praised or scolded, caterpillars being susceptible of such varying moral interpretations in the eyes of adults.

Arthur, feeling deserted and acting petulant, had told Swinburne (now his sole companion) that he would *not* like a Chelsea bun, but Swinburne, kindly, had not believed him, and had gone into the shop and bought four. They sat down to look at the boats and eat the sweet buns, and Swinburne asked him what he would be when he grew up.

"I don't wish to be anybody," said Arthur guardedly.

"Oh, but you must do something. Everybody must do something. Would you like to be a soldier?"

Arthur, intent on not losing any of the crumbs, shook his head.

"With a horse," Swinburne persisted, "and a musket, and a tall black shako with white waving plumes?"

"No." Arthur felt impelled to hold his position. "I *wouldn't* like to be a soldier. Would you?"

"When *I* grow up, you mean?" he answered, inclining his head to a comical angle. "Oh, but I have grown—all that I'm ever likely to—and it wasn't enough by half. But yes, I should have liked that."

"What do you do then?" Arthur demanded to know.

"Nothing. Someday I may do something, but now I am still at University."

"Do you fancy it?"

"I used to fancy it very much when I was at Eton. The masters are very strict at Eton, you know, and it is a rare boy who escapes being caned now and then. But . . . you must simply grit your teeth and take your swishing like a man. And then you will fancy Eton." He gave a tight-lipped grimace of a smile by way of confirmation.

Arthur was not persuaded, but was not inclined to argue either. "What I should like to be, I believe," he said, reverting tactfully to the earlier question, "is a painter. But you must promise not to tell Papa that."

"He doesn't approve of painters?"

Arthur shook his head. "No, he doesn't."

"He would prefer you were a writer, like himself?"

"I don't know. But my mother says that writers are always poor, and it is *wrong* to be poor."

"Indeed! And painters are not poor, then?"

He hung his head. "Oh, I probably shan't be a painter, you know. That is only what I'd *fancy*."

"And people cannot always have their way. True enough."

"I told Mamma I should like to go with her, when she goes away— but I must stay with Papa."

"Would you rather be with your mother?"

"Oh yes. But you must promise not to tell Papa that either."

"I promise."

"He's very jolly, but . . ." The character of the antithesis eluded him.

"Is he too *strict?*" Swinburne suggested, giving once again that peculiar emphasis.

"He *doesn't* let me play out of doors," Arthur conceded. "I can play out of doors when I am at Grandmamma Nicholls'. But Papa says I shan't return there again. I mustn't go anywhere where my mother may be, not anymore."

"Ah, that is a pity," Swinburne agreed uneasily. "But your Grandmamma Meredith—possibly you will stay with her for a while?"

Arthur shook his head. "*We* are the only Merediths there are."

After a long pause Swinburne suggested that perhaps they had better return now to Hobury Street. Arthur offered his hand regretfully, as a prisoner might, resuming his manacles.

As they were approaching the King's Road, Arthur screwed up his courage and asked his companion if *he* had seen his little brother, Harold, and what he was like.

Swinburne confessed he had not had the privilege, pointing out that he had only that afternoon made the acquaintance of Arthur's mother.

"But you *came* with her," Arthur noted skeptically.

"Not precisely true. We simply happened to come to the door at the same moment. I'd come by to give your father this book." He showed Arthur the book he'd been carrying, tightly tucked under his left arm.

"Let me see it," Aruthur insisted. "I can read most anything."

"Not this, I'll wager." Swinburne handed him the book.

They slowed to a saunter, while Arthur scrutinized, frowning, the first page of text.

"It's in French," Swinburne explained. "That is why the words are queer."

Arthur sighed. Then, politely: "What is it about?"

"It's about—it is about a woman, Emma Bovary, who is married to a surgeon and—um—they live in a small town in Normandy where very little ever happens. And that's all it's about, really."

"Did you *fancy* it?"

"Oh yes, enormously. It is written with such super style. And that is why I brought it for your father to read. However, on second thought, I believe I shan't be leaving it with him."

"Why?"

"No reason. Don't tell your father that, though. He might be annoyed. You keep *my* secret, and I'll keep yours. Is that fair?"

Arthur nodded cheerfully. "Shall I promise?"

"If you would."

"I promise."

"Thank you."

At the door of No. 7 Swinburne returned his young charge to the keeping of the resident dragon, who informed him that Mr. Meredith had not yet returned. Swinburne left his card and departed with a wave to Arthur, who stood, once more, within his melancholy frame of curtain tassels, a model prisoner.

# CHAPTER SIXTEEN

# A Day in the Country I

## 4 JULY 1862

A Friday like many other Fridays that summer—hotter perhaps than those the year had thus far yielded, and without the threat of rain (for which everyone whose livelihood was connected with Cremorne Gardens must be thankful).

At Cremorne, though the gates were open daily after three, wet or dry, at one shilling admission, the turnout could be very small indeed when the skies of London threatened to drench each lovely gown and mar the lanes with puddles. Indoor entertainments abounded, to be sure, in order that visitors be guaranteed value for money regardless of the weather—tonight, in addition to the usual fare, an operetta, *Le Mariage aux Lanternes*, presented in English in the Grand Concert Hall (paired with a ballet version of *The Elixir of Love*)—but the weather, as we have indicated, offered no impediment to outdoor pleasures.

If your tastes or principles did not incline you toward such entertainments as Cremorne offered, you might, for half the price, go instead to the Horse Repository, Holborn, where for a limited time it was still possible to view "that extraordinary animal, the Mammoth Ox, weighing upwards of 490 stone." Amazing, but there were the figures in black and white in the pages of the *Evening Standard*, which went on to report the animal's length to be a gargantuan twelve feet, three inches.

Few residents of Chelsea would be inclined to venture so far afield to save sixpence, but one might be tempted in such bright weather to stroll as far as the Crystal Palace, that Aladdin's cave of the Modern Age, where for half a crown one might attend the Great Rose Show and hear a military band. However, those eager to witness the skill and derring-do of the "Female Blondin" (her namesake, the Frenchman Blondin, was other times to be viewed in the same arena) must return the next day, when that celebrated young woman would perform on the low tightrope.

Today the Female Blondin, or "Mademoiselle Genviève" (to her neighbors, Lucy Young), rehearsed on the sparse lawn behind her parents' home on Davis Place, witnessed by her most faithful audience, Tinnie and Alice Greaves, who sat complacently or fidgeted on the brick wall that separated the Youngs' and the Greaveses' back gardens. Though, truly, she'd have preferred privacy, the Greaves girls must be endured for reasons of the heart: Lucy Young had formed an attachment to her next-door neighbors' eldest son, Charles, which all her recent celebrity with its concomitant attention from young men of the sporting persuasion had not been able to diminish. Lucy's mother loudly deplored this romance, pointing out that Charles could never amount to more than a common boatman like his father—that his brothers were even worse: layabouts, would-be painters (and not of the useful wall-and-house variety either). Even for a young woman without so promising a future in the theater, this would make an unwise family alliance. Yet who can sway the heart's election?

So, despite gapings and gigglings, she began with the simplest limbering exercises on the coarse matted grass: touching the tips of her toes; bending still lower to touch forehead to knee—then in a single smooth motion bending backward nearly double; squatting low on her haunches, rising quickly to full stretch, first on both legs, then alternating left and right until her calves fairly glowed with conscious strength. Only after forty-five minutes' warming up did she run through the actual sequence of tomorrow's performance: the awkward (but crowd-pleasing) "clog dance"; the more sprightly "basket dance" (without real eggs in the basket); then a series of ever-more-rapid cartwheels down a line of empty stout bottles (at the Crystal Palace, they would be burning candles); then the several feats involving chairs; the "flag dance"; and finally, the "drum polka," during which she took one of her rare false steps—which she was quick to dissimulate, however, as a graceful descent from the tightrope.

Twelve-year-old Alice, alone on the brick wall (Tinnie had simply seen it too many times now), offered her mite of applause. To tell the truth, there had been an element of disappointment for her in today's private matinée: Lucy had not worn the red- and white-striped pantaloons with the flaring overskirts that were Alice's favorite article of clothing in the world, but only a work-a-day version in soiled gray muslin. It put her in mind of spirits and table-rappings, especially since all of Lucy's dances were executed in silence, with never a note of music. She'd love to see her at the Crystal Palace, with a real brass band, and all the nobs in their finery—though it *might* be hard to see over the hats. It had been just such tall black hats that had nearly prevented her from witnessing the accident last summer when the Female Blondin crossed the Thames on the high tightrope. Shortly before reaching the Chelsea shore, the aerialist had experienced an unnerving slackening in the wire, preceded immediately by a tug to one side: one of the guy wires had loosened—it was even said that someone had done some tampering—and Lucy would have fallen and probably been crippled for life had she not kept calm, considered every possible solution, and finally, with quick good sense, discarded her balancing pole and grabbed the swaying tightrope, letting herself slowly down to a boat below by means of the still-stationary opposing guy.

Since that day Alice had no longer coveted the career of an aerialist, and yet the desire to own, to be seen wearing, the red- and white-striped pantaloons remained as passionate as ever.

Often there would be another pair of eyes studying Lucy from the uppermost back window of the Greaveses' house, scrutinizing her with an intentness of purpose that mere desire, whether for striped pantaloons or for Lucy herself, could never have brought to bear. Walter Greaves's purpose was simply to capture in the inflection of a line the corresponding line of the rope dancer's statuesque attitudes.

Today, however, was Walter's sixteenth birthday, and his father had told him at breakfast, quite unexpectedly, that he was to have the day for a holiday. Accordingly, he had borrowed his brother Henry's best suit and betaken himself to Berners Street, where a new art gallery was exhibiting works of William Frith, Augustus Egg, and Daniel Maclise, among others less notable. It was on account of the last-named artist that Walter was making this pilgrimage to (as he believed) the heart of London—the gallery was just a few steps north of Oxford Street—for Maclise was the greatest painter living in Chelsea. Just as his sister dreamed of a future in which she might wear those amazing pantaloons, so Walter had visions of somehow becoming the great man's protégé. Never mind that Maclise was reputed reclusive and peculiar. The same had been true of old "Puggy Booth," who'd belatedly been discovered to have been no less a personage than the president of the Royal Academy, Joseph Mallord William Turner. And had not Turner taken on any number of promising lads as apprentices at one time or another? That was how the trade of painting was organized. The only problem was how to demonstrate one's own bright promise: if (Walter daydreamed on his long way to Berners Street) he were to show Maclise one of his least-botched watercolors, the one of Chelsea Old Church perhaps . . .

At the gallery, however, Walter was destined not to see the painting that had drawn him there, for his attention was first engaged by something altogether odder. It was a study of a woman in a white cambric dress standing before a white muslin curtain. It could not be called a portrait, since Walter recognized the woman in the picture, with her red hair tumbled about her shoulders, as a professional model who lived in Chelsea, Joanna Hiffernan, or "Jo." Portraits weren't painted of models but of the wealthy and the families of the wealthy—people with money to spend on such luxuries. But if it were not a portrait, then what could it be? What *story* lay behind its enigmatic plainness?

Walter was not alone in asking such questions. Several people were similarly puzzled as they paused before the painting, though most of them dismissed their puzzlement with a laugh or a sarcasm. At last Walter had to know, at least, its name. He approached a solitary gentleman who carried the catalogue of the exhibition and asked him what the painting was called. *The Woman in White*, he was told, "by that young American puppy, Whistler." Not much help there. The woman in white, Jo Hiffernan, stood on a bearskin rug. The bear's mad glass eyes glared from the bottom of the canvas like the eyes of a thwarted demon. But the fur . . . he squatted on his haunches the better to admire the execution of that fur.

A moment later the director of the gallery, alerted by the man whose catalogue had been so little useful, suggested that he leave. Walter complied without challenge, without asking a reason. He knew his brother's suit was not adequate to the occasion of Berners Street.

The afternoon was not necessarily lost. For the price of a shilling Walter might go to see the reputed masterpiece of William Holman Hunt, *The Finding of Christ in the Temple*, which Hunt had painted, as it were, from life, having actually gone to the Holy Land in order to ensure the last degree of accuracy in the representation of the Temple and the Sanhedrin. Or, for the same price, he might take in whole rooms full of paintings by Rosa Bonheur, including the celebrated *Horse Fair*.

In the event, he exercised neither of these alternatives but idled away a curious hour at Mr. W. S. Woodin's Cabinet of Curiosities, and afterwards booked a rear balcony seat at the Royal Alhambra Palace, where, after a comic song and a tearful ballad, he watched Nathalie, Reine des Gymnastes, perform, in the words of the broadside on the street, "marvellous feats of muscular power." Loyally, he considered Nathalie in no way equal to Lucy Young.

While Walter sweltered in the balcony of the Royal Alhambra Palace, Miss Joanna Hiffernan had stopped at the office of *The Athenaeum* to get an advance copy of tomorrow's edition of that weekly journal. As soon as she was outside, she turned to the correspondence page and discovered to her relief and delight that Jimmy's letter had been printed. That was certain to put him into a jollier temper.

The letter read as follows:

> 62 Sloane Street
> 1st July 1862
>
> May I beg to correct an erroneous impression likely to be confirmed in your last number? The Proprietors of the Berners Street Gallery have, without my sanction, called my picture "The Woman in White." I had no intention whatever of illustrating Mr. Wilkie Collins' novel; it so happens, indeed, that I have never read it. My painting simply represents a girl dressed in white, standing in front of a white curtain. I am &c.,
>
> *James Whistler*

Members of Parliament, at that hour—the few who were present in the House—mopped their brows and melted within their clothes as they discussed the wisdom, convenience, and cost of a proposed embankment road to be laid along the Thames. The first stretch of shore to be thus transformed was that between Charing Cross Bridge and Wellington Street, but eventually the embankment was planned to extend upstream to the Houses of Parliament and downstream as far as Blackfriars. A question was raised concerning the fate of the Temple Gardens, and a Member who had once resided in the Temple assured the questioner that the embankment road would pass *in front of* the Temple Gardens and therefore would not endanger that "pleasant recreation ground for the people." There were cheers from both sides of the House.

Also at work in the Houses of Parliament that day, though not within earshot of the cheering in the Commons, was the painter whose contribution to the exhibition at the Berners Street Gallery Walter had been prevented from seeing, Daniel Maclise, R.A. Maclise had exhibited few works in the galleries of late. All his time (ten hours a day, six days a week) and all his energy (which had begun to flag, alas, now he was fifty-six) had to be given to the work perpetually in hand, this damned vast mural of *The Meeting of Wellington and Blücher after Waterloo*. Better call it, thought Maclise, *The Murder of Daniel Maclise*. And when this was done, there would remain to do, on a corresponding scale, *The Death of Nelson*. From where he stood on the scaffolding Maclise considered the great gray latency that must become the deck of the *Victory*, then turned back, with a sigh of weariness and boredom, to the face of a Prussian subaltern reverent before Field-Marshal Blücher's victorious posturing.

Few matters could have been further from the mind of Dante Gabriel Rossetti as he passed along the Chelsea waterfront that afternoon than the deliberations of sweltering Members of Parliament, and yet the activities of the House at that moment would, in effect, literally crumble the foundations of both his past and his future. One of the first buildings to come down making way for the new embankment road would be the house on Chatham Place, which had been his home until only four months ago, when his wife had committed suicide. And in little more than a decade the embankment of the Thames would extend (with interruptions) as far upstream as Chelsea; would pass before the very doorway of the house he had lately committed himself to renting. "Tudor House" it was called—or, even more grandiloquently, the "Queen's House."

Not that foreknowledge of these changes would have altered Rossetti's decision. Ten years was an unthinkable gulf of time to one who made it his pride that, like the lilies of the field, he took no thought for the morrow. He lived alert in a present compounded, this July moment, of the repeated, varied verticals of masts of anchored boats, the broad horizontals of beached scows; of the pleasure to be taken in fanning his sweaty forehead with a black, wide-brimmed wide-awake; of the odd, romantic desolation of the riverside streets, where not a soul stirred but the Brimlicombe boy flinging a bucket of spoiled milk into the river.

Moved by the spirit of the moment, Rossetti opened the saloon door of the *King's Head and Eight Bells* and at once discovered how the neighborhood had emptied itself of the usual rabble, for here they all were: workmen and wives, scullery maids and children, crowded into the public bar beyond the partition of oak wainscoting, hiding in the only spot of public shade to be found along the noontide streets. He ordered a stout and, settling himself at the nearest empty table, opened his sketchbook. But instead of drawing the woman who'd taken his fancy (who was, after all, rather coarse), he fell to admiring the sketch he'd done the previous afternoon at Simpson's cigar divan and then had promptly forgotten. Nothing to refine or frame, but the humor of it still struck him—and might amuse Christina, for it had been inspired by a phrase in a review of her book, *Goblin Market*. "Miss Rossetti," *The Times* had pronounced, "can point to work which could not easily be mended." To misconstrue (by way of illustrating this accolade), Gabriel had shown his sister, or her nightmare approximation, smashing crockery and hurling banknotes into the grate. Would it amuse her? They teased her for her temper. Yes, she'd be cheered. More to the point, he would enclose the two reviews she would not have had occasion yet to see, those from the *National Review* and the *British Quarterly*. Though the latter did puff his pictures rather more fulsomely than her verses. A problem arose (when does one not?): Would Christina judge him vain for forwarding what was in essence *his* good review? Or would she, nonetheless, enjoy the reviewers' somewhat tepid praises of her own contribution? Christina could be draconian in her judgments, especially on the score of vanity. Had she not given up playing chess because of her "inordinate pleasure in winning"? Ah, but she forgave easily. He would send both reviews *and* the drawing. *Basta*.

Without having properly savored its singular flavor, he found he'd emptied his mug of stout. Not wanting another particularly, he left a copper on the unwiped table and returned to the hot street.

As he followed the river downstream, he noted that a bank of clouds had arisen in the western sky and was being borne by the higher winds across the blue-white zenith to screen Rossetti and Chelsea, and soon all London, from the full force of the summer sun.

And there it was—his own house. Though not until the autumn. Now, and for the remaining months of the Exhibition season, it belonged to interlopers. Carpenter: he'd caught their name at the renting agent's offices. Even as he stared, with wistful covetousness, at the house that was not yet his own, he saw a human shadow pass before one of the sitting room windows on the ground floor. A man, a woman, gentleman, lady? Only a flash of summery white.

Carpenter: the word carked him like the first twinge of a headache. Carpenters, begone! Rossetti, be patient.

At any other time the sound of the singing proceeding from the *King's Head and Eight Bells* would have caused Carlyle a breach of concentration and brought down his responsive lamentations upon the public house, but Jane was not home to lament to, and, oddly, today he could truly wish that his upstairs "soundproof" study were less quiet. In effect it was a double room, one set of walls within another, and, while this sealed out the extraneous noises of the street most effectively (though not organ grinders and pub singing), it also sealed *in* the heat. There was no way to combat the immutable laws that govern the movement of gases, no point in opening the doors of the inner, the windows of the outer walls. The day itself was still and airless. Without a breeze, the leaves of the lime trees couldn't comfort him with the suggestions of their rustling, nor would his study be ventilated.

All that his efforts, earlier, had brought forth was a great burly bumble bee, entering at the garden window and refusing all gentler persuasion with impromptu foolscap fans and atlas map to return to its natural demesne. Instead, like a demented scholar (not without good intentions), it had buzzed from bookshelf to desk to bookshelf, favoring the brighter bindings. The beast was too devil-resembling self-willed to leave by the power of suggestion, and it became necessary to summon Maria, who arrived in a state of emotion, yet armed with a long-handled twig broom and inchoate cries eminently suited to the exorcism of bees.

Thus for an eyewink, bee's, bell-pull's, and besom's combined upheaval had caused some air to circulate in the otherwise airless room;

but the heat persisted, and with it, a "continual chaotic restlessness" that would not allow thought of the steady and focused order which *Frederick* required.

Three volumes were published, a fourth was in galley proofs, and the fifth (and final) volume had advanced Frederick's story almost to the Peace of Hubertsburg and the end of the Seven Years' War. Now the end was so clearly in view, one might suppose there should be a downward-rushing momentum—but it was not so. Still Carlyle lived in "the Valley of the Shadow of Frederick," in whose dusty purlieus he had lived the last full decade of his life. He felt a weariness beyond words—for indeed his *words* must ever express a contrary meaning; must moisten the arid wastes of Formal History and make it spring to new green-foliated life. And—adding pain to well-established pain —his private words must now belie all inner desolation, for Jane's nerves were so often jangled, her health so much impaired, that he must moderate his old proclivity to lay his troubles at her door: her own quite filled it.

Curious, how she could be present in his thoughts almost in inverse proportion to her physical presence in the house. The newest of her daily letters had already become buried beneath Burney's *Present State of Music*, but he fished it out, opened it again. The wretched, absorbent paper drank the sweat from his fingertips, and here and there a letter or a word grew fuzzier.

Her stay at Folkestone with the Ashburtons in their hotel suite seemed to be doing her a wealth of good: so little complaining, so much good cheer. Long walks by the sea with Lady Louisa—if it had been Lady Harriet entertaining her, one can be sure her letters would have had a very different tone. Not that Jane would ever have *willingly* set off to the seaside with that *bête noire* of so many years. Yes, a relief no more to be assailed by her in those sad fits of jealousy (mixed with melancholy), though what a price to have paid! Nothing less than the lady's death—five years a-gone now in the unyielding past. In Paris, as she was dressing for dinner. Now the new Lady Ashburton dressed for dinner, Lady Louisa, and had become Jane's dearest and most particular friend. Jane's accounts of each passing day at the West Cliff Hotel made Folkestone seem a very Elysium: the sea-bathing, the games of whist, the leisure to sit evening-long beside a fire (how much cooler it must be if fires were even thinkable!), reading Mrs. Oliphant's *Life of Edward Irving*. Odd it must be to read a biography of the man she once almost married! Though no odder than reading her husband's, and Jane would, doubtless, enjoy that sad pleasure ere long. Ah, but it did sound restful there in Folkestone with its absence of barking, quacking, and crowing elements, *mirabile dictu*. No liver-confounding French sauces on the table, but good honest unpretending fare: loin of mutton and boiled chicken. And according to the report of this letter, the only reminder of life in the metropolis was a copy of this month's *Cornhill*, substantial with review (albeit horror-stricken) of the latest volume of his *Frederick*, a review which Jane loyally belittled. She made no mention of the first chapters of George Eliot's *Romola*, serialized in those same pages, though surely she had read them. Everyone —even those who knew her true identity and the scandalous facts of her life—read the woman's books: living as the "wife" of an already married man (a former disciple of Carlyle's, it must be said in shame). He *would* enjoy having someone to talk to besides Maria, something to fix his mind on besides the Peace of Hubertsburg.

As a final inducement for him to join them, Jane said there was a horse.

He *would* go. Meanwhile, reaching down the right volume from the highest shelf, he would satisfy Lady Louisa's curiosity (as per Jane's request) concerning Saltwood Castle. Then possibly Cobbett would have something to say anent Folkestone and environs, or Defoe. . . .

And so, surrounded by new legions of dusty books, he began his holiday by the sea.

Both as the son of a baronet and as a physician of some distinction, Dr. Blakiston was not accustomed to being denied a reasonable and civil request such as he had put to the man behind the locked gate of the Physic Garden. But the fellow was enamored of his own authority and refused to allow the doctor and the lady accompanying him within the garden upon any consideration or condition. A pity, for over the high wall separating the garden from Swan Walk one could not obtain any sort of view of the towering cedars to either side of the river gate. Two hundred years old they were, nearly. If a visit to Chelsea yielded no other results, there would have been a satisfaction in having made the acquaintance of two such venerable trees. But Dr. Blakiston was not one to brood upon symbolic injuries: the fellow was only performing his duty, after all. It was perhaps as well that mere curiosity-seekers be excluded from the grounds, since they could not but hinder the Physic Garden's established purpose as a source of botanical specimens and *materia medica* for the Apothecaries' Society. Dr. Blakiston's philosophy, while not one deeply meditated, was one that reconciled him very well to everyday disappointments.

His lady companion, a modestly pretty woman in her fifties, dressed in black (with crapes), meanwhile, was conducting an argument with herself beneath the ineffectual protection of a pagoda-shaped parasol. Sometimes she told herself: *I can. I must. I shall. Having come so far, I cannot turn back now.* But then she would remind herself that, indeed, she *could* turn back, that the whole idea of visiting the Carlyles was a folly and futility. Twenty-eight years had passed: Mrs. Carlyle would not remember her. She had been the lady's servant, not her friend (though a part of the old Bessy protested that she *had* been her friend). Was it not vanity that prompted her now to want to flaunt the match she was about to achieve, a match so far above her reasonable expectations? Poor Bessy Barnet, who had been ruined by Dr. Baddams, was now to be Dr. Mrs. Blakiston. There were few remaining in the world who knew the circumstances of her youthful disgrace except the Carlyles: was this visit, then, a way to lay that old ghost? If only she could be sure of her own motives. It had seemed so clear while the miles still stretched out between herself and London: an impulse of kindness, a glow of long-remembered gratitude, a dim concern for Jane's well-being (for if she'd been so prone to sickness at thirty-three, how would she fare now at sixty-one?), but here on the old streets the clarity of distance was gone; instead, this ever-shifting uncertainty, like the dirty waters of the Thames.

"Well, my dear, have you been able to decide?" asked Dr. Blakiston, still good-humoredly.

"I'm sorry." She shook her head in self-reproach. "Something tells me I shouldn't. Not today. And not in this dress, the dress was a mistake. She'll think I've come to show it off!" A smile, at once melancholy and coquettish, played across her lips. "I suppose I've come to show *you* off, really."

"And why should you not, my dear? The Lord knows I have shown you off frequently enough. It is a legitimate pleasure for a betrothed person. Yet, if you have had second thoughts, another day will serve as well as this." He paused for a moment. They were standing now at the corner of Swan Walk and the Queen's Road. To turn left, in the direction of the charming prospect of aged trees and the river, promised a glimpse of Bessy's past, familiar vistas, faces grown old but still recognizable, landmarks appointed by the heart; to turn right meant to deny the eye its several near-won prizes, hurrying up the Queen's Road to Sloane Square and away. The elderly physician cleared his throat. "I have heard tell that the Cremorne Gardens serve an excellent tea in pleasant surroundings. Shall we?"

Her smile was instantaneous and bore the satisfaction of relief.

"I daresay the gatekeeper there will accept my shillings."

Miss Jewsbury had opened the two windows of her room from need of air, but then drawn the curtains to restrict its flow, reasoning that the outside air might be the cause for her eyes' hurting so—despite that she wore dark-tinted spectacles and a blue eyeshade. The sensation was neither a burning nor an itching quite, but rather one of dryness, intense pressure, abrasion. With the deadline for her review so close upon her, she could not take off time for a nap: it must be at the offices of *The Athenaeum* no later than Monday morning, and the second of the two novels still waited, all unread, beside her bed.

She'd misplaced her small supply of cigarettes—or run out altogether. She could not remember. Her nervous ink- and nicotine-stained fingers searched among the litter of papers on her writing table, earlier drafts of reviews and readers' reports for Bentley; letterless envelopes, and here, in its place of honor at the right-hand corner, exempted from the other clutter, *his* latest letter.

It bore the neat handwriting, one would think, of a cautious person, and had been franked in New Zealand. There were other, similar letters about, indeed rather a number, though nothing like the profusion she had written to him. He, Walter Mantell, was her "Matara" (the closest New Zealand's Maori natives could come to pronouncing his surname), while she, having passionately requested her own exotic pet name, became "Manu" or bird. She could never wholly accept his not returning her love, though three years had passed now since that matter had been so exhaustively considered. She touched the brittle paper and wondered: Was it only compassion, courtesy, idleness that drew him out?

Dipping her pen, once again, into the battered silver inkwell, she continued where she had left off: ". . . talks a great deal too much, wearies the reader, and is a great clog on the pleasure of reading the book." She paused—dipped the pen again, and proceeded to scratch out all she had written.

After having snuffed out the single candle, she removed both spectacles and shade (for they too made her hot) and, like someone quite mad, she stooped down to the floor to tuck her head between the curtains and the open window, eyes tight shut, wiping away a rash display of tears. What would any sensible person think, happening to pass through Markham Square and view her displayed thus—an elderly, overweight, distraught child. It was a day for Ilkely, the hydropathic establishment on the Yorkshire moors, surely. If only there were time.

A Friday like other Fridays that summer in Chelsea: bumble bees among the trellised roses of a back garden, milk spoiled before noon, horses' dung baking in the sun, and then at ten minutes past four a shower. The rain obliged Jimmy Whistler to take shelter for its duration under the arch near the Old Church, where he discussed the chemistry of mud with a washerwoman. He noticed, while she spoke, how in profile her chin was exactly the chin of his mother. A day, one might think, of no importance, yet no day passes that does not, somehow (or in some far-away place), add its distinctive and shapely detail to the broad mural of History. An ocean away from London, the inhabitants of another city (Whistler's mother among them) on another river breathed their first cautious sighs of relief as it became clear that Lee's army had succeeded in repelling McClellan's invading forces—at what cost of life none knew better that morning than Mrs. Whistler's younger son, who tended the maimed and the dying in a Richmond hospital.

There is, however, another history less grand but no less significant; it is not constituted of monolithic basalt blocks of victory and defeat but is a composite of leaves and pebbles and broken bricks, of vagrant moments that somehow impinge on a single consciousness and form by slow accretions the spiritual monuments of nations. A shot may be fired, not on the field of battle but by a gamekeeper sighting a rabbit on the weedy bank of an inland river. The shot is wild, the rabbit runs some fifty yards in panic terror, then (pausing for only a moment) darts down its hole into those dark intricacies that the rabbit's indelible image (bringing to mind some painting by Landseer) will in time elicit from the imagination of the bemused Charles Lutwidge Dodgson.

Dodgson, in white straw hat and white flannel trousers, did sense, however, even in that first glimpse, some inner congruence between the vision and his favorite child-friend Alice. Many times already she had figured as the heroine in tales he'd improvised for her entertainment, so that she had become, most certainly, his muse. He, the Dodo of their last outing's fairy tale (for D-d-dodgson was afflicted with a stammer), would place Alice in the most extraordinary situations (in defiance, usually, of one or more laws of nature, while proving a principle in logic). She was not like any of the other children whom he had entertained in this wise. In the eyes of Alice Pleasance Liddell was a candor surpassing that of all other children, an ability to surrender her innermost self to the world of imagination—and still to go one step beyond. There were times when her spirit did not seem earthbound, when he believed that she had been born free of any stain of original sin, that she could see, with earthly eyes, the naked soul. This was a fancy which pure Anglican orthodoxy must, of course, disallow, but Dodgson was not one of those ministers of the Gospel, so common of late, who disturb their consciences with scruples as to Faith and Doubt.

Across chessboard and croquet landscapes peopled with Queens and Knights, their animals animated by conundrums in logic, and with manifold grotesque metamorphoses of the redoubtable Prickett, the dread governess of the Liddell nursery, Dodgson's stories moved. They continued endlessly. Or as endlessly as the stories told to King Shahryar by the beautiful and wily Scheherezade. And again, today, as the small boat passed up the Isis with its party of five—Dodgson, Alice, and their three chaperones (Alice's not much older sister Lorina, the younger Edith, and Dodgson's colleague at Oxford, Duckworth—the "Lory," "Eaglet," and "Duck" of their latest adventure)—Alice insisted that he take up the thread of "the story about Alice."

It was five o'clock, and nothing of the day's heat, or of its brightness, had abated. Mrs. Liddell, wife of "the Greek lexicon Dean" and mother of Lorina, Alice, and Edith, was pacing from the sitting room of the Deanery to the dining room, thence to the hallway, and back to the sitting room, circuit upon circuit, meditating all the while upon her cause for alarm—for today there was little to be done but pace the carpet. Had she spoken to the Dean of her misgivings, he would have dismissed them with a peremptory "Rubbish!" And so she'd said nothing. For how could such a thing be said? Certain phantoms of the imagination resist all summonings to become manifest.

But the letters! Had she dared to show them to her husband there would be no question of "suspicion"! But the Dean was immured in the running and the rituals of the College and saw his children only through a haze of other concerns. Now it was too late—the letters had been destroyed: in her own unthinking anger, she'd burned them in the nursery grate. And afterwards she'd spoken to Dodgson: the look he'd given her—like a rabbit about to dart into its hole! The fear.

But what she hadn't seen then was the cunning of the man. Though, in retrospect, it was clear how he had always been duplicitous. His pretended interest in Prickett, his praise for her "attainments." Yet all the while, even then, he had been engaging Alice—a child!—in fantasies . . . unspeakable. Gross innuendoes. Horridness.

And now. Now he had her to himself again.

If only she had had the presence of mind, when he had asked, to invent some plausible reason why he might *not* take them out boating on the Isis. Prohibit it on the pretext of his having let them be drenched on the last expedition. But no. Cunningly he had kept his proposal of another boating trip in abeyance until just the moment. At the reception after Duckworth had been singing. In Duckworth's presence, amid the hyperbole and fuss. Cleverly including Duckworth in the plan—*and* in the presence of the Dean. Put her foot down? How could she?

So Alice was his, and no telling *what* the result of it might be.

# CHAPTER SEVENTEEN

# The Lexicon, the Leprechaun, the Dragon, and the Drone

## 12 MAY 1863

### 1

Rossetti rolled over onto his back and by a wiggling motion of his head shaped a more accommodating hollow in his pillow. How if he painted a "Death of Dante"? On the steps, it might be, of Ravenna Cathedral, or better, before one of its ancient mosaics; but no, his namesake had died a lingering death, and therefore certainly in bed. It would have been a stately bed, doubtless, a fourposter large as this, the wood carved and gilt. Might the spirit of Beatrice be present? Again, no—it wouldn't do to suspend a woman, albeit a spirit, from the rafters of a bedchamber. Angels were another matter. But he could see the picture literally visible as Macbeth's knife, or like the synopia of a fresco roughed in on the white plaster of the bedroom ceiling: Dante *en déshabille*, Beatrice in crimson and green, the dying poet's son propped respectfully in one corner (young Knewstub might pose for that), cradling the completed manuscript of the *Commedia*. A pretty thought. Perhaps.

But a better idea, surely, would be Dante on the actual morning of his thirty-fifth birthday, respectable in the robes of his civic authority. He would have come to visit Beatrice's grave in the nave of whatever chapel in Florence (he'd have to find out); to Dante's left his own Beatrice, aged five or six, kneeling at her mother's side—the daughter rapt in prayer, the wife waiting resignedly for her husband to finish his visit of duty. And behind the three, primitive frescoes: perhaps a portion of a Last Judgment. Frescoes would not present so great an obstacle to his brush as mosaics.

A distinct possibility. But he could not *see* it: light shone too strong upon the ceiling, or possibly his mind was now too wide awake. Half-closing his eyes hardly helped: no forms grouped themselves on the blank canvas of fancy. At night it was always so much easier to summon up the spirits of not-yet-painted paintings. Was it the darkness? Or being at the edge of sleep's *selva oscura*?

He would put it to the test. He would paint the ceiling black! Or an exceedingly dark blue without the distraction of stars (unlike Topsy's contribution to the Oxford Union's ceiling). The very thought brought him directly back to a radical black—from the paneling up—and heavy velvet draperies over the windows, enclosing the bed. He would have a kind of cave, a crypt, fit for one of Mr. Poe's frail, foredoomed heroes.

And if it did not serve the purpose, he would have it all painted white again.

He reached behind his head and tugged the tassel of the bell pull, then with a sigh surrendered the warmth of his bedclothes for waistcoat, trousers, and jacket, huffing as he bent forward to lace his boots and encountered the cumbersome bulk of his own stomach. There was a rapping on the door, and when he went out into the uncurtained Maytime glare of the breakfast room four brilliant yolks gazed up at him from four limpid (and still rather liquid) whites. Steam flowered from the spout of the china pot. He poured himself a cup, tasted it, and wolfed down the four eggs; only then, with his unused knife, did he slice open the letter from his mother, which was all that had come in the morning's post. She wished him a happy birthday and hinted that he ought to return the photograph of old Cairo he had expropriated from her parlor to serve as a model for his Troy. Now Troy glowed complete, down to the last bright flame that leapt from a ship at anchor in its bay, but Helen, whose beauty was the proximate cause of the ship's launching and later combustion, wanted some final modulation. Annie would come round in the afternoon to sit, et cetera, and as it was Monday, George would stop by in the evening, and William as well. He would tell Mrs. Weir to bake a good Madeira cake (despite her already proven disability to produce even a passable Victoria sponge). He would tell Knewstub to begin painting the bedroom at once. He would fill the hours of his birthday so full of eventfulness that the blue devils of boredom would not be audible anywhere in Chelsea. He would thrive.

The two Walters, Knewstub and Greaves, had met in the course of Rossetti's one excursion on the Thames. Meredith, after scolding Rossetti all winter for his obesity (which was blamed at mealtimes on his diet and at other times on lack of exercise), had organized a boating party on the first plausible day in March. Meredith, an accomplished oarsman, had taken charge of the boat with William and Fanny, while Knewstub had gone with his mentor and the boy (the other Walter, Walter Greaves) in charge of renting the boats. For five minutes Rossetti had rowed with fierce, uncoordinated energy and then, collapsing, had left it to his assistant and the boatman's boy to keep pace with Meredith and his brother as far upstream as the leafless grounds of Cremorne Gardens.

Twice since the outing Knewstub had stopped at the Greaveses' boatyard and chatted with the fellow, who, for a whelp of only seventeen, was a worldly, talkative young man (bearing in mind, always, that he was a cockney). His family had lived in the neighborhood time out of mind, and he could tell amusing stories of the days when Turner had walked these streets—and John Martin as well. Knewstub remained skeptical of some of Walter Greaves's tales, for they had the ornamented air that comes of having been told many times over. Still, he could not resist liking the boy—for he was an original. What most conduced to their friendship (though of this Knewstub was unconscious) was Greaves's quick, graceful alternations between extremes of deference and camaraderie, toadying and bluff equality, a manner (and a social strategy) that mirrored Knewstub's own, though he, with the advantage of many more years of experience, had polished his to a much higher gloss. Still the resemblance was there, and both Walters felt the peculiar fascination of finding one's self mirrored in another human being. To their credit, neither made the common mistake of confusing this fascination with love.

Further, Greaves evidenced a more than idle curiosity about painting, even spoke of "setting up in the trade" himself. Though this might seem absurd in the son of a waterman, Knewstub's own birth was not so exalted (his father was a tradesman) that he could regard young Walter's ambition as a joke. Indeed, Knewstub rather savored the

opportunity to be authoritative about art. Never mind that he had not
yet made his own way in that world (for though he was talented, he'd
come to a sense of artistic vocation in late youth); never mind that he
was the unpaid (even—ignominy!—the paying) assistant of a man
only three years older than himself. In the eyes of Walter Greaves,
Knewstub was a person of consequence, a former student at the Royal
Academy school, the intimate acquaintance not merely of one man of
acknowledged genius but, through him, of a whole parliament of
notables. Knewstub had even dined with some of these, both artists
and patrons, when there had been a chair to be filled at the table. As to
the exact nature of his relations with Rossetti, Knewstub need not be
overprecise. He had implied to Greaves that he was, like Swinburne
and Meredith, a kind of lodger at Tudor House. There was even a sort
of truth in this, for did not the poet and the novelist both take a share
in the household expenses? Admittedly *they* were not obliged to labor
long hours copying the great man's masterpieces, nor set to such in-
glorious tasks as this business now of painting the bedroom. But as to
that, it would be enough to tell Greaves that it was Rossetti's birthday
and that he was undertaking to transform his bedroom as a surprise.

When Knewstub approached him, sitting among the beached hulks
of his father's boats, Greaves was only too happy to surrender the
responsibility of the boatyard into his older brother's hands and set off
to Tudor House for what Knewstub assured him would be a lark. The
proffered wages were trifling—four shillings for a full day's work. For
Greaves the attraction was simply the gratification of a curiosity that
had become almost passionate. Since the painter had moved into the
neighborhood last October, the stories circulating in the *Adam and
Eve* and the *King's Head* concerning his carryings-on had become
steadily odder and more outrageous. To be invited to enter Rossetti's
inner sanctum was not an opportunity Greaves could refuse. As for the
money, he supposed Knewstub was pocketing part of his wages, but
that was simply the way of things. Not for a moment had Greaves
given credence to Knewstub's claims to equality with the other denizens of Tudor House, who were all of them, in their loose, sloppy, new-
fashioned way, swells of varying degrees of heaviness, while Knewstub
was clearly in the category of flunky. Greaves supposed him to be a
bohemian sort of valet with a subsidiary knack for sketching faces. He
would have been shocked to learn the truth Knewstub was so careful to
conceal—that he paid for the privilege of being Rossetti's lackey.

The work of preparing the bedroom was already in progress when they arrived with the buckets of paint they'd mixed in the washroom. The bed had been stripped, its mattress protected by a huge and unattractive old counterpane evidencing a history of other, brighter house-paintings. The lighter furniture had been moved into the adjoining breakfast room. Only the walls remained dressed in their accustomed attire of small watercolor drawings in plain oak frames. Greaves, who had never seen Rossetti's work before, assumed these to be a sampling. Knewstub watched, blank-faced, as the younger man studied one and then another. As Greaves's dismay grew, so did the need to deny it. At last he burst out with what he hoped would pass muster as praise, that the drawings were done "by a real poet," but this equivocation did not conceal his true opinion, that they were not the work of a painter.

Knewstub nodded. "Lizzie *was* poetical. It shows in everything."

"Lizzie?"

"His wife, that was. He was married, you know, before he came to live here."

"Yes, I'd heard something of a marriage," Greaves blurted out, then blushed for it, since the only knowledge he could have had of Rossetti's marriage, other than what Knewstub might let drop, was the pub talk of the neighborhood. "But only that Mr. Rossetti took it very deeply, when his missus died," he added. In fact, what he'd heard was that Rossetti's wife had taken her own life with laudanum, and that the coroner's jury had papered this over with the fiction that her death had come by mischance. Such had been the tale purveyed by a couple who'd served at Tudor House last autumn. However, as they had been fired within weeks of their hiring, their testimony was not above suspicion.

"It was a great tragedy, her dying so young," Knewstub said, with the professional *gravitas* of the better sort of undertaker. "But she'd been consumptive since she was just a girl, so I've heard. I never met her myself, though I was with Gabriel the very night she died."

"Truly?"

Knewstub began gathering the dead Mrs. Rossetti's watercolors from the wall. "Truly. They'd been to dinner at a new restaurant in Leicester Square—the three of them, for Mr. Swinburne was with them that night. Mr. Swinburne was as fond of Lizzie, you know, as her own husband, and went about with them everywhere like a member of the family. Though there was never, you know . . . anything improper."

Walter nodded soberly.

"But that's neither here nor there," Knewstub went on. "After the dinner Gabriel took Lizzie home alone, and then he set off for the Working Men's College on Great Ormond Street. It was a Monday night, you see."

"He taught there?" Greaves asked.

"He was the best teacher they ever had," Knewstub averred with real faith. "Miles ahead of Ruskin. I've had them both, and there's no comparing. Ruskin has a wonderful, smooth line of talk, but it hasn't much to do with the real work of painting pictures. It's as though he was writing his books aloud. In practical matters there was no one come up to Mr. Rossetti." Knewstub, in his sincere idolatry, did not even notice that he'd lapsed from the familiarity of "Gabriel." "Color!" he went on. "Rossetti is the King of Color. You should see him sometime matching a particular tone from a few ha'penny oils. No approximatings, never a dab more than's wanted: just bang on target every time. Amazing man."

"I *would* like to see that," said Greaves wistfully.

"It's a shame he's stopped teaching," Knewstub agreed with patronizing earnestness. "I suppose there's still profit to be had going to the Working Men's College. Brown's a good teacher for drawing, though he will make you swot with his plumblines and his thumb-measurings. I dare say we all have to go through that. But with Rossetti . . ." He sighed, and removed the last of the watercolors from the wall.

Feeling amply fed with this much gossip (but with every intention of gathering more), Walter Greaves dipped a wide brush into the bucket of blue-black paint. Then, with a delicious sense of sacrilege, he slashed a rough horizontal bar of darkness across the yellowing plaster wall.

He was not, after all, in a frame of mind to return to Troy. The sunlight entered the studio too pleasantly and refused to accommodate itself to the turbid twilight that his Helen's head inhabited. Nor was Annie disposed, on such an afternoon, to calm herself to the condition of statuary. For an hour he drew desultorily, while Annie adopted a succession of poses all expressive of Sabbath-like impatience and constraint. At last, yielding to necessity, they made love on the sagging holland-covered sofa, a relic cadged from the library of Grandfather Polidori. Annie, still in a contrary mood, lay back languid as a lily on a pool—until he thought to tickle her. Whenever she was tickled, Annie indulged in the same happy mock hysterics that his sister Christina had given in to in the long-lost era of giggles and pinches, riddles and puns. Annie would curl herself into a ball and wrap her arms about her legs so as to prevent his fingers from approaching the zones of greatest hilarity. After such therapy, Annie replied to his ardor with ardor of her own, though she would never be swept away as Fanny was at times, closing her eyes to enter the realm of delectable inwardness. It was rather as though Annie sought, wide-eyed, in each embrace, some evasive substance—some essence of joy—neither of them could name, though each believed at last to be discoverable were they to consummate a perfect union. It was the sharing of this faith that had made it impossible to break with Annie, though the liaison had cost him the friendship of Hunt and the censure of most of his acquaintances— whomever he'd allowed within the high walls of his privacy.

No such exception was taken to his more comfortable and quasi-matrimonial arrangement with Fanny—except, oddly, by Swinburne, who, while he was willing to entertain the possibility of Vice, could not bear to associate it with such quotidian realities as Fanny's soiled slippers lying in the corner of a room, or the sight of her slowly combing her hair as he declaimed his poems. Doubtless it was her sincere, uncalculating indifference to his art he could not tolerate. She was equally indifferent to Rossetti's paintings, even his many portraits of herself, but Rossetti was proof against the opinions of women in the matter of his art. How, after all, should a woman (except she be as wanton as Annie) be able to recognize in his Helens and Lucretias, his Venuses and Liliths, the meaning they conveyed to the least reflective man? that these were the embodiments not of woman's nature but of man's desire, their parted lips promising the brief eternity of what Rossetti, not quite candidly, called a "kiss":

> *At length their long kiss severed, with sweet smart:*
> *And as the last slow sudden drops are shed*
> *From sparkling eaves when all the storm has fled,*
> *So singly flagged the pulses of each heart.*

Like a kind of envoi to their intercourse, the lines of his sonnet tolled in his mind, telling the plain truth of every tryst's tristesse.

Lines that would never, sad to say, reverberate in any mind but his own and such of his friends who had read and still remembered—gone now, literally, to the tomb, dedicated to oblivion. Lovely word, oblivion. How if he painted the moment when Dante, on the summit of Mount Purgatory, swoons into the stream of Lethe, unable to bear the contrast between his own remembered sins and the sight of Beatrice transfigured?

"Gabriel?" Annie brushed his disordered hair out of his eyes.

"Mm?"

"I've got to be off, love."

"No, wait. The light is right for your hair now."

"I promised to be at Boyce's at four thirty, and if I come much later the light'll be spent. So I must."

"Five minutes," he said, pulling on his trousers and crossing to his easel. "And then I'll pay for a hansom."

Annie sighed, flexed her back, and submitted to the pleasant necessity of indolence, while Gabriel, with the quick automatism of an old woman knitting the simplest of stitches, mixed on his muddied palette the precise five colors of Helen of Troy's hair.

Escaping to his own bare bedroom from the fumes of the paint, Knewstub was in time to see Rossetti and his model pass through the paved courtyard of Tudor House and out through the tall iron gate. Now was the moment, if ever, to take young Greaves into Rossetti's studio. No one need know and no harm could come of it. They had to clear their heads somehow, and better the studio than to ask the fellow in here to witness the marks of his penury and the meager fruits of his own artistry—a *Gypsy Maiden*, an *Ophelia and Laertes*, a *View of the Thames*. The last was, in fact, the view from this very window, and rather suffered by too close comparison with its original. The hesitantly rendered trees warred with the broad opaque swathes of water. The wharf seemed to have wandered here from another painting; the boats on the bank to float some few inches above the mud. The sky, striving to be limpid, looked like a high blue wall. Landscape was not Knewstub's métier.

As they descended Tudor House's single stairway—a narrow, meanly carpentered contrivance much out of keeping with its well-proportioned Georgian amplitude—Knewstub cautioned Greaves not to touch the railing or anything in the studio with his paint-stained hands.

The strong north light, softened and diffused by the spring foliage of the garden, gave the oddly shaped room the air of a chapel, though a chapel celebrating profane rather than sacred love.

"Blimey," said Walter Greaves, with the utter candor of his seventeen years; and again, approaching nearer the easel which supported Rossetti's *Helen*: "Bly-*mee*."

"She's a stunner, in't she," Knewstub agreed.

"It's old Annie Miller, from the *Cross Keys*."

"You know her?" Knewstub asked skeptically.

"Oh, the whole village knows Annie Miller. Her father's a pensioner up in the barracks, you know. Or was, till he passed on. Well, I'll be blowed." Then, adjusting his manner more to Knewstub's sense of the decorous, much as he might hike up his trousers when they rode down off his hips, he observed: "I'm glad to see Annie looking so prosperous. There was a time when she had taken up with another bloke, likewise a painter, and there was talk she was going to be his wife, but he went off to Egypt—so I heard. I was just a lad, but I remember thinking how I should like to see Egypt and the Plagues. And why's this here behind her, the burning ship?"

"She's meant to be Helen of Troy."

Greaves nodded and smoothed his downy moustache with a knowing finger until he remembered the condition of his hands.

"It's a spiffing piece o' work," he announced, after further study. He moved to another painting and made an appreciative purr. "This as well, though it's strange, in't it? Seems to glow like gaslight."

"That's Lizzie."

"His wife as was? Why is it so misty-like compared to the other pictures? Did she die before he could finish it?"

"She died before he started it. He does it all from memory, though he has sketches to work from. There's a whole drawer in that cabinet over there with nothing but drawings of her. But as for the finish, that's deliberate."

"It's strange," Greaves insisted, and then, when this elicited no further explanations, "Does it mean something? Is she supposed to be somebody, like the other one, Helena Troy?"

"Rossetti calls it *Beata Beatrice*. Beatrice was the woman Dante loved as a young man, and this is supposed to show her in a kind of death trance."

"That's 'is name, in't it—Dante?"

"It was his middle name, but lately he's turned the order round, that's true. His father was a great Dante scholar, and over the years Gabriel's painted several pictures of Dante and Beatrice, though this one is . . . well, it's hard to say the *best* . . . perhaps what you said—the strangest."

"And that red bird with the flower in its beak—is that a part of the story I ought to know?"

Knewstub equivocated tactfully. "It relates, I think, to Lizzie's story, more than to Beatrice's. The flower is a poppy."

Greaves refused to draw the inference. "A poppy," he repeated blankly.

"Poppies are the source, you know, of opiates. Mrs. Rossetti died of taking an excess of laudanum."

"By mischance, was it?"

"A coroner's jury thought so, though in the nature of these things, I don't suppose one is ever completely sure. She'd seemed very gay that night, Mr. Swinburne says. But she had a vein of . . . is it fair to call it morbidity? You saw her watercolors. Whether by mischance or by her own hand, the tragedy for Mr. Rossetti has been the same. He takes it very hardly."

Greaves glanced sidelong at the portrait of Annie Miller in classical décolletage, then at the other similarly opulent denizens of Rossetti's studio. They were, he would admit, a rather melancholy lot, but there are many men who fancy them quiet and mysterious, just as there are men who fancy them plump and jolly. What was clear to Walter Greaves (clearer probably than to Rossetti's patrons) was that all these beauties were being offered for the same sort of admiration as the can-can dancers in the tent at Cremorne or the beauties leaning from the windows of waiting cabs in the Haymarket. *Look at me*, each one insisted. *Imagine my kiss.*

## 2

Whether in conscious mockery of *The Awakened Conscience* or simply because the logic of furnishing a small parlor leads inexorably to a single conclusion, Fanny's parlor in her own little mews cottage at 36, Royal Avenue, was a virtual replica of the parlor in Hunt's painting—especially on a sunny spring day such as this. It might have been accounted a clear instance of nature imitating art but for the great likelihood that Fanny had never seen the painting in question. True—Gabriel had, and it was Gabriel who'd provided the large gilt mirror and the little glass-domed timepiece on the spinet, but it was Fanny who'd arranged all these elements in this evocative fashion.

She'd known at a glance when he'd walked into the room (for since he paid the rent he felt dispensed from the necessity of knocking) that his call was prompted by sociability more than desire. This was regrettable in a way, since it reflected on the perishableness of her charms, but it also was more comfortable not to be ever awaiting summons. Their relationship extended beyond the customary bounds of man and mistress, artist and model, even of householder and housekeeper (for Fanny spent much more time at Tudor House, directing—and assisting —the servants, than she did in her own little cottage). Mondays, however, were Fanny's day away from Tudor House, for the evident though unspoken reason that they were Meredith's day in residence. Fanny did not like George Meredith.

Rossetti, in the spirit of his own birthday, had bought a present for Fanny when passing through Sloane Square, after he'd dispatched Annie Miller into a hansom. Fanny took off its wrappings with an obliging sense of drama, and when it was quite unwrapped showed herself suitably mystified. It was a book without words—just one creamy-white blank page after another. Suitable, possibly, for someone as little inclined to read as Fanny, but still . . .

"What's it for, then?" Fanny demanded, with the glint of a smile, as though asking the answer to a riddle certain to be amusing.

"It is an album. Every young lady of the better sort has one, you know. Especially young ladies in literary circles."

"But what is it *for?*" she insisted.

"Why, for visitors to sign. And if they are writers, or clever, then you must insist—as those young ladies do—that they write you a sonnet, or at the very least a couplet, of polite compliment."

"Then—" She plumped the book squarely in his lap. "—*you* be the first. And nothing you know by 'eart, mind. Make it something you never writ before—and put my name in it."

"As my lady commands." From the inner pocket of his jacket Rossetti removed a fat black fountain pen, took off the cap, and wrote quickly and without a single pause, in a flowing hand across the first page of the album. Finishing, he handed the album back to Fanny and bade her read the verses aloud.

*"May the god of visitations*
*Send you callers from all nations—*
*Poles and Frenchmen suave and dapper,*
*From the wilds of Illinois a trapper,*
*Scotsmen staunch and Irish sturdy,*
*And sometimes a hurdy-gurdy,*
*But may your doorway never darken*
*Or your ears be made to hearken*
*To visits of Ruskins*
*In . . . "*

She faltered.

" 'Tragedy buskins,' " Rossetti prompted.

She continued:

*"In tragedy buskins*
*For he is such a twit, and a prig, and a bore.*
*This, for Fanny, I implore!"*

After an appreciative chuckle, Fanny asked, "What is 'tragedy buskins,' then?"

"It used to be when actors were playing in tragedies they'd wear a special sort of footgear to make them taller and nobler-looking. Now, if you say that an actor, or anyone else for that matter, is in his buskins, it's as much as to say he's ranting."

"A 'am, in other words."

"Precisely."

"Well, that's very cruel to Mister Ruskin, but I'm surely glad you didn't let 'im come and live with you." She kissed his cheek in thanks for the present, which she placed on a near table and promptly forgot forever.

"Has 'e been bothering you again—Ruskin?"

"No, he's become quite cool to me since I said he could not be adopted into our little family. He was dead-earnest to do so. But can you imagine what that would have been like? How he'd have hectored and bullied and wanted to manage us all? It's quite bad enough when he's in Chamonix and must rely on the post to instruct me in my everyday duties—to have him actually here in the house!"

"Well, I know 'e thinks I'm a evil influence. . . ."

"Oh Fanny, he was always careful to say it wasn't of *you* he disapproved per se, but rather your modeling for me. You were not—I believe his phrase was—'an elevated subject.'"

"But for all that, you know, I can't 'elp feeling sorry for 'im. 'E's like these preachers what go round rescuing fallen women—whether they wants it or not. So shy, but so sure of themselves too. It's funny, in't it, about writers and painters?"

"How's that?"

"Well, Ruskin is a writer, and 'is wife leaves 'im to run off with that John Millais, and it's the same all over with Meredith and '*is* wife. And I'll say, if it'd been me as married either o' them, I'd of done just the same. There is something so much *kinder* in painters, some'ow. I always thought 'Enry Wallis was, leastwise, though I never sat for 'im but the once."

"And what of me, then? Do you think of me as a writer or as a painter?"

"Oh, no doubt about you, love. You're a painter. And if I was a writer, and 'ad a pretty wife, I should be sure to keep 'er at a safe distance too."

An uncomfortable silence ensued.

"Someone must 'ave just walked on me grave," said Fanny brightly.

"Or on mine perhaps," said Rossetti.

"Something is eating at you, Rissetty. And if you 'adn't come 'ere particular to tell me of it, then you wouldn't be throwing out 'ints. What was that little poem you was telling me—not yours but that friend of yours, Mr. Gilchrist."

"Gilchrist? He's no poet, Fanny. You must mean Blake. Gilchrist was editing an edition of Blake when he died, since when I've been helping his widow finish his work."

"Blake, Gilchrist, whichever one, you said 'e was the poet most like you that ever lived 'ere in London, though the poem wasn't much like yours, more like what people remember for adages. It was about your being angry."

> "I was angry with my friend,
> I told my wrath, my wrath did end.
> I was angry with my foe:
> I told it not, my wrath did grow."

"That's the one."

"God knows, Fanny, it's true enough."

"Then tell me 'ow I've offended, love."

"Oh, good Lord, Fanny, it isn't you. Though the poem comes aptly enough. It's bloody Meredith, against whom my wrath has grown . . . beyond the point, I think, where the mere telling of it will put an end to it."

"I said, didn't I, that you'd 'ave trouble with that one? What did 'e do?"

"Remember two weeks back, when I got up that dinner for Leathart and Rose?"

"And 'ung those nice chintzes, oh yes. That was the Wednesday Tim came round 'ere, drunk as a rolling fart, and all but stole the clock off the mantel: would 'ave, if I 'adn't given 'im what-for. 'E thinks, 'cause 'e's made me an honest woman, that 'e can come and rob me blind whenever 'e goes off the rails. Men." Fanny shook her head in complacent reprobation. "But you was saying, about your dinner."

"Oh, it doesn't concern you, Fanny."

Fanny dismissed this with a wave of the hand.

"Well, in a nutshell then, what happened was that Meredith was there too, though Wednesday is not his usual day in town. Some ten of us all told. And I laid on a smashing dinner, served up on the best pieces I had. It was a feast out of the Arabian Nights, if I do say so myself. And all the while I could tell that Meredith was fretting that we were dining in *his* sitting room. He's only there, after all, one day of the week, and it is the most commodious room in the house, except for my studio, and I couldn't very well serve the dinner there. Well, as the evening wore on, we started, naturally enough, to talk turpentine. Boyce started in on Ned Jones, who'd just sold a painting to Old Man Ruskin—"

"'As 'e? Good for Ned!"

"—and Boyce was telling of how once, when he went round to Ned's studio, he'd said—as a joke of course, quoting the sort of things they say about us in the newspapers, that he had just begun to fill up an empty canvas with 'flagrant violation of perspective and drawing, and crude inharmonious color.' Which is the sort of thing Ned will say when he's feeling inharmonious himself. But then Meredith takes it up seriously, and says that that's the problem with modern painting generally, that we haven't received the grounding in fundamentals of the old masters, and he cites *Found* as a prime example of *my* incapacity in perspective. In front of Leathart, who's commissioned me to finish it!"

"Is that the one of me and the calf in the cart?"

He nodded. "And as though that were not damaging enough, he brings up something I said once about how I'd never been able to get the knack of painting with oils, which was once true enough, perhaps, but a look at the pictures on the wall of the room should have been sufficient to give the lie to that canard."

"I should say," said Fanny consolingly.

"He would *not* let off. Swinburne, gamely, tried to swing us round to talking of France by bringing up Jimmy Whistler—they've just come back, you know—but Meredith would not take a hint and went on ragging me."

"Oh, I'm sure no one gave 'im any 'eed, love."

"But they did, he was in good form that night."

"Sounds to me like 'e'd over'eated 'is flues."

"That was his excuse, of course, the next day. He posted me a note apologizing for 'unremembered indiscretions' and had the gall, in the same scrawl, to suggest that it might have been a case of *in vino veritas*. The apology scarce improves on the original insult, though at least he didn't publish it in *The Times*. Ye Gods."

"Well, love, all you 'ave to do is bid 'im farewell. It's your 'ouse; 'e's just a lodger, and the last you said 'e 'adn't even paid up."

"It's not as easy as that, Fanny. For one thing, he did finally settle his score and he's square till August now. For another, he did apologize, however lamely, and if Swinburne is to be forgiven his bacchanals at something like weekly intervals, then Meredith ought to be allowed a single fall from grace. After all, I do *like* the fellow. . . ."

Fanny arched a skeptical eyebrow at this, as who would say, "There's where you're wrong."

"No, truly, Fanny, I enjoy his company. When I'm not the butt of it, there's no one whose wit I more admire."

"Then you must forget and forgive, love—it's that simple. Despite what Mr. Gilchrist said in 'is poem."

"*Not* Gilchrist, Fanny—Blake, William Blake. Born 1757. Died twelfth August 1827. Nine months to the day, Fanny, on which I was born. And was there ever a more potent argument for the transmogrification of souls?"

Fanny exploded wetly into laughter. "Oh Lord, Rissetty. I swear, you must 'ave been weaned on the dictionary."

Rossetti frowned somewhat petulantly. He knew it was too much to ask of his mistress that she should appreciate the remarkable coincidence of these dates, but her laughter was nonetheless wounding to his poetic *amour-propre*.

Fanny sensed his grievance and subdued her mirth. "Happy Birthday then, Gabriel." She never used his given name except when she meant to be especially affectionate. " 'Ow old are you?"

"Thirty-five."

Fanny sighed philosophically. "Well, we're none of us getting any younger, are we?"

3

Two stops before Sloane Square the woman who had been sitting next to Meredith in the omnibus and enveloping him with her immense, encroaching skirts departed, and at once William Rossetti, who had been sitting all the while three rows back, took her place. With a smile of greeting and an inner groan (for he thought the younger Rossetti rather a dull dog), Meredith put aside the manuscript of the novel he'd been reading, a piffling, breathlessly written tale palpably derived from *Lady Audley's Secret*, which he had resolved not to recommend for publication.

Having agreed that such good weather ought not be wasted, the two men descended at Sloane Square. William paused outside the fishmonger's to light his pipe, and Meredith, inspired to remember that this evening's dinner was to be no ordinary occasion, went inside and purchased two dozen oysters, then to be on the safe side, a dozen more. He felt a pleasant moral tingle emerging with his well-wrapped (but nonetheless redolent) parcel.

They set off down the King's Road and walked past the modest terrace of houses that faced the grandiose piles of Whitelands Training College, on whose well-tended, flowery lawns a hundred or so of the future schoolmistresses of the nation strolled decoratively or sat on benches reading by the light of a sky-filling pink and gold sunset. Reaching Butterfly Alley, Meredith insisted on stopping to admire the tiers of potted plants outside Davey's, which was (unless that honor belong to Colville's across the alley) the best nursery garden in all London.

"What think you?" he asked William, as they pondered a young rhododendron. "There is that bare spot at the turn of the path in the garden. . . ."

"Yes, and the same fate that came to the rosebush will meet this, doubtless, if you plant it there: the peacocks will tear it up. It is where they like to scratch."

Meredith accepted this caution gratefully, for he had not really wanted to squander the sum likely to be asked. In any case, Rossetti was quite traditional in his floral preferences: roses and lilies.

They continued on their way southwestward.

"Oh, I have something I *must* tell you," said William Michael, clenching the stem of his pipe in a toothy smile. "The other day at the office I did something I'm sure would please you. My superior was waxing lyrical over some recent Confederate victory. He's rather an old fogey, our Brown, and with a sneaking partiality for the Southern cause, which he won't bring quite candidly into the open. Instead he will wonder aloud as to whether the Nigger is in fact gifted with an immortal soul like to our own. Rather in the vein of Carlyle, I always think, though I'm sure Carlyle wouldn't welcome comparison to such as our Brown, for he is neither a hero nor a worshipper of heroes, but rather that new breed that has eliminated the need for all heroism whatever, the breed of Members of the Board."

Meredith, feeling some response was called for, but unable to manage even the smallest chuckle, said, "Ah-ha." He regretted having got off the omnibus so early now that he sensed the dimensions of William's anecdote. Brevity was not a virtue much cultivated by the young excise officer. There was always pith to what he said, weight, merit—but no wit, and Meredith, in social moments, preferred *brio* and *allegria* to any quantity of moral earnestness.

"Well," William continued, trailing a thin cloud of tobacco smoke, "at some point in the argument, when Brown was deploring the policy of our Foreign Office in the matter of the *Alabama*, I thought to mollify him by remarking, 'In action Wisdom goes by majorities.' Brown was so struck that he asked me the source of the adage, for while it seemed quite familiar, he could not at all place it. Nor could I."

"Why, it's mine!" said Meredith, beaming satisfaction.

"Yes, as I recalled later in the day. Dutifully I went up to Brown's office to report that it was neither from Shakespeare, as he'd supposed likeliest, nor from Goldsmith, which was my guess, but rather from *The Ordeal of Richard Feverel*. Brown duly noted the title in his memorandum book, though I doubt he will go so far as to read it. To my certain knowledge he hasn't read any novel more recent than *Pickwick*."

"But how delightful to be mistaken for both Shakespeare and Goldsmith on the strength of one aphorism. I must cull out more of them and make a garland—*Meredith's Maxims for the Modern Age*, printed one to a page in a very slender duodecimo volume."

"It needn't be all that slender," said William blandly. "In *Feverel* alone there was quite a stock of maxims, adages, what have you, that have stuck in my mind like burrs—*with* their proper attributions."

"My own favorite (though as a parent I ought not to declare to having favorites) is: 'Kissing don't last: Cookery do!'"

William nodded. "Mine was, 'I expect that Woman will be the last thing civilized by Man,' though, mind you, I don't at all agree."

"Nor do I. Nor does Dickens necessarily subscribe to all the opinions of Sarah Gamp."

"There are days, Meredith—" William removed his pipe to signal the importance of what he was about to say. "—as I'm sure I have told you before, when I look up from the papers on my desk and ask myself what I am doing there. I should like to make literature my whole career, instead of a pastime. But when I read one of your novels and consider the difficulty of minting new maxims, new epigrams, new memorable phrases, I am much reconciled to my own duties."

"Few epigrams are new," said Meredith, now fairly in his stride. "They are mostly old truths, and if the world were used to honesty, no one would ever establish a reputation as a wit."

"Mm. But there is a kind of cynicism in most such sayings, and it is not enough to say that it is Sarah Gamp who speaks, and not our dear Boz. It *is* Boz. And it is you."

Meredith shrugged regally. "If it is cynical to be clear-sighted and to express concisely what one has clearly seen, then all good writers are cynics of the darkest dye."

"Is George Eliot a cynic?" William countered. "Or Carlyle?"

"No—*they* are prophets. Prophets are clear-sighted but lack brevity.

One can't presume to divine afflatus without the risk of seeming windy at times. But I don't presume to prophesy, not at least in Carlyle's grand manner. Miss Evans is, in all respects, an anomaly. To set oneself up as a moral instructor to the age all the while one lives in open adultery with a failed *philosophe*—and what's more amazing, to succeed at it! It passeth understanding."

"Agreed. But as to your novels, I'm surprised you should disclaim *any* prophetic intent. Surely you won't fob me off with saying you only write to *amuse*."

"I write," said Meredith, "for the same reason your good brother gives for his painting: need of tin."

"Bosh," said William, in the friendliest way. "And in that, my dear fellow, I include my brother."

They walked on down the King's Road as the sunset swelled to still larger dimensions, turning the bricks of the terraced houses to a dusky rose, making the flowers in the window boxes clamor for attention. But Meredith's attention was turned, for the moment, inward.

George Meredith, the handsomest English novelist of any established reputation, was a man in whom self-examination had usurped the place of conscience. Further, he knew this of himself, and deplored it. He should have liked to have been a simple, sturdy yeoman with staunch moral principles, an iron digestion (his own was finicking), and an independent income of, say, £500 a year. Self-consciousness, however, is not the same as self-knowledge, and so for all his musings on the intricate excellences and inadequacies of his own nature, the view he took of himself in the *Galerie des Verres* of his moral indignation corresponded very imperfectly to the view that others took of him, for the world (in the person, say, of William Rossetti) mainly saw Meredith as the person he wanted to be—that is, as a man of the middle class and middling sensuality, a very gentlemanly bully, and, despite all his intellectual graces, a bit of a Philistine in his heart of hearts.

Meredith, of course, was not examining himself in such fundamental and unbecoming terms. He was considering, rather, the moral dilemma posed to him by the existence of *A Woman Wronged*. Should he recommend its publication to Chapman and Hall, or should he insist on his honest conviction—that it represented the worst style of the present taste? In absolute terms there could be no question: he should consign it to a merited perdition. But he had two years ago dealt in like rhadamanthine fashion with *East Lynne*, which had gone on to earn a fortune for a publisher with a clearer eye for the public's appetite for melodrama, whatever absurd excesses it might run to. If the same thing should happen in the case of *A Woman Wronged*, Chapman and Hall might begin to have misgivings about Meredith's aptitude for the position of reader. The book was unmitigated rubbish, but the dramatis personae were similar to those of *East Lynne*—a compromised wife, a vile seducer, a noble but unforgiving husband, with the further twist, in this instance, that the wife's honor remains unstained all the while she must pretend (in order to protect her deceased mother's reputation!) to have consorted with the wicked Lord Vizard. Would not the subscribers to Mudie's Library who'd reveled in the bathos of *East Lynne* abandon themselves as shamelessly on behalf of this twaddle? And could he say so to Chapman and Hall without utterly compromising his own reputation for probity?

These questions had a way of turning round and leading back to their own beginnings, labyrinth-like, and Meredith was still groping blindly among them when he saw approaching on the King's Road from the opposite direction a figure that seemed to have been summoned up by these very deliberations, a woman set apart from all the other women up and down the King's Road (which was becoming rather a thoroughfare) not by any distinction in her attire, which was sober and genteel, nor even by the peculiarity of her dark-tinted spectacles, but rather by a certain mannishness of bearing or of gait, an air of conspicuous independence.

But perhaps this was all imagination, for Geraldine Jewsbury was, in a small way, Meredith's nemesis. She it had been who, when the manuscript of *East Lynne* had been rejected at Meredith's behest, had strenuously urged Bentley, the publisher for whom she read, to publish. Bentley had published, and the rest was history, though a history never referred to by either Meredith or Miss Jewsbury on the various occasions when the life of literature or the fact of being neighbors had brought them together. That her own novels had enjoyed a notoriety and success in their day (such as *his* novels had never known, though he'd have wagered his life that his were better) did not make her any dearer to Meredith, though in view of the common report that Miss Jewsbury had ceased to produce novels, it was hard to feel any bitterness of rivalry. Indeed, if her eyes were failing, as the dark spectacles would seem to suggest, then even the meager resource of being a publisher's reader would be denied her. A thought dark enough to bring a pang of fellow feeling to Meredith's heart when, on approaching nearer, he raised his hat and bade her good afternoon.

Some of his warmth of feeling must have penetrated to his voice, for Miss Jewsbury was disposed to stop and chat.

One of the advantages of Chelsea as against the more metropolitan districts and thoroughfares of London was a certain freedom of manners—not a bohemian disregard of decorum so much as the confidence that comes of living in a village in which all one's neighbors are known quantities, in which a woman is not compromised by the lack of a pair of gloves when she does her marketing, nor a man by the scent (and it was now quite pronounced) of the oysters he is bearing home.

"Oysters!" cried Miss Jewsbury with unfeigned enthusiasm. "Are there still oysters to be had? How splendid—ah! I see *A Wronged Woman* has found its way to your doorstep. I recognize the stain on the binding (my own spilt coffee, I believe)."

"Then you did not find this a near-equal to Mrs. Wood's masterpiece?"

"Oh my dear Mr. Meredith! Don't suppose, because I advised its publication, that I am unaware of the failings of *East Lynne*. Let us reserve such terms as 'masterpiece' for your own novels, which are not embarrassed by absolute claims."

Meredith inclined his head, accepting the compliment, which his smile, however, seemed still to call into question. "You do me too much honor, ma'am."

"On the contrary. *Feverel* is a great achievement, as I have already said in the pages of *The Athenaeum*—though I found the ending too painful to bear. I hope your next novel is not so tragic!" She smiled at William Rossetti, belatedly acknowledging him, and poked gracelessly at her snooded hair. "But I'm astonished to see you actually bearing away *A Wronged Woman* from the office."

"There were passages," said Meredith, quickly improvising a believable lie, "that I could not resist reading to my friends."

"Ah yes, the delights of bathos. I confess that I'm too susceptible to the rush of almost any story that captures my fancy to stand at the distance that laughter requires. You'll think me the veriest Philistine, but *East Lynne* did reduce me totally to tears. I'll confess, for all that, that almost the greatest charm of the book was having the honest old country lawyer who figures so largely in the story—and is such a stick!—called 'Mr. Carlyle.' I could not stop slipping the *real* Carlyle's physical presence into the role, and the whimsy of it quite conquered my judgment. I'll tell you both in confidence, *Mrs.* Carlyle, herself, found the book amusing, and solely on that account. But that will not excuse me in your eyes, I fear, for having played midwife to such rubbish."

By way of including William Rossetti in their talk, Miss Jewsbury turned the conversation toward a consideration of who had written which unsigned review in which recent periodical or newspaper, a subject on which Miss Jewsbury's conjectures (and confident misinformation) outdid those of either of her fellow reviewers. They parted with a promise on Meredith's part to call on Miss Jewsbury some day soon at her residence in Markham Square, scarce two hundred yards from where they stood, and on her part to call upon the fishmonger who had supplied Meredith with May oysters.

Sitting before the tarnished mirror, combing out the bird's-nest tangle of his hair, Algernon Swinburne felt stirrings and rumblings within of what might be either sex or poetry. As yet they were too indistinct to be certain which way they tended, and in any case he had already had excess of both this afternoon, having accomplished a sizable part of the recalcitrant third chapter of his novel, a scene at dinner in which Lord Charles is rather carried away with reminiscences of being flogged for false quantities in Latin poetry. Lord Charles's drolleries had led by insensible degrees to four pages of freely flowing verse on the same theme, and such had been the power of suggestion of his own verses that he had concluded the labors of the afternoon with some ecstatic reveries beneath the sheets of his bed, after which he had lain drowsing until he'd heard Meredith entering at the front door, neighing with laughter like one of Swift's Houyhnhnms. The chief drawback of having this bedroom was its propinquity to the entrance. Meredith's voice was soon subsumed into the house's concerted murmurs and silences, but the thought of him lingered like an unsettling odor. Indeed, Swinburne was so sure he could detect an actual smell that he put his hairbrush on the dressing table and went out, naked as he was, into the dimness of the hallway to take an investigative whiff.

He smelled the sea, his favorite smell, and returned to his room.

To do what? There had been a purpose in mind, only moments

before. To find his drawers? To write a poem? Not another epic of caning; for the while he'd rid himself of that urgency. But in the same broad vein of comedy. It was there, he could feel the rhythm of it, iambic lines freely seasoned with anapests. But there on top of *Leaves of Grass* were his drawers, and he pondered, as he pulled them on, how odd it was one so little felt the lack of a metrical interest in Whitman. A button was missing without which the drawers were no longer useful and so he dispensed with them altogether, stepping into the cruel abrasion of his trousers. Really, what need was there for drawers at all? He would wager that Whitman did not wear drawers! Perhaps he found meter similarly unessential. Surely such a treasure as "A Voice from the Sea" would not have been improved by corseting it into heroic couplets? Swinburne slipped into his shirt in the same direct spirit. It galled him, it truly did, how Meredith had been so self-righteously abusive about his simply walking from his bedroom to his sitting room without taking the trouble to wrap himself in a dressing gown. Wasn't the entire point of their sharing Tudor House that they should be free and unconstrained by such considerations? It was not as though he had indulged in some Corybantic excess—he had been searching for his notebook, and there'd been no time to piddle with dressing gowns. It was a question of class, doubtless. Not having been born to a gentleman's estate, he was overnice concerning the protocols of daily life. No wonder his wife had left him for Wallis. A prig. Yes, despite his poetry, despite his commendable zeal for the liberation of dear Italy, despite a gift for manly foolery that would have been the envy and admiration of any sixth former—a prig of the first water.

The poem had quite vanished, if it had ever been there, but his shirt was buttoned, and his boots were on. He went into the hall, then followed his nose onwards and downwards to the kitchen, where, prey to any passing predator, a great many oysters were heaped in a blue china bowl.

### 4

As the two widowers sat facing each other across the length of the table, with William and Swinburne between them, they constituted a kind of family, but a family in which the feminine and maternal element was unfixed and fluctuating. Rossetti and Meredith each found in the other the qualities of the missing spouse. Like Lizzie, Meredith would badger, criticize, pester, and harass—all with the lightest grace, the brightest wit, and an honest, almost evangelical urge to reform his friend's work habits, his diet, and his physical regimen. He tried to lure Rossetti along on one of his marathon walking tours, rhapsodized over the pleasures of mountaineering, and denounced Mrs. Weir's rich puddings as "sweet poisons." After each Monday that Meredith spent with him Rossetti felt he'd undergone a week of matrimony. What he most resented was Meredith's evangelizing for a strenuous life of Indian clubs, cold showers, and Spartan meals as though these pursuits were innately virtuous. To Rossetti's way of thinking such an obsessive pursuit of one's own fitness was no more inherently noble than a miser's hoarding of gold coin, and misers at least have the decency not to proselytize.

By way of retaliation Rossetti would indulge in caprices of freedom calculated to chill Meredith's conventional blood. In the first flush of tenancy he had taken to keeping peacocks and other exotic fauna in his back garden. He paid extraordinary prices for Chinese porcelain ware and insisted (correctly, as time would prove, for Rossetti was a born entrepreneur) that they were a prudent investment. Further, he would dine off his acquisitions as though they were everyday china. He bought expensive clothes and took such little care of them that anyone coming to call would not have supposed him a gentleman. Indeed, he was not a gentleman, except by virtue of his professional accomplishments—and even concerning these Meredith had his misgivings. Rossetti had taken to painting his vaunted "stunners" almost exclusively now, and while he did them very well, one had to ask whether it were an activity worthy of large artistic gifts. In these several ways Rossetti rubbed against Meredith's rawest nerve—the memory, which he could neither bury nor come to terms with, of the errant Mrs. Meredith. Being, however, a staunch believer in a double standard of morality, Meredith could not offer the same objection to Rossetti's liberties that he had to his wife's. On the contrary, there was a side of his nature that applauded, envied, and timidly would emulate Rossetti's pococurantish ease, his Falstaffian gusto.

As in most families, the two spouses contended most energetically on the battlefield of their children's lives. The only child of this union was assuredly Algernon Swinburne. William Michael Rossetti was too unalterably Gabriel's brother, though one might have thought him, from his baldness and general deportment, an older rather than a younger brother. Truly, William was so precociously grave and reverend that his role in the larger, hypothetical family seated at dinner would have to be Grandfather, all elder wisdom, quiet toleration, and doting love, tempered by occasional outbursts when his established prejudices were violated within his own purview (which, of course, the other members of the family were careful not to do).

But Swinburne's fitness for the role of child was so correspondent at so many saliencies of character that it would have been difficult to deal with him in any other wise. To begin, he was short and slight, delicate in manner, and nervous in mannerism. But for his wisp of a moustache he seemed, still, an Etonian—of one of the lower forms. Like a child he craved the perpetual attention of those about him, and like a clever child he had learned how to obtain that attention willingly. He was sprightly, charming, and given to temper tantrums and prankishness. He had been a prodigy throughout his childhood, and his intellectual character was that compound of arrogant erudition and quirky enthusiasms that is the mark of the precocious adolescent, to which was joined a rhetorical power that even Rossetti and Meredith might envy. In short, he was just the elfin child that a poet steeped in Shelley and Wordsworth might wish to have for his own, a very Ariel of a fellow —and what's more (though this was a consideration only for Meredith) the grandson of a baronet!

Time out of mind it has been the tragedy of parenthood that doting affection is not reciprocated, and so it was for Meredith, both in reality (Arthur, his son by Mary, remained obdurately unloving) and in the livelier realm of fantasy here at Tudor House. Meredith was the most indulgent of parents—a tireless listener, a jolly playfellow (within the bounds of what he allowed to be play), forgiving of peccadilloes, and able to follow the nimbly mounting flights of the poet's fancy to whatever altitudes of inspiration. Yet despite all this it was Rossetti whom Swinburne loved with a love that was filial and true, while toward himself he felt, at best, the tolerant but guarded affection due to a solicitous stepmother, who, whatever she may do, will never be asked for a kiss at the end of the day's adventures.

After the port had passed into history (there had been but half a bottle), they returned to champagne, of which Rossetti had laid in what seemed several seasons' stock, thanks (he declared) to the more generous credit made available to the tenant of Tudor House—or

"Queen's House," as he gave it out to shopkeepers. The conversation had turned, mellowly, to childhood, of which Gabriel and his brother shared a stock of anecdotes as inexhaustible as the champagne. Gabriel told of how he'd imagined a spectral Dante Alighieri haunting the darker corners of the staircase of their home on Charlotte Street and how his father's copy of *La Vita Nuova* had seemed to glow with its own eerie light (for Dante and his endless conundrums of allegoric meaning had been his father's hobbyhorse before his own).

William recalled to mind the table, now resident here in his own bedroom, which had been the cave of Gabriel, the dragon, and from which he had threatened his sister Christina (Maria, the eldest, had refused to be terrified).

In the course of this reminiscence Swinburne had exclaimed, "The Dragon!" in a tone suitable and only comparable to a cry of "Eureka!" —and at once excused himself from the room and the danger (to him ever a real one) of indulging too far.

This placed an added burden on Meredith's already uncomfortable shoulders. Childhood was not his favorite theme. Though in most well-bred company there might have been little to choose, in terms of respectability, between a father who had been a professor of Italian and a father who had been a tailor, Meredith remained sensitive on the point of his origins. Yet it would not do too violently to veer from the course that had been determined, so when his own turn came round he was prepared with an anecdote of schooldays in Lowestoft, when he would escape the dullness of the Sunday sermons by inventing chivalrous adventures for a rather unsaintlike St. George. William noted wryly that it had been providential for the dragon under the table that he'd never ventured so far afield as Lowestoft.

Chivalry itself then became their theme, and Swinburne returned with an ostentatious folding of paper and tucking it into an inside coat pocket. Most uncharacteristically, when asked what he had written, he was coy but firmly unforthcoming.

"Nothing at all," he insisted, pouring himself a fresh glass of champagne and spilling an equal quantity on the damask cloth. "A note to myself when I wake in the morning and am *moi-même encore. Mais continuez: la courtoisie défraye la conversation.* I say, Meredith, do *you* suppose Walt Whitman wears drawers?"

"Algernon . . ."

"Very well, if chivalry is our theme (and not linen), say why it is that the legends of chivalry are so taken up with forbidden love. I've often asked myself the question; now I put it to you."

"Are they?" asked William. "So taken up, I mean?"

"There is Morris's *Defense of Guinevere*. There is Tennyson's *Idylls*. There is my own *Tristram*, if I am ever able to write it. All the protocols of chivalry concern nothing but the behavior of a gentleman toward someone else's wife—usually his suzerain's. Or the behavior of the injured husband. Think of what Arthur suffered in that not at all joyous regard."

"Well, Reggie," Rossetti boomed in a mock-pontifical tone, "there is a very simple explanation for the interest of that theme then or now— the human condition. What, after all, is the alternative? To write, as our more genteel novelists choose to, of the love of men for virgins? While that can be a very satisfactory sort of love it ends, whether happily or unhappily, with the ending of virginity. Thereafter a woman is either a wife or a subject of public disgrace—like poor Hetty in *Adam Bede*. But adultery, since it cannot be so surely detected, may continue so long as those involved are circumspect. Launcelot and Guinevere went on for decades, didn't they?"

"One objection," said Meredith, "from a practicing novelist: it is not always *our* choice to be genteel. It is the public's demand. Look what happened in France to Flaubert for his attempting to treat such a theme without the tinsel of chivalry about it."

"Infamous!" Swinburne shrieked. "Truly infamous."

William chose to believe that Swinburne was denouncing the book rather than the government's prosecution against it. "The scandal was compounded in that case," he declared from within a Delphic haze of pipe tobacco, "by the fact of the protagonist being a woman, and by the fact that she goes more than halfway to meet her seducer, and indeed *becomes* the seducer in the second instance. I can't say I altogether object to such a book's being prosecuted. If it must be published, let it come out clandestinely, like the rubbish of that other silly, scabrous Frenchman, Marquis Who's-It."

"Oh, really!" Swinburne protested, for he had lately discovered, in the library of his friend, the once Monckton Milnes, now Lord Houghton, the works of de Sade that William was denouncing. "You cannot be serious, William. Between the one writer and the other there are worlds of difference."

"What is your test?" Rossetti demanded of his brother. "The same as Pecksniff's—whether the book will bring a blush to maiden cheeks? And if it does, shall none of us, man nor woman, maid nor matron, be allowed to read it?"

"Would you offer the book to Christina?" William asked.

"No, for Christina's own self-prohibitions would forbid her to read it."

"But there are other women, you know," Meredith said, "who are not so sternly self-regulating. Women of mature judgment and women merely curious as well. And I am not altogether persuaded that a dose of Flaubert, even for the curious, would be less improving than such a book as *East Lynne*."

The naming of his nemisis slowed Meredith sufficiently for William blandly to put in: "Oh, under my government that book shall be outlawed as well."

"I rather liked it," said Rossetti. "It was lurid, but the same can be said of Dickens."

"Gentlemen," said Swinburne, rising unsteadily, "I give you Charles Dickens." He lifted his glass and tried to lead them in a cheer, but the other three men regarded his "Hip, Hip, Hurrah!" mutely.

"Flaubert *excuses* Emma Bovary," William insisted dourly. "Mrs. Wood *punishes* her erring heroine."

"He makes us privy to Emma's own self-extenuations," said Meredith. "That is another matter."

"I believe," said Swinburne, still standing, "that the troubadours were correct: a love is possible between a man and another man's wife that is at one and the same time passionate and non-*duleress*." He corrected himself: "Non-adulterous. Such was Dante's love for Beatrice." He did not add that such had been his love for Lizzie Rossetti; there was no need.

"But not all husbands were as fortunate as that good lady's husband," said Rossetti.

Once again Meredith felt the swerve of the conversation approaching the shoals of a personal smart. It was common knowledge that his wife had run off with Henry Wallis, returning to England only to die. Yes, and to die begging to be allowed a visit from her son Arthur, which Meredith had permitted only after there could be no doubt as to the course of her consumption. A sorry tale, which he had made it his aim to efface from memory, an aim in which his friends usually assisted. It was Swinburne, damn him, who had introduced the subject of adultery (though Meredith had himself to blame for introducing the figure of Madame Bovary). The fault was no one's, he decided. The fault was in the wine.

"Gentlemen." He rose. "I hope you will excuse me. I need a breath of fresh night air."

"The fog, you mean," said Rossetti, "and you're welcome to it. Only don't let any in here. For my part, I was thinking of lighting a fire. If George won't mind our bacchanal continuing in what is, after all, his drawing room?"

"As you like, Gabriel. After all, we are here to celebrate *your* birth-day." Meredith left the room.

The moment the outer hall door leading to the garden steps could be heard to slam, Swinburne collapsed onto the sofa and burst into gales of laughter. "Oh, did you see him!" he shrieked. "Did you *see* his face?"

"Has the naughty boy been up to tricks again?"

Gales abated to hiccoughs, while as though by some private law of conversation Swinburne began simultaneously to agitate his hands in almost epileptic fashion and twist his legs into serpentine knots—a mode of behavior which neither of the Rossettis seemed to view with any alarm.

"What did you do, Reggie?" Rossetti insisted.

Swinburne took a deep breath. "You know how he is always complaining of Mrs. Weir's cuisine? But no, I mustn't implicate the poor woman: the blame's all mine, if blame there be."

"You poisoned him?" Rossetti asked.

"He must have thought so, the look on his face was that distressful. The oysters: there they were, I helped myself, and then, seeing Knewstub with that fellow he'd brought in to help him paint, it seemed only natural to reward their labors with something, and there was only that very indifferent sherry that one can't really serve to company. Which left rather too few oysters for dinner: seven too few, to be exact. So I began to experiment with isinglass and egg whites and . . . and that was when Mrs. Weir returned: I explained my purpose to her, and she succeeded wonderfully. As to texture, that is."

"All six oysters Meredith ate were nothing but white of egg and isinglass?" William asked incredulously.

"No, no, no, all six of mine. He had only the one, but that providentially was the last of them."

"Did he *eat* it?" William asked. "I'm sure I shouldn't in a like case."

"George Meredith has too high an estimate of his own good form ever to remove anything that has gone into his mouth," Rossetti pronounced. "Have you ever seen him picking at his fish in fear of bones? Besides, these were oysters *he'd* supplied." He shook his finger at Swinburne. "Twenty strips of the birch for you, my lad."

This was calculated further to convulse the young poet—and had precisely that effect. Then, like the drowsiness that follows sexual release, Swinburne sighed, slumped, and slept.

"I believe," said William, "that if the directorship of Bethlem Hospital should fall vacant, I have ample qualifications."

Gabriel knew from his brother's tone that this was only a pro forma complaint and made no effort to mollify him. "What do you think friend George is up to?" he asked.

"He? Running, doubtless. When last we drank together he tried to persuade me to do the same as the surest preventive of paying the morrow's penalty."

"Bacchus of the time table," Rossetti scoffed. "Never was a man so systematic in his pleasures."

"Yes, he wants marrying again. Bachelorhood doesn't hang well on him."

"Every Monday I think it is as though old Ruskin had managed to sneak in with us by disguising himself as a virile youth. Virility aside, there *is* really not much to choose between the two of them."

William clenched his pipe stem in a concurring smile, from which his brother was given to understand that *he* would have no objection to encouraging Meredith's departure.

The third time round the path, just as the chill night air was beginning to hone his senses to their proper sharpness, Meredith fell over a peacock. The bird woke with a cry that seemed to break directly from the lower circles of Hell.

Elbowing himself up from the gravel, Meredith's first concern was for the knees of his trousers, since he had no others in which to make his journey back to Surrey. His trousers were also the peacock's first concern, which, in the fury of awakening, acted with a savagery one rarely associates with peacocks.

"Whoa!" shouted Meredith, feeling a peck at the back of his knee. Before the beast could lunge again, he caught hold of its long neck. The peacock loosed a still more terrible scream than the first, and began to attack Meredith with its spurred and taloned feet. This time Meredith had enough presence of mind to repress his own instinctive battle cry, but meanwhile the *other* peacock had responded to his mate's alarums. Meredith lifted the first peacock by the neck and swung it from him with his full strength—then took to his heels. The bird did not pursue him, nor did he encounter its mate.

Both Rossettis were standing at the opened garden door.

"I frightened the peacock," Meredith explained, brushing at his trousers and feeling, surreptitiously, for rents.

"By attempting to murder him?" Rossetti inquired coolly.

He felt too abashed to protest. "I was running round the garden. The first two times the damned thing wasn't on the path."

"How long are they likely to go on like this?" William asked his brother.

"Till George apologizes to them, I daresay, for robbing them of their sleep."

"I'm sorry, Gabriel. It never occurred to me that . . ." He could not bring himself to round off the absurdity of it: "that I might step on a peacock."

"Quiet!" came a voice from the farthest darkness.

But the peacocks would not listen.

"We'd best go in," said William.

"Quite right," said Rossetti; "then the neighbors may suppose it is someone else's peacocks making all this racket."

"Oh Christ," groaned Meredith, which was for him (although an unbeliever) the supreme oath of his adult life. "I *am* sorry, Gabriel."

Rossetti put an arm round his shoulder and led him through the wide doorway. Meredith did not know whether to feel flattered at the warmth of the gesture or condescended to as a drunk who could not be trusted to negotiate his own path. His heart was still pounding with the excitement of the peacock's attack, and his knees trembled.

Even with the door closed behind them, the cries were acutely audible in the drawing room.

Swinburne had awakened—into the extremity of drunkenness. "*Is that?*"

"That," answered Rossetti, "is Argus. Unless it is his wife."

A gleam of intelligence pierced Swinburne's stupor, and he began to recite . . . something in Greek. Of its appropriateness to the occasion only Swinburne himself might have judged, for Meredith and the Rossettis had long since unlearned the little Greek they'd studied in their youth.

When Swinburne had come to a sonorous conclusion, William, with the pride that is born of humility, said: "I'm afraid you'll have to translate that into plain English for me, old chap."

"In plain English," said Meredith, "*tout comprendre c'est tout pardonner.*"

"Toot, toot, toot," agreed Swinburne, grinning and squirming out of his jacket with a single twist of his bottle-shaped shoulders. As he wore no waistcoat, he commenced to unbutton his shirt.

"I believe it is time for beddy-bye?" suggested Rossetti, with the dulcet inflection (his mother's) he habitually adopted for his role as parent.

Meredith twined his arm under Swinburne's and round behind his neck. "I shall help him up to his room," he announced.

Though the wrestling hold in which Meredith had pinned Swinburne was more disabling than helpful, it had prevented his further disrobing. Swinburne accepted this polite coercion with the grace of the often-bullied and hobbled off where he was pushed. Halfway up the dark staircase Meredith himself stumbled and they both nearly careened in unison down the steps, but with his free arm Swinburne had a firm hold on the banister.

"Sorry," said Meredith, releasing him.

Swinburne assumed an attitude of dignity, which was more possible standing two steps above his companion. "*Tout comprendre,* my dear Meredith, may dispose one toward forgiveness, but friendship may be out of the question for all that."

Meredith stood where he had stumbled, stricken and admiring in equal measure, while his friend—former friend?—continued unassisted to the top of the stairs, where he turned round and with great decorum dropped his trousers and waved his small, flaccid penis in derision. The spirit of the staircase had quite abandoned Meredith, who without so much as a shake of his head retreated defeated to his drawing room.

There the full-bodied flies of May were feasting on the remnants of the birthday dinner, some nibbling crumbs of the Madeira cake, others sipping the dregs of wine. A large white-and-gray moth assaulted the frosted glass chimney of the lamp on the dining table.

Swinburne's cast-off jacket lay in a heap by the sofa. Meredith picked it up, and, in a spirit of quiet self-mockery, examined it with an eye for detail that owed something to his being the son of a tailor. It was a lounging jacket of the three-seamer variety, single-breasted, the collar rather narrower than Meredith thought proper to this style. The workmanship was all of the best, especially as to the lining and the inner pockets.

There was a single folded piece of paper in the inner breast pocket.

Guiltlessly, even with perverse pride in his own piratical spirit, Meredith removed the paper and unfolded it. It was not, as he had hoped, a letter; rather, a poem entitled fulsomely, "The Lexicon, the Leprechaun, the Dragon, and the Drone." It had every appearance of having been dashed off in a white heat and would require study to decipher, so before he settled to the task, Meredith took care to close the door of the drawing room to avoid interruption by the return of either Rossetti. Then, by the moth-varied light of the burning lamp, he read the following poem:

## THE LEXICON, THE LEPRECHAUN, THE DRAGON, AND THE DRONE

*The Lexicon, the Leprechaun,*
 *The Dragon, and the Drone*
*Decided to live together*
 *A life that was all their own.*

*For Lexicons can tire*
 *Of their lexographic skills*
*And Dragons grow dull in the evening*
 *Unless they are drunk to the gills,*

*And Leprechauns are apt to need*
 *Correction and control,*
*And a poor Drone is ever buzzing:*
 *"If I only had a soul!"*

*How if in their life together*
  *The four of them should find*
*That Lexicons, Leprechauns, Dragons, and Drones*
  *Are never of one mind?*

*For Lexicons are loquacious*
  *And given to scoff and to scold,*
*And Dragons tend to be testy*
  *In proportion as they are old,*

*And Leprechauns resist the bonds*
  *That bind the likes of Lexicons,*
*And a drone can buzz but a single song*
  *Of honeycombs and hexagons.*

*And thus when they joined together*
  *The lesson they took to heart*
*Was that Lexicons, Leprechauns, Dragons, and Drones*
  *Should live their lives apart.*

## 5

The walls were dry at last—and black as Night herself might have desired, black with the slightest infusion of indigo, as of blood glowing through ebony skin. Was there such another room in all of England? Not a glimmer through the window, for the moon and stars in sympathy had drawn a veil of wet weather across their faces; not even a candle's glimmer in view anywhere among the distant back windows of neighbors who overlooked his garden. He felt a curious comfort from it, a sense as of having become invisible.

There were Lizzie's pictures on the table, waiting to be hung, and there was the great expanse of pictureless wall. No, they must find another place of honor. If her spirit meant to be at him ever and always, very well, he would not resist; but he would not offer it the invitation of these damned watercolors. He wished he had the strength to burn them—but even the thought sent a thrill of guilt through his veins. No, he would hang them in Meredith's drawing room, which would not be Meredith's much longer—that much seemed clear. How the ultimatum was to be announced he had not yet resolved. Perhaps simply the hint of these pictures on the wall of his room when he next returned might be sufficient. He hoped so. For all Meredith's gibes at the dinner for Leathart, Rossetti bore no animus against him. Indeed, he was incapable of bearing grudges. In that respect he was more Christian than all the women of his family assembled in a single pious pew. He would, however, have his way, and in that he was not at all Christian.

Meredith would go. The pictures would go—from this room at least. And he further resolved, or foresaw, that he would work no longer at *Beata Beatrice.* For if Lizzie haunted him here, by the frail power of her own art, how much more did she haunt him there in his studio, where, for minutes or hours of every day, her face became the object of his meditation. He was not abandoning the painting; no, it was finished. Let the greatness of the painting be its very rawness, its nearness to the dear and dreadful hours when his brushes had the entire fire of creation in them.

His past was behind him. Lizzie was behind him. He would not look back at her, even when she called to him. He would return to the daylight—or, like Dante, to a sky of stars:

*e quindi uscimmo a riveder le stelle.*

Such thoughts may be entertained most safely in a bedroom where one is invisible.

A single aureole of yellow light swayed upon blackness. The river waters below, in spate from weeks of rain, purled in unseen eddies among the wooden pilings of the bridge, the very sound, it seemed, of philosophy. He would have to take his stand with the pre-Socratic who named water the first, the wisest, of the elements. It was also the least heroic. Yet what would be the point of forcing the issue with Rossetti? Indeed, what issue was there to force? That Swinburne had pierced the armor of his *amour-propre* with a remark that was not only wounding but perfectly true? For too intimate acquaintance with those we believe to be our friends may in the end preclude the possibility of friendship —this had been the burden both of Swinburne's parting shot on the staircase and of his nonsense verses. One would like to think that as people knew one better, liking and sympathy would grow; alas, not inevitably.

Why "Lexicon"? If he could but understand why Swinburne had settled on that epithet for him, he would not feel this ridiculous, this childish, this thoroughly unworthy sense of having been unfairly dealt with. Why that and no other word? Each of the other cognomens in the poem had seemed self-evidently appropriate. Poor William *was* a drone. For all his talk of wanting to devote himself to Art and Literature, it must have been evident, even to himself, that his greatest contribution to that cause was to have kept his brother out of bankruptcy court and supplied with a sufficiency of paint and creature comforts; secondarily, perhaps, to have provided a roof for his sisters' and mother's heads. Admirable deeds—for whatever would become of the hive without the drones?—but not the ideal basis for friendship. One was always aware, at one's finer moments, either of trimming one's sails to accommodate William's slower movement through the waters of intellect or else of plunging ahead regardless. As to "Leprechaun," that fitted Swinburne like a glove—though of course in the way of the nicknames we give to ourselves, it also flattered egregiously. "Dragon" evidently had been suggested by Gabriel's anecdote after dinner, though it suited him well enough that no other reason need be cited than Rossetti's generic resemblance to the mythic beast.

Well, then, why "Lexicon"? What had the poem said about the Lexicon? (He regretted now that in the first forlorn and furious moments after reading the manuscript he had given in to the impulse to burn it, for not only had he no right to do such a thing but it had, as well, prevented a closer study.) Loquacious and a scold, it called him. Undoubtedly he *was* too much in love with the sound of his own voice, but surely Swinburne and Rossetti were no less so. The inspiration of their living together was precisely the possibility of a kind of parity of genius, an egalitarianism of titans. As to being a scold, he did not like to think it true, but say it were? That still didn't explain the basic riddle of "Lexicon." Meredith was quite certain that his effective vocabulary was no larger than his companions', and while some critics may have found his writing overelaborated (or simply overblown), it was not a charge he could imagine being leveled by Swinburne, who had, after all, written that splendid letter to the *Spectator* defending *Modern Love* against that journal's critic. Therefore, why "Lexicon"? Simply to meet the demands of meter and alliteration?

He ought to stop thinking about it. All this bootless worry over some lines of wine-inspired doggerel.

It had been a mistake to pack his bag and set out from Tudor House at 2:30 a.m. There would be no omnibuses into London for hours yet, the bag was too heavy to carry for any distance, and as to hansoms,

Meredith made it a rule to take cabs only in company, never on his own. (He observed the same rule with respect to alcohol.) So the choice was either to wait for dawn and omnibuses here on the bridge, or to return to Tudor House and risk the embarrassment of an explanation or the pain of mutual recrimination. Sooner would he jump into the Thames! He really must steady his mind, fix it on something external, objective, true. Nature could be such a resource.

But tonight Nature remained obdurately invisible, mantled in her thickest fogs, and Meredith perforce must keep returning to the events of the evening that had sent him forth, an outcast, a criminal. . . .

For there was the rub: in one heedless moment he had committed a wrong as grievous almost, to his authorly eye, as homicide. He had destroyed the only existing copy of a fellow writer's work. Reduced it to ashes. Never mind that it was a piece of inconsequence. Never mind that it would never have appeared in print. His guilt remained unmitigated.

True, Swinburne, sober, might not even remember having scribbled the thing. All that he wrote, drunk or sober, came out of a kind of trance, a mode of working that appeared as mysterious and unlikely to Meredith as the original *Fiat lux!* Possibly, therefore, Swinburne would not even think to look for the incinerated manuscript, nor hope, when it was given up for lost, to reconstruct it from memory.

All the more heinous, if so, the crime Meredith had committed! He tried to imagine what he would feel if he'd learned that any of his friends had done such a thing to him.

There had been exactly such a case once—not to him, but in this very neighborhood: John Stuart Mill (rumor had it) burnt the first manuscript of Carlyle's *French Revolution* (or some part of it) and Carlyle had simply taken up his pen and written the book again. An apocryphal tale, almost certainly; to compare it to his own case was to compare great things to small. Still, the novelist in Meredith would dearly have loved to have eavesdropped on the soul of Mill during the hours immediately after he'd perpetrated *his* deed.

But really—all this anguish, this soul-searching over a scrap of nonsense verse that didn't even keep to its own meter from one stanza to the next! His conscience was too tender. Some of Swinburne's manuscripts would be the better for having been burnt: this new, rubbishy novel on which he was wasting his time, and those endless schoolboy jingles about swishing and caning were—both novel and jingles—so obviously the superflux of the erotic daydreams of Swinburne's privacy. It would be a kindness to their author if one of his friends would destroy those productions before they could be used against him—as they surely would be if they ever became public. Not *all* the world had attended Eton and would take Reggie's obsession with ritual flogging as a normal human peccadillo.

But this comforting train of thought was brought up short by the realization that it represented the most egregious rationalization. In those verses, now destroyed, no line could have been construed as offensive in implication, but to himself. And William Rossetti.

Had guilt precipitated his flight from Tudor House—and not the fine scruples he'd imagined at the time? Might he still return there, confess his crime, like Richard in his own novel, and be restored to fellowship, friendship, and primal innocence? The loss of Rossetti would be sore to him. The man's magnanimity was a tonic to his own less than expansive spirit. What had he said at dinner, *vis-à-vis* some false economy of Mrs. Weir's: "Money is the root of all parsimony"? The shoe fit Meredith's foot all too precisely.

With the first tingling flush of shame came the memory that had eluded him all these hours, the answer to "Why 'Lexicon'?" It had happened some weeks earlier, before Swinburne had gone off to Paris, possibly. They had become embroiled in an argument over the etymology of the word "honest." Meredith had declared (correctly) that when first used in English it had referred rather to high rank and estate than to any intrinsic ethical qualities, which Swinburne (who ought to have known better) bitterly denied. Meredith, in a vainglory of certitude, had said, "Let's look in the lexicon, shall we?" And it was in the inflection of that "lexicon"—he could hear it again, his own voice—that Meredith had betrayed the shopkeeper in his soul. That was the source, and there was its meaning. The smug triumph of that moment, as though he'd been seen to exult over winning at a round of tosspenny! The baseness of it. The shame went beyond the power of any apology. He could not return to Tudor House, knowing how Swinburne—both Rossettis, as well, probably—regarded him. Knowing, moreover, that he deserved such scorn.

Yet even as he pronounced exile on himself he felt a kind of glory stirring in his soul—for he had broached the meaning of the riddle. There was nothing he loved more than to arrive at a conclusion.

# CHAPTER EIGHTEEN

# A Day in the Country II

## 7 OCTOBER 1863

"I'd like to keep the tree," Dodgson insisted, poking his boyish head out of the camera tent to address his assembled subjects. "The leaves will have a disembodied air, rather like lily pads in a pool. If we can count upon the breeze to k-k-keep still."

William Michael Rossetti (whose stone-smooth pate flared forebodingly whenever, momentarily, the sun pierced through its coverture of cloud) communicated by his slouch and glazed fixity of expression a polite, Sabbath-like gloom. The Great Goddess Photography was unyielding in her single, all-encumbering demand: Keep Still. His natural impatience at such constraints was exacerbated by a mild itch of resentment, for he knew very well that his presence was dictated by courtesy alone, that the young cleric made these exertions wholly on Christina's and Gabriel's accounts. Doubtless, despite other accomplishments (Dodgson was a maths lecturer at Oxford), he aspired to authorship himself. William, since he suffered from the same affliction, could always sniff out would-be writers.

Maria Francesca, the eldest of those Rossettis assembled—except, of course, for their mother Frances—sat complacent as the moon on the cold steps leading down into the Tudor House garden. Though in much the same position as her younger brother with regard to worldly accomplishments, she was less inclined to dwell on such disparities—or at least better schooled in the Christian (and womanly) discipline of self-effacement.

Mrs. Rossetti, seated on the garden chair with its aerial-balloon motif, practiced a dutiful smile.

"If you like," Christina called out to Dodgson, "I'll keep the branch steady with my hand." She gave William a cheering glance.

Recumbent against the doorframe, Gabriel yawned a long, deep-chested, nasal yawn—the sort of yawn one must adopt during the quietest moments of a concert. Now he wished he hadn't let himself in for this succession of disruptions. Christina, Maggie, and the Antique all at a go—the dinner still to come!—and this Dodgson: like an invasion of four women instead of three. Altogether an unwelcome strain on the natural rhythms of the household, what with Fanny exiled to Royal Avenue and a day's work lost.

And yet the fellow had an eye. Even if the day's portraits found their way into no one's album but his own, he'd promised—seemed genuinely eager—to devote tomorrow to photographing drawings. A useful record to have when the originals were sold.

The siege, now in its seventh day, had all been Munro's doing. The sculptor-medallionist, wanting to have *his* portrait etched in collodion for posterity (but lacking the requisites of private sunlight and a lawn whereupon to pitch the apparatus), had brought the young don and Gabriel together. With no suspicion of what sort of gift horse he was allowing within his garden walls, Rossetti had made his grounds available for a week's carte blanche—even dangled the bait of a meeting with Browning, a meeting which, to the intense disappointment of Dodgson (who was quite dotty to be introduced to any luminary), had not materialized. The week began, inauspiciously, on Monday afternoon when Dodgson arrived two hours after the appointed time of noon abubble with apologies and excuses that Gabriel perforce must listen to. He'd spent the morning with Tom Taylor, the playwright, whose small son—"the naughtiest, most intractable child in all England"—had withstood his parent's and Dodgson's combined efforts to dress him in the costume Dodgson had brought all the way from Oxford, a darling little plumed helmet and for his spear an angling rod. But willful, wicked Wicliffe Taylor, once he'd been coaxed from screaming, would not put off his sulks. The entire morning. Only the servants had been at all cooperative, and as a reward (providing, as well, an object lesson for the naughty young man) Dodgson had been obliged to put off his departure for Chelsea in order to record their henceforth immortal images.

Across the garden the raccoon shook the bars of its cage in an access of rage so passionate (and sudden) that one of the peacocks, preening itself nearby, was moved to answer the challenge with a scream.

Frances Rossetti started—not so much from fright, for the unearthly screech of a peacock was no longer new to her, but at the thought that another photographic portrait might be in progress. She distrusted almost as much as she marveled at this mysterious process of treating sheets of coated glass with ether and other noisome chemicals so as to produce an image, like a mirror, more uncannily close to life than any of the paintings her son had ever painted. To her relief she noted that Christina was still moving about, making any record of the moment impossible. "Here," she said, stooping forward from her chair to remove a leaf from the hem of her daughter's broad skirts.

"Did I not see a chess table in the upstairs sitting room?" said Dodgson, popping out from beneath the tent like the Punch in some streetside puppet show. "Might it be brought down here? And another chair. Oh, never mind—there's one that will do quite well." He pointed to the weathered mate of Mrs. Rossetti's, leaning (where it had been left by Swinburne a week ago) on two legs against the mulberry trunk. "Miss Christina?"

"Yes, Mr. Dodgson?"

"May I ask to see you standing . . . there." He pointed to the left of the steps. "This time I should like your profile, hand on the banister? Just the one hand. Or possibly both. I can't decide. Yes. That's very pretty—but now I should like you to face more nearly to where your mother—no, Mrs. Rossetti: in just a moment all shall be explained, but *you're* not to stir. Miss Maria, you may remain on the steps. Facing me. However, turn your head just a bit counterclockwise. So."

"Poor Raccoon," observed Christina, "he wants his portrait taken as well."

"Actually, I believe it's Gabriel's wide-awake he fancies," William ventured.

The new servant, whose name only the absent Swinburne could remember, appeared at the top of the steps (the door held open by Mr. Weir) bearing the intaglio table with all the chess pieces upright and in position.

"Ah, splendid. Place that, would you, immediately beside Mrs. Rossetti. And now, Gabriel, if *you* would be seated opposite."

"What fun," said Christina, with quiet conviction, for despite the prohibitions her conscience imposed on her there was nothing she relished quite so much as a good game of chess.

Dodgson directed William to stand behind the chess table between his brother and his mother.

Christina looked at William, then at Maria, who wore the same blandly unfathomable expression she'd evinced since arriving. "Maggie," she whispered, "do take heart!"

With a glance of reprobation toward her younger sister, Maria stiffened her spine and gazed sibyllike into the camera's soulless and insentient lens.

Christina understood her sister's glance all too well but could soothe her conscience with the excuse that her apparent warmth toward Dodgson was the outgrowth of longer acquaintance: she had met him yesterday and even been photographed. The shyness she'd experienced then, both in herself and in him, had spent itself so that now her somewhat diffused sang-froid in the role of photographic model gave her, relatively, a tactical advantage over both her sister and mother. But if they had seen her yesterday. . . .

Clearly he stood in awe of her, or rather of *Goblin Market*, the merits of which he inventoried by way of compliment; he was courteous as Castiglione, well spoken (despite a dreadful tendency to screw up his face fearfully when he stammered, as he did regularly, especially at a hard "c"); not without wit and even a childlike quirk of producing seemingly unconscious *bons mots*. Yet something about Charles Dodgson in that first, difficult meeting, seeing him look up from the lens he'd been polishing—she might have mistaken him for the new servant had he not been attired in a cleric's collar—seeing his face blanch—that, the unseemliness of such timidity in a grown man, had "shut a door" in her. As it had been at Gabriel's urging that she had come, so it was for him that she had lingered on about the half-assembled camera, feeling for all the world like some piece of merchandise on a shelf (Item: marriageable sister, one of a pair). Save me, she'd prayed, dear God, save me from a brother's good intentions— listening even as she prayed to Dodgson's dry amenities, scrupling not to seem to notice his stammer and its attendant tics, and all the while, really, hearing none of it, listening more keenly to sounds that issue from the near beyond—the creaking of a floorboard far above—and instead of voices, the paralyzing under-silence of the room.

Dodgson, within the protective darkness of the tent, was comfortably deep in the difficulties of his art. Too much furniture, too many figures. He called out to William, then motioned him to step forward from the shadows where his head hung like some disembodied apparition, forgetting that the chess table stood in the way. Standing to the side of Mrs. Rossetti, his bald pate beamed like the beacon of a lighthouse. He must remove himself from the composition altogether—there was no other answer.

In the next photograph the chess table, one of the chairs, and the obdurately uncharmable elder sister were removed to see if four Rossettis might be arranged more tastefully than five. Still the problem persisted of William, the tree trunk, and its shadow conjoining into a single Caravaggesque murk. Only after developing the plate within his little dark-room pyramid did he note the anomalous trapezoid behind Christina Rossetti's head, which he at last deciphered as her shawl, hanging on the iron banister. Ruined. But possibly not: the accident imparted an air of life. As for William's jacket, that could be darkened with pen and ink to help it emerge from the jumbled grays. If not life, then art. "Splendid," he proclaimed.

"May we see the result?" asked Mrs. Rossetti, who ordinarily excelled in her ability to disguise either eagerness or anxiety. What if the camera made them look like fools?

"Until I've bathed the plate in a fixing solution, you shall have to rely on your imaginations." Dodgson's voice emerged muffled from the tent surrounding his head, torso, and the Ottewill's secret workings. "In any case, I can't show you positive prints today, as the plate must first be varnished." A lengthy pause ensued. "But if you'll note which ones you wish (or which portions, for one can edit photographs like manuscripts), and how many copies of each, I shall post them to you promptly."

"It is sad," remarked Maria, in a rather acerb tone, "that we still have not succeeded in producing one of the five of us."

"Perhaps one might cobble something together from separate prints," Christina suggested. She had already begun to imagine some of the droll hybrids that might be created in this way (Gabriel playing chess with Gabriel), when Maria curtailed such fancies with a frown. Christina sighed and reached behind her absent-mindedly for her shawl. "I do believe it means to rain."

Maria looked up at the accumulation of gray-edged clouds. "Yes, it is darker than only a minute ago: I can look at the brightest part of the sky without squinting."

Christina crossed the leaf-littered space to the raccoon's small cage at the edge of the unkempt lawn. "Poor Raccoon. Gabriel, won't you take pity and let him have the run of the garden—just while we're here to watch.'"

"Mamma?" He felt confident that in deferring to Mrs. Rossetti he would be spared having to issue an order of release. His mother, after William, was the least animal-foolish. The raccoon could be unpredictable: recently it had been inspired to declare its territorial supremacy by ripping a pair of red curtains to shreds. Henceforth, though the peacocks were still allowed brief holidays indoors (they did brighten a room wonderfully), the raccoon had been exiled to the garden. Here, although there were no draperies or carpets for the creature to savage, there were fewer means of controlling its actions.

Frances Rossetti tried to remember the habits of the raccoon which she'd been obliged to study and comment upon so often at the Regent's Park Zoological Gardens when the children were young. This one, though not so large as the Zoo raccoon, seemed considerably less subdued. "It would be a kindness—and perhaps he will feel less anxious, if you let him exercise his curiosity."

Gabriel and Christina exchanged a quick, complicitous smile.

"I say, Mr. Dodgson, would you object if Christina were to let the raccoon out for a moment? If he is especially quiet, you might wish to do his portrait."

Dodgson, engrossed in the process of coating a new plate with collodion, made no audible response.

Gabriel removed from his pocket a small key and tossed it to his sister. The raccoon became instantly quiet.

Christina's skirts ballooned as she stooped down to place the key in the lock. A delicate little hand with long nails reached out ready to divest the cell of its iniquitous bolt—or merely to help. She gave it her forefinger, and the wrinkled, dark, reduced hand clutched it only long enough to decide that this was not the actual key, then groped excitedly for any hard object. She inserted the key and turned it counterclockwise. Two bright eyes studied her own.

"Do you suppose," asked Maria, "he might climb the wall or a tree and never come down?"

"He may climb a tree—he has before—but there's one thing guaranteed to bring him back to earth: a raw egg."

Just as the lock slipped loose, the raccoon grabbed the bars of the cage's door with both hands and gave them a desperate shake, stealing the glory of his liberation from Christina—the door gave way. He was out instantly combing the grass; skittered over to where one of the peacocks stood watching the scene nervously (making it scream); retreated, stopping to look up either appreciatively or judiciously at Christina, who shared his own delight equally, before veering off in the direction of the inscrutable tripod and trousers culminating in a weathered canvas pyramid (which was, surely, the most uncustomary object in the garden).

"He's lovely, Gabriel," observed Christina, "but I'm afraid there is little chance of his keeping still for the forty-five seconds a portrait requires. I wonder, would he object to my picking him up?"

"He's quite sociable, as a rule."

The raccoon, realizing that the legs beneath the canvas tent terminated only in another human being (one who carried his own nest about with him, it appeared), swerved off sideways to a patch of long grass likely to be inhabited by a range of comestible insects. Christina reached down and swept the dominoed creature up into her arms. He offered token resistance, then lay back looking admiringly into her eyes, holding her hand, with great interest, in both his own.

"You're only a baby," she declared.

"A baby who is also a bandit," said Maria, who had approached quite near.

Their mother stood timidly apart from the raccoon's range of action.

"He has the softest hair, Maggie—just feel. But his teeth are like needles."

Maria formed her arms into a cradle ready to receive the animal. The transfer was effected, and now it was into Maria's eyes the raccoon so disarmingly gazed.

"A proper goblin, that's what he is," Maria announced, just as the raccoon, tiring of playing the baby, proceeded to climb unceremoniously to her shoulder, the better to view Mrs. Rossetti.

"Oh dear," said Gabriel.

"Just look at him—he's waving at me!" said Mrs. Rossetti, waving back at the raccoon.

"I daresay he fancies the ribbon on your cap, Mamma," said William Michael. It was really Gabriel he was addressing: a note of fair warning.

"And he fancies my nose as well," said Mrs. Rossetti, who had lost all trepidation. She gingerly put forward an index finger and the raccoon took it, peering straight into her eyes while shifting his weight on Maria's shoulder. "Are your *hands* clean?" she demanded to know, not quite sure what counted for polite conversation among placental mammals, family Procyonidae (long years as a governess had fixed her memory of the Latin names for most animals to be found in the Zoo).

The raccoon cocked his head, seemed to beg her pardon for some as yet uncommitted crime. He gave her finger an unmistakable tug.

William stepped forward. "I believe that will be enough."

She had only the opportunity to say, "You're quite correct, William," when the raccoon, realizing William Michael's intent, summoned his courage and leapt from Maria's shoulder to the top of Mrs. Rossetti's head, and then, after no more than a second's pause, straight to the lowest bough of the mulberry tree. Before the frightened woman had quite recovered from her shock, the raccoon had found his way through a network of branches to the top of the garden wall. Without a backward glance he was over the wall and gone.

Again Dodgson immured himself within the camera's tent, and again they heard the tell-tale clink of glass plate against the Ottewill's rosewood frame. "Now," he said, with familiar finality, "are we all ready to remain absolutely still for . . ." All eyes but Dodgson's considered the lowering sky. ". . . one entire minute?" It was to be his final attempt to capture all five Rossettis in a single tableau.

They were ready indeed.

Dodgson removed the lens cover in a single, smooth motion:

Time Stopped.

At once Christina regretted the smile on her lips, a foolish, slipshod sort of smile that she was doomed for the next minute not to vary by the slightest alteration of a muscle. She foresaw the scene with Maggie when the print appeared: "Imagine—" (in that quietly reproving tone of hers) "—being remembered by posterity as the poetess preeminently noted for this grin!" A small blessing that now, as they were posed by Mr. Dodgson, with her head in Maggie's lap, only God and Dodgson could judge just precisely what species of oddity she represented. Where had it come from, that smile? Had much of the minute passed? William (she guessed) would be counting off the seconds in his head. Was it possible to keep from blinking so long?

Maria Francesca's mental motions during this interval were neither so rapid nor so varied. Her thoughts were fixed upon a single, poignant image: a table spread for an ideal tea of scones, butter, clotted cream, and strawberry jam. She imagined the butter melting into and moistening the white flesh of the opened scone—and sighed inwardly, for she knew Mrs. Weir would not extend such unprecedented largesse to Gabriel's guests. There would be nothing but the usual Tudor House weariness of bread and butter, bread and (very little) butter. Better, then, to fix one's thoughts upon the unvarying, if only platonic, truths that would, in any case, rise unbidden to the surface of her mind: warm scone, melting butter, the little cloud of cream in its white bowl, strawberries ecstatically crimson.

Not only God and Dodgson but her mother as well, by virtue of position in profile to the camera, could see the smile on Christina's face. It did not strike Mrs. Rossetti as odd or silly in the least. Mirth and whimsy had little part in that smile. On the contrary, it seemed (in this sidelong view) a smile of the highest seriousness; and gentle, especially about the eyes, so that Frances was put in mind of the "light" John refers to in his first Epistle. The light of love. Could Christina be in love? Love of the other sort; not the Christian love she must feel toward William Michael, her brother, for example, or toward the world at large. Love that is also longing and sadness (for that could be read, as well, in the lines about her eyes). But for whom? Any properly attentive mother ought surely to be able to frame a likely guess, and yet—this Mr. Dodgson? After a day's acquaintance? Not possibly. Charles Cayley then? He had been so assiduous in his attentions. One mustn't dismiss him on the grounds cited by Gabriel: because his talk was "dull," his coat "ragged," and his published translations "uniformly uninspired." Still, there was the volume of Cayley's verse, which even William Michael was hard-pressed to praise. William, however, did not mock his sister's "dear mole," nor did he announce (as had Gabriel) a blanket refusal ever to accept Cayley as a brother, should the situation arise. Indeed, William clearly inclined to favor a match, on the ground (which he was much too polite to state) that Cayley might take one of his sisters off his hands. But would he, in fact? At forty to have met with such small success in so many undertakings did not conduce to that buoyancy of confidence that seems (if unfairly) to be a precondition of success in the world, even of mere social survival. William might well end with one dependent *more* rather than one less. Yet Cayley was a pleasant, earnest man, despite his spells of silence in the presence of quicker wits; in that regard he'd suit Maria far better than her sister. He could discuss fine points of Greek grammar with Maria for hours on end. If Maria ever intended to find a husband . . . but it was clear that she did not. Christina, however —and Cayley? No, she *was* in love; her smile proclaimed it, but not with Cayley.

William counted the minute off (as his sister had imagined) in hippopotami. He had reached the thirty-seventh hippopotamus, when his subvocalized chronometer was thrown out of all reckoning by a sudden welling up of anger.

Ten pounds Gabriel had spent on that raccoon, and still more tin for the cage: all gone, all lost, escaped over the garden wall! And next week Gabriel would begin to wheedle more tin for some new folly. He spoke of zebus now—and lions! William felt his face growing hot with resentment; then cool, as a breeze (reckless of Dodgson's prohibitions) fanned his flushed cheeks and lifted the lappets of lightest tulle from their fixed position on his mother's bodice. How could a minute stretch on so? He resumed counting the seconds to make them pass more quickly: one hippopotamus, two hippopotami, three . . .

For Gabriel, leaning on the banister, the minute's enforced stillness passed painlessly, scarcely heeded, one monad in the uncharted plenum of things observable. Without any special accounting he saw the greens and umbers of the untended garden; the odd silhouette of the camera; behind it the no less odd silhouette of a tailless peacock; Dodgson with his stopwatch; belated daisies sprung up in the grass . . .

Muffled by the intervening maze of brick and plaster walls, the front bell of Tudor House punctuated the minute's silence with its jangle of summons.

That, thought Gabriel, would be the Munros arriving, conveniently late. He hoped Weir would know better than to bring them straightaway through into the garden—and spoil the picture. Surely the minute must be at an end?

Christina leaned with her head in her sister's lap, not knowing, not caring for once *who* could be at Gabriel's front door—the day was so mild. The leaves floating above seemed themselves aware of photography's demands. The day's gentleness bespoke more of spring than midsummer—the belated, unexpected spring that might greet a solitary visitor to Northumberland.

*Alas! that we must dwell, my heart and I,*
   *So far asunder.*
*Hours wax to days, and days and days creep by. . . .*

Five years of creeping days filled with the memory of a picnic lunch, the touch of a hand, the smell of sea, and waiting (as though for a holiday that had been banished from the calendar), culminating in a single, problematic communication—Gabriel, writing home from Newcastle-on-Tyne, sullying the waters of remembrance: "The fearful Dixon got wind of my presence, and though discouraged, duly turned up one evening. He is exceedingly anxious, among other topics, as to the allegorical meaning of *Goblin Market,* so Christina knows what she has to expect when next she sees him." But did she? After five years can there still be expectations? He'd become a mere phantasm in her mind. A fancy. Any thought of marriage to him must be counted as absurd as her loving the zookeeper, or Gabriel's greengrocer! His interest in her book had—to tell the other side—cut to the quick: it presumed to question the mask, acknowledged that there must be a human face behind, and behind that face a soul. Rubbish. And yet after five years the mention of his name had precipitated, in the cloud-lands of her soul, showers of verses (in Italian, in order that, should a member of the family happen upon them, his first conclusion would be that they were addressed to the innocent Cayley, who had been her father's favorite student in that language). She'd destroyed those that seemed most compromising and hidden the remainder: a trousseau twice-removed.

Dodgson covered the lens.

Excusing himself, Gabriel hurried into the house to see to the visitors. William Michael helped his mother to her feet.

"I'm afraid I twitched when the bell rang," said Mrs. Rossetti.

Maria Francesca, rising from the steps, held out the palm of her hand as though to receive change. "It is beginning to rain," she announced.

Christina regarded her younger brother—two drops glistened on his forehead—with sudden, pregnant silence. "William," she said awkwardly and in a tone unguarded enough to command, at once, complete attention. "Do you know, there is a marked resemblance between you and Thomas Dixon—I'd never noticed it before."

"I beg your pardon, Christina?"

"The cork cutter of Sunderland. We each encountered him on our separate visits to Mr. Scott some five years ago? Oh, but I can see you're furious about that raccoon!"

Ten pounds, thought William, and that not including the cage. "But you must cover yourself. It's starting to rain in earnest now." He took her hand and shepherded her up the steps.

"Hurry, both of you," said Frances Rossetti, within the doorway. "You'll be drenched. Oh, look at poor Mr. Dodgson. His apparatus is really more than a single pair of hands can deal with all at once. William, do go and help him, that's a dear."

"It's quite ruined, I'm afraid," said Dodgson elegiacally. He held the plate up for Mrs. Rossetti to examine.

While she and her daughters looked at it, Dodgson dried his hair and forehead with a flannel cloth. Weir stooped, mopping a puddle of developing solution from the bare wood floor with scarce-disguised indignation on his employer's behalf.

In their haste to bring the Ottewill out of the rain, William and Dodgson had overturned one of the vials kept within its traveling dark-room, only discovering the accident after a pool had formed on the hardwood floor (fortunately not on the carpet, inches away). The plate, whether having been subjected to droplets of rain or chemical solution, was splotched beyond repair.

"William," mourned his mother, "your face—and my hands!"

Christina crowded close to her mother. Though the *tout ensemble* might be lost, a face or a figure could still be saved from the wreck. It was difficult at first (as when one enters a darkened room from the light) to make out any image whatever on the negative plate. Each detail was the opposite of itself: the men wore suits of luminous whiteness, their faces all were those of blackamoors. But even so she felt an altogether forbidden fascination looking at her own metamorphosed mirror image. No claim to beauty there—at best, a kind of dreaminess. Her vanity hungered for an image enlarged and reversed again to the world's usual order of dark and light. Then, realizing the unseemly nature of her impulse, she stepped aside, affording Maria a closer look.

"A fair likeness of Christina, if one may judge by a negative image," she observed. "What a pity to have lost it."

"N-n-not a bit of it," interposed Dodgson. "I shall make a print of K-K-K—" His eyes rolled up to show only their whites; he drew a breath, and resolutely stammered his way to a triumphant "—Christina! *and* yourself, and I d-d-dare say no one will ever be the wiser." He patted his damp hair and offered a smile of professional encouragement, the counterpart of his collar. "*And*, as soon as the rain lets off, we may have another go."

William sighed.

Dodgson brushed away nonexistent crumbs from the corners of his mouth (he had not tasted the bread) with the serviette, and addressed Christina in a tone of almost confessional confidence. "I wonder, Miss Rossetti, if I might confer with you on a matter of *professional* interest. Though perhaps I employ that word prematurely. My own efforts have yielded little of a finished nature, as yet."

"Dear Mr. Dodgson, rest assured, nothing so gratifies me as an opportunity to appear professional. It is not my usual role."

Dodgson waved his serviette deprecatingly—and continued his interrupted preamble: "As the authoress of so charming—and pretty!—a work as *Goblin Market* (which has already a claim to the status of a classic, and not only among the youngest readers), I defer to your g-g-genius and experience with regard to a little story, or rather a fairy tale (perhaps, one day, a book), which I have set down at the special request of a child-friend. To come quickly to my point—I am in need of a title!"

"I see," said Christina gravely (the while she repressed the whimsy, *Would he prefer "Lord," "Sir," "Viscount"?*). "How *curious*—to have written a story without having a title already in mind. I tend to *begin* with a title." She laughed dryly.

"My own starting point, in this instance, was coercion. You see, I am the f-f-fond c-c-captive of a certain very young lady who demands that I tell her stories in which she figures as the heroine. One day, not this past summer but the summer before that, again finding myself constrained to entertain the very young lady and her two charming sisters, I c-c-c-c-conceived a place, a world so exactly like and yet *un*like our own (all underground, you see), that my fancy quite ran away with itself, and Alice (that is my child-friend's name, in fact) begged me to write it all down, just as I'd told it her as we were boating on the Isis."

"Indeed. And this world of likeness and unlikeness is underground, you say? But how do people see?"

"Oh, that offers no problem: people see with their eyes."

"Perhaps dark is light there, and vice versa, as in your photographic plates."

"Metaphorically that is precisely so." He raised the teacup to his lips, blew gently on the milky tea, and replaced it, untasted, in its saucer.

"Well, I do hope little Alice will allow you to share her story with the world beyond the Isis. I should like to be allowed to read it myself."

"Oh, you're too kind, Miss Rossetti. Truly, I had never *any* thought of imposing on adult attention; yet in the meantime, since I first set it to paper, I have, I confess, allowed one grown-up friend, and then another, to see whether it amuses them—and they all do urge me to publish. I've even set about drawing my own illustrations—nothing so fine as those your brother accomplished for you, but on a par at least with Mr. Lear's endearing scribbles. I do lack a title, however; or rather, of the dozens I've considered, none seems predestinately right. The nearest, perhaps, is 'Alice's Adventures Under Ground.'" He looked down into his tea so as not to seem to be studying her reaction.

Christina tried the words on her own tongue: "'Alice's Adventures Under Ground.' For the uninitiated that may have a more ominous ring to it than you quite intend. Of course, I haven't read the text . . . how long is it, may I ask?"

"Not very long at all. A fraction of the length of Mr. Kingsley's *Water Babies*. As long, perhaps, were I to let it grow to its ideal length, as one of Mr. Dickens's Christmas books."

"And what other titles have you been considering?"

"'Alice Among the Elves'?" He dared look up to see what response she made to this, but except for a smile as dry as toast she remained impassive.

"How does your Alice enter this Hades or Under-Ground Kingdom?"

"Down a rabbit hole. But there, you see, this is no Hades. Not a k-k-kingdom of the d-d-dead. No. You see, she is in pursuit of a White Rabbit who is fearful of being late for an appointment—and accordingly carries a pocketwatch. There were no pocketwatches in Hades, I am sure."

"But your first title will surely have that connotation for other readers than myself. 'Alice Among the Elves' would do far better."

"Or possibly 'Alice's Hour in Elfland'?"

"I think I might prefer that. 'Hour' is a magical word: of all the units of time it is the most imponderable. Either it is interminable, or so fleeting. One finds it difficult to believe there are a full two dozen in a day."

"Better, you think, than 'Alice's Doings in Elfland'? That is another contender."

"Much the better, I should say. But the latter title does suggest to me a pertinent question: What sort of adventures under ground does Alice pursue with these elves? What *are* their 'doings'?" She wondered, watching Dodgson's eyes retreat into the folds of the serviette he now began to twist in his fingers, whether she had gone too far.

"How peculiarly embarrassing! I must c-c-c-confess there are no elves, as such, in the entire tale. A number of other odd creatures, but no elves. Though if one were to encounter elves anywhere, I suppose this is the sort of place where one would find them: a world of fancy."

"A wonderland."

"Yes, yes, a topsy-turvy sort of world. A wonderland." He cleared his throat. "What think you of . . .'Alice's Golden Hour'?"

"Very pretty. Very pretty indeed. *Slightly* elegiac."

" 'All in a Golden Afternoon'?"

"Oh, I do like that, but then you lose the 'Alice' altogether, and I assume you'd prefer to hold to that, if only for the child's sake. Of all the possibilities I believe I prefer 'Alice's Golden Hour,' despite the sadness of the suggestion that only one hour of one's life—of one's youth!—should be golden."

"And is it as light as—" Mrs. Rossetti, who sat at the center of the table, nearest the centerpiece, had risen to remove the cover. For a moment she stood stricken, cover in hand and the piece of china itself quite forgotten: within the smooth white womb of the elaborate piece was a furry animal, rather larger than a rat, fast asleep.

"That is Wombat," said Gabriel, in the manner of an introduction.

"Do you think he would fancy some bread and butter?" Mrs. Munro asked with candid eagerness.

"As a marsupial (but not a mammal, you know), he *will* eat milksop," said William, "but only late at night. While the light lasts, he sleeps."

"What a dear, individual creature he is," said Christina. "Not at all like a rodent of that size."

"More in the nature of a small bear, I should say," ventured Maria. "The resemblance is more notable when he opens his paw and you see the claws: a paw is not a hand."

Gabriel pushed back his chair and bent across the table, holding up his forefinger in a pantomime of silence. "If you listen very, very closely, you'll hear him snoring. The most discreet little snore you would ever want to share a bedchamber with. Not so, William?"

"*His*—oh, yes."

"Don't be horrid, William," said Christina.

"Ought we to be talking like this," whispered Mrs. Rossetti, still holding up the pagoda-roof of the centerpiece, "when the poor creature is trying to sleep?"

"Oh, he can sleep through *Swinburne's* declamations. Have no fear on that account."

"Dear Mr. Swinburne," said Mrs. Rossetti, setting the china cover down on the superbly polished mahogany tabletop. (Weir neglected the other furniture scandalously, to Mrs. Rossetti's way of thinking, but he was fierce in his devotion to the dining table.) "Do tender my good wishes to him."

"And mine," agreed Christina.

Maria, rather from a natural disinclination always to form a trio in the forms of courtesy than because she actually disliked the man (though she did, rather), did not chime in.

Dodgson, who had been intent all this while on the sleeping wombat, asked whether he might be brought out into the light (for the rain showed signs of leaving off) to sit for his portrait.

"I rather think not," said William. "Wombats are not fond of direct sunlight."

"Apparently," said Gabriel, "there is always conversation going on in wombat burrows (so they learn to sleep through it), but very poor fenestration. Somewhat like life below stairs, I should think."

"What a pity." Dodgson's disappointment seemed genuine: the wombat had captured his fancy.

"Without the shock of sunlight, however, I believe he might be persuaded to interrupt his dreaming for a moment. Would you like to see him awake, Mother? It matters little, our awakening him—he will fall immediately back to sleep."

"Oh, not on my account, Gabriel!"

He smiled indulgently. He loved to see his mother being disingenuous, for then he could condescend. He left the dining room, went down the hall to his studio, took a cigar from the box he kept there, and returned to his guests. At the sight of the thick cheroot his mother raised a categorical objection: cigar smoke made her ill. It also made Christina and Maria ill. They confirmed this. Even Mrs. Munro, when pressed, admitted that she found the smell distasteful, though it did not make her actually ill.

"William, *you* explain. Mother will listen to you."

Frances Rossetti raised her hand with queenly authority. "William!"

"Mamma, there is no need to set the cigar aflame. I shall merely rub it so. . . ." Placing the cigar near the pierced windows of the pagoda centerpiece, he rolled it (clumsily, for it was square-cut) in his fingertips.

One paw opened, and a tremor passed along its claws, like a piano arpeggio. The other claw uncurled, stretched. The nostrils quivered, and the two paws reached up in unison to rub consciousness into his eyes.

"Oh!" said Dodgson, transfixed. "Oh my dear."

# CHAPTER NINETEEN

# Arrangement
# in Flesh Color and Black

FEBRUARY, 1864

"Are you cold?" he asked the naked Sarah.

She said she was not.

He stared at the tip of the needle, then at the smoke-blackened ground of the plate, seeming scarcely to apportion her gooseflesh a glance. "Are you comfortable?" he added in that peculiar "Dixie-land" drawl that set him apart from all other men of the housemaid's acquaintance. "I don't want you declaring, in a minute or so, that your ahm is breaking off."

She nodded her head.

"Whatevah you do, sugah, please, please don't move." The muscles about his left eye tightened convulsively around the monocle (for he was very near-sighted) and his teeth clenched in a grimace of a smile; then he etched the first line with the needle, laying the copper bare in a long curve that described the ambiguous boundary between her loosened hair and her long neck.

"You have a fine neck," he announced, looking up, cutting another line from the black ground, looking up again, "as fine a neck as Jo's, I daresay. A *puh*fect neck."

The etching progressed—quickly for Whistler, slowly for his model, who was not at all accustomed to this line of work. She wished now that she had not insisted on remaining upright: at least a half of her would have been warm if she'd been lying in a tumble of bedclothes like the Venus he'd shown her when she'd first resisted his temptations. The studio, despite the fire she'd built, was a cold room; a lack of ordinary furnishings made it seem even colder. Who would suppose that simply standing still, with a hand on one's hip and the other

dangling loose, could be such *work*! The worst of it wasn't the physical
discomfort, it was the way he looked at her: one quick squint after
another; not the least glimmer of affection or even interest—
though she stood naked as the proverbial cuckoo and unable to move
as though he'd put her under an enchantment. Was there ever anything
odder?

"I hope you won't think I'm being forward . . . sir, if I say that I *do*
feel queer."

His eyes were fixed on the copper plate before him, which she
construed as tacit permission to continue:

"I shouldn't mind having a go with you, sir." Sarah arched her
eyebrow knowingly. "There's no harm in it—that is, as long as we
each remember our relative stations, and it does put us on a friendlier
footing day to day, which makes life pleasanter all round. But I do feel
awkward doing *this*. I mean, it's so *heartless*. Isn't it?" The "h" of
"heartless" was superbly aspirated.

"Hush, Sarah, please. I need all my concentration. There's a crinkle
in your forehead when you talk that throws me en-tah-ly off my stride.
I must have your face *smooth*. Do try, sugah. And then later we can
have all the serious talk you like. You know I enjoy your company—I
truly do."

At this urging the crinkle disappeared, but Whistler continued, at
odd moments, to offer up such fragments of his thoughts as would
yield themselves to language—the unpremeditated overflow of the
quick communications passing wordlessly between eye and hand. Long
ago he'd learned that this was the surest way to keep a restless sitter
sedate and amenable. "I love the line, just they-ah at the curve of your
knee—that line, oh yes." Any such murmuring Sarah was pleased to
construe as a tribute to her beauty, and so for half an hour the sitting
prospered: line by deliberate line, copper gleaming through the blackened ground, the image formed. He caught the anxious flex of the wrist
that pretended to hang limp, the twist of the neck, the averted glance,
every subtle sign of her embarrassment. And the way the light fondled
the full curves of her naked flesh (for she was not *so* young) like an
old voyeur, like some superannuated Patron of the Arts.

So Miss Spartali's indisposition had proved a blessing in disguise. A
day, or several, would not be wasted. The painting must wait, but . . .

He'd forgotten the confidence of mastery he felt with a needle in his
hand; not at all the same as brush and palette. Color added a dimen-

sion of . . . no name for it. But line, pure line—no name for that either. He fell silent (within as without), sensing that Sarah had at last passed into that realm of timeless, tireless passivity, the limbo of models.

Eternity was interrupted by his mother, who entered the room without even the preliminary portent of a knock (the teatray she bore was all the apology required). "Jemie?" A brief silence ensued. The half-open door screened from sight the housemaid standing unclothed on the dais. As she stepped forward and her eyes met those of Sarah, the two empty cups rattled forebodingly in their saucers. "Excuse me, Ah'm sure Ah didn't mean to—" But she chose not to instigate a crisis then and there. "—intrude." With a defiant glance at Sarah, Mrs. Whistler retired from the studio as precipitately as she'd entered, leaving behind only the faintest aroma of green tea and a suggestion of brimstone.

He found her, an hour before dinner, bundled in black shawls, in what had become since her arrival two months ago her "withdrawing room," though the presence of *his* easel in the brightest corner indicated that the boundaries of hers and his were still in dispute. The blue-and-white upon the shelves, the painted fans disposed in delightful asymmetry above the bright fire, the very placement of the brass fittings before the hearth bespoke his sense of decorum, while hers was amply conveyed by the stricken smile on her thin lips and her stiff posture in a rush-bottomed settee that would have looked more "at home" in Puritan New England than here in the London of Queen Victoria—as would Anna Whistler, herself.

"Oh, Jemie," she whispered, with an expressive shaking of the lace lappets hanging down to either side of her head like long ethereal braids.

"Now, Mummy, it's not what you may think."

"Ah should hope, my dear boy, that Ah have *no* such thoughts! May Ah never be given cause to do so."

"Then why upset yourself? You know it is in the nature of my work that I must have models, and it was one of the conditions of Sarah's employment here that she should sometimes act in that capacity."

"Ah suppose that is the reason she is paid double the wages a maid of her degree would receive in any household but this."

"Yes, and she'd be a bargain at twice the price."

"Oh, Jemie—that's what you say of all your extravagances. Those old Dutch pots you came home with—Ah've nevah mentioned them befoah, but Ah have heard you say to Mistah Ros-set-ti—" She pronounced the name with exaggerated care, as much as to say, "the Italian." "—that you spent sixty pounds on them. Sixty *pounds*! Jemie, you could buy a horse for that!"

"They are not Dutch, Mummy; they are Chinese, as you know very well, and they are particularly admirable examples of their kind and worth much more than I paid. In terms only of prudence, I could not have made a sounder investment. I suppose you'd have me put my money in railway stocks and become a bankrupt—"

"—Jemie, Ah will not he-ah you speak ill of your poor fathah's occupation. Mistah Whistler was not to be blamed that Ah was left unprovided fo-ah. *Relatively* unprovided fo-ah," she thought to add.

Whistler sighed theatrically.

"Your fathah was a good man," she insisted, "and the Czar *wanted* to honor his memory. It was my own decision to return to America when Mistah Whistler dahd, a decision which Ah have nevah regretted, whatevah it may have cost in worldly terms."

"And in that, Mummy dear, I take after you. In any case, sixty pounds doesn't buy much of a horse, nor am I (as you know) much of a horseman, whereas I *am* a very good judge of Long Elizas. Bless my soul."

"Jemie Whistler, Ah am a tolerant woman—as you know—but Ah will not sit in this chair and hear you speak profanely."

"Mummy, a Long Eliza is nothing more than the English for '*Lange Lijzen*'—which is to say, one of those very large blue-and-white pots."

"Jemie, you are *willfully* misunderstanding me."

"I daresay I am misunderstanding you, but not by choice, Mummy. What *other* profanity did you mean?"

"Ah won't stoop to repeat it, be assured. In any case, Ah don't know how you managed to *sidetrack* me again." She tossed back her lappets proudly as she used this bit of railroading argot. "Ah did not intend to speak to you about the price of *rahd*ing horses, nor to dispute your dear fathah's honor, may his soul rest in the Lord, as Ah'm sure it does. Ah wish to discuss another matter entah-ly."

"Yes?" Whistler inquired cautiously. Though he was grateful to have the matter of Sarah's posing already relegated to the vast oblivion of all that was ummentionable between them, he could sense, in the set of his mother's firm small jaw, that a subject at least as awkward was about to be introduced.

"The matter is of your sister Deb'rah," said Mrs. Whistler in her most genteel and direst tones.

"What is wrong with Deb'rah?"

"Deb'rah is quite well. She has the constitution of an ox (lahk all the Swifts). But gives me to understand, by letter, that it will not be possible for her to visit me so long as Ah resahd at Numbah 7, Lindsey Row. She offahs no explanation except . . . Mistah Haden forbids it— mah own daughtah! Really, Jemie, Ah can't imagine what it all may be about."

Whistler breathed a heartfelt curse, but softly enough that his mother could pretend not to have heard. He understood all too well both the ostensible and the true reasons for his brother-in-law's prohibition. To begin, Deborah Haden was the daughter of Mr. Whistler's *first* wife. Ostensibly, she was to be denied access to her stepmother's domicile because it was (or had been, until Mrs. Whistler's recent arrival and Jo Hiffernan's consequent departure) a Haunt of Sin.

In reality, Deborah could not abide the company of her stepmother, and it was surely at her own instigation that Haden had pronounced his interdict. They could not be together fifteen minutes before the old woman had found some way to make her "Dahling Debby" seethe. One of Whistler's earliest memories was of a Sunday morning in Springfield, Massachusetts, when his mother had locked away Deborah's favorite storybook (a collection of fairy tales), thereby provoking her into an hour-long tantrum. On the Sabbath, in the Christian household of the Whistlers, the Gospel of St. Matthew was not to be supplanted by the Gospel of Cinderella.

Whistler could sympathize with his half sister's reluctance to confront this dragon from her childhood after seventeen years of relative autonomy as wife and mother. Mrs. Whistler had set out to reform the Haden household immediately she had arrived in London, conducting prayer services for the servants from her sickbed, interrogating her granddaughter, Annie, in all the particulars of her own and her mother's faith and morals. Only Mrs. Whistler's removal to her son's home in Chelsea had prevented outright revolution against her autocracy.

He sympathized—but even so, he did resent the manner in which the Hadens had chosen to proclaim their independence. That Haden, himself a regular visitor to Lindsey Row in the days when Jo had presided there as its (and Jimmy's) mistress, should formerly have proscribed his wife from following him across that threshold had then seemed to Whistler a natural enough exercise of conjugal authority, but that the proscription should remain in force after Jo had been made to decamp, as though her presence lingered in the rooms like some moral bacillus—to use such an excuse, *that* was a piece of arrogance and Pecksniffery.

Mrs. Whistler, who understood these matters quite as well as her son, though she would have described them rather differently, interpreted the sudden rush of angry blood to his face as due and proper shame. She was pleased to think he might have begun to experience a moral awakening, and as this was more than she'd hoped to achieve, especially after the way he'd dismissed the grave matter of Sarah's "posing" (she was not fool enough to suppose for one moment that it went no further than that: Sarah was much too attractive a woman), she felt inclined to let him, temporarily, off the hook.

"Ah know what it is, Jemie: it's me. Rathah, it's Debby. Ah've nevah been able to make her love me. Not truly love me, like my own flesh and blood. It's a terrible thing for a mothah to have to confess. Lord knows, Ah've tried—tahm and again Ah've tried—but to Debby Ah'll always be the wicked stepmothah in the fairy tale."

This was cue enough for Whistler, who assured her that, on the contrary, Debby was her darling. The difficulty lay with Seymour Haden, who (Whistler was suddenly inspired with a plausible half-truth) had taken it into his head that the house on Lindsey Row had been tainted by the sometime presence there of—whom do you suppose?—Alphonse Legros!

"Alphonse Legros?" Mrs. Whistler repeated with some uncertainty, yet marveling in advance at her son's powers of improvisation. "Ah'm sure Ah've heard the name befoah . . . but whey-ah?"

"I've mentioned him in letters—he's one of the three members of the most exclusive club in Paris: the Society of Three (the other two members being Fantin-Latour and myself)."

"Oh yes, of course, now Ah recall. He's the bearded figure, isn't he, in your painting of Wapping? Fahn painting—even Ah can see that, and with mah poor failing eyes. But what has this Alphonse Legros to do with mah Debby's not coming here?"

Confident of his audience now, and with a conscious relish for the

shape of the tale about to unfold (he'd told it many times to other
audiences, both in French and in English, and he knew its shape and
texture as well as if it were some *objet d'art* long owned and deeply
pondered), Whistler sat beside his mother on the rush-bottomed settee,
placed a hand upon the two of hers folded in her lap, and commenced
to cast his spell.

"Back in, I believe, 'fifty-nine—" When he spoke to his mother, or
other Americans, Whistler slipped free of his Southern drawl and
spoke an English pure as any Etonian's. "—when I'd first come here
from Paris on holiday and fallen desperately in love with London's
weather and *La Tamise*, as our French friends call the Thames, I
persuaded some of my Parisian *confrères* to join me here, so that I
need not be torn between the delights of their company and those of
Rotherhithe and Wapping. Seymour was good enough to put my
friends up at Sloane Street, not altogether for reasons of altruism,
however. My brother-in-law, as you know, fancies himself an artist.
Indeed, his vanity on that account makes him rather a laughingstock
among the artists he so assiduously cultivates as friends, but as Rossetti says, we must be grateful for patrons, whatever shape they take.
Ha-ha."

This Ha-ha was not so much a laugh as a quick sketch of the *kind* of
laugh that might properly be prompted by his friend's remark, a sketch
heightened in its effect by a quick raising and lowering of his bushy
eyebrows. Such interpolations were not intrinsically humorous; rather,
one thought, "What a curious fellow he is, this Whistler!" Even his
mother—or perhaps she especially—could not resist his drolleries, his
teasing out an anecdote into an entire vaudeville complete (at his most
inspired moments) with songs and dances. Her principles were never
proof against him for long.

"And he did deign, before ever meeting Legros, to patronize him.
You may have seen the painting; it is hidden now in the hallway on the
second floor, *L'Angélus*: some women kneeling in a country church. A
bit too Barbizon for a modern taste, but we were young, and the
Barbizons had just come into their own, and there can be pleasure in
bringing off an *hommage* that captures just the tone of *l'homme à qui
l'on présente ses hommages*. Howsoever, Seymour bought Legros's
*Angélus*, had it framed in a gorgeous frame that cost easily twice what
he'd paid for the painting, and it was given the place of honor above
the mantel in the drawing room. Well, Legros followed his picture to

London, and naturally his first call was at Sloane Street, where, after being duly impressed with the frame, he discovered that Seymour, that great dilettante and tamperer Seymour, had repainted the entire floor of the chapel in the painting, thinking he would correct some mistake in its perspective that his pedantic eye had detected. Needless to say, he'd made a terrible botch of it. Seymour's etchings are quite bad enough, but his oils: oh no." Whistler lowered his eyelids in mock dismay and shook his head.

"Well!" With a suddenly brisker tempo, as he neared the resolution of his story: "In the face of such a crime I acted as a young man of honorable Virginia blood ought to act. I snatched the painting from Seymour's drawing room, and took it and Legros forthwith to my own studio, where he was able to scrape off Seymour's desecrations before the man himself arrived—who, confronted with the fait accompli, had the good grace to accept it without *open* rancor, only asking that Legros repaint what he'd rubbed out and do it better, to which Legros replied with a *'oui'* that stopped just short of a slap in the face. And that is how Seymour decided that my friend was the most degraded type of bohemian and a being whose presence in *this* house made it unfit for Deborah's delicate foot to step therein, thereafter. But I ask you—ought he not, by the same token, to debar my sister from her own house? For Legros has been a guest there too." Whistler concluded his performance with a *moue* of comic inquiry, and his mother, while putting no credence at all in his story (though it was, in fact, a true one), conceded it an approving chuckle.

A few minutes later Whistler took up his hat and excused himself, saying he meant to take a stroll in the night air. Mrs. Whistler knew quite well that his stroll would take him to Sloane Street, where he would have it out with Seymour Haden. Moreover, she thoroughly approved his intention, indeed, rather hoped they would come to blows, since Jemie would certainly emerge the victor from any such contest. It was really too much! Forbidding Debby to come to Lindsey Row because her son's mistress had lived here! As if the whole point of her own coming to live here weren't precisely to make it impossible for Jemie to go on leading an openly disreputable life. Well, he could be counted on to deal with Haden. The English were easily bullied. And, once she had her strength back, she would deal with Debby herself. Fleeing north through the battle lines of the war and then the crossing in the worst possible weather had taken the stuffing out of her. By spring she'd be able to reassert herself and regain some of her lost authority. In the meantime, she took pleasure of a sort in surveying the ground: it wasn't going to be easy to reform her son and make a proper marriage for him. Always there would be a maid to cow or a model to drive off. Significantly, he'd resisted her will in the crucial matter of becoming an artist, and with such success that even Anna Whistler had had reluctantly to recognize it.

In any event, it was too late now to make a civil engineer of him, or anything else entirely respectable. He was an artist, and so it was *as* an artist that he must now be broken to the curb of marriage and the saddle of a diligent, prosperous professionalism.

She gave the bell pull a purposeful tug. The serving maid would be respectably clothed again by this time.

She appeared at the door in cap and apron.

"Sarah, come ovah here a minute. Ah want to talk to you about Christ."

# CHAPTER TWENTY

# *Pain*

---

## FEBRUARY, 1864

As Carlyle entered the hall, the pregnant cat who went without a name lifted her head and stared luminously at him without stirring from her billet on the third step of the darkened stairway. Carlyle placed his open umbrella delicately on the hall carpet to dry, then mounted the steps, atypically hugging the wall in deference to the cat's comfort. The door leading from the upper hallway to his wife's bedroom was closed, but there was still a lamp burning in the drawing room.

Jane's friend Geraldine, hair gathered in a snood, looked up from the book that lay unread in her lap. When Carlyle seemed to hesitate outside the door connecting drawing room and bedroom, she shook her head.

"You'd best not," she whispered. "I gave her a second draught earlier. She's sleeping."

He looked about for somewhere to deposit a folded slip of paper, limp from the night's all-penetrating damp. Little by little, as the management of the household had given itself over to other hands than those of Jane Carlyle, the room had come to seem a churchyard chaos of lifeless forms.

"What is that?" Geraldine asked.

A smile broke over Carlyle's theretofore worried face, but then, like the sun slipping behind thin clouds, paled to extinction.

"*Ignis fatuus*, dire pealings of cracked bells—in plain talk, a tract." By way of disposing of it, he added it to the accumulation of books on the bookshelf. "When she wakes. Better she should sleep."

Geraldine nodded in thoughtful agreement, but then was overcome by curiosity and reached to retrieve the bit of paper. "*Awake, ye drunkards, and weep,"* she read aloud, unable to repress a tone of moderated incredulity, *"and howl, all ye drinkers of wine!"* She looked up to Carlyle for some reason why he thought it might interest Jane.

"If it scrupled to continue on to the end of the verse," he said, quickly providing an exegesis, "which, if I am not mistaken, reads, *because of the new wine; for it is cut off from your mouth,* the sentiment would, presumably, not appeal to the Christian Temperance Union of Stonington, Connecticut."

"I daresay." Geraldine squinted at the damp scrap of paper through her dark spectacles, wondering how it happened to have traveled the long watery distances from the American shore to Chelsea. She still couldn't understand what positive effect it could have over her suffering friend.

Jane was dying. Though no one but Jane herself ever stated the matter so bluntly, they were all certain her suffering could not continue at such a pitch much longer. Already she had lain immured in her bedroom for five months of the bitterest winter that anyone in Chelsea could remember; for five months endured malignancies of pain such as the Inquisition itself could not have exceeded, pain for which there was not even the solace of an explanation. The torn sinew she had suffered last September after being struck down on the street by a careering hansom had long ago mended, since when the specific pain of that injury seemed to have flowed with her blood to every tissue of her body. The doctors diagnosed "neuralgia," but only by way of giving a name to their ignorance and incapacity. No remedies served. Even with morphia she could not hope for more than three hours of sleep a night. All food repelled her, and she had withered to a skeleton.

Geraldine scarcely blamed Carlyle for hiding from such a memento mori in the (for once, blessedly) endless labors of his *Frederick the Great*. What use to Jane to have him on hand to witness the moans she couldn't restrain, the tears that would burst from her haunted eyes? The worst moments, though, were when the pain had passed and she was left exhausted—exhausted and yet in an agitation of fear of the moment when the pain would return—for it always did, with the unscheduled regularity of an in-law living in the same neighborhood. What can one *say* in such a case? What use are assurances of love or counsels of hope? Especially from such as he, who had long ago abandoned the God he'd grown up with, a God with whom one could bargain in one's prayers, a God susceptible to the bribe of a life reformed? Geraldine pitied him, and pitied herself, and despaired for Jane. Yet even so she was shocked to see him bring home a *tract*—as though he were declaring his own stony principles to be as bankrupt and barren as the age he'd made it his lifework to denounce.

She was completely at a loss, therefore, how finally to respond to it: Had he meant the tract to have *amused* Jane? And if so, in what manner was it to have accomplished so extraordinary a feat?

"I should explain," Carlyle said, unbidden, "that the peculiar interest of that bit of paper lies in the person of the giver—a poor soul once (long ago, and very briefly) in our employ. There she was posted just outside the *King's Head and Eight Bells*, now a grown woman. I was only turning from the river to make the last stage of my way homeward—"

The bell sounded, summoning Jane's attendant. Immediately Carlyle broke off his tale and followed Geraldine into his wife's bedroom.

"Jane?" Geraldine whispered.

"Geraldine: light the lamp. Carlyle—oh, that's better. Carlyle, who *was* it?"

He smiled awkwardly.

"Who was it gave you the tract?" Jane said, with an impatience at once sincere and exaggerated (for she knew in her ever-conscious heart that nothing was likelier to cheer her husband and Geraldine than to act in her accustomed manner).

"Then you were listening?"

"What else should I do while lying here awake? Do forget *me*, and continue with the tale. Oh, and where is the tract? I shall want to see *that*."

As Geraldine went back to the parlor to get the tract, the maid entered the bedroom, hair frowsy and drying her hands in her coarse cotton apron.

"Mum?" she inquired.

"Oh, Helen—it wasn't for you I rang."

"Are you feeling better, mum?" Helen asked with an artless hopefulness that made Carlyle blush for having thus far failed to ask that all-compelling question.

"Except I feel the lack of sleep."

"Then could I bring up a cup of broth?"

"Not now, Helen, it would only confirm my insomnia. Perhaps Carlyle or Geraldine would like some tea—would you ask them?"

Carlyle shook his head signifying that he would not, while Geraldine, from the drawing room, said a cup of tea was a splendid idea. She waited until Helen had come out to the landing, then told her in a whisper to bring up hot broth with the tea: an often-reenacted scene in the continuing conspiracy to tempt Jane to eat.

"Sometimes I wish she were not called Helen," said Jane, when the maid could be heard descending the stairs. "It always sets me to worrying what became of Helen Mitchell—no doubt drank herself to death, without a friend to console her. How *she* cared for me! I can still feel the tears on her cheek—ever deciding who was fit to be a visitor here, lining up the 'unladylike ladies' and the 'uncommon genteel.' It doesn't seem fair they should both have the same name. The one handing out tracts . . . it wasn't our Helen?"

Carlyle shook his head gravely. Helen Mitchell had had to be sent away more than ten years ago. "Well, Jeannie, I'm cheered to see you so lively. So like yourself."

"So like the self that is so lively, yes. Oh, is that it?" (taking the limp tract from Geraldine) "You were approaching the corner where she stood, but I still do not know who *she* was."

"It was Sereetha."

"Who?"

"The wee cockney craiture we took in, on a temporary basis, when Bessy left us—during your mother's visit. 'The Peesweep.' She told us her name was Sereetha, and it wasn't until I questioned her closely that I ascertained her name to be Sarah Heather, an appellation several syllables weightier than so little a maid might bear—seven years of age."

"I recollect vaguely . . . a child standing on a stool."

"Just so: Sereetha. Now grown to woman size."

"I'm surprised you recognized her. Nearly thirty years have passed."

"She knew me: 'Is it Mr. Carlyle?' says she, as shy as a child."

"Ah, poor soul," said Jane with a sigh.

"Contrarywise, she seems quite thriving."

"But to be handing out tracts before a public house. Only a reformed drunkard goes to such lengths of enthusiasm—"

"Or the wife of a drunkard," suggested Geraldine.

"That was my supposition first," continued Carlyle, "but her case is otherwise. I know, for I was obliged to hear her history, in minutest detail, from the day she left our kitchen to return to her mother's arms, to events of an hour past in some *airtist*'s studio off beyond Battersea Bridge."

"Ach!"

"Not on her own initiative was she distributing these tracts, but at the insistence of her employer's *mother*."

"Then she is a housemaid?"

"The lass stressed her role as model."

"She must be nearly forty now."

"But she has a face like my own dear little woman, a face that shows no age."

It was not like Carlyle to proffer his hidebound tendernesses other than through the post, and Jane was, accordingly, more nearly distressed with the compliment than touched—but managed not to show it; indeed, she treated the word of flattery like a bibelot that has lived for years on the same out-of-the-way shelf and so become invisible. "She lived over a fishmonger. I remember that as clearly as if it were yesterday. But something else is there now instead of the fishmonger. I can't remember what. Are you sure it was Sereetha?"

"*Sairtainly,*" he answered with good nature, "and she asked most particularly to be remembered to you, and was grieved to hear of your accident. She knew of it already."

At the mention of the accident the interest he'd awakened vanished, to be replaced by the familiar, far-off look of awaited pain.

"She offered to supply a kind of jelly she avers to be an infallible remedy for sciatic pains. Whistler's mother—that is the painter's name —uses it."

Of a sudden, Jane grew agitated. "Oh, Carlyle—you *didn't* say she might!"

"No, no, never fear—"

"I can't bear company now. Not a servant who has worked here. Please! And if Bessy calls again, she must be told I'm dead! I won't be sent to an asylum."

"Jeannie!"

"Promise me."

"St. Leonards is not an asylum—it is Dr. Blakiston's private dwelling place."

Just then, as Jane was about to collapse in tears, Helen arrived with the tea and the steaming broth. Jane wrinkled her nose in disgust at the thin brew and asked quietly to be left alone.

"If you would let me help your puir self," Carlyle said from the doorway.

"No one can help," Jane stated flatly. "Please close the door."

Two weeks later, at her own request, Jane was removed (by hearse-like "sick carriage") to St. Leonards to live in the household of her former maid Bessy and Bessy's distinguished husband, Dr. Blakiston. The Blakistons refused to accept payment for her lodging or treatment. Dr. Blakiston seemed to hope for the *réclame* of Jane's cure, for since the death of Lord Ashburton (news of which had prudently been withheld from her), she had the thankless distinction of being London's most discussed invalid. However, neither the salt air nor the Blakistons' well-meaning attentions wrought the change that had been hoped for, nor yet did the progress of the weather from winter to spring exert its usual power of suggestion.

Carlyle stayed on alone at Cheyne Row, already a widower in his imagination; grieved, in both senses—of anger and of sorrow; careless (for the first time in his life) of his own apperance and of the house's management.

This carelessness came most opportunely for Mary Callaghan, the senior of the two serving girls, an Irishwoman who seemed much older than her twenty-five years, by reason both of her matronly figure and the boorish character of her face. Mrs. Oliphant, who had visited often during the course of Jane's illness, insisted that she had seen the twin of Mary in a painting by Ostade (in an Amsterdam gallery) depicting peasants reeling drunkenly in a country inn. "And so I am not surprised to learn," she later declared, when the truth was made public knowledge, "that Mary was not the noddy she pretended to be. It is never wise to credit a servant with stupidity, for it is invariably an affectation."

But that is to anticipate. Interestingly enough, through all the time Carlyle lived with Mary and Helen as his daily companions, he never once saw through the efforts Mary took to conceal her disgrace. Finally, despite all that corsets could do, her disgrace had proclaimed itself so boldly that Carlyle's neighbors had to suppose his silence on the matter represented a tacit understanding: after all, between the labors of finishing his *Frederick* and a dying wife, he would not now want to take on the difficulties of finding and breaking in a new cook— he who couldn't boil water! This was surely Mary Callaghan's view of the matter, and she accordingly began to indulge still greater license, inviting her lover, Jimmy Hannah, an Irishman who kept both a coffee stand and a wife in Hammersmith, to spend entire weeks at Cheyne Row (such times as Carlyle would be away at the cottage he'd rented in St. Leonards). Mary did not feel she was taking undue liberties. A death in the family, particularly when it was one's mistress who was dying, always offered the servants a sort of holiday, and so long as they observed due proportion, where was the harm? Mary saw to it that her lover never filched silver or china, and she prudently conserved a portion of the liquor the Carlyles' friends had given them (for, sad to tell, they rarely laid down any bottles themselves). But she could see no reason why she must sleep on a thin straw mat in the kitchen when the mistress's ideally comfortable bed lay open and inviting; nor why she should not take her tea in the good china; nor why, if the curtains were drawn, she might not entertain a few of Jimmy's friends when the rain made a marsh of Cremorne Gardens.

As to her pregnancy, Mary had naturally felt some anxiety since she knew it might cause her to be dismissed at the very time when her position had become so advantageous. But if Carlyle looked the other way, and if his wife lingered on in St. Leonards, Mary felt confident that she could deal with other potential enemies. Helen, in *her* rare moods of rebellion, sometimes threatened to inform against her, but a simple counterthreat of poisoning Helen's food put the kibosh on that idea. Helen, after all, was enjoying the Carlyles' absence quite as much as she, and it was only such times as Jimmy became uproarious or the bed fell apart (it was easily fixed) that Helen needed a bit of nerving up.

Mary's other enemy was not so manageable. Henry Larkin was a ticket collector on a Chelsea steamer, who, from idolatry of Carlyle or sheer love of drudgery, had become the great man's unpaid secretary. He indexed and proofread galleys of *Frederick*, did the more inconvenient and dusty forms of research for that book, and kept the Carlyles supplied with flowers from his own garden. This garden was visible from the Carlyles' back windows, for Larkin, apostolic in his devotion, had moved himself and his mother into No. 6, the next house up Cheyne Row, so as to be more completely at Carlyle's beck and call. When, with the improving weather, Carlyle had gone off to join Jane at their rented cottage in St. Leonards (Jane, by resisting the miracle of an immediate cure, had outworn her welcome with the

Blakistons), it fell to Henry Larkin to keep his master's house and servants under surveillance, which he did with his customary unimaginative diligence. For Henry as much as for the paid servants Jane's illness was an inadmissible blessing. He luxuriated among books hallowed by Carlyle's touch; he had a second garden in which to potter; he could make all the rooms of the shrine his own (except, from an uneasy sense of deference to the mysteries of womanhood and death, Jane's bedroom, which he would only look into to make sure it had been dusted).

The keys to the house had been entrusted to Henry in May, when Mary was already into her seventh month, well past the point when corseting was an effective deceit. Her first child, which had come when she was only sixteen, had not swelled her up so, but then she had not been so handsomely provided for during that pregnancy. Perforce, when Carlyle's factotum appeared (never with the least warning), Mary was obliged to betake herself to the kitchen and twiddle her thumbs for the duration of his visit. Fortunately, Henry's curiosity did not extend below stairs, and he chose not to notice that it was always Helen who answered his ring. Fortunately, too, Henry had to rise early for his job on the steamer and so could be counted upon not to linger longer of an evening than eight o'clock. Only once did he turn up when the guilty father was on the premises, and Mary herself, corseted almost to apoplexy, had been able to pass him off as a man come to check the flues (since which time anything to do with the functioning of the chimneys was sure to provoke a round of laughter).

It seemed that Mary would be able to come to term right there in the Carlyles' house, might even call in a midwife—and no one ever the wiser. But then her luck turned. Jane, whose insomnia had pursued her (together with her husband) to the Kentish coast, decided to flee it again, this time to Scotland, whither for the time being Carlyle was not inclined to follow. Jane passed through London without looking in at Cheyne Row, whose rooms had come to seem the concrete form of her pains. Never, she had told her husband, did she wish to enter No. 5, Cheyne Row, again—which he interpreted not so much as a reflection on the thirty years they had spent there together as an admission, even a warning, that she was now hastening to Scotland to die, as salmon return to the stream in which they were spawned.

That Jane meant to accomplish this business of dying in Scotland was, of course, welcome news to Mary. Not so the letter announcing Carlyle's imminent arrival on the 19th of July.

On the 29th of July, Carlyle returned home from his afternoon constitutional accompanied by Geraldine Jewsbury. Helen barely had time to close the doors between the dining room and the smaller breakfast room before Carlyle had entered the dining room and rung for tea, for himself and his self-invited guest. Helen fidgeted, then tried to persuade him to take tea in the garden—it was such a nice, cool day—but Carlyle was not in a suggestible mood. Quite the contrary. In addition to having given in to "the fluff of feathers" (Geraldine), whom he would decidedly rather have left at her door, his bowels had been in a state of rebellion for quite two weeks, a discomfort which, in Jane's absence, he could complain of only to the empty air. He'd, moreover, been exasperated at lunchtime by a letter from Emerson, whose Abolitionist rhetoric had grown unconscionable now that (as he maintained) the North was certain of victory; so exasperated that he'd ripped the letter up. Exasperation with himself was only now setting in for having thus created a lacuna in the carefully preserved file of their correspondence. Nevertheless, having accidentally encountered Geraldine in the King's Road and told her of letters at home from Jane, he was now obliged to let her see them, for there could be no making light of Geraldine's concern. It was she who translated his "Sometime hence you must see them," to their taking tea together that afternoon, even undertaking to supply cakes herself from the baker on Duke Street.

Meanwhile behind the double doors leading onto the breakfast room, Mary Callaghan had begun to feel her labor pains in earnest. Thinking to be safely solitary, she'd come there to rest in her favorite armchair, the softest in the house, having taken the usual precaution of locking the door to the hallway so that Carlyle might not catch her by surprise if he should suddenly arrive. When the first contractions had begun she'd called out to Helen, who'd reached her side just as Carlyle (accompanied by the loquacious Geraldine) was arriving. Helen had had the presence of mind to close the double doors connecting dining room and breakfast room behind her, leaving Geraldine to wait alone in the front room while Carlyle fetched the letters, but she neglected to bring with her the duplicate key to the door between hall and breakfast room. Now, unless Mary's pains ceased long enough to allow her to unlock the door herself, she was trapped there.

Far from ceasing, the pains grew worse. Stifling any outcry, Mary made for herself, out of a great tumble of table linen, a kind of damask cave beneath the assembled portraits—some glowering, others benign: Voltaire, Coleridge, Goethe, Cromwell's wife—in the small china clost at the rear of the room. To keep from crying out she stuffed a serviette in her mouth. The taste of the starch seemed, for an instant, blissfully delicious. Then the pains were renewed.

"What a thing for your brother to have said to Jane!" Geraldine declared, having tucked the last of the three letters back into its envelope. "It's as much as to accuse her of malingering—to say that no *poor* woman could ever be so afflicted. To accuse Jane—of all people! —of having never *done* anything in her life . . . , and in the midst of such sufferings! It is too cruel."

"Just so I told my poor darling when I wrote to her: 'cruel and absurd,' I said."

Geraldine seemed somewhat mollified by his ready agreement but still alert for any hint of equivocation on his part. Dr. John, Carlyle's brother, was a perfect dunce, or, in the words of old Sterling, "not a man at all but a walking Cabbage," and yet Carlyle himself had in the past shown an unswerving loyalty toward this "problem" brother. Her own theory for Jane's malady was that anyone obliged to live years of her life with a man of Carlyle's querulous, self-regarding temper must eventually pay a mortal price, just as a plant that lives in arid soil will wither and die. Though it had never come to an open quarrel between them, he must have had some sense of her reprobation, for he was not without powers of observation. It would not do, therefore, to engage him in any serious discussion of the matter. Instead, in the manner of a wise governess, she tried to direct his behavior by making a parable of her own intended course of action.

"I shall indite a letter to her tonight," she declared, as Helen entered to lay the table for their tea, "and I shall endeavor to be very *cheerful* and *positive*. For it cannot be of any comfort to her to read my complainings about, for example, the troubles I've been having with my *eyes*. No, I must think of something I have *done*, some *event*—the sort of thing *her* letters spin out so well."

Carlyle concurred silently, morosely sensing that she meant to chatter.

The table was set. Helen stood nervously before the closed double doors to the breakfast room. Without straining, she could hear Mary's serviette-muffled cries. (Why couldn't *they?*) Again she suggested the garden for their tea, but Carlyle dismissed the suggestion with a grimace of annoyance.

"But it is so *difficult* at times," Geraldine went on, "to recall to mind what has happened in one's life that bears mentioning. I did have an adventure of sorts yesterday—"

"Oh yes?" Carlyle inquired, pouring the tea.

"I took a ride on the new Metropolitan Railroad, the one that runs *under* the Marylebone Road. It was the strangest experience. One proceeds down a stairway at Baker Street and eventually finds oneself in a cavern, which becomes very *steamy* as the train approaches, much like the Hades I imagined as a child. The train moves so quickly that in moments I was at Euston Square."

A cough hinting of his disapprobation was Carlyle's sole comment.

"You don't approve of underground railroads?"

"No, the milk is curdled; it's spoilt my tea. Just another example of the mismanagement that grows here daily with Jeannie away. For that matter, I don't love railroads *under* the ground, *on* it, or a mile *above*, should some blockhead devise a means of routing them through the Heavens. Londontown needs no new source of steam, smoke, soot, and uproar, nor does it need to grow larger. Soon enough Chelsea, even, will become no more than a borough of a single, sprawling, formless, clattering, money-mad metropolis—Excuse me, I must find another cup."

But before he could rise from the table, Helen, who had been listening all the while outside the door, forestalled him: "Please, sir, let me," she insisted, slipping into the breakfast room.

To her astonishment, the room was empty. Only after testing the hall door (still locked) did she notice the closed door to the china closet.

"I'm sorry about the milk, sir," she said, returning with a fresh cup and saucer and placing them before Carlyle. "It was got fresh from the dairy this morning, but the weather's been like an oven."

"Ay de mi," Carlyle moaned in his most martyred manner.

But Geraldine was in no mood to pity him. "For *my* part, I regard the Metropolitan Line as an unalloyed blessing." She took a deliberate sip of tea. "But you'd have to be a *woman* to understand."

He shook his head forlornly, as who would say, "Impossible to reason with such an one."

"*Jane* would surely understand. If she'd been on the railway platform instead of in the midst of the bustle of the street, she wouldn't have had to dodge that speeding hansom, and wouldn't *then* have slipped in the mud of the street. Indeed, were it for no other reason than for cleanliness, the Metropolitan Line must be applauded. Men could understand *that*, if they had to wear skirts that sweep the pavements."

"If they *did*," Carlyle replied testily, "they wouldn't be fiddle-diddling every which way—they'd have enough good sense to pick them up!"

"Assuming there were a servant at hand to carry one's parcels," Geraldine answered laconically.

During the brief silence that followed her remark, a human sound (half grunt, half cry) seemed to issue from without the house. Both heard it, though neither made a directly related comment.

"Ach, poor Jeannie," said Carlyle, now lachrymose. " 'Tis true, just as ye've said, she should have had her own barouche."

"Was *that* what I said?"

He rose from the table. "You'll have to excuse me, Geraldine. I canna think of anything but my puir Jeannie and what she's suffering. . . ." Tears formed in the corners of his eyes. "I'd like to be more civil, but—" He shook his head.

After Helen had shown Geraldine out the door and knew Carlyle to be safely upstairs, she returned to the breakfast room. "Mary," she whispered, outside the still-closed door to the china closet.

"Come in," said Mary weakly, "and bring a cuppa tea?"

Helen opened the door and saw her friend spread out unceremoniously on the linen-strewn floor with her newborn son nestled just where God had placed him, in the Carlyles' best tablecloth.

"The master's gone," said Helen, lifting the child gingerly. "Did he never cry?"

"Not once," said Mary. "It was as though he knew he shouldn't't."

# CHAPTER TWENTY-ONE

# *Resurrections*

## NOVEMBER, 1864

"To confess the greatest change," said Jane, sitting in her own brougham (Carlyle's gesture of thanksgiving at the return of her health) beside Lady Louisa, "I have come to believe fervently in the Resurrection! Formerly I doubted its literal truth, but now—having experienced my own unhoped-for resurrection—how may I continue to doubt! Despite, as you can see, that I am still too weak to walk even this short distance, words cannot express the relief I feel each new day that I persist in being *well*."

"Yes," said Lady Louisa, "it is extraordinary. I am so happy."

"It is as though—" Jane titled her head back, searching for a metaphor; with her left hand she touched the wrinkled flesh of her neck meditatively. "—as though I had awakened from the realms of Purgatory to a world positively radiant with things beautiful." Jane winced, hearing herself give voice to what Carlyle, if he were present, would have called "unprincipled blockheadism."

Lady Louisa (her mind elsewhere) did not reply except by a smile, innocent of implication.

The houses at the foot of Cheyne Row flanked the stage of life, Jane fancied, across which she glimpsed, as from a balcony seat, carriages and characters entering and exiting. The same sun that lighted the autumn-dappled cobbles inflamed the roses of Lady Louisa's hat—but the significance?

"I do not mean to claim sainthood," Jane went on, conscious of her friend's complacent expectation that *she* maintain the momentum of the conversation. "However open wide my eyes may be, I am still the doubting soul you have known formerly. When Mrs. Southern materialized on the doorstep and told me how my house had been managed in my absence—I *did* tell you of Mary and Helen?—my temper flared like that of a woman of three-and-thirty! I descended to the kitchen; would listen to none of their pleas for forgiveness; I huffed and fuffed like Jehovah Himself (I mean Carlyle, of course. I would not blaspheme here in my own carriage!), all the while hardly keeping myself from laughing. Ach! There was a detail which came forth only yesterday when Mrs. Southern came to help me instruct the new girl: early last month *after* I'd returned (but before I discovered the depths of Mary's perfidy), my appetite had diminished to such a degree that the only beverage I could bring myself to taste was that lovely champagne you and Bingham supplied us with last winter. As soon as I'd declared my preference, Carlyle, who has become quite promiscuous in his indulgence of me, vowed that there should always be a bottle at hand, cooled and ready to open (he thinking, of course, that a full dozen bottles remained). And so when (true daughter of Eve that I am) within three days I'd depleted all the bottles *actually* extant, Mary was obliged to replace, in greatest haste, all that she and her man had consumed! And how do you suppose she accomplished this Great Work?"

Lady Louisa pursed her lips.

"*Helen* was dispatched—the power that Mary had over her I shall never understand!—to pawn my good china! So as to supply *me* with more champagne. Accordingly, in a week I had drunk up *all* my best porcelain, and if Mrs. Southern had not come bearing her tale, we should now be eating off crockery from a high street peddler's cart!"

Lady Louisa laughed prettily. "Oh, it is such a delight to hear you again. All the while you were away that was just what I missed so much—your voice, and the stories."

"I daresay that is what I missed most myself. Disease renders all the truisms truer, and among them the injunction to *Know Thyself*. In my sickbed (better to say *death*bed) I learned just how gregarious I am—I need the companionship of old friends as much as a plant needs water. Returning to London has been, as I say, a resurrection."

"I'm glad to know that you mean to be social, still. My mother, after her long pleurisy, became very reclusive. But I suppose she'd always inclined to be solitary. When I was a girl, she always resisted coming up to London for the Season."

"Oh, social I shall be—an intrepid lion-hunter!"

Lady Louisa laughed, rather more heartily than before. "But that is most ridiculous, Mrs. Carlyle! You are the lion! A lioness, I should rather say."

"Nonsense. I have simply been privileged to live in the thick of things—call it Civilization. Being married to Carlyle is tantamount to having an ideal place in the stalls at Covent Garden—and yet one is still amongst the rabble—as opposed to sitting in an actual *box.* To give credit where due, the stall's view cannot be surpassed, while Scotland, though it gave my health back, was comparable to a place in the most distant row of the balcony. There, I thought long and hard about my former life. I became quite voracious in my hunger for human speech—and *not* of the countrified variety! That, Lady Louisa, is my reason for so shamelessly stalking this young Rossetti."

"If you had ever made known to me, my dear, your desire to make this acquaintance, I should have arranged it long ago."

"Had it ever occurred to me before, I might well have! I did many years past enjoy the dubious pleasure of watching his father, '*the* Dr. Rossetti,' make a perfect fool of *him*self reciting bad poetry. We shall see what the painter-son has up his sleeve by way of an improvement!"

"I am sure," said Lady Louisa, "I've spoken of him to your husband—"

"Oh, Carlyle has no curiosity about painters, and almost none about poets. Also, I deduce that what he *has* heard of him through Ruskin and Browning has not disposed him to cultivate the acquaintance. In point of fact, I sit here today with you in Sure Risk of crossing my own husband! Yet now I am to have my own way in Everything: fresh milk each morning from the rector's cow, this wonderful brougham, and (best of all) freedom to call upon whomever I like! Tell me, do *you* like him—do you like his work?'

"Oh yes, quite—what I've seen of it. He doesn't show in galleries, and won't submit to the Royal Academy, so it is only those things one's friends have purchased and chosen to hang that one may judge by."

"But you *have* visited him at Cheyne Walk previously?"

"Yes, with credit again to Mr. Munro."

Jane knew that Lady Louisa did not like to express a judgment in possible defiance of some as-yet-unknown consensus, so rather than press the question, she continued in her soliloquizing vein:

"You know of his marriage—and how it ended?"

"Yes, a terrible misfortune."

"I am told by my husband (who learned it directly from Ruskin) that when the poor woman was laid out in her coffin he placed with her a volume containing the only record of all his poems."

"Really!"

"Carlyle said that in that way he buried *all* the indiscretions of his youth. Without knowing either the poet or the poems (not to mention the dead lady), the judgment seems both cruel and unjust. When I told this to Geraldine—you have met Miss Jewsbury?"

"Indeed."

"Geraldine cannot resist a mystery, and when I told her of the buried poems, she promptly burrowed into the periodical file of Bentley's, for whom she reads, and discovered in some magazines from the 'fifties a sampling of what the world presumes lost forever."

"And?"

Jane's shrug was dismissive without being disdainful. "For such a young man as he then must have been they seemed accomplished. Well-turned phrases, clever enough rhymes, a superfluity of morbid fancy, yet none of the spasmodic puffery that even Mr. Browning was prey to in his youth. Do you know, I am not entirely sure but that I heard and saw this Mr. Rossetti when he was still a child, in the same context as the father—at the anniversary of Mazzini's Italian school."

"But what were they *about?*" Lady Louisa insisted. "The *poems.*"

"That is the difficulty: I almost couldn't say. One concerns a very decorative sort of woman, waiting for her lover to die and join her in Heaven. Another, a ballad, was written in imitation-medieval style. Oh, and there was an excessively pathetic poem on the death of his sister Margaret at Christmas Eve."

"I don't believe he *has* a sister Margaret."

"Geraldine liked them better than I. He adopts a tone of seeming to resent (but not to resist) the world's ills—including his own. I believe he did well to bury them! Is that your Mr. Munro coming up the walk toward us?"

"Yes!" Lady Louisa opened the door of the barouche and signaled with a wave of the hand to the long-awaited mutual friend (hers and Rossetti's), who had agreed to accompany the two ladies. Introductions were made and Munro was summoned by Mrs. Carlyle to take the facing seat. Then, with a rap at the forward-looking window to rouse Sylvester from his nap, they were on their way to 16, Cheyne

Walk, before the elaborate iron gate of which they arrived punctually at the stipulated hour of two o'clock.

The man who greeted them at the door, shooing away his own servants (and then calling them back again to take the wraps), was neither so young nor so uncommon as Jane had been led to expect. Only his beard, in its scruffy irregularity (like a hedge gone wild), pronounced him a bohemian. The drawing room into which he conducted his guests was of a similar character: a prevailing genteel shabbiness enlivened by vignettes of permitted disorder; piles of things (mostly books) so firmly established as to be invisible to a servant's eye; in the darkest corner—none were bright—a feather duster had been placed in a vase and allowed to pose as a bouquet. Lower window panes shone noticeably cleaner than those above; likewise the lower portions of the many mirrors. A household of bachelors. Though not disgraceful; not even (Jane took the seat she was offered) uncomfortable.

While Lady Louisa repeated her account of their morning's odyssey of shopping, to which Munro responded by chronicling a jumble sale he'd attended the previous week in Pimlico, Jane tried to identify the smell inhabiting the room—a smell at once elusive and familiar. An unhealthy smell, yet oddly not altogether unpleasant, distantly masked by the combined odors of oils and turpentine.

Soon after the first amenities had drifted away into silence, like coals that have not taken fire, the airless peace was rent with a gargling shriek.

"Dear God!" cried Jane, "What is *that?*"

"That," said Rossetti in sepulchral tones, "is my last peacock."

"He doesn't sound at all well. Shouldn't we look to see that he is not trapped between the jaws of a sea turtle?"

"In point of fact," said Rossetti, twiddling the scraggy ends of his beard, "he is dying."

An awkward pause ensued, as it did regularly now when anyone mentioned death or dying, however obliquely, in Jane's presence. It was up to her to rescue them.

"That is the dark side of making friends with animals. Their lives are both shorter and, in town especially, more precarious than those of humans. We lost my poor wee Nero. A lapdog. Eleven years together and such sufferings he put me through! So many times he was either lost or stolen. Twice he attempted suicide by jumping from an upper window of the house, and once, to his ultimate undoing, he was mangled by a butcher's cart in the street. When he died (he'd been suffering so for days that I gave him up to be poisoned), a sampling of humanity made characteristic suggestions: that I switch to *cats* thereafter—or that I might have Nero stuffed and put in a glass case! Imagine. I commenced to feel like Miss Squeers in *Nickleby*, 'hating the world and wishing everybody in it dead.' Others urged me to accept the present of a *new* dog—once, *six* were offered in succession!—but I could never undergo another such bereavement, and had to decline."

Lady Louisa made a face of public confusion.

"You mean to say, I have Tiny now. Yes, that is so. But I've given him to understand that he is obliged to outlive his mistress. Still, it is almost as painful to think of the poor child—all pets are children, you see," she noted, with a shrewd glance at Rossetti, lest he suppose that she were unconscious of her own doting. "To think of Tiny left behind without me, after I've taken such pains to make myself the center of his existence! The Indian practice of suttee, morally suspect as it is in the human realm, seems the most satisfactory way to deal with pets."

"Perhaps," said Rossetti, with a smile of applause. "At least in the case of such affectionate pets as your Nero must have been. As for my peacock, I have never felt any kind of sympathetic bond between us. He hasn't even a name. I doubt, indeed, he knows I am anything other than an occasional intrusive presence. And yet he is very beautiful, and that makes him welcome. Or he *was* beautiful until he lost his tail."

"I see you have salvaged a feather," Lady Louisa remarked, indicating the single slender and iridescent outcropping from the brass spittoon to one side of the fireplace.

Munro, accommodating the glint of interest in Jane's eye, got up to bring the feather for her closer inspection and, as though by foreordination, the sun came out from behind a cloud, making the room's mahogany furnishings reply with a responsive glow.

Rossetti had evidently been waiting for the better light, as he at once marshaled them up from the sofa and down the long dark hallway to his studio. Jane, on Munro's arm, which he'd offered as though they were going to dinner, followed at her own slower pace. As an invalid she had the prerogative of dawdling. Not that there was anything of interest to linger over. She simply wanted to draw out the pleasing theatrical tingle of curiosity certain soon to be gratified by the parting of the curtain.

The curtain parted: "Bravo," declared the voice of consciousness, as she passed across the threshold from the hall's darkness to the studio's light, which seemed to issue from the paintings as much as from the high-reaching windows. Rossetti was a consummate show-man, no doubt of it. He had done well to insist so particularly on the hour they were to arrive and then to keep them waiting for the best light. The paintings, six of them, were positioned in a louvered pattern slantwise down the length of the room, each on its own easel with draperies disposed behind it. The few pieces of furniture were huddled against the bare white walls like poor relations at a wedding reception. The paintings, liberated from those walls, glowed like extravagantly polychromed porcelains, an effect as intense as it was unnatural. They were, at a glance and in a word, luxurious, and they chose to represent women, singly and in decorative groups, all arrayed in costumes sumptuous and somewhat antique. The effect, for Jane, was of a very melancholy costume party to which no men have been invited. The women languished and sulked and combed out immense tangles from their abounding hair.

"This," said Rossetti, introducing them first to the lady with the comb, the nearest of the six, "is *Lady Lilith.*"

Lady Louisa nodded, as though Lady Lilith were an acquaintance of long standing. She did not, however, linger before the lady's portrait, but passed on to the next painting. "And this?"

"I call it *The Loving Cup.*"

Lady Louisa praised the colors.

Jane lingered by the door, puzzling over the effect of the paintings *en masse.* Both in matter and in manner they seemed calculated to put one in mind of the Renaissance, and once one got round the unnaturalness of that ambition, they succeeded at their task well enough, though the Renaissance one was put in mind of was not one that Jane could approve—*not* the Renaissance of Florence with its great intellectual audacities, but rather of Venice, the Venice for whose merchant princes Veronese and Titian had painted their endless successions of courtesans, represented both in their own disreputable character and as Olympian goddesses. Carlyle, apropos the writings of his protégé Ruskin, had often and roundly denounced the fleshpots of Venice, and though Jane did not appropriate *all* her husband's opinions to her own use, she had always felt uncomfortable in those rooms of the National Gallery where the Venetians reigned supreme in their sybaritic pomp. Fleshpots: exactly. And that seemed to be the sole commodity that Mr. Rossetti trafficked in. What could anyone, especially of the female sex, politely say of such celebrations of bosoms, of such paeans to the twin arts of hairdressing and seduction?

Lady Louisa's answer to this question seemed evasive, not to say hypocritical: "Such a *glow*, Mr. Rossetti!" And then, before the next canvas: "What sumptuous *flowers*!" As though flowers were in any way at issue.

With a sense of controlled aversion, as though looking behind a cabinet where bugs are suspected, Jane approached *Lady Lilith* for a closer examination.

Mr. Munro, who had taken it upon himself to be Jane's companion (she, after all, was but an onlooker; Lady Louisa might very well buy), pointed out to her that on the back of this unfinished painting, glued to the wood of the stretcher, there was a sonnet (also Rossetti's), which interpreted the painting's not at all obscure meanings; and indeed it did. The last six lines were particularly explicit:

> *The rose and poppy are her flowers; for where*
> *Is he not found, O Lilith, whom shed scent*
> *And soft-shed kisses and soft sleep shall snare?*
> *Lo: as that youth's eyes burned at thine, so went*
> *Thy spell through him, and left his straight neck bent,*
> *And round his heart one strangling golden hair.*

The poem and the painting seemed altogether to prostrate themselves before the prospect of Lilith's kisses—but in such a sniveling way. Bobbie Burns had, doubtless, celebrated as many of *his* Lady Liliths in his bawdier verses, but at least he'd done so with gusto. So, upon considering it, had the painters of Venice. Rossetti seemed positively to revel in morbidity, to exult over it, to caress it. Still, one had to allow that the result had its fascination, albeit an unseemly one. That last line in particular stuck in the memory: "And round his heart one strangling golden hair." Jane wondered whether she would have liked the wife—what had she had to suffer from him?

When all six paintings had been surveyed, Rossetti, as a last *coup de théâtre*, was prevailed upon by Munro to show a seventh, which stood, by a wonderful convenience, upon an easel in the brightest corner of the room. Rossetti had only to whisk away the remnant of damask that had veiled it and, "Oh *my!*" Lady Louisa declared (prophetically, as the event would prove). "I say," said Munro.

Jane continued to keep her own counsel. Though relieved that the unveiled picture did not represent another latter-day hetaera, she could not at once unriddle the subject, which thus seemed much stranger than it would have with its title spelled out, gallery-wise, in a cartouche at the base of the frame. To Jane's eye, its most salient feature was simply the extraordinary length and thickness of the young woman's neck. She held a sword to the side of her face—by way, it would seem, of emphasizing her Grecian profile, though even so it was the wonder of that neck to which one's eyes returned. *Then* Jane observed a pair of feet pendent from the upper right corner of the painting—feet oddly *smaller* than the hands that clutched the sword; these feet (she realized, with a wince of distaste) must belong to a giant, unseen crucifixion. A lily lay on a damask cloth, the original of which had been the painting's covering—and served now for backdrop. The sheen of the woman's armor and of so many rich and varied yardgoods imparted a sense of luxury equal to that of the other paintings, if more chaste.

"I've never seen," said Lady Louisa, "a more inspired Joan. *There* is a woman I can believe able to lead armies."

The lily, the sword, the armor, even the feet of Christ—Jane felt an idiot not to have taken their sum.

"I assume (because I like it so) this has been sold," said Lady Louisa.

"It belongs to Mr. Anderson Rose, my solicitor. I have it, as it were, on loan."

"Is not that always the way of things. You *knew*, didn't you, how much I'd like this?"

"Kind of you to say so, Lady Ashburton."

"Your *Lilith* is quite admirable, and for all I know of such matters possibly a better painting. But she is not someone I should want to *live* with as a daily presence."

"Indeed," said Rossetti, with a smile of coy, almost boyish complicity.

"She is not Shakespeare's Joan," Jane could not forbear observing.

"No, not at all," Rossetti replied earnestly. "Shakespeare was woefully mistaken about Joan, who was neither a witch nor a hoyden, nor yet a lunatic. I have often thought, reading Michelet's account, how much more suitable a subject Joan would be for your husband's pen, Mrs. Carlyle, than for my brush. She was that rarest of combinations —a soldier and a saint; the Cromwell of her age, one might say."

"*You* say so, Mr. Rossetti, and your picture says so very handsomely—" (This was as near as she would come to a compliment.) "—but I'm sure that my husband would say otherwise. He'd never have tolerated her abandoning of petticoats, for example. I remember during the days of Mrs. Bloomer (you'd be too young to remember her) how incensed he became on the subject. No, if he had been alive then, he would have been among the English who signed the warrant for Joan's execution."

They laughed, glad for the opportunity.

"That's not *quite* true, of course," she added, as though relenting. "He's much too shrewd a politician to have made a martyr of an enemy. He would have had her locked up in some out-of-the-way dungeon, more likely. I think I would have, too."

"Jane, you're not in earnest," Lady Louisa declared.

Sudden as a shift of light, fleeting as a remark overheard on the street, Jane felt a pang of headache. Before she could twist her head sideways (in an exploratory motion), the sensation vanished. Even so, her dread mounted, for the possibility had been stated. It was as though that overheard remark had revealed some misfortune directly pertinent to one's own welfare—the death of a friend, the bankruptcy of the bank in which one's life savings were on deposit.

"Excuse me a moment. I must . . ." She tightened her lips in a humorless smile, a plea to be left alone. ". . . sit."

"Should we—" Lady Louisa began, but Jane forestalled the question with a peremptory wave of the hand.

"Are you quite all right, Mrs. Carlyle?" Munro insisted, as though (were she not) he was empowered to offer a remedy.

Rossetti, to do him credit, simply nodded a casual acquiescence, then (after a quick glance of appraisal) turned his attention back to Lady Louisa.

Jane retired to an aged sofa inexpertly covered with rough brown holland. The unbleached cover was stained on one arm with a daub of the same gaudy red-orange that glowed from the square beads about the neck of the girl in *The Loving Cup*. Jane sat down cautiously, and the cushion seemed to sink beneath her weight almost to the floor. As it was pressed down, there appeared, to her side, rising from between the cushions like a revenant, a dirty glass. Hastily she thought to press it beneath the adjacent cushion; then, thinking what might befall the next person to sit (likely as not Lady Louisa), changed her mind. The smell she'd noticed in the drawing room asserted itself distinctly: it was that of laudanum. But to be certain, she lifted the glass to her nose, keeping her eye fixed on Rossetti, who faced the other way. Yes, laudanum—and judging by the deposit that rimmed the glass, a powerful infusion in its time. She bent forward and tucked the glass under the skirts of the sofa, with a *frisson* of reprobation—directed not at Rossetti (whom she assumed to be the opium-eater of the household) but rather against the housekeeper who could permit dirty glasses to be seeded about the rooms like so many public confessions. That laudanum *was* a vice, Jane reluctantly allowed in theory, but as it was a vice she had shared, she was prepared to be generous toward any fellow sinner, who was sure to be, as well, a fellow sufferer. Rossetti seemed a robust man, but the pain of migraine and the tortures of insomnia were no respecters of strength or health.

A pity it was not a matter open to discussion, for she was curious to hear his story. Yet it went too deep, cut too close to the quick of the heart. In any case, if one is a careful listener, eventually, all curiosities and questions are answered.

The smell of the glass beneath the sofa seemed to have quite penetrated the room, overriding the pungency of turpentine, defeating even the scent of smelling salts in the handkerchief she wafted defensively under her nose. Perhaps it had been the smell that first brought on the shadow of that migraine, which was now (however she might bend her neck) quite vanished.

"Her special appeal," Rossetti declared, placing what he thought the choicest morsel of bait on his hook, "is that there have been no other great paintings of Jeanne d'Arc for me to follow. If I painted St. Catherine, there needs must be a wheel; if St. Lawrence, a griddle. But Joan has been a discovery of our century, and so there is no established iconography."

"I daresay the Roman Church will be grateful to you, Mr. Rossetti, for repairing that omission."

"I doubt it. Joan is a Protestant martyr lost in the darkness of the

Catholic past. I doubt her church will honor her with sainthood: it was they who burned her alive, after all."

"Such a thought," murmured Lady Louisa, with a glance toward Jane, whose possible sufferings, more than Joan's, concerned her. It was not like Jane to remove herself so suddenly.

Rossetti, too, was acutely conscious of Mrs. Carlyle, whose withdrawal he interpreted rather as a slight to his paintings than as symptomatic of any larger distress. One can tell when people don't like one's work: whatever praise they may feign, their eyes do not light up, no involuntary smile comes to their lips, they do not linger within the picture's field of enchantment. A pity, but he must not allow himself to be regretful now, with the hook only half-baited.

"Yes, that awfulness, as you say, was the special problem of the painting, from an iconographic point of view. How to suggest her fate without being lurid? A fire burning in a grate in the background would not do."

"I can see that."

"I thought of a flamelike pattern in the draperies, but my friend Mr. Morris—you do know William Morris?—who makes a study of such matters, assures me that there were no such textile patterns in the fifteenth century."

"Now I *see!*" exclaimed Lady Louisa. "The candle on the altar— that's been snuffed out."

"Yes, but even more the censer, here, in which incense is burned."

"Is *that* what that is? Of course."

"Because the meaning of martyrdom must be, I believe, that it leaves a sweetness behind it. The pain, like the incense, is a sacrificial offering, an imitation of Christ. And then too, the metal of the censer can be harmonized with the metal of her armor—but that is a more painterly consideration."

Lady Louisa (her eyes alight, a smile on her lips) turned her head to one side and then the other, as the painting dictated. The hook was well in, but even so she must be allowed to run with the line.

"Lady Louisa, if you'll excuse me . . . ? I don't want to seem to neglect Mrs. Carlyle, and indeed I'm eager to make her closer acquaintance. Perhaps you would join us in the drawing room, in a few minutes, for tea—that is, if you don't mind my leaving you in the studio alone?"

"I should like nothing better. In any case, Mr. Rossetti, before such a painting as this I shan't be alone."

Munro required no other hint than a lifted eyebrow, and they converged at the same moment upon Mrs. Carlyle, who all too readily agreed to return to the drawing room.

If Mrs. Carlyle had exclaimed as fully over each of his seven paintings as Rossetti felt they warranted, it is doubtful that even then he would have felt a full warmth of welcome toward her, for his *amour-propre* was sensible of the slight of her husband's absence, a slight all the more stinging for his having read, over the years, almost the entire oeuvre of Carlyle. There is such a disproportion between the attention that writers and that painters lay claim to! People think nothing of spending days, even weeks, in thrall to a book, but how much attention do these same people accord a gallery of paintings? An hour or two, while they mostly stroll and talk. Carlyle, by his wife's account, did not concede the other arts even that faint acknowledgment, for Mrs. Carlyle, by way of extenuating his absence, had claimed that he was blind to painting, deaf to music, and professed little sympathy for any poetry since Robert Burns. Truly, thought Rossetti, here was the prophet the Philistines of England deserved!

For over two years Rossetti had been the Carlyles' neighbor; for far longer they had shared innumerable friends. His remaining at home on this occasion could *only* be accounted a snub. Blast him. This was, however, distinctly the wrong frame of mind for engaging Mrs. Carlyle in polite conversation. All he could think of was how, on the morrow, she would deliver her report on him over the neighborhood's back garden walls—the neighborhood not of Chelsea, but the one they more truly shared, the neighborhood of Arts and Letters, where it has been established on the populous slopes of Mount Olympus.

Mrs. Carlyle's thoughts must have been following a parallel evolution, for as they entered the drawing room, where the tea had already been laid, she said, in a tone intended as placatory, "I understand, Mr. Rossetti, that you do not choose to exhibit in galleries, and that you do not offer your work to the exhibitions of the Royal Academy. So I am sensible of the honor you do me by allowing me to come here, where your works may be seen to best advantage."

"You're very welcome, ma'am—the honor is all mine." Though he did feel placated, he could not resist a bit of teasing—and asked the quite impermissible question: "And what did you think of them? Were they what you'd been led to expect?"

Jane pursed her lips, and this warmed to a smile, as though, after taking thought, she were inclined to welcome his candor more than to reprove his importunity. "Well. I have heard you spoken of as a painter of historical subjects, and I'd imagined pictures more in the line of our other local artist, Mr. Maclise. To do your paintings justice—to begin to understand them, that is—I should have to follow the example of Lady Ashburton and study them. I heard what you were saying to her concerning the symbolic significance of the details in your, as it were, portrait of Joan. I confess I do not always seek out such meanings when I peruse a painting."

Rossetti poured tea while he spoke. "Exactly, Mrs. Carlyle. Half my effort as an artist has been to escape such significances. A painting that interprets itself at a glance has no mystery and, hence, little interest."

"Yes, but the most mysterious canvas would be like the night, or the grave—uniformly black. I was very puzzled, at first, by your painting of Lilith. But when I read the sonnet which accompanies it, the picture itself seemed more interesting, because more comprehensible. I doubt that I should ever, without the hints thrown off by the poem, have come to understand the painting in the same way."

Rossetti, not knowing that Mrs. Carlyle had been shown the sonnet, was dumbfounded. How had she thought to look behind the painting? Would she likewise peek into his desk and open cabinets?

"In its own right," she continued, "the poem is quite as mysterious as the painting."

"I took the liberty," Munro said, sensing his friend's misgivings, "of pointing out the sonnet to Mrs. Carlyle."

"Oh-ho!" It was out before he'd realized, with a blush, the implication: That explains it.

"It is unusual, is it not," Mrs. Carlyle asked, "for any very accomplished painter to be equally accomplished in a literary way?"

"Perhaps more in England than elsewhere. Michelangelo's sonnets are quite admirable. But even here there has been one artist, in our own time, of the very highest genius both as poet and painter, though perhaps I should rather say draftsman. In fact, I have lately had the satisfaction of assisting at the man's biography."

"Was he a notable poet?" Jane asked.

"The greatest of his day, I should say, although I'm prejudiced, since I consider him my spiritual forebear, and I'm inclined to discover all sorts of uncanny correspondences between us."

"I must confess, Mr. Rossetti, I can't guess your riddle: Who *was* he?"

"Have you heard of William Blake?"

"Ah, yes."

"You know his work then? I'm surprised."

"A short poem called 'The Tyger,' but nothing else. I have heard that his long poems are . . . obscure, and as to his being a painter, or a draftsman, I'd no idea at all."

"You're not alone in your . . ."

He hesitated long enough that she could say, "Call it ignorance—for that is what it is."

Rossetti grimaced. "Truly, Mrs. Carlyle, it is only Blake's reputation that is obscure. His poems are lucid as crystal. I hope that Gilchrist's biography, now that it has finally appeared, will win Blake the readers he deserves. Unfortunately, Gilchrist died before he could finish his work, and his widow and I did our resolute best to sort out what notes he left and work them into a form he could have approved. But it is unfortunate he could not live to witness the vindication of his work."

"I shall certainly read the book. But you pique my curiosity—what are the 'uncanny correspondences' of which you speak?"

"Oh, it is nothing but a hobbyhorse of mine, a fancy."

"He is the reincarnated Blake, Mrs. Carlyle," Munro volunteered in the accents of a believer. "Or he could be. The dates work out perfectly."

"Really? But that is extraordinary! *How* perfectly—not to the very day, surely?"

"To the day," said Munro.

"Well, no," Rossetti demurred. "I was born in May of 1828, and Blake died sometime earlier."

"The twelfth of August 1827, to be exact, and Gabriel's birthday is the twelfth of May, in '28. A rail schedule couldn't be more precise than that."

Mrs. Carlyle looked at Rossetti, who blushed. Then came understanding, and with it a nervous impulse to giggle, which she tried unsuccessfully to stifle with her handkerchief. The giggle swelled to laughter just as Lady Louisa returned to the drawing room with a look of pleasant expectation—rarely did her friend surrender so utterly to the power of humor. She was much likelier to be the cause of laughter than its source.

"Oh!" Mrs. Carlyle brought out at last. "You must excuse me. I didn't mean—" She caught her breath, controlled herself, stopped.

"That's quite all right," he said, coloring still higher, though more from anger than embarrassment. Munro ought to have known better than to spell out the matter so explicitly, though the fault was really his own for having dropped the hint.

"It isn't that I thought that you . . . or rather . . ." She was thoroughly flustered now, and seemed also in danger of another fit of laughter. "Simply, I'd never thought *through* the idea of the transmogrification of souls before—of course the moment of conception must be the point of the soul's translation!" There. She had said it, and the danger of laughter was past. "It is a very Dantean idea, in fact," she added, in an almost sober tone.

"Oh, I assure you, Dante would put me directly into the circle of his heretics if he ever heard such a notion. The Roman Church doesn't tolerate the idea of reincarnation. It is my own fancy entirely. Lady Louisa, may I pour you some tea?"

"Please." Then, with a sense that it would be best to wait until later to ask for the joke to be repeated, she addressed herself to other matters: "I am afraid, Mr. Rossetti, you are going to be very angry with me."

"How is that? Milk?"

"Please, but no sugar. Because I mean to ask you to do what I know no artist very much fancies. But I so admire your Joan that I'm determined to make her mine."

"Ah, but she's not my Joan any longer—you will have to approach Mr. Rose, who is rather possessive about her, I fear."

"And rightly so. No, I don't aspire quite that high. But I hoped I might persuade you to make a copy. I know you probably have other and more pressing work, but if you possibly could see your way to it . . . ?"

"In oil or watercolor?" he asked.

"As you prefer."

"I shall have to ask Mr. Rose whether he will be willing to extend his loan. If he is—then yes, I should be happy to make a copy for you." He handed her a cup of milky tea with a sense of having safely netted his fish and got it into the boat. He smiled at Lady Ashburton and lifted his teacup in salutation.

"Well," said Lady Louisa, when they were once again in Jane's brougham, "what did you think?"

"Oh, he is a very clever young man, and very personable."

"He's not that young, really. He's as old as I am, or nearly."

"In fact, he told me he was thirty-six. Though he does seem older. It's the beard, I suppose."

"You didn't like his paintings much, I take it?"

"Why do you say that?"

Lady Louisa smiled knowingly.

"I didn't buy one—if that is what you mean."

"You believe I was mistaken to have done so."

Jane hesitated. "I thought his effort to sell one was uncommonly transparent. I suppose it is something artists are obliged to do—though why he can't put his paintings into a public gallery, as other painters do, I don't quite understand."

"Some painters have thicker skins than others. If he doesn't exhibit publicly, he can't be reviewed. I think it's as simple as that."

"What do *you* think of his paintings? In general terms."

"Oh, I think them well executed. And curious—in some of the ways that *he* is curious. He's not really English, but he's not quite Italian either."

Jane knew better than to press for a more developed opinion than this, so she tactfully resumed her own postmortem. "I *don't* think I shall pursue the acquaintance, though he is a nice young man. But that is the problem—he is too nice. He makes me feel like an ancient mother being humored by her dutiful son."

"You?" Lady Louisa exclaimed. "You are one of the *youngest* women I know. There are debutantes in London for their first Season who are not as young as you."

Jane placed her hand on her companion's. "Pretty of you to say so, and it's *good* of you to make me feel a child so often, as you do—but the truth is that I more nearly belong to the generation of Mr. Rossetti's avatar than to his own—did you know he is the reincarnation of William Blake?"

"Indeed, I did not! Were you laughing at that when I came into the room?"

"Wasn't I awful! I couldn't help myself. I burst out at the absurdity of it."

"Oh, Jane, you must tell me."

"Really, it doesn't bear repeating."

Lady Louisa laughed—a well-modulated contralto trill that any professional actress would have been proud of. "What *did* you think of his paintings?"

"Must you know?"

"Yes—since you refuse to tell me the reincarnation story—and I also insist on knowing whether you think him *a lion*."

"Well. I *didn't* like his paintings, and, by the way, I think you're a fool to buy them—but that is none of my affair. As to his being an Actual Lion, I fear Carlyle would eat him for breakfast the first time they met. What else would you have me discuss!"

"I have come," said Anderson Rose, "to reclaim my heart's desire."

Rossetti took Rose's hat and looked for somewhere to put it, but the table in the hallway was piled high with books and china, the plunder of his afternoon's expedition to three antiquary shops. Unceremoniously, he put it on his head, and led his patron-cum-solicitor down the hallway to the studio.

"Ah," said Rose, entering. "My beauty! My saint!"

Rossetti had repositioned the painting of Joan so that it now was the first to claim the attention of someone entering the room. *Lady Lilith*, which was destined for another, wealthier collector, had been relegated to the position of least honor and drama. There was no purpose in exciting an appetite that could not be fed.

"You're going to be vexed with me," Rossetti said, slumping into the sprung sofa. "I've bad news."

"Then we're square. I've bad news for you as well. What's yours?"

"Joan won't be free for another month. Possibly two."

"You still haven't finished the copy for Miss Heaton, is that it?"

"In fact, I have. It's finished, paid for, and dispatched. But today Lady Ashburton was here, with Mrs. Carlyle, and demanded a copy. If I do a watercolor, rather than oils, it will require only another month —would that be all right? It redounds to the glory of your original, you know."

"Indeed, indeed. I shall want it for Christmas week, however—so be quick if you can."

"What is my bad news?"

"You asked me to inquire of the possibility . . ."

". . . of exhuming my wife's grave, yes." The hat, a full size too large for his head, tilted forward.

"Well, I'm afraid it can't be done without a written release from your mother."

"My *mother?*"

"She is the registered owner of that plot in Highgate Cemetery."

"Yes, but Lizzie was *my wife!*"

"I've spoken to the director of the cemetery. It would require something like an Act of Parliament, or a letter from the Home Secretary, to circumvent the statute."

"Damn!" Rossetti flung the hat on the sofa. Then, contritely: "What am I to do?"

"Some of the poems have appeared already in print, have they not?"

"Yes, but in drastically different forms. The *perfected* poems were in that book."

"You couldn't reconstruct them from memory?"

"It would be easier to reconstruct *The Divine Comedy* from memory. I've studied *that*. Once a poem of my own is done, I try to forget it. And even if I could reconstruct something like the originals, I would never be sure they weren't less than they might be. No, I must have the poems *in that form,* and if I have to hire a pair of damned resurrectionists—"

"As your solicitor, Gabriel, I'd advise you not to entertain such thoughts."

"Very well then," he said angrily. "The poems are lost. Forever."

"When your mother dies?"

"You'd have me wait for her death like some damned legatee? That's a degree worse than robbing graves, I should say."

"What sort of differences are at issue? A comma here or there? A word?"

"A word different is a world of difference. 'Real effect,' Blake wrote, 'is making out of Parts, and it is Nothing Else but that.' Change the parts, by howsoever minute a discrimination, and the Whole changes too."

"I'm sorry I can't be of more help."

"Blake is always right," Rossetti said dourly.

# CHAPTER TWENTY-TWO

# Five Chairs

## JANUARY, 1866

"An' have ye saved nary so much as a biscuit forr yer own faather, when he's come all this way (an' the wind blawin' so bitter) at yer own behest? What, not even a cup o' tay? Ah, Jo, 'tis sharper than the serpent's tooth to have a thankless child."

"I wish you would make your mind up, Father, whether you are King Lear or a Stage Irishman. You can't be both at once."

"Well then, Lear, me dear—and do poke the fire up and give it some coal. Tom's a-cold. O! do, de, do, de, do, de."

"If you'd come at five, as I asked, there'd have been fire, tea, *and* biscuits enough. I shan't build up the fire now, when I'm due to go out at any moment. But if you'd like some whiskey, Jimmy left a bottle in the pantry, no doubt with your health in mind."

"If it be so," declaimed Patrick Hiffernan, exiting from the sparsely furnished sitting room, "it is a chance which does redeem all sorrows that ever I have felt."

"Bring a glass for me," his daughter called after.

"It is unusual," he said, returning with the whiskey and glasses on a chipped lacquer tray, "for you to *ask* me to come calling. I had begun to think you viewed me as an encumbrance. Oh, in the most loving way—I wouldn't deny that. But the fact is, my Jo, I *am* an encumbrance." He lifted his glass, handed her hers. "Cheers!"

"Nonsense, Father. You're taking the role of Lear too seriously. We all encumber each other, and there's no help for it—except to help each other. That's why I asked you here—I need your help."

"Don't tell me that son-in-law thinks to dip into me pockets! There's a fine how-de-do!"

Joanna sighed. "I wish you would retire that joke, Father. The gloss is quite worn off it, while for me the sting remains. Jimmy has no intention of becoming your son-in-law. Ever. At all."

"*He* was the first to make the joke, Jo. So when I serve it back to him, he is obliged to take it in good part, as between two men of the world."

"Two thieves, more like."

"Americans do tend to obscure the difference between thieves and gentlemen. Or better, like me own dear countrymen, they can see the points of likeness. Jimmy Whistler is a clear-sighted lad, and I think for that reason he may come round in time to make our little jest come true. You shake your head, Jo, but stranger things have happened: that friend of his, the Italian—Rossetti—you were telling me once that *he* married one of his models?"

"Yes—and then promptly drove her to suicide. Not a fate to envy. But it was about Rossetti I wanted to talk to you, in point of fact."

Patrick Hiffernan downed his whiskey and poured another for wisdom.

"We have been calling up spirits," continued Jo, "the four of us, and Rossetti stands poised on the very edge of wholesale credulity. I should like . . ." She pursed her lips at the rim of the glass.

"To tip him over the edge."

"Precisely."

"Why?—if that's not an impertinent question."

"I don't really know why. For the amusement of it? It amuses Jimmy too."

"Not with any notion of profit in view, I hope. You're into much too good a thing with Jimmy to jeopardize it that way."

"No, no. My spirits shan't solicit contributions for me. There is nothing, I know, so certain to undo one's good work."

"As poor Bridie so often learned to her cost."

"It is about Aunt Bridie I want to question you: you worked with her sometimes?"

"For a lark, sometimes, yes."

"So you could tell me some of the tricks of the trade, so to speak?"

"You conveniently forget, Jo, that ten years ago you were offered an apprenticeship to the trade, and turned it down."

"On your advice, Father."

"Because I knew you were meant for better things, my Jo. You have your mother's gift—a beauty that doesn't tarnish. Which was why Bridie wanted you to work for her, of course. What sort of séance do you mean to undertake? No materializations, I hope. That can't be done without a great deal of preparation and practice."

"Only a bit of table-rapping."

"Is your toe in practice?"

In answer, Jo slipped her foot from its satin evening shoe, pressed her big toe into the instep of her other shoe, and produced, by the popping of the joint, a remarkably distinct report.

"Very good," Patrick Hiffernan declared. "If you don't throw your toe out of joint, by overuse, which poor Bridie was ever and again complaining of; and if you can keep a straight face, I don't see that there is much more advice I can offer—except: Don't get caught. Does Jimmy know what you're about?"

"He does and he doesn't. He likes to pretend that . . . well, he likes to pretend to *think* there's something in our séances, much as he likes to hear ghost stories."

"Faith, an' there *may* be something in it! Your Aunt Bridie always swore to me there were matters that passed her understanding—messages she'd be inspired to deliver that were uncannily accurate."

"But she did make it her business to seek out little points of information, things she presumably couldn't guess of?"

"Of course—that's the commodity a medium mostly trades in. On that score, I remember that Bridie was always quite particular not to cut too quick to the bone. If there are real skeletons in this Rossetti's closet, you'd do well not to rattle them. At worst he'll think you mean to blackmail him; at best you'll make him uncomfortable. What have you got on this Rossetti, if you don't mind my asking?"

"Oh, nothing in particular: pet names, tit-bits of gossip I've gleaned from various mutual acquaintances. He won't suppose either Jimmy or I could know any of it—and there's the fun."

"When you're done having your sport, I have a friend in Hammersmith—Mrs. Marshall (you'd remember her as Emmy Harris)—who'd appreciate a bit of business being thrown her way, together with any pertinent information you'd care to contribute."

"First, you counsel me not to fleece Mr. Rossetti, and then you ask me to conspire in Emmy Harris's doing just that."

"Oh, Emmy's appetite is small, and she puts on a good show for the price. Not just raps, but tiltings and levitations. Spirit voices, too.

Emmy's game, and will try her hand at whatever's demanded. She gives herself out to be a washerwoman, and then transmits messages (in a trance, of course) in almost perfect French. What the theater has lost in Emmy the etheric world has gained."

"I will mention her to Rossetti's friend Howell, possibly. I don't believe the suggestion should come directly from me. Aren't you drinking too much?"

"I'm not half-screwed, Jo, me daarlin', but if ye can spare a half-jack, I'll go elsewhere to fortify meself." He held the whiskey bottle out questioningly over his glass. Jo offering no other objection than a caustic smile, he poured.

The bell rang, and Jo went downstairs to open the street door. While she was out of the room, he emptied the glass and filled it quickly to the same level, recapped the bottle, and settled into the room's one comfortable chair. Patrick Hiffernan's chief objection to Whistler as (so to speak) a son-in-law was the Spartan style of his domestic appointments. It wasn't meanness: the house on Lindsey Row, where he lived himself (and over which Jo had presided as mistress until being displaced by the painter's mother), was furnished just the same, with straw mats on the floor, straight-backed chairs, and thin chintz curtains, for all the world like a summer cottage at the seaside. At Lindsey Row this sparseness had the dubious merit of setting off his own (to Hiffernan's eye) equally dubious paintings, but here in Jo's exile on Queen's Row there was nothing to be set off but a single trifle of an etching over the fireplace. The man had such a fantastic conceit of his handiwork that he wouldn't let it out of his keeping. Hiffernan's secret hope was that his daughter would take up with the other painter fellow she was seeing tonight. Rossetti was, by all accounts, a queer beast, but he produced more paintings, sold them for better prices, and lived like the Shoreditch Toff. All in all, a much better bargain than Jimmy Whistler. It was too soon, however, to put a flea in Jo's ear. If she had not scented the possibility herself, she was no daughter of Patrick Hiffernan.

The woman who now entered the room with Joanna, Fanny Cornforth, was the single most cogent reason for supposing Rossetti a likely prospect. Hiffernan knew Fanny from the days (long vanished now) when they had tippled the champagne and sherry of Cremorne Gardens together. In those days, Hiffernan had acted in burlesques and played a cornet in the dance pavilion; Fanny, for her part, had followed the traditional calling of the ladies who, unaccompanied, frequented Cremorne. On one drunken occasion Hiffernan had enjoyed her favors, but even then she had been ampler in her development than he quite fancied. Now she was a full-pooped frigate and seemed to take on more ballast every week.

"Lor-a-mussy!" Fanny exploded. "If it ain't Paddy 'Effernan!"

"An' who else should it be, Fanny," he returned, slipping on his brogue as easily as an old slipper, "here in me own daughter's parlor? I haven't had time to warm me toes at the fire an' she's tellin' me I must be off."

"You've 'ad time enough to soak your clay though, by the look of it."

"It's the only bit o' warmth me daarlin' daughter would give me. Where are yer manners, Jo? Old Fanny'll be wantin' to brighten her nose, won't ye, Fanny?"

"Listen to 'im, the old scrub," said Fanny, with tacit, affectionate consent.

Jo fetched another glass, and Fanny, with a look of misgiving, settled herself on one of the spindly straight-backed chairs. For several comfortable minutes she and Hiffernan reminisced about the golden age of Cremorne and traded ancient catch phrases. Then, coals and bottle both exhausted, Jo sent her father on his way, slipped into a long, sleeveless cloak, extinguished the two gas lamps, and set off with Fanny to the séance, which was to be held tonight in Rossetti's house on Cheyne Walk.

As Whistler prepared (changing into fresher linen) to depart for Rossetti's séance, the atmosphere at 7, Lindsey Row, was distinctly less amicable, and indeed, this evening quite poisonous. The cause of this was the presence of his younger brother Willie, whose all-inadvertent fault lay in providing a pair of ears for Anna's motherly lamentations. Of her two living sons, Willie had ever been the more tractable, having become not only a surgeon, as per Anna's instructions, but as well an officer in the Confederate Army, in whose services he had braved the Northern blockade to bring dispatches to England. Before he could return to his doomed cause, the war had providentially ended, and Willie had stayed on in London to develop a medical practice—once again, as per Anna's instructions. Anna naturally wanted to have her sons about her, and since Jimmy could not be pried loose from London (except to junket off to Paris, which, as being Papist, was unthinkable as a residence for Anna Whistler, staunch evangelical that she was), she (and Willie) must defer to necessity and live in London themselves. The climate did not suit her, but what was the alternative? To return to America would be to choose between one or another bitterness—life in her devastated but still-beloved Southland, or among unmannered Yankees, who were smug with triumph and (worse) *righteous* on the subject of slavery, which had been abolished now, by Constitutional amendment, in all thirty-five states. Anna could not bear to be excluded from the ranks of the righteous, but it did tax one's wits to strike an attitude of moral superiority on the issue of slavery, especially in Stonington, Connecticut, where her sister lived.

If London it must be, Anna was determined that it should be a more moral London than the one she had discovered on her arrival. She was bent on reforming Jimmy into a respectable member of (if not Society) the Royal Academy at least, to which end she made increasingly broader hints as to the undue width of his hat brims and the too unconventional cut of his moustache, even venturing so far as to question the wisdom of all facial hair whatsoever (Willie's included). Jimmy and Willie were united in the defense of their hair, but Willie supported his mother in thinking the sums that his brother spent on fans and jugs and other Japanese bibelots were excessive. Concerning the paramount bone of contention, the matter of the company Jimmy kept (or, more precisely, the mistress), Willie had so far—till this evening—remained neutral, or at least silent.

So long as his mother had possessed no other allies than the Hadens in her campaign of reform, Whistler had not been excessively incommoded. Having early in life declared his independence, first by dropping from West Point, then, on attaining his majority, by throwing up a "good job" with the Coast Survey in order to become an art student in Paris, he was confident of his ability to steer his own course, however Anna might exert herself to take command of his moral rudder. But now, with Willie marching under her banner (and living in the house), he could not so readily rule the arrangements of his private life. Willie was given to soul-searching, brandy-steeped conversations on the subject of the Conduct of Life, and the needs for a New Chivalry and a Good Wife (a search he had already begun to undertake himself in the circles to which Whistler had introduced him). He could also become exercised, as a medical man, on the dangers of disease and would cite powerful cautionary examples of the awful price exacted by a life of venery. Until today, however, Willie had taken care not to overstep the bounds of polite generality.

What had caused him to break from his precedent had been a meeting on the King's Road with Rossetti's brother, William Michael, who'd taken a liking to Willie, who not only shared his Christian name but also the tribulations of growing up in the shadow of genius. William Michael, having a voracious and not very discriminating appetite for table-rapping (he sometimes spent the price of an opera box on consulting mediums), had organized tonight's séance—and so felt free to invite Willie to come with his brother. Grateful for any social occasion, Willie had accepted, only to discover at home, from Jimmy, that the notorious Miss Hiffernan was to be among the company at Rossetti's. Willie thereupon declared that Honor demanded he decline the tainted invitation; he thought, moreover, that it would be better if Jimmy spent the evening home as well. Hot words were exchanged between the two brothers, as the question of Jo's personal merits became inextricably confused with the larger question of spiritualism, which Willie swore was buncombe. Unforgivably, at the height of his rage he called his brother a slacker, a yellow-back coward, and a traitor to the Confederate cause. While Willie had been risking his life fighting with Orr's rifles in defense of his fatherland, his brother had been a mere epicurean, or, not to put too fine a point on it, a whore-monger—then and now. With this Willie had flung out of the studio, only to return five minutes later to offer an abashed and quite inadequate apology. Whistler was grateful to be spared the inevitable scenes with his mother that would have followed Willie's forced departure, but Willie's words, though formally rescinded, were gall and worm-wood. Whistler had attended West Point long enough to have developed a manly susceptibility to questions of honor. Whatever his reasons, the fact glaringly remained that he had *not* fought in the war that Willie—and most every other young man in America—had risked his damned-fool neck in. Therefore, in a strictly de facto sense, Willie's imputations were not "damnable lies," though if it had been anybody but Willie who'd thrown them in his face, his honor would have answered for it. Whistler was as capable as any man (as capable as Willie, certainly!) of facing enemy fire, enduring hardships, and covering himself either with glory or with six feet of topsoil. At least he supposed so.

For Willie's aspersions on his sexual conduct, Whistler felt no such lack of self-certainty. Willie was too provincial, too much Anna's son, to know whereof he spoke concerning Jo, who was anything but the *femme fatale* he imagined. She was not marriageable, of course (Whistler had long ago conceded that to Haden, to Willie, even to Anna), but the bond between them exceeded mere lust. Jo was no piece of kid leather. Their intimacy was fine and rare, and went deeper (he dared swear) than obtained between most husbands and wives in proportion as Jo herself went deeper than most women. What other woman understood the enormity of the task he'd set himself as a painter? None! Or knew so well the essential art of stretching shillings into pounds? Some few there might be, though Anna not among them. Since his mother had taken over the management of the house, his day-to-day expenses had got quite out of hand. Jo was a regular brick.

Whistler was not a believer in love, that commodity of unfledged youths and lady novelists. He thought it, at best, an illusion necessary for the perpetuation of the race, at worst, bait for the trap of an imprudent marriage. Nevertheless, in his own fashion he loved Jo, and he certainly didn't intend to abandon her on his family's account. Why wouldn't they leave him in peace? Why must they try to destroy a woman whose only fault lay in her having been born to the wrong social class? The worst of it was that Anna's determination to rout Jo from his life (as she had already from his house) had made him unable properly to concentrate on his work. Only when he'd shipped Anna off to Torquay for her health, permitting Jo to return temporarily to 7, Lindsey Row, had he been able to paint with any of the old fire. But as soon as the weather permitted Anna's return, his Muse went back into retirement. In the autumn he'd gone off with Jo to Trouville, where at once the most sublime seascapes had poured forth: three masterpieces, in rapid succession. Clearly Jo was as essential to his painting as his hands or eyes. He'd be damned if he would sacrifice her on the altar of Anna's respectability.

But before he left the house to go to Rossetti's, he did look in on his mother, and when she begged the trifling concession of a cup of tea together (pointing out that they had exchanged but five words the whole day), he agreed, making himself half an hour late for the séance.

"Do the spirits object, Rissetty, if we indulge ourselves in some *liquid* spirits before'and? I've a thirst for a nice 'od of mortar."

"There's no porter in the house, Fanny," said Gabriel, with a wince that went unnoticed. Rhyming slang was one of Fanny's few vulgar allegiances he couldn't interpret as bucolic charm. "And so far as we know, no spirits of the bogey variety either."

"I rather hope there *won't* be," said Jo, "though I know it is the point of our sitting around the table. Even so."

"Oo, I know just what you mean, love. When those raps start in, I come all over goose bumps. One time, not so long back, we thought we was in touch with something, only it wouldn't answer any of our questions. But you could feel it stirring about, like a draft in the room, though it's not a room as usually 'as a draft, is it, William? 'E felt it."

"I felt something," William Michael confessed.

"An' then, you know what it did? It yanked on me 'air! Like as if a boy was to pull at your 'air when you was a girl—a proper 'eadacher it was. I let out *such* a yell."

"You did that, Fanny," said Rossetti. "You gave *me* such a fright, I practically went over backward in my chair. I expect you won't do that again. In the dark a scream can be very disconcerting."

"It wasn't my doing, was it, love? It was the bogey."

"Have *you* ever experienced such a violent manifestation, Miss Hiffernan?" asked William Michael.

"No, nor should I fancy to, I'm sure. It sounds quite upsetting."

"Oh, it was, love, it was. Rissetty, it doesn't 'ave to be porter: some sherry would do. I'm sure Miss 'Effernan could do with a drop o' sherry 'erself. 'Oo knows 'ow long we'll 'ave to wait for Mr. Whistler."

"Very well, Fanny." Rossetti got up from the divan which he and his mistress nearly filled with their combined bulk. "Excuse me. I shall have to fetch it myself, as I've given the servants the night off. I didn't want them about if there should be . . ."

"Any 'anky-panky?" suggested Fanny, filling in his nervous ellipsis.

"I understand from Whistler," said William Michael, "that you have a distinct gift for mediumship, Miss Hiffernan?"

"Oh, Jimmy thinks I'm gifted every which way, and I don't try to undeceive him, I'm afraid. There have been raps and such, when we've conducted our little experiments at home, but I'm sure there is a perfectly natural explanation. An old house is full of all manner of creaks and groans, which we never listen for and accordingly never hear."

"Not creaks and groans that answer questions that are put to them," objected William Michael. "I agree that there *may* be a natural explanation, but may there not be a supernatural one as well?"

"What I object to," said Fanny, "is the waiting. If there *is* bogeys about, I wish they'd just speak. It's not much fun sittin' there in the dark reading out letters, trying to think what they add up to. Sometimes I wonder if these say-antses isn't just Rissetty's way of makin' a scholar of me."

"Of *you*, Fanny?" said Rossetti, returning with the sherry and glasses.

"I agree that waiting is tiresome," said Jo, "but at least when the spirits keep us waiting, there is some excuse. For Jimmy there is none. Half an hour!"

The doorbell jangled.

Fanny laughed. "I 'ope you 'ave the same power presently with bogeys."

The two women exchanged a smile of open complicity and mutual distrust.

While Fanny and Jo went off into Rossetti's studio, so that Fanny might vaunt the latest of the gowns Rossetti had had made up for her sittings, the three men stayed in the parlor under a canopy of smoke from William's Havannah.

"I thought your brother was to have come as well," said William Michael.

"He had second thoughts," Whistler said with the careless grace of a skilled liar. "Or rather, my mother did. She disapproves of spiritualism strongly, though during the first craze for spirit-rapping in America I believe she dabbled in—as she now regards it—the Black Art. She would deny it, of course."

"How does it happen that you're allowed to be here if Willie must stay at home?" asked Rossetti.

"Willie is simply that much more fully under her thumb."

"It can be difficult," said William Michael morosely. "I know. Half the time I am under the same roof as my mother and sisters. Then I am here for a night or two, and it is like entering another atmosphere."

"With those cigars," said Gabriel, "it certainly *becomes* another atmosphere."

"He means I'm not allowed to smoke at Albany Street, and so I rather overdo it here. Lord knows, Gabriel, I pay a fair share of rent for the privilege." William was especially grieved with his prodigal brother, who only yesterday had sent his manservant round to the office with a note to co-sign so that Gabriel might borrow money to pay a long-overdue bill: £50 to the butterman—it scarcely seemed possible.

"I'm not complaining, William. Indeed, I'm grateful to you for assuming the lion's share of the burden with respect to Mamma. I don't have Jimmy's strength of character: when Mamma is about, I'm stricken half-dumb. I'll invent any sort of excuse to be out of the house. Not that I don't love them all with a filial and a fraternal love: I very much do. But I could not go back to living with them, having known the taste of freedom. I wonder that you *can*, Jimmy."

"What choice have I? If I were as well set up as you, and had patrons clamoring for *copies* of old pictures—"

"Not that you'd ever condescend to *do* such pot-boiling work, I daresay," Rossetti observed.

"How would I know before I am tempted? I'm not complaining, mind. I'm happy with my work; it's going well, moving forward; and it supports me. But it won't support a separate household for my mother. Once Willie's on his feet professionally, and before he can start filling up his rooms with children, I shall insist that he assume responsibility for her. Meanwhile it is up to me, and in a way, you know, I rather enjoy it."

"Yes, there's that," said Rossetti. "Your mother's no fool; no more is mine. But doesn't that make them *harder* to live with, as being less easy to fiddle?"

"What it is I enjoy is simply my *ascendancy*. An awful admission, doubtless, but the fact remains. As mothers go, mine was rather martinetish: we kept the Sabbath very strictly; I wasn't permitted to read or draw. For years she set herself against my becoming a painter, though it was evident to everyone who knew me that I'd never be good for anything else."

"But a parent who didn't oppose such inclinations would be remiss," ventured William. "For every painter who succeeds, as you both have—"

Whistler rapped his knuckles on the mahogany tabletop.

"—there must be a score who come to nothing, or struggle along like poor Knewstub, who is no longer, after all, very young. When I have children, if I ever do, I fully intend to discourage them in every possible way from becoming artists."

"Hoping all the while that they'll defy your prudent counsels and go on to become a tribe of Universal Geniuses in the Rossetti tradition," his brother countered.

William sighed. "The Rossetti tradition!" And shook his head, exhaling a long serpentine curl of cigar smoke.

"My mother's reasons were more in the nature of horror than of prudence. What she most wanted me to become was a parson. Failing that, a railway engineer like Pa. Painter was never even at the bottom of the list, though she has learned to swallow it."

"And you *enjoy* her discomfort?" William Michael asked, not quite able to avoid a tone of disapproval.

"Rather, yes. I sometimes think it's as though I'd spent several years in jail and she'd been my jailer. Now that I'm at liberty, her presence is a constant reminder of what I've been freed *from*. For instance, on Sundays I used to accompany her to the door of Chelsea Old Church—but not inside. I'd go back home and *work*."

"She didn't complain?"

"Oh, bitterly. But I simply told her flatly that like most educated gentlemen these days I could not subscribe to the Thirty-nine Articles of the Church of England, and that as long as I could not, it would be hypocritical in me to attend its services."

"And what did she say to that?"

"She wanted to argue each of the Articles on its merits right there at the church door, and I refused to. Whereupon she said that she would *pray* for me unceasingly till God should be inspired to restore my lost faith."

"It doesn't sound as though you ever had it to lose," said Rossetti.

"Ah, but I'm here tonight, ain't I?" Whistler grinned, gave a vigorous twist to his moustache, and produced a deep-throated and utterly uninterpretable Ha-ha!

"Such *sleeves*!" exclaimed Jo. "Why there must be three yards of material in the sleeves alone. And *such* material. Oh, *do* put it on. With the coral necklace, just as it is in the painting."

Fanny's quick demur was candidly insincere, and a very little more coaxing was required to persuade her to put on the silk damask gown (gold and crimson on a ground of white) that Rossetti had designed for her to pose in. "D'you like it?" she asked, shaking out her thick red hair to give it a similar amplitude.

"My dear, you look as though you'd stepped right out of a Veronese."

Fanny fluttered her feather fan appreciatively. The comparison was not lost on her: Rossetti had more than once taken her to the National Gallery to study the way the models of those days had carried themselves in their ancient crinolines. Of all the models they'd looked at, those who'd worked for Veronese had had the most in common with her, with regard not only to figure but to their coloring as well, which was high.

"You must wear it to the séance," Jo said decisively.

To this, too, Fanny was persuaded after the feeblest of protests. The sherry and the flattery together had put her into such a good disposition that she dared ask Jo the question that she'd kept herself from asking these many months: Why were her skirts so narrow? Why with so fine a figure did she not take the trouble to dress fashionably?

"Ah, but you see, my idea is that I shall *set* the fashion."

Fanny laughed good-naturedly at this paradox. Fashions, she knew, were followed, not set. It was patent absurdity to think one might make the whole world abandon crinolines by going about as though one had just got out of bed.

"I'm quite in earnest," Jo protested, while seeming to share the joke. "If I were a respectable housewife or moved in Society, it would be another matter: I should wear crinolines always a little larger than any my servants possessed and count myself innovative for following *La Mode Illustrée*. But as I cannot be taken anywhere but to restaurants or the seaside, why then I shall dress as it suits me. Jimmy likes a Grecian profile, I know: he says it reeks of the boudoir. And of course it's less dear. I shudder to think what Mr. Rossetti spent on the magnificence you are wearing: those gold pins, the crystal pendant, the coral, the pearls. It's awesome."

"But where am I to wear it, love? This won't do for a restaurant, nor yet for the shore at Brighton. I wear it when I sits to 'im, and that's all."

"Well, I do envy you that," Jo reassured her, quite offhandedly.

Fanny, however, interpreted the remark otherwise. "Would *you* like to sit to 'im, then?"

"I? Heavens no. I mean, of course he's a fine painter. But I am quite busy enough sitting for Jimmy. It's dull work at best: I shouldn't care to double it."

"Mm." Fanny nodded, unconvinced.

How, politely, could she reassure her that she was not a rival for Gabriel Rossetti? It wouldn't do to say she didn't *like* Rossetti, that she found his mind and waist alike too thick. It equally wouldn't do to protest her loyalty to Jimmy, since Fanny evidently didn't think much of him and could not, therefore, imagine him commanding the loyalty of any woman who stood to make a better bargain elsewhere.

"I shall tell you what it is, then," said Jo, "but you must promise that it goes no further. It is his beard."

" 'Is beard!"

"I suppose you think me a perfect fool, but I really can't abide beards."

" 'Ow odd."

"Isn't it? But there it is, and I can't help it. Some people can't eat tomatoes. Others can't bear the feel of silk or the smell of a stable. For me it has always been beards. Please don't tell Mr. Rossetti. Men are so sensitive about their appearances."

"Oh, not '*im*. 'E could let 'is appearance go 'ang. Beards—now I've 'eard everything!"

"But you won't tell?"

Fanny patted her hand. "My lips is sealed, as they say. Now—" (with the broadest of winks) "—what do you say, shall we start rapping on that table?"

Rossetti's bedroom was desperately cold, for ghosts are known to be shy of all forms of illumination, even the glow emitted by embers of coals. After sitting in the frozen silence until she'd started shivering, Fanny was about to rise from the table and take her leave (as from a restaurant where one has received no service), but just as she was rehearsing what she would say to Rossetti, should he object, the first rapping came. A much finer, crisper sound than any she'd ever been able to produce by rapping her knuckle surreptitiously on the underside of the table. She wondered how Jo did it.

The ghost was made to agree that "Yes" would be one rap, "No" would be two, while three would mean either "I don't know" or "Maybe." Then they started in on the alphabet, and the ghost identi-

fied itself as EROSS, which was shown to be a cipher of Lizzie's full
(but transposed) name, Elizabeth Rossetti Siddal. Gabriel asked if she
were happy, and she rapped one rap: Yes, she was happy. Was there
one person present she especially wanted to talk to? Yes. Who? William started off through the alphabet until the ghost stopped him at G,
then at U, and again at G.

"Gug!" Gabriel cried out. "That was our pet name: she was Guggums, I was Gug!"

Fanny dimly remembered an evening, just after Lizzie's suicide,
when Gabriel, having drunk a great deal of brandy, had talked about
his dear lost Guggums, but "Gug" was a new one. She wondered how
Jo had ferreted out such a tit-bit, and from whom. Howell, probably.

What did Guggums want to tell her Gug? The letters emerged in
solemn succession: P, and A. I, and N.

"Pain?" Gabriel inquired distressfully.

But William went on calmly chanting the alphabet, and another
letter was added to the first four, a T.

"Paint," said Whistler. "She is urging you to paint."

"Paint," repeated Gabriel. "Boring. Is that it—just paint?"

The ghost rapped a Yes.

Did the ghost have a message for anyone else at the table? It did.
Moreover, to signal its intention, the table was tilted—toward Fanny,
who had begun to feel (despite that she suspected this was all Jo
Hiffernan's doing) just the slightest bit uncanny. One can't sit for an
hour in a cold, pitch-black room pretending to talk with spirit voices
without at least a twinge of . . . something.

"What is your message?" Fanny asked.

"HELP ME" was what the letters spelled.

Fanny would have left it at that, supposing that by whatever means
Jo could produce such whipcrack rappings, she was now tiring and had
taken this means to enlist her cooperation. But Gabriel was not satisfied. "Help you do what?" he demanded.

And the reply: "LOV."

"Are you still there, Lizzie?" Gabriel demanded, when William's E
elicited no rap, nor any of the succeeding letters.

At last Fanny broke the silence, tapping the large opal onyx on her
right ring-finger against the underside of the table. It produced a much

more satisfactory sound than her bare knuckle, not so loud as Jo's raps, but as though the spirit had withdrawn to another room.

You could almost believe in it, if like Rossetti you were in love with the idea of belief, if you craved some large and permanent truth to illumine a mind so often merely stagnant or idly speculative. You could almost avoid the suspicion that these ethereal rappings might be a contrivance. But by whose agency?

There was ample time to consider the question while his brother hummed his monotonous ABC's and EROSS spelled itself out, letter by slow letter; then the names of their sisters, revealing where they were to be found at that exact moment: HOME IN BED.

Fanny? But she'd not been present when this spirit first had been manifested at Whistler's. She'd been on hand here at various times when she might have had her bit of sport, but this evening's bogey was somehow more authoritative. Even the sounds it made were louder. "Paint," it had bidden him; Fanny would not have told him that.

Jimmy, then? Yankees were notorious for their practical jokes, and it was Yankees who'd invented the pastime and made it so popular. If *all* séances were frauds, then the number of mountebanks in the world did not bear thinking of. *Some* were cheats, surely—but *all*?

"Gug," Lizzie had called him in the early days of their living together, long before the marriage—and she alone. No one here would have known that pet-name, not even Fanny. Besides, he'd talked to Jimmy about this business of calling up bogeys and sensed in him the same equivocal feelings he felt himself, the same well-dampered dread shading off into a warmth of wistful benevolence. Jimmy was not such a good actor as to be able to feign the eloquent incoherencies they'd exchanged on the subject of their half-belief.

Jo? At first she seemed the unlikeliest candidate of all, for what reason could she have for exhuming a stranger's deepest-buried griefs, awakening his wounds to the pain he'd almost managed to forget? But then, consider: Is it possible to know the motives that impel even those we think we know best? Would he ever understand why Lizzie had taken her own life? To say Jo had no reason to tease him so was not to say she wasn't doing just that at this moment.

Suppose it were Jo, for whatever prankish or malicious reason. Could it not be, even so, that she were, as they say, the medium through which Lizzie chose to speak to him? Could Lizzie have found in all London an apter representative than Jo Hiffernan? She was Lizzie's moral *Doppelgänger*, perfectly: the mistress of a painter beginning to make his way in the world, a man who'd resisted as fiercely as he'd resisted it himself the idea of an imprudent marriage, but who could not, for all that, extricate himself from the knots of love, guilt, and simple predilection that united them more firmly each month they continued together. Oh, the parallels were everywhere, even to the color of her hair, the same ever-changing red as Lizzie's, which became flame in sunlight, auburn in a shadowed room. Jo might believe she was acting on her own accord when in fact she was moved by impalpable impulses and promptings that Lizzie could work like the invisible strings of a puppet.

"I am thinking," said Whistler, "of a common word. It is five letters long. Can you tell me, spirit, what that word is?" Rossetti claimed that his ghosts had often searched the haystacks of his thoughts and found such needles. Of all the tests one might set, this seemed the toughest, the most impossible to explain away by any but a supernatural hypothesis. Whistler did not expect the spirit to pass his test, but he couldn't resist tempting miracles to happen.

The word (it was "chair") had come to him earlier, seeing Jo standing next to Rossetti's rosy "Elephant" in her preposterous jumble of jewelry and feathers, a forged Veronese in the flesh. Whatever became of her, Whistler knew that Jo would never let herself sink to such a sorry condition, so that a flight of stairs left her short of breath. Jo's wealth was her flesh: proud flesh, *la chair fière*, as he'd heard his friend Legros say of a family in Paris whose entire social cachet lay in the fact that for three generations all their women had preserved their beauty well into their sixties. No common roses they, perishing in the first heat of summer, and the Hiffernans sprang from similar perennially vigorous stock. One could see in her father's figure, still athletically trim, and in his face, still animated and handsome, and even in his hair, still as thick and red as hers, that she would age as nobly. A scoundrel he might be, in a small way, and a rogue, but residing in the Hiffernan *chair fière* one couldn't help but like him. His spirit preserved the virtues that sort with vigor, passion, and good appetite, which were the virtues Whistler himself most prized—from a sense, probably, that they were not part of his own natural endowments. His father had died relatively young of overwork; his mother seemed to wither and weaken along an even downward gradient of decay. And he was her son, flesh of her flesh. He would go down the same path. His vision would fail him, as Anna's was failing her now. Since childhood his lungs had been weak, and last year at Trouville he'd nearly drowned from not having the strength to resist the currents that swept him ever farther out to sea: it had been Jo who'd rescued him.

Sitting in the dark, waiting for the spirits to announce themselves, that French word had returned to him as English, not translated but letter for letter: chair. Odd that he'd never noticed the visual correspondence before. Here they were, five *espèces de chair* in . . . five chairs, pretending to speak with a sixth, who'd left her chair and now circled the table restlessly.

William Michael began his recitation of the alphabet, and was stopped at B.

Whistler felt a pang of disappointment as acute as that moment when one knows that a painting has been botched beyond redemption. The ghost had not guessed his word—was not, therefore, a ghost.

The next letter was R; after that, I. He was able, at once, to guess the fourth and fifth.

" 'Bride,' " William Michael announced. "Was that the word you were thinking of?"

"No. No, it was not."

"Does it relate to it, possibly?" William insisted.

"I shouldn't say so, no. My word was 'chair,' which bears no relation I can easily imagine to 'bride.' "

"Maybe the spirit didn't think it was interesting," said Fanny, speaking aloud for the first time. "And 'ad this message to give you already on 'and, and didn't wait to spell it out. Maybe?"

"Do you think Jimmy's to find himself a bride at last then?" Rossetti asked, unable to resist a bit of teasing.

"Why not ask 'er if that's what she meant?" Fanny suggested.

"Very well," said Whistler (making an effort to keep any trace of annoyance from his voice). "Gentle spirit, tell us, is that what you meant by 'bride': Am I to marry soon?"

Fanny immediately rapped a single rap with her ring on the underside of the table: Yes.

By the cracking of her toe, Jo changed the Yes to a No. She knew that Jimmy would have interpreted "bride" as her own private message to him. Best and wisest to scotch that idea at once.

But then, for the first time that evening the ghost answered with three raps: Perhaps.

"I wish," said Jo, when they were again alone in Rossetti's studio, where Fanny was changing back into the clothes of her own century, "you hadn't done that—I assume that was your doing?"

"Done what, love?"

"Rapped that third rap. I don't want Jimmy to think I'm herding him into wedlock. Because I'm not."

"If 'e asked you, you wouldn't say no though."

"I might, in fact. But he's not about to ask."

"Any'ow, love, it wasn't me. The first was me—for which I beg your pardon if it didn't come welcomely. But the third time I don't know 'oo it was, if it wasn't you. 'And me that brush by the pot, love."

"It wasn't Jimmy, that's certain."

"Ta." Fanny took the brush and set to combing out snarls. There was nothing like a stiff brush for thinking out a problem. Not the problem of the third rap—that was of no consequence—but the problem of whether to tell Jo Hiffernan what she had overheard that afternoon between Gabriel and Jimmy Whistler. As a rule, Fanny didn't interfere in business that didn't concern her, and this was a particularly ticklish business. Jimmy Whistler was going off to South America, on the other side of the world, as far away almost as Botany Bay. They were intending to have some sort of war there, and he wanted to fight in it, having missed the chance to fight in the war they'd just had in his own country. That was what he'd said, anyhow. Fanny had her own idea of his reasons, being of the commonly held opinion that all men are rotters at heart.

The problem was whether to tell Jo. Possibly she knew of his plans already, but Fanny doubted that. And she certainly couldn't know that Whistler was intending to leave her all his pots and paintings and his bit of money in case he should be killed off in the fighting. That had been his reason for telling Rossetti about it. He wanted him to act as *executioner*, along with their solicitor, Mr. Rose.

She decided to be indirect.

"Death," she said, solemnly putting aside the brush, "ain't anything

I like to think about for long at a time. I wish Rissetty would leave off these say-antses. Not that I'm afraid of bogeys, mind, since it's usually been me as was doing the rapping—though sometimes there's one that don't come from nowhere, like the third one tonight. But I don't like to think of it: it ain't natural. It ain't natural for 'im to be thinking of 'er always."

"But the messages he receives from her seem to be of a consoling sort."

"Oh yes, I see to that."

"Well, isn't that a woman's duty—to deceive a man into being happy?"

Fanny laughed. "Oh, Miss 'Effernan, that's a wicked thing to say."

Jo blushed and looked away. Fanny blushed as well, realizing belatedly that in addressing Jo as her superior she'd destroyed any established intimacy. But how to help it? It was the way Jo talked, not just the "lardy-dardy" tone of voice, but the way she had of being so smooth and nasty all at once. Rossetti's friends took that tone too, especially the ones who wrote books, but Fanny had never known a woman so eager to sound like that sort. Surely it was a mistake. Men might enjoy that kind of talk for a while, but they don't want to live with someone who's always trying to be more clever than they. That was the reason, at heart, that Meredith had been booted out of the house, and Fanny could see the same thing in store for Swinburne. Rossetti could only be comfortable with someone like his brother or herself, people who didn't always put him through his paces. But how to explain *that* to the likes of Jo Hiffernan?

It was too much bother. Fanny decided to let her learn about it in her own way, which would probably be waking up some morning and finding a letter with ten quid slipped under the door.

"It was Rossetti," Jo announced, with a wag of her finger expressive of sudden conviction.

" 'Ow's that?"

"The third rap was Rossetti's."

"What makes you so sure?"

"No reason. Or call it intuition."

But just before she left to brave the winter night with Jimmy, Jo found out her intuition had been wrong.

Jimmy and Rossetti had gone off to the latter's studio on the pretext of seeking a lost pair of gloves. Fanny had developed a one o'clock craving for Stilton and gone off to raid the pantry. Jo was left alone with William Michael, who had so far succumbed to the lateness of the hour as to have removed cravat and collar. Now, with a catlike smile of apology, he yawned, stretching his arms up over his head, lacing his fingers together, and cracking his knuckles loudly.

Their eyes met. She began to smile just as he began to blush. It was as good as a written confession.

# CHAPTER TWENTY-THREE

# The Death of Jane Carlyle

APRIL, 1866

When the hansom came within view of the river, Carlyle pulled the check-string and asked his brother John, after the driver had drawn over to the curb, to continue on to the house alone. John attempted to protest, but Carlyle, lifting his still-unseasoned knobstick like a scepter, overbore him with wordless, peremptory power.

His head seemed filled with darkness as the hansom rattled away from him down Cheyne Walk. Yet once its form and sound were muffled by the night and the rising damp of the river, once he felt himself fully alone, the darkness relented, lifted from his spirit like a garment plucked from his shoulders. If he'd known how, he would have clutched it to him, for he took no delight in nakedness—even (or especially) the nakedness of his own close-chambered feelings. Already he regretted having dismissed John, whose unremitting banal homilies he had had to endure now for three full days; how much *easier* to bear such brotherly botherations than to face the blank, utter Nothingness, the *Nichtigkeit* of his own night thoughts. For a moment his mind tongued the Teutonic word, as though it were a coin worn smooth by decades of commerce, but the coin fell from his grasp and was lost in the mud of the street.

Thought was useless, yet almost in proportion to its uselessness it was profuse: like Ixion he was bound to the revolving wheel of his own mentations; denied all respite of tears or of sleep; and on those rare occasions when sleep came, it was a dreamless sleep that brought no manna of merited grief to his soul. This was the reason, doubtless, that he cringed before the certain prospect of Forster's ever-ready lachrymations, of Geraldine's Corybantic anguish. These two friends had, in Carlyle's absence, jointly taken responsibility for the obsequies. Her, especially, he dreaded, as another man might dread confronting the known but unacknowledged lover of his wife across the chasm of her open grave. Not that any honest husband *should* have aught to fear from lovers, known or unknown; but still he did.

He must walk. He let his feet choose the path, flinching with grateful pain each time he made his recently sprained ankle support his full weight, taking no advantage of the walking stick. Past Old Chelsea Church, through the arch, down Duke Street. Coming to Battersea Bridge he remembered—it seemed particularly important—the rumor that soon this bridge would be swept away in the name of Progress to be replaced by chains and links of brutal ironmongery.

He proceeded out upon its broad, well-weathered planks. Eastward all London glowed, immense with the noise and purpose of its intricated lives—to him no more than a wasteland, a charnelhouse, a shambles. It had been the same earlier, arriving at the rail station and passing through its gates as through the gates of Dis: the mad faces, the roiling smoke, Pity and Horror rubbing shoulders in the crowd and never acknowledging each other, so busy with their business. Then, as quickly as brother John could enlist the service of a cab driver, off through the ghastly gas-lighted streets that bore no witness—none—to the change that had been wrought forever within this single monad in their midst. Every grimace, every footstep, every word exchanged seemed but the swarming sound of the human hive: *Schwärmerei*, the Germans called it; mere bedlamite crowd-madness to him. Once when the hansom had been halted by perpendicular streams of traffic, he had wanted to leap out and assault, Samson-like, the Philistines milling about; which rough justice (needless to say) he had not performed, though the stick in his hand still trembled with the effort of restraint.

The loutish men he'd seen loitering in doorways—madmen, fools, knaves—Moses coming down from Mount Sinai must have seen his fellow Hebrews so: craven, honorless, giving the name of religion to their drunken adoration of a golden calf. Carlyle could appreciate the earlier prophet's impulse to shatter the stone tablets; each time he returned to London from the Sinai of his family's Scotsbrig farm he felt a kindred impulse to shatter, denounce, vilify; to tell every scoundrel and imbecile of his acquaintance the precise nature of his stupidity— as, to John Stuart Mill he would say, "You, sir, and the whore you've made your wife have sinned against the Holy Spirit, which is of all sins the guiltiest. You have violated your own self-trumpeted ideals of intellectual probity, fidelity to Truth. To the Pit, then, with both of you!" Then, to Browning, "You, friend, are an incorrigible fool made blind by taffeta of petticoats, the slave of a woman who, even in death, corrupts your judgment and tempts you to those lies you call Art! Your mind, that might have been a force for virtue, becomes the mere refined plaything of an idle coterie. Away with your rhymes and liquid pleasing measures!" And to Dickens, "Popinjay adulterer! Wastrel—of your own great talents, of your children's lives, of a nation's trust! England does not need more fantastications and goblets of drugged wine, more flute-spittle and dribblings, more Art, though the Millions may adore it. What do the Millions know but the inchoate urges of their untempered and untaught appetites? You pander to those appetites and still would claim the praise and attention of thoughtful men? Away with you! Away with all your tribe of novelists, journalists, small-beer chroniclers, and ballad-singers! Away!"

Thus Moses, upon descending from Sinai; thus Carlyle, returning to his home in Chelsea. But the author of *Exodus*, in the terse manner of ancient narrative, had neglected an aspect of his hero's life—to wit, the influence of Zipporah, Moses' wife. For when the false idols were smashed to powder and strewn upon the water and the children of Israel had been made to drink thereof—surely then it had been she, Zipporah, who had lain at Moses' side and counseled him to relent, to remember that his people were children of God, though divorced from Him by the sin all men inherit. She exhorted him not in the accents he used when he addressed the Israelites, but in sweet domestic parables, in scraps of gossip—a joke, may be, at the expense of Joshua's vanity in having waistcoat buttons of fools' gold; or she might imitate (how tellingly!) brother Aaron's stutter (for Zipporah and Aaron never could get on together). The sum of all Zipporah's guileless gossip was to reconcile her prophet to the people he would otherwise have abandoned in the trackless wastes through which they sought their Promised Land. She it was who sat at home while the people danced in shame and nakedness before their golden calf, watching them carefully, conscious of every ignominy, but through it all the source for him (when he would need it, coming down from his attic study where he wrote the endless tablets of God's law), the living fountain of his faith in that most problematical object of fidelity, Our Fellow Man.

Of all this the author of *Exodus* says nothing, nor does he speak of Moses' suffering when, after forty-one years of marriage, after long illness, Zipporah died.

Geraldine sat in the middle of the horse-hair chaise longue, her skirts spread wide to either side. Her dark glasses made it easy to pretend to be reading. She had no desire to talk with Carlyle's brother John, whom Jane had always, or nearly always, particularly disliked.

The blinds were drawn, as both the hour and the presence of death required, but John could not resist stopping in the midst of his pacing from time to time to lift one louver from the supporting web and peer out into the undifferentiated blackness of the street, a beacon to his wayward brother to return and rescue him from the company of Miss Jewsbury.

"Really, Miss Jewsbury, there is no *need* for you to remain. It would be impossible to say how long my brother may stay away."

"No matter," Geraldine replied, turning a page of the unread lending library novel she'd taken from Jane's bedside. Then, looking up with a formal smile: "However, if *you* would like to retire, do not on my account suppose you must pace the carpet."

John glowered. Earlier he had virtually commanded Miss Jewsbury to leave the premises, and she'd refused outright, insisting that she had information to impart to Carlyle that could not wait for the morrow. He suspected that it had been her probable presence that had originally prompted Carlyle to send him on ahead, as scout and skirmisher, and it piqued him at the very center of his pride to be so casually defied. "Do you mind," he asked, not in a questioning tone, "if I smoke?"

He was already moistening the cigar on his lips, when she answered, "Not at all. But you must go into the garden. Jane never permitted anyone, not even herself, to smoke in the drawing room. It would not do much honor to her memory, would it, to initiate another policy tonight?"

"No, of course not." John put away the cigar in his case. "*She* smoked, you say—regularly?"

"Indeed. I taught her to."

"Really. I prescribed it for her stomach more than twenty years ago, but I had no idea that she smoked for pleasure."

His tone was so priggish, his lifted eyebrow so stern with rebuke, that she could not resist baiting him. "Does that surprise you?"

"It is not . . . customary. Though, of course, London's customs and those of Dumfries must be divergent at many points."

"Undoubtedly. Though Jane once told me that *your* mother was fond of a clay pipe."

"So she was—to my wife's sometime distress."

"Though you smoke yourself."

"When I am permitted, yes."

"Do feel free to go into the garden. If you like, I'll join you. I would often go into the garden with Jane. Or when the weather did not allow that, we would sit at her bedroom window, blowing the fumes of our cigarettes out into the rain."

"Miss Jewsbury," John said with sincere distress (for there were tears trickling out from behind the woman's dark glasses), "do not—"

But how should he prohibit her from crying? Indeed, under the circumstances were not her tears more apropos than the mere nervousness he was evidencing? The Carlyle clan was not a family much given to overt expressions of sorrow. John had not known their mother to shed a single tear on behalf of their father, not in illness or in death, though she had *grieved* for him quietly as well as any wife of the tenderer variety. Consequently he disliked tearful people, though as a physician he had learned how to deal with them in a practical way.

"Perhaps I will go into the garden," he said, accepting defeat. "When my brother comes—"

"I shall tell him you are there."

John nodded.

Carlyle did not come home for two more hours, by which time John had retired to the guest bedroom and was soundly asleep. Geraldine, to stay awake, made herself read the novel in her lap. Regularly, as the hour was struck on the dull bells of Chelsea Old Church, she would climb the stairs and enter Jane's bedroom. On the first of these visits she extinguished the candles burning on either side of the coffin, for they'd gone close to the sockets and hadn't an hour's light left them. When she returned, an hour later, she relighted them, certain that Carlyle could not decently put off much longer the inevitable moment.

When he entered the drawing room, he did not seem surprised to find Geraldine in possession of the house rather than his brother. There was a pressure of hands, murmured condolences, and then, as though he might not find the way himself, she led him up the stairs to the bedroom.

While she remained in the doorway, he advanced to the foot of the bier-supported coffin and touched the smooth unvarnished wood. Forster had argued volubly for a more sumptuous casket, but on the subject of superfluous expense Geraldine knew Carlyle too well to suppose that he could be swayed by what Forster called "the World's opinion." In any case, Jane was to be buried with her own family in Haddington, far away, and so the world whose opinion mattered to Forster would have no opportunity to view Jane's funeral nor to judge of its expense.

"Candles?" Carlyle asked with hushed sarcasm.

She smiled, having wagered with herself that this would be his first point of inquiry. "Do you object?"

"I object to nothing." He drew back from the coffin. Like a nervous fly, his gaze refused to fix itself upon his wife's dead, candle-lighted features. "Why have you stayed on so late, if not to explain these trappings?"

"I thought you would want to know the circumstances of her death in more detail than a telegram could convey. That is why I stayed. I shall be in the sitting room when you wish to speak with me." ·

He nodded his reluctant acquiescence.

She left the room in a rustle of silk, closing the door with the conscious cruel justice of a jailer locking a prisoner into the cell in which he is doomed to spend the rest of his life. So, at least, Carlyle felt it.

Death had been tolerably kind to Jane, unlike life. All undone and smoothed away was the painful handiwork that illness had wrought upon her flesh, wrenching the mouth askew, crimping the forehead, wrinkling the skin about her eyes. She seemed the wife of his youth again, with respect even to the mockery of her smile. He had meant, the moment he was first alone with her, to mark this last reunion with a kiss, but now he felt unaccountably shy, as though in death she had a power (one he never suspected when she was alive) to detect the merit and sincerity of his least action. No kiss could encompass the confusion of his feelings—the love, the loss, the bitterness of having been left to face alone whatever span of years. A smile served as testimony to her having triumphed in this ultimate conjugal combat, the race the finish line of which is death, and no protest, no apology, no explanation could gainsay its silent enigmatic scorn.

Only her upper torso was visible; the coffin's lower half-lid was already screwed shut. The mere physical presence of death had never before exerted such a force over his imagination—the unnaturalness. He would have left the room at once, were it not for Geraldine's presence on the floor below. If only his brother had not been routed from the drawing room. He could have *talked* to John: there would have been a relief in that as easeful in its way as a Papist's recourse to the babble of rosaries. They could have continued to say the simple, consoling things they'd said all throughout the anxious weekend of waiting (the news had reached him late on Saturday, and trains did not travel on the Sabbath). To wit: how fortunate that death had come suddenly, that Jane had been spared another agonizing illness; what a dear wife she'd been, what a sweet, thrifty Goody, what a neat manager of all domestic trifles. These truths and their numerous corollaries would have seemed much less potent in the presence of Geraldine, whose regard for Jane was based on other considerations. Had he begun to commemorate his love in this vein, she would quickly have picked a quarrel with him. So, although he knew he must eventually descend the stairs to hear what she was determined to tell him, for the time being he chose to remain with the corpse, as the lesser of two discomforts.

He did so far exert himself against the morbid tendency of his thoughts as to leave his station of duty, four paces from the foot of the coffin, and go to seat himself at Jane's desk. At once her living presence asserted itself. Here was the ordered workshop of her wit: the stoppered, almost empty inkbottle, the little tray of blackened pen nibs, the paperweight of antique glass (a gift from Ruskin) atop a small mound of unanswered correspondence. Beneath the paperweight, first in that mound, he found the many-times-folded galleys of the address he'd delivered three weeks ago in Edinburgh on the occasion—momentous, as it then had seemed—of his being installed as Rector of the University. How death had dwarfed *that* dignity. Yet before he could well consider this vein of lamentation, he remembered the promise he'd made to Jane on the day of his setting out for Edinburgh that he would deliver that address again for her private edification and delight as soon as he returned to London. A small recompense for the anxiety she'd been made to share beforehand, since Carlyle, not permitting himself the ease of a prepared address, must make his speech extempore—direct, as it were, from the summit of Sinai. In the event, his preparatory anxieties had proven unfounded. The Israelites—that is, the students of the University who had chosen him as Rector—had cheered, laughed, and applauded with discernment, and the press (in reporting the address) had acclaimed him in terms embarrassingly close to his own highest, and most inexpressible, self-estimate.

Should he—could he—keep his promise? No, the idea was absurd. Jane was dead, and he did not believe in an afterlife. All promises between them were at an end, all vows, all trust, all secrets, all name-able reciprocities. And yet—he considered—in reading the address to her he might find his way to the relief of tears. He took up the galleys —some thirty octavo pages of close-printed prose—and turned to the coffin.

But what of Geraldine? The likelihood of her overhearing (and judging him another sentimental fool like herself) argued against any reading until he had heard her out, and sent her away.

He went down the stairs and entered the drawing room with a renewed sense of his own masterfulness, but fate seemed determined to thwart him in his least assertions: instead of Geraldine (who'd gone down to the kitchen to make tea), he found Tiny, Jane's dog, in possession of the drawing room. Tiny whined and shook his long ears defiantly. Carlyle grimaced.

He was no lover of animals, least of all spoiled lapdogs. Years ago he had so far overcome his own nature as to reach an amicable—even loving—understanding with Tiny's predecessor, Nero. Nero, however, had been a spunky, playful animal, eager to please, whose brute stupid-ity could be pardoned on account of his general moral character. Tiny was a whiner, a hider in corners, a barker at strangers (including, all too often, Carlyle), the sort of dog that, if it had been a child (as Jane sometimes pretended), Carlyle would have immured in a nursery, as in a tomb, and not spoken to twice in the week. In short, a most unlik-able dog, which for Jane's sake he had been obliged, this year and a six-month, to live with on terms of feigned tolerance.

"Down, dog," Carlyle ordered brusquely; and when it would not budge, "DOWN!"

Tiny, sitting on Jane's favorite chair, wagged his tail placatingly.

Unmoved, Carlyle crossed the room and swept the dog to the floor with a stroke. Yipping, Tiny skittered into the hall, appealing to Geral-dine's black silk skirts, then reentering the room behind them.

"Poor thing," said Geraldine coolly, placing the teatray on the table by the lamp. "He's so upset. They understand death as well as we do. Or as poorly. Did you want tea?"

"No."

"You'll excuse me, then. I do."

"There was no need to remain this late, Geraldine. Certainly once my brother had arrived . . ."

"The need, perhaps, was mine. I did not want to leave Jane until you were here. I couldn't say why. When my feelings are *very* strong, I see no need to examine them. Also, I wanted to tell you, in more detail, the circumstances of her death. I've spoken with the coachman at some length."

"For that you have my thanks. It is not a task I would have wanted for myself. Was there anything untoward in the circumstances of her death?"

"Not at all. She died in the carriage at some point in the course of her drive through Hyde Park. She had got out of the cab by Victoria Gate, when Tiny, poor thing, was struck by another brougham (you may have detected, he has a bit of a limp); that was the last that Sylvester can positively testify to her being alive. When she returned to the carriage, he drove some distance about the park. Finally, when he had received no orders for some time, at Hyde Park Corner he thought to turn round, and something in her attitude alarmed him. He asked a passing lady to look into the brougham. She was already dead."

"The telegram said she was at St. George's Hospital?"

"That is where Sylvester brought her, since it was so near by."

"I don't understand what there is in this story that could not have been told as well in the morning." There was more of curiosity than of criticism in his tone.

She poured a cup of tea for herself, looked up inquiringly.

"Oh, very well."

She poured tea for him, handed him the cup.

"There would have been an autopsy but for Forster's intervention. Did you know that?"

"I beg your pardon."

"It is established routine when no attending physician has certified the cause of death. There would have been an inquest and a physical examination."

"Without *my* authorization?" All Carlyle's self-possession seemed to have deserted him in an instant.

"Even if you'd been here, I doubt there would have been any way you might have prevented it. But Forster, as you know, is a lunacy commissioner, and he knew whom to speak to. At last the matter was arranged, and the hospital officials agreed to accept a statement from Dr. Quain as to the probable cause of death."

"A coroner's inquest?" Carlyle demanded, as though the possibility still actively threatened. "God! They would have done that? As though there was a doubt as to the circumstances of her death?"

"Forster knew you would not have wanted such a thing. He exerted himself greatly."

Carlyle placed his cup of tea, untasted, on the tray. "Of course I would not want such a thing. Would any husband? A stranger's hands to—the idea is infamous! To become the object of low gossip, of filthy innuendoes?"

"But it wasn't done, and there can be no scandal now, thanks to Mr. Forster. That is all I wanted to tell you. I'll go now. Your brother says you'll not set off for Haddington for yet another day, so I'll return tomorrow for my last farewell. I should have liked to have been able to make the journey with you, but—"(In point of fact, she hadn't been asked.)"—I cannot spare the time away from my work. Nor, for that matter, the railway fare to Scotland and back just now."

"Then, good night," said Carlyle. Despite the hour—it was after one a.m.—he did not offer to see her home. She had stayed so late on purpose to ruffle his composure; she had done so, and he felt no debt to her for it.


Alone once again with Jane, the notion of reading his address to her unhearing ears did not possess the same sentimental attraction it had earlier. But it was a purpose he'd formed, and Carlyle was not one to shirk a purpose. He took up the galleys again.

Outside the door of the bedroom Tiny began to whine, and then to scratch at the door.

He could not do it. He could not read thirty pages of sage advice to his wife's corpse.

He went to the door and let in the dog. It circled the foot of the bier twice, whining and casting anxious sidelong glances at Carlyle, who began at that moment to understand the nature, quality, and extent of his own sorrow.

# *Envoi*

The hawsers were slipped from the moorings and fell with elephantine grace into the frothing waters of the slip. She'd spoken to the landlady, given the postman a small remembrance: a watercolor of the azaleas in the rear garden. Now, with the ropes dragging in the water, Jo was no longer connected to the land—not in any physical way—yet even this could not signal the definitive moment of departure, for at Tilbury she needs must step on English soil again. And—who could say?—she might return.

That was still her fondest hope. All but those times when her anger would rear up, like the head of a monster rising from the sea, and she would wish him dead—killed in his absurd war in Chile—herself heiress to more than twenty unsold canvases, which, in her fantasy of vengeance, she would then, like another Dido, immolate upon a pyre. But the monster barely had time to suggest one fiery breath before Jo felt the knot of tears close about her throat—not at the thought of Jimmy Whistler's abandoning her, but at the thought of willfully destroying those paintings, familiar to her as the Thames itself seen from the studio's windows in every weather. As to being abandoned, it wasn't to be wondered at. Without the specific irritation of his mother's presence, Jimmy might have prolonged the liaison for as many years as it had endured already, but sure as a loaded pistol he would have gone off some day, just as irrevocably (if not so far). Her father had said it would happen; her friends had warned her; she had never doubted the outcome. Better that it should happen now, before her dowry of beauty had quite exhausted itself, and while she had a standing invitation from Monsieur Courbet.

Though his wits were not so sharp as Jimmy's, nor his waist so trim, nor his brush so delicately attuned to every nuance of shadow, nevertheless he was a fine enough painter and his pockets were deep. Working for Courbet would be a more comfortable self-sacrifice than any other she could imagine. Until her French was much improved even his schoolboy jokes would seem cleverer than they were. In that respect (for what it might be worth), he was no worse than Gabriel Rossetti.

It was Rossetti's house, or rather the pediment of pink brick peeking out from the screening foliage across the water, that had put her in mind of him. And there, far upstream from the Cadogan Pier, all but out of sight, was the Greaveses' boatyard. And there, behind, known—even visualized—but unseen stood the house on Lindsey Row. Anna Whistler would be awake and about by now; for her this day must be much like any other.

Just inland from the pier, only a few doors up Cheyne Row from her point of departure, stood the home of Thomas Carlyle, and a few steps farther inland lay the house where Leigh Hunt had lived with his large family. She'd walked past it only yesterday.

Faces, names, histories, memories: how less charged with laughter and tears places became once one was gone from the land. How merely actual they appeared from out here in the middle of the river—a landscape of chimneypots, shingles, and sagging roofs! Oughtn't it to be more painful, seeing the entire village pass in review, knowing that soon it would fade from sight forever? No, surely not forever—though it might be many years till she returned, and time would have razed wide swathes of what she now thought as permanent and imperishable as the sky. Like as not, the friendly old river pub, the *Adam and Eve* with its rickety river stair, would come down (there was talk of it now, an embankment scheme). Painted names peeling from signboards would flake away, to be replaced by new, unfamiliar names painted in brighter colors. Corresponding changes would have occurred in herself—of amplitude, of fortune, even of name—it was not unthinkable.

But would her eye resist time's metamorphosing power? It had been the best of gifts. A knack. Would she lose that? The ability to see the world exactly as it was, coolly conscious of colors and intervals: the gesture of a chimney or a course of bricks, the several gradations of smoke as it melts into haze, and then in turn the more subtle degrees of density perceptible as haze arches across the horizon. "To see the world," Jimmy had said once, "just as it is painted."

Not that she wanted, in her own case, a painterly eye for its own sake. After the first excitement of learning to use the brush had come the disillusionment with her own untowering talent. But to *see* like a painter (whether one painted or not) was to see with more interest and attention. It was a way of keeping ever alert to the possibility of blessedness in a moment. Painters, as a rule (and he chief of all painters she had known), had that knack, and she had learned over the years with him how best to provoke him to bring the knack to bear. She knew how even better than he. The knack was hers—insofar as it was a gift of the eye and not of the hand.

A doubtful gift when one's eye was turned toward such imponderable entities as trees, clouds, blue distances of space, but one had only to turn one's attention to something closer by and the use of the knack, in a practical way, became apparent. A woman, wearing double skirts of altogether Gargantuan dimensions, lingered alone at the railing (for the custom was light today, and the benches in the center of the deck were scarce a quarter filled). Such voluminous skirts must be a penance to wear, especially in summer weather, and yet how wonderfully they expressed a meaning that would not have been expressible any other way. Lacking a vision of the world, Jo would have dismissed this woman's fashionable foibles without another thought, but having the knack (and having passed so many years in the company of another who possessed that knack), every ruffle, every posy and pose, every smile (however stiff or easy) had its own readable meaning.

The ticket examiner, a thick-waisted man with a drooping moustache and drooping eyelids, asked to see the ticket of the woman in the double skirts. At first she could not find it, bit her lower lip; suddenly found it, smiled: the impress of her teeth still visible, for a moment, on the flesh of her lip.

The examiner stuffed the ticket into his jacket pocket. But supposing, thought Jo, he had let the ticket fly off with the breeze, to flutter and soar upwards, out over the Thames until it appeared to be no larger, no more identifiable, than a single dot of confetti? The knack could make nothing of that. Impressions could, after all, be *too* ephemeral.

While there, just downstream from Rossetti's house and the Physic Garden, resting on its green lawns, set well back from the shore, was one of those Supreme Objects that the knack might feed upon endlessly: the Royal Hospital.

They had stood before it once, she and Jimmy—but on the other side, having walked down from the King's Road—in a magnificent March rain, sheltering beneath a single stout umbrella. How they had taken it to pieces—taken, that is, the *idea* of it to pieces: how ridiculous it was to build a monument—a palace, virtually!—for no other purpose than to house old soldiers, who might have lived much more comfortably, as other people had to do, in a row of ordinary houses. But Jimmy, ever the Yankee patrician, had countered that the Chelsea Hospital was the pleasantest thing in Chelsea and that it mattered not at all what use it was put to, so long as it was there, lending its awesomeness to the lives not merely of its residents but of everyone who must walk by it and whose minds were made, for the moment, larger and livelier; as though—he had said—a string orchestra began playing in the middle of the street. That afternoon they had returned home absolutely soaked, still arguing (about the Royal Family now). Jimmy declared himself to be their most loyal subject, and for the same reasons, basically, that he'd offered in defense of Christopher Wren's Royal Hospital (and, indeed, all heroic architecture): for being Large, Visible, and Interesting.

Such walks they had taken! By comparison, despite *its* large, visible objects of interest, Paris would never be able to match these Chelsea streets, rife with a lifetime's associations.

Disheartened, her spirit suddenly quite withered, Jo left the railing and took a seat among the benches in the middle of the deck. Melting into the morning light as the boat moved slowly downstream was Battersea Bridge, its warm wooden tones now muted and cooled to a single gray by distance.

Once, on Battersea Bridge, many years ago, she had encountered Thomas Carlyle. It was the only time they'd ever spoken. She was not drunk, but had the courage that comes with drink (having spent the earlier part of the evening at Cremorne tippling with her father in the pavilion), and had stepped out on the wooden bridge to watch the sun set. It was all over and done in a flash. Not the sunset—which, in point of fact, seemed sullenly to draw itself out, as though to mock her lèse-majesté—but the encounter. After a quick apology for intruding, she confessed how much she'd admired his short book *Past and Present*. Actually, she'd read only a bit more than a third of it, then stopped because it seemed to lose its magic. But she had intensely liked that part. He had dusted, stripped down, and scrubbed clean for her a single relic of history so that it gleamed with truth. He had led her safely across the chasm of seven centuries. Not that the *Jocelini Chronica* mattered at all to her—but he had taught her how to look at the past.

"Thank you," he'd said with a look of high disdain, then turned on his heel and walked away—never looking back, not even after he'd descended from the bridge. A snub. Horrid man—with his stiff neck, rough-hewn face, the long, unseasonable surtout, arrogant to the shop-keepers, a tyrant to his servants, and withal the assurance (solid as the Chelsea Hospital) of an inviolable independence.

Perhaps she *had* been drunk? What if he were sitting, now, in the empty space next her?

"Why, Mr. Carlyle!" turning sideways and affecting surprise. She would know from the first hesitant word of his reply that this was not the man who'd snubbed her one evening summers past. "Pardon me," he would say, "I don't remember—"

"Miss Hiffernan," offering her ungloved hand. "Miss *Joanna* Hiffernan," and matching his constrained smile with one perfectly equal. "I am not certain I even introduced myself on the last occasion of our meeting. I offered a word of praise for your book *Past and Present*, and then you were *swept* away."

She stood. The uncrinolined silk frock fell smoothly over her hips. Now the steamer had almost left Chelsea behind, and she hurried again to the rail. A barge stacked with bales of fermenting hay obscured the grounds of the Royal Hospital, and yet the cupola still dominated the horizon.

Though she might leave it now, she would not lose it: that was what she wanted to believe, and almost could. Chelsea, yes, she must leave that. But she would keep the knack, the clarity, the steady eye. Though of course one might still make mistakes. She'd judged Carlyle too harshly, perhaps—she'd even been wrong about the absurdity of crino-lines, for there was something truly monumental in that woman's dress (she still stood by the rail), with which Wren's cupola would find itself in accord. But there was almost always a possibility of blessedness, and the knack kept one alert to it. One moment one walked along the pavement without a thought, and then there it would be, bright and shining: the great, merry, gracious jumble of lives and rooftops, of purposes certain to be defeated and leaves pushing their way past other leaves into the rewarding light.